Solaris:
The Rising

nole lacour

Dedication

*To the creative minds that wander the world in wonder
and the hearts that accept knowledge, growth,
and love.*

*But, most of all, to the family
that allowed me to dream.
Mine.*

Prologue

A young man walked through the woods one chilly night. The cool winds nipped at his nose and ears as he gripped his sword tighter in the eerie silence that engulfed his bruised but muscular body.

Loneliness hung in the air and fell upon his shoulders like a weight. The man longed for the same tranquility that lingered in the smooth melodies of the swaying forest trees and the quiet chirps of crickets.

He shivered and whispered to himself, "Winter is coming…"

He only wore a thin tattered rag as a shirt and ripped hide pants but no shoes. The thick locks of his curly, brown hair fluttered in the air. With each subtle step he took, a small follicle pricked up on the back of his neck. Someone or something was watching him.

The man suspiciously glanced all around him as he progressed forward, moving slowly so he would not alarm his mysterious predator.

Suddenly, to the right of him, a loud rustle came from the bushes. Before the young man could react and unsheath his sword, a large brown wolf jumped out of the brush and pounced on the suspecting man.

Startled, the man lost his grip on his sword, fell backward from the powerful leap of the wolf, and stared into the furry creature that stood on his chest. The wolf's teeth were long and sharp, drool dripping from each treacherous fang. The wolf snarled in the man's face.

"Hydo, your breath is wretched!" the

young man shouted as he tried to push the obtrusive wolf off.

The wolf cocked back its head, howled, then replied, "It's not my fault that we've had nothing but rotten deer meat for the past week. Maybe you should improve your hunting skills, Viril. Your breath doesn't smell like flowers either."

The wolf walked off the young man and sat on the ground.

"With the terms of this war," Viril spoke as he sat up and brushed the dirt off his shirt. "We are lucky to even have found that deer carcass, or would you rather starve?"

The mighty wolf licked his beaten down paws. There were many scars and cuts hidden within the dense fur coat. Hydo did not respond to his companion's question.

Seeing the lack of compliance from Hydo, Viril continued, "And why are you parading around in your Neo form? You know that only increases your chances of getting caught by the Ander forces. They may be winning this war, but at least we can outwit them for a little while in our human forms."

Hydo, still stubborn, turned his head away from Viril and snapped back, "I do not wish to be seen in *that* form. Even if the rest of Pangea chooses to walk these grounds on two legs rather than four, I will not succumb to the Anders' despicable shape."

"But, Neos have been roaming Pangea as humans for decades now, even before the war. Haven't you seen the motions of development since we, Neos, have chosen to utilize the human body?"

"And what progress is that, Viril?" Hydo returned coldly. "War? If that's progress, I want nothing to do with it."

"True, the result of the crossbreeding has turned into an unfortunate event," Viril whispered softly. "But, I have to hope that one day, creatures, Neos and Anders alike, will be able to work together and make positive strides to a better future."

"Then you are crazy," Hydo muttered as he lied steadily on the ground, closing his eyes under the silver moonlight. "With that attitude, you'll be dead before too long."

"Well, I would hope you'd come to help me," Viril joked.

"Let your hopes and dreams save you, Viril. You will see. Our kind have already started to rebuild. That's why we're going to the Great Crossings, isn't it?"

"The rumors of the Noble Organization being reestablished..."

"Yes! There is news that the Nobles have contracted the help of the nomadic wizards from the enchanted lands, as well. Soon, the Neos will regain their power and strength, and we will take back this land and what is rightfully ours."

"And what would that be?"

"Freedom, brother. Freedom," Hydo stated bluntly but impassioned.

Before Viril could open his mouth to announce another glimmer of hope within his passive heart, a dozen men leapt out of the surrounding bushes where Hydo, himself, hid.

All the men carried a weapon of some sort: a spear, a sword, an axe. Standing tall, they bore shiny armor plates covering their chests, thighs and biceps. Their burly builds only added to the intensity of their numbers.

"What a beautiful discussion between brothers," the tallest man announced.

He had a shiny, bald head that shimmered

in the moonlight and a thick red beard that soaked in the reflected beams from his skull.

Hydo and Viril stood erected, prepared to fight.

"How touching that you believe that your people will rise again," the sarcastic soldier announced. "But, I don't think you should set your wishes so high in the stars."

Inflamed, Hydo took a bold step toward his offender.

"Shut your mouth, you filthy-"

But, as soon as Hydo set his paw down, an arrow flew out of the trees and landed directly in Hydo's paw. He yelped with pain. Viril rushed to his brother's side and pulled out the arrow while the surrounding attackers laughed.

"Just like a mangy mutt," the tall red bearded man continued. "Too quick to think and without a brain. I'd be careful of your next move, boys. I've got a handful of archers stashed in the canopies."

Viril tried to hush his angered brother.

"Let's just hear what they have to say, Hydo."

"Yes," the stranger echoed. "Listen to him, *Hydo*. Maybe we just came to talk in terms of peace."

Hydo snarled at the man's snide remark. Viril stood up and confronted his bald opponent.

"What is it that you wish with us, sir?"

"Sir? Listen up fellas! This half-dog believes he has manners! What a riot!"

Once again, the men laughed.

"I'll tell you what we want," he continued. "We want to dispose this land completely of you. What kind of sick creatures are you anyway? Half animal, half human..."

"We are Neos," Viril replied calmly.

"Ah yes… The New Breed. Well it's disgusting."

Fed up with the man's rude statements, Hydo piped up angrily from behind his diplomatic brother.

"Our people were the ones that gave birth to you, you fowl ass! How do you consider yourself the better species when you have ruthlessly killed your mothers and fathers? You've even killed off Anders that embraced the Neo heritage they came from!"

Unable to return the banter, the red bearded man withdrew a small dagger and swiftly jabbed it into Viril's stomach.

Viril's eyes widened in shock, and his already milky white skin turned paler than the fluffy white snow that began to fall around the commotion. Hydo screamed at the sight. He jumped to his brother's rescue, but two of the offenders pounced on Hydo's back, slamming his aching body to the hard soil.

The stranger pushed Viril off of his blade and turned around.

"C'mon, boys. Let the wolf live. Allow him to swallow his words as an appetizer to his pride."

The two large armored men peeled themselves off Hydo, and Hydo immediately crawled over to Viril's dying body. Within seconds, the band of Anders left, and Hydo was left alone to mourn the fleeting life of his beloved sibling.

Still in the form of a wolf, Hydo rested a careful paw on Viril's heaving chest.

Viril coughed.

"Hydo, do not be angry."

"You cannot be serious," Hydo fought back.

"It is only in fear that they resist us."

"That fear has grown into hate, Viril. Why can't you see that?"

Viril coughed one more time and sighed.

A rising chill swam over the two brothers, cooling the last bits of warmth in their exhausted spirits as the empathetic skies sifted a flurry of snow from its wispy clouds. The lightness of the sparkling white spots reminded Viril of his innocent youth and the vibrant hope that lingered in his heart. The cozy feeling felt nice against the wintry atmosphere encompassing his body.

Viril stared up at the marvelous sight and blinked the light snowflakes out of his long eyelashes.

Not answering Hydo's question, Viril whispered, "I was right. Winter is coming."

With that, Viril closed his eyes forever.

Hydo did not blink. He did not cry. Instead, Hydo bowed his head at his brother's kind heart and turned to leave as the fresh snow around Viril's body became tainted by a crimson pool of blood.

The steady snowfall continued to gravitate to Hydo's back, making small white sprinkles in his dark coat. Soon, the faint traces of his footprints were left behind in a thin layer of snow as he continued his journey to the Great Crossings. Although his tread was solemn now, Hydo's spirit was lifted, for his brother's wishes for unity would not be wasted.

There will be a change, he thought to himself. *Things will be different, and freedom shall be achieved.*

Hydo's slow pace transformed into a hastened run. The beating sounds of his paws onto the firm ground echoed in his flapping ears. He breathed in and out, faster and faster as he continued to race south through the forest.

Hydo's heartbeat was thumping furiously now and tiny beads of cool sweat trickled down his thick coat. The brisk air breezed past him as Hydo cut through the rushing winds so fast that he felt as if he were flying.

Then, the world around him began to disappear. The burning cut in his paw from the arrow no longer tingled with pain, the coldness of the oncoming winter no longer chilled his bones, and the sight of the snow and blurring forest no longer crowded Hydo's vision.

But, how could this be?

Hydo had finally allowed himself to cry, overcome by the ambition Viril had tried desperately to instill. The tears swelled in the corner of Hydo's eyes and fell down his furry cheeks, freezing in his matted coat like tiny icicles on a pine tree.

He threw back his head and howled, spirit charged, at the ivory moon as he ran toward his future, his newborn hopes and dreams, and… his freedom.

A New Era

"I now claim Pangea… under the Lionship!"

The crowd cheered, and a steady applause sang throughout the Great Hall as the magnificent King Ashos raised his glass of wine into the air. Nobles from all five lands had gathered to celebrate the end of Tournament XI.

"These past five years we, Neos, have been lucky to have been guided by such a great leader, my dear friend, King Delver of Wolf's Reign. Had he known that he would be in charge of steering our army in a war against the Anders, I'm sure he would have reconsidered his championship at Tournament X, but at least, he was blessed with one year of peace upon the end of his term. I raise my glass to the man who sits at my right side tonight, King Delver. To him, I raise it high with respect, honor, and thanks. And to you, my humble court, I raise it high with hopes of a brighter tomorrow and the beginning of a new era… To Pangea!" the king roared.

"To Pangea!" the crowd echoed.

"Come! Let us feast on this magnificent meal!" Ashos commanded cheerfully.

Another wave of applause saturated the air and bounced off the Great Hall walls.

The Great Hall was built when the Nobles were first united a century ago. Its purpose was to have a place where all five lands could meet and celebrate the new coalition, as well as lavish parties and mirthful balls. It was the central castle on Pangea, and though located in the Savannahs territory, the Great

Hall was saturated with boundless acres of gardens, ponds, and enough rooms to fit all the Noble guests. It was a true oasis.

The dining hall, itself, was glorious, as well. The sand-colored marble floors were shined and polished daily by the Majesty Crown's Court. The gleaming finish reflected the artwork on the ceiling so perfectly that it seemed as if the ceiling had fallen to the ground, radiating just as beautiful as it was sitting in the heavens. Long, crimson velvet drapes hung beside each tall window and were fastened by the embrace of thick goldenrod cords. Hundreds of lustrous lamps and chandeliers sparkled, emphasizing the glossy finish on the cherry-wood furniture.

On the nights when feasts were held, like this particular event, the amount of food seemed endless on the hundred foot long table. Trays and dishes were stocked and piled high with a rainbow selection of fruits and desserts. Bowls were filled to the brim with hot delicious soups and steaming pastas. Succulent chicken, pork and beef were grilled until the skins were a crispy brown, and all meats were glazed in honeys and sugars, garnished with heavenly spices. The rich aroma of these lavish dinners added to the color and life of the Great Hall, the walls dancing in the party's hue as the feasting continued.

"Ashos, you're lucky. Had I not broken my foot in battle, I would have beaten you at the five mile race and kept the crown for another half decade," Delver laughed.

Ashos threw back his thick blonde locks and laughed with his comrade.

"A man is not made of luck but of the fate he makes for himself. Besides, I *am* the more handsome of us. Had we tied, I'm sure the ladies' votes would be mine by a hundred-fold or more."

"Don't flatter yourself," Delver returned.

They laughed again, clinking their glasses in good humor.

Embodying his human and Neo form, King Ashos was a brilliant sight with his long dark blonde hair, a mane thick enough to shield his noble head from any attack. As a human, his tan skin glistened in the sun as he roamed his savannah. Even as a lion, during the colder days, Ashos' smooth coat would exude the heat of his masculine body to surrounding entities. Majestic was more than adjective to the this tournament's victor, it was a way of life.

King Delver was right on par, though he had a more rugged character. His deep brown eyes and brooding aura played against his striking smile. The contrast of the two only extenuated his warrior build and confident strut. At night, his dark skin absorbed the moonlight while as a wolf, his fur would fly with the stars, flexed muscles pacing his every stride.

They truly were a handsome pair.

Then, a woman's gentle voice from across Delver's seat broke the laughter.

"How typical of a Head Nobles man."

Delver took a large swig of his wine and raised a comical eyebrow to the lady across the table.

"What is, my dear Irutia?"

"Thinking your seat at the head of the table relies on your looks. How low of you both to think so superficially."

"Ah yes… *This* coming from Pangea's greatest beauty, the Phoenix Queen, herself," Ashos sneered.

Queen Irutia was, indeed, the pure definition of an elegant lady. Her delicate features teased any soul, man and woman alike, as her lips were full of passion, her eyes full of wonder, and her heart full of devotion and love. She was petite in height and width and had short black hair that cupped lightly just below her chin. When she inhabited Pangea in her full phoenix form, her feathers carried her effortlessly through the skies and graced the air with a cooling and calming sensation for even her words tread lightly to her listener's ears.

She smiled as she replied back to the Lion King.

"Then I suppose *I* should have won," Irutia mocked.

"Ay, Irutia. Who would ever vote for the likes of these two with mugs like that?" King Oldar cackled as he nudged Delver playfully in the side.

King Oldar was older than Ashos and Delver but no less striking. His silver feathers graced the winds as he flew, much like his humorous spirit that uplifted any sad or upset heart. As a human, the Great Falcon King was also very tall and muscular with an arm span large enough to engulf three or four of his enemies at once, and despite his entertaining wit, his piercing blue eyes were always sharp and focused.

"What do you think, Bellor?" Oldar continued. "Or perhaps we should remind these young'uns that like wine, the older one is, the finer the countenance!"

"Well, if that is the case then I would not be so hasty in calling yourself wine, my dear friend," Bellor coolly responded with a subtle smile. "I believe aged cheese is more suitable for you. Repulsive at first look and smell but surprisingly delicious if one gives you a chance."

Bellor, the Black Bear King, was the eldest of the Head Nobles. His age was blessed with a surplus of wisdom, and his heart was charged with love. However, in the heat of battle, Bellor's strength was infinite and driven for a man in possession of so many years. He was of larger size but solid as a rock, a sturdy and governing body, and his wooly black beard was just as dominating.

All five Head Nobles were drowning in hysterics, as was the rest of the Noble feast. The Great Hall was filled with two hundred of the Nobles finest, from statuesque soldiers to gorgeous maidens and from holy priests to naïve children.

Even the Noble Court, that was in attendance, was there, dressed in their absolute best for the potluck.

Each Head Noble line had its own Court, its royal workers. The Lionship had the fluent and agile Gazelles, Wolf's Reign had the fierce yet nimble Bobcats, Phoenix Rule had the wise and poised Foxes, Falcon's Order had the ever so colorful Peacocks, and finally, Bear's Sovereignty had the sly yet aggressive Snakes.

The bond between the Nobles and their Court was unbreakable. Both sides had an irrefutable amount of respect for the other. The Court served with the utmost loyalty to their Nobles, and in turn, the Nobles worked hard to provide health, prosperity, and safety from the Anders, for it was only about half a decade ago when chaos first stirred in Pangea. The years were filled with war and the lands were soaked in blood, but since the reformation of the Noble Organization, peace was restored and victory over the Anders was won.

"Tell me, my dear Majesty Crown," Oldar said as he teasingly bowed to Ashos. "Pray tell, what is your first declaration? Surely, after this long war you intend to reinstate our annual balls, for it has been too long since all Nobles have gathered in one place without the scent of battle swelling in their noses. Heaven knows we are in dire need of jubilation."

"It is most certainly top priority," Ashos agreed. "Our people have seen too much war, and our children have been born in fear for too long. Take Bellor's son, Ceros, for example. He is but twenty years old and has already been in combat when his youth should have been spent chasing pretty Neo girls and raising hell for his father."

Ashos winked in the direction of the young man sitting next to Bellor.

Ceros was not like his father in character by any means. Ceros was impatient, irrational, and quickly angered. Not to mention, he was reckless in battle, hardly paying attention or showing respect to his comrades. Even Bellor had a hard time managing his son's temperament.

But, like his father, Ceros' physical build was enormous and ruling for his age. He had dark, thick curly hair with tanned skin and deep brown eyes that easily penetrated another being. His strength was massive and continued to grow which made his love for conflict disturbing. In fact, there was such a darkness surrounding his presence, that mostly everyone referred to him as, "the Black Prince."

"I actually enjoyed the fighting, your majesty."

"Did you now? Why is that?"

"Battles have an air about them, don't you agree?"

"Yes, but the air is drenched in confusion, fear, and hate. Surely that is not the type of air you wish to breathe, my boy."

"It is the only air my lungs know how to inhale. With a sword in my hand, I demand order. With every swing, I create it and make it mine. I slaughter all fear and glow when I watch it bleed before me."

"Hush now," Bellor intervened. "Ceros, my beloved son, this is no topic to discuss at a time of rejoice and elatedness."

Oldar leaned over the table and whispered to Ceros, "Especially in the presence of a lady."

"I heard that you feathered coward," Irutia jested.

The Head Nobles laughed again, all but Ceros. He quickly grabbed his glass and guzzled his ale to keep from unleashing an annoyed verbal defense. His father watched from the corner of his eye, and a familiar unsettling feeling swam through Bellor's body.

Still chuckling, Delver began, "As we are on the discussion of battle, my friends, I'd like to introduce you to one of my soldiers for he is to take my place upon my death as King of Wolf's Reign."

Delver turned to his Bobcat Courter.

"Delby?" he summoned.

A middle-sized bobcat with a burnt-sienna fur coat covered in black spots approached the Wolf King's chair and bowed.

"Yes, your highness?"

"Did you fetch him?"

"I did."

"Brilliant! Bring him then, and thank you, Delby."

"There is but one problem."

"And that is?"

"After I brought him to the Wolf's room to change, he disappeared."

"Disappeared?"

"It seems that way, your grace, but he left a parchment saying he would return before dinner concludes."

"Lost another soldier, eh, Delver?" Oldar bantered. "What's so special about this one? Other than his disappearing act?"

"He is-" Delver started but caught glimpse of a beautiful girl approaching the head of the table. "Why, Princess Therene. It is nice to see you again."

A young woman appeared behind the Phoenix Queen and curtsied. The Noble men stood and bowed in return.

"Of equal niceness to see you, too, King Delver, as is all of your highnesses."

"Where have you been?" Irutia queried as the Noble Princess took her seat.

"I was out by the pond reading, and I fell asleep underneath the Great Oak tree. Please forgive my tardiness."

Bellor smiled.

"No need to be apologetic, Princess. It is easy to doze off under the shade of trees, as your mind and body are fooled into thinking it is night time. We are all so happy to see you; war has kept us apart from innocence too long. You have grown up to be a beautiful young woman. How old are you now?"

"Eighteen in two months."

"A woman indeed!" Bellor exclaimed. "Is she not, dear son?"

Ceros looked up from his dinner plate and was instantly taken aback by Therene's loveliness. It was no secret that she was Irutia's daughter. She was just as elegant and classy, but her youth made her fair skin and her almond-shaped eyes seem more alive. Her neck was tall, as her posture was, and she had long black hair that draped over her shoulders, decorated with tiny flowers. As she smiled, and what a marvelous smile she had, so did her ivy green eyes.

Ceros felt his breath escape him every time she moved.

"Yes… She is."

Ceros smiled slightly at Therene, and she politely returned it. Ceros knew, at that instant, he had to win her heart even though having intimate feelings for other Neo species had been forbidden for years.

"Though you may not take my apologies for my late arrival, then take them for interrupting darling King Delver, as I do believe he was speaking when I made my entrance."

"Don't worry, Princess," Oldar started. "Delver's star Neo soldier has yet to be unveiled. I think he wants to remain a mystery."

"Or perhaps he does not exist at all," Therene played back.

Ashos chuckled, "I see she has also inherited your wit, Irutia, as well as your allure. Well, Delver? Now, you must describe this man to us, as we are all curious and eager to create his image in our heads."

"His name is Rysul, and he *is* real. He is young, but he has a passion and a burning fire in him unlike any elder I've seen. His movements are swift and clean, and he has a keen precision touched by grace. His speed is as fast as lightning, and his calmness in battle is that of a pond in spring."

"It sounds like he has warrior's blood coursing his veins as I do," Ceros declared.

"I thought it to be so, as well, but when I speak to him, he pronounces that he has that of a poet's heart."

Peaked with interest, Therene propped her elbow on the table and rested her chin in her hand.

"A poet?"

"Yes, a poet," Delver laughed.

The table of Head Nobles stayed silent in bewilderment.

"If I read your faces correctly," Delver continued. "I was as astonished as all of you, but yes, he says he is a poet, a true lover."

"How could a poet be such a great fighter?" Ceros asked furiously. "The two roles are contrasted so much in nature!"

Bellor interjected, "That is not entirely true, for both roles are rich in a special kind of passion. It is a passion that is derived from a pure and just heart. A poet writes justice whether it be for politics or for love, and a warrior fights for freedom and change."

"Ah yes!" a strange voice sounded from the front doorway.

The Head Nobles all turned to see who it was.

Standing in the entrance was a tall teenage boy wearing a brown tattered cloak. His beige skin sparkled under the chandeliers, and his shadowy hair glistened. The combination was captivating. He bore soft hazelnut eyes and a dashing smile that overwhelmed its audience as he walked closer

to the stunned table. His strides were solid
and confident, and as his pace increased, his
cloak flew off his back to expose a wide array
of flowers in his hands.

"These are for the ladies."

The guest bowed and presented lovely
bouquets to Irutia and Therene.

"These are remarkable!" Irutia exclaimed.
"Did you make these yourself?"

"I fear not, my lady. Mother Nature
deserves all the credit."

"Well, I thank you anyway. Therene, dear,
say thank you."

Therene looked up from her floral wonder
to the stranger's face. At first, she was
hesitant, for reasons she was unaware of, but
proceeded to smile.

"Thank you, sir, and what might we call
you?"

"This is Rysul!" Delver proclaimed in the
young poet's place. "The poetic warrior I was
just telling you about. These flowers are
proof of his romance."

"So, you *do* exist?" Oldar joked.

Rysul howled and replied, "I do, King
Oldar."

"I see. For a moment we were giving
Delver the run-around for making you up. Your
entrance was supposed to a few moments ago."

"My apologies. Delby did bring me here on
time, but as I was changing clothes, I looked
out my window and saw the sun beginning to
set. Needless to say, I made my way outside to
the hill to properly wish it goodnight."

"So, we've got two daydreamers among us
tonight?" Oldar said slyly. "Rysul *and*
Princess Therene should enlighten us as to
what we are missing out on."

Rysul turned to Therene.

"I should have guessed a goddess like you would be like me, a victim of our minds. I can't even begin to imagine the engaging thoughts spinning in your head."

Therene briskly looked down to her plate, trying to hide her blushing cheeks.

Seeing this, Ashos smiled and changed the flow of conversation.

"My boy, how old are you exactly? If you are as good as Delver says, surely you must be at least twenty-five years of age."

"You flatter me, Majesty Crown, but I am only sixteen."

"Sixteen?!?" Ashos exclaimed. "Delver, you let him fight in battle? He is just over a child's age."

"He insisted upon it. I was leery at first, but when I saw him wield his sword and engage in combat, my doubts were just as slain as his opponents."

"That is fascinating," Ashos continued. "It is almost a shame that we have no more enemies to wrestle tonight, as I would love to watch you create your art in battle."

"Perhaps the next war," Rysul chuckled, as did the rest of the Head Nobles.

Even a pleasant giggle escaped Therene's mouth. She looked up at Rysul, whose stare was fixed on her anyway, and he winked at her. Her blushing returned, but this time she did not look away.

Noticing this, Ceros became enraged and wildly jealous. At the speed of light, he stood up and slammed his fist on the table so hard that everyone in the Great Hall was instantly silenced.

"I challenge you…" Ceros whispered.

"What was that, my Prince?" Rysul asked.

"I said, I challenge you! I challenge you

to a dual!"

Silence hung in the still air, so much that one could feel the impact of a pin dropping upon their skin had one fell.

The quiet remained until Bellor mustered up his voice to say, "Ceros, son… why do propose such a match?"

"Well Father, his Majesty Crown suggested it. He wishes to see Rysul fight, and I am now eager to, as our conversation earlier initiated my thirst for it. Unless… Rysul is too tired from watching the sun set that he forfeits?"

All eyes then turned to Rysul.

"On one condition, if the Princess agrees to it," Rysul replied calmly.

Rysul turned to face Therene.

"The winner is honored by accompanying the lady on a night walk in the Great Gardens. Truly, that is a prize worth fighting for. What do you say, Princess?"

All eyes then shifted to Therene. She closed her eyes, took a deep breath in, and stood.

After opening her eyes, she neatly said, "I shall award the winner my hand for the night."

Ashos stood as well and announced, "It seems to me that we have a dual! Gazelles, quickly prepare the Great Gallery for a sword match."

With those last words, the Great Hall bellowed in cheering as the Gazelle Court hurried to the next room to arrange the proper setting.

Ashos sat back down and whispered, "This is quite the stir you've created, Ceros. Though I must say, this will put an interesting end to tonight's celebration."

"And an entertaining one at that!" Oldar chimed in as he bit into a candied apple.

"Whatever pleases my Majesty Crown is more than enough to please me. If you excuse me, I must go to my room and grab my armor and sword."

Ceros bowed and made his way up the Great Staircase to his quarters.

"You have a spirited boy, Bellor," Ashos commented.

"That I do, Ashos. That I do."

Meanwhile, Rysul had made his way to Therene's chair; he knelt down beside her.

"Thank you for agreeing to the terms of war, Princess. I know if I win, this walk will give me much joy. I already know how bright a phoenix shines in the sun's fire she was born of, but I'm more intrigued to see what she looks like under the shimmer of my moon."

"I certainly hope you do more than wish to win, Rysul. I had only two reasons governing my decision tonight. One, was to please his Majesty Crown and two, to have the chance to talk with you. You've already done an extensive job at presenting your poetry through your intrepid remarks, but I am more intrigued to see if your actions match your performance."

"Well said, Princess. In that case," Rysul took Therene's hand and pressed his lips to it. "In that case, I shall win with full certainty. Now, I must go prepare."

Rysul stood and also started towards the Great Staircase, but Therene grabbed his hand and whispered, "Ceros is a fearless fighter. Some even say he is relentless and a madman in battle. Also, he has four years on you… You will be careful, won't you?"

Rysul spun around to look at Therene once

more.

"Princess, there are many types of fearlessness. One is merely created through power, the inability to see truths, and you think yourself invincible. Another type is to know a love so strongly that the self actually becomes invincible. Prince Ceros has his fearlessness, and I have mine. In that aspect, it really will be a fair match."

Rysul smiled once more and went back to his room.

About an hour passed before the guests, Nobles and Court alike, were situated in the Great Gallery, anxiously awaiting their recreational surprise. King Ashos stepped forward into the middle of the Great Gallery, and the crowd hushed.

"My fellow Nobles and Court, tonight we are lucky to witness what will be a grand fight, a fight between two of Pangea's most passionate soldiers. On one end we have Prince Ceros, son of King Bellor! On the other end we have a new warrior from King and Captain Delver's private forces, Rysul!"

The gallery shook with booming cheers and applause as Ceros and Rysul entered the room.

Ceros was wearing the classic Bear Sovereignty armor, black steel shined and polished to perfection. Each armor plate was outline with cardinal paint and trimmed with pure gold. His sword lie quiet in his sheath, but everyone knew that the blade was sharp and deadly when Ceros wielded it.

To everyone's surprise, except for Delver, Rysul was simply protected by a thin leather covering over his chest. His thin but muscular arms and legs were exposed with only his shirt and pants as a shield for his flesh. The crowd began to whisper their doubts and concerns.

King Ashos approached the young warrior.

"My boy, is that all you choose to wear? You are aware that tonight's victor is declared by the first sign of blood? With this dressing, you might as well surrender your title now."

"I know what I wear may look to be foolish and ignorant, but I assure you that my outfit was carefully selected. Armor has proven to be too heavy and limiting for me. My movements are swift and need the ability to be fluid. The less weight I carry on my shoulders will confirm my intentions as well as my delivery."

The Nobles sat at the front of the room. Rysul snuck a peek at Therene who was full of worry and was sitting at the edge of her chair, clutching and fiddling with her diamond necklace.

"Well-reasoned," Ashos smiled, and walked to his seat amidst the Head Nobles. "You may start upon my command."

The room went still, as everyone was eager to hear the first clashing of swords and see the breaking of sweat from the two combatants.

Ceros unsheathed his mighty sword and steadied his hold. The single golden stripe that divided the blade in half radiated in the flickering candle light.

Rysul inhaled deeply and closed his eyes, arms and hands resting at his waist. He was syncing his mind and body to the make shift arena and his opponent. The stale hush of the audience soothed his nerves and caressed his skin as he waited for an attack.

Ashos' eyes wavered back and forth between the two Nobles waiting for the precise moment to yell…

"Begin!"

With that, Ceros let forth a wild scream and charged forward to Rysul. The crowd regained its frenzy and roared with him. Rysul's eyes remained shut as he felt Ceros presence become stronger and stronger, closer and closer, until he could feel Ceros' sword move upward, preparing to strike down upon him, but with one swift motion, Rysul drew his blade and blocked the downward thrust of Ceros' ferociousness.

The room went wild, each spectator's body tingling as if they held the clashing sword themselves. Ceros was growing more and more incandescent with every blow Rysul shielded himself from. Ceros knew his strength was of enormous intensity and that he was clever in his attacks, but he could not figure out how Rysul was able to block every shot.

The two warriors whirled around the room as their swords continued to sing.

On the sideline, Oldar leaned over to Bellor and whispered, "Is it just me, or does it look as if Rysul is dancing upon our marble floors?"

Bellor calmly replied, "Yes, but it is not an appearance. He *is* dancing, and that is why my dear son will lose."

Rysul carried his actions like water, free of constraint and allowed to move as he see fit. Ceros' irritation was growing exponentially by the second. He broke apart from the closeness and took a few steps back to catch his breath and gather his plans of attack.

"What I heard of you is correct," Rysul shouted. "Prince Ceros, you really are a fantastic swordsman. I applaud you."

Further livid by Rysul's compliments, Ceros made another head on charge towards Rysul.

"I do not need your pity!" Ceros yelled as he thrust his sword forward, but Rysul quickly stepped aside to avoid the blow and stuck out his foot.

With the momentum Ceros gathered from his charge, he tripped easily and fell forward, his sword leaving his grasp and retreating underneath the seats of the audience.

Both embarrassed and infuriated, Ceros stood and turned to face Rysul who had abandoned his sword.

"I want this to be a fair fight, dear Prince, so the combat shall travel to our hands instead."

Ceros was actually pleased with this turn of events, as his fists were much larger and his body more massive than Rysul's. Surely, Rysul's bones would crumble under his mighty hold. Ceros sneered.

"Perhaps not as fair as you would hope, wolf."

Ceros made his way towards Rysul and launched his fist forward, but instead of hearing the anticipated cracking of skeletal framework, Ceros fist was met by a shocking amount of strength stemming from Rysul's defensive grasp on his wrist.

Before Ceros could contemplate his disbelief, a speedy fist was hurled upward underneath Ceros' chin, putting him flat on his back. Rysul mounted Ceros, pulled out a small dagger and nicked Ceros' eyebrow just enough so that a single drop of blood emerged.

Rysul stood up and reached out his hand to the defeated Ceros.

"I do not wish to cause any more harm to

you, brother."

Not wanting to raise suspicion or an upset, Ceros begrudgingly took Rysul's hand and stood.

Everyone in the Great Gallery were standing now, hooting and squealing with excitement. Even the Head Nobles were erect and clapping. Rysul and Ceros turned to Ashos and bowed.

"My, my, my! What a terrific treat you have given us, this evening," the pleased Majesty Crown exclaimed. "Both of you are fine soldiers that I am proud to call Noble. Such exemplary skills and courageous talent!"

The crowd cheered again.

"But, I imagine young Rysul here is eager to take his walk with Princess Therene."

"That, I most certainly am, your Majesty," Rysul said proudly through a wide grin.

"Well, don't let me keep you!" Ashos roared with laughter.

Rysul smiled and walked up to Therene.

"Princess, may I have the honor of accompanying you on a walk?"

"You may."

With that, the Phoenix Princess and Wolf Warrior made their exit to a wave of cheering.

Ceros returned to his father's side.

"My boy, you fought very well tonight."

"Do not patronize me, Father. You know how I despise that."

"Despite your disappointment, I am still proud of you."

"Your pride means nothing to me when mine has been cut down. I'm going to my room. Do not disturb me for the remainder of the night."

Bellor watched with sadness as his son

made his way into the excited crowd and up the stairs to his chambers. Bellor sighed and felt an arm wrap around his broad shoulders.

"Don't fret Bellor," Delver comforted. "He is growing still, and you know as much as I do, when there is a woman at stake, we all become crazed little Neo boys."

The two friends laughed as they walked to the Great Parlor with the other Head Nobles to finish the night with a round of the finest cherry wine and the final dialogue before bed.

As the noise from the Great Gallery began to dissipate, and the crowded bodies diffused into their individual bedrooms, Rysul and Therene made their way to the rose garden's Wishing Fountain. Therene sat on the edge and grazed the surface of the tranquil water with her fingertips.

"Rysul, I've never seen someone fight like that before… I would be lying if I said I was not impressed."

"My thanks, but I must tell you that I had already been impressed by your fervent comeliness which is why I suggested this walk in the first place."

"At dinner? I did not say much so I'm confused as to how you found me so attractive."

"To be honest, I saw you prior to my entrance at the Great Hall. You heard how I sat on the hill to watch the sun set?"

Therene nodded.

"I saw you there. I saw you reading under the Great Oak tree and was instantly captured by your radiance. Forgive me, for my eyes could not part from you."

Slightly taken aback but complimented, Therene replied, "You are forgiven, sir, so perhaps you should have wakened me when I dove into an early slumber. If you had, I could have avoided a lecture from my mother."

Rysul chuckled.

"Forgive me again, but as soon as I saw you lay your head down on the grass, I made my way to the gardens to fashion the most stunning bouquet for you. I wanted to present you with the same beauty you unknowingly presented to me, but alas, no flower could blossom as supple as you have."

Feeling red in the face, Therene stood up, and turned away from her moonlight poet.

"I don't know what this is," she whispered to herself.

"What?"

"This feeling I have in the pit of my stomach. It's as if an earthquake shook rocks loose from my heart and caused a vibration throughout my body, resting at my canyon. Though the movement of the rocks have stopped, the shaking and trembling in my body has not."

Therene still had not turned back around to look at Rysul, so he stood and put his hands on her waist, but she quickly escaped.

"No!" she screamed.

"What is it?"

"You know this is against the law. More so, it is against nature."

"I don't see how earthquakes are against nature," Rysul cleverly responded.

"I'm not joking!"

"Neither am I."

Rysul took a couple steps closer to Therene and cooed, "Listen. Do you hear that?"

Therene's small ears perked and heard nothing but the stillness of the cool night.

"I don't hear anything."

"Exactly. If Mother Nature was so opposed to how you're feeling, she would have responded by now. She would have sent heavy rain clouds, saturated with lightning to strike you down or blown a gust of wind so great that your feet would leave the ground, and you would be sucked into the sky. Yet, you are still here."

A brief silence hung in the air until Therene cleared her throat and asked, "What about your feelings? You've only heard me blubber about mine."

Rysul took the last steps toward Therene.

"Sweet Princess, heaven could kiss you for how arresting you look under the starry light. It is a shame that it can't, but it is in my luck that I have the honor in their place."

Rysul rested his hands on Therene's waist again as he pressed his forehead to hers. She quivered under his warm touch.

"But, you know what cross-breeding leads to…" she said worriedly. "The shame, the disgrace, the-"

"Shh… All I know is this. All I need to know is this. *You* were my fearlessness tonight."

One of Rysul's hands made its way up to Therene's jaw as he slowly tilted her lips to his. She did not resist him or refuse him. His handsome charm had swayed her completely so that all Therene knew was magnetism. They kissed under the stars, the only witnesses to their magic and love.

As the lovers stayed snared in each other's arms, the Head Nobles enjoyed themselves in the Great Parlor.

The Great Parlor was a fairly small room, but it was still lavished with finely carved furniture and gold accents. A polished brick fire-pit was centrally located in the room as the Head Nobles gathered around it, sipping their wine, and comfortably relaxed in large velvety cushioned chairs. It was a place where only Head Nobles could go; it was their sacred escape together.

"That Rysul you have," Oldar started. "Is a wonder, if I ever saw one. Almost godlike."

"Indeed he is," Delver replied.

"And such grace, chivalry *and* charm. It's astonishing that he has no female suitors," Irutia exclaimed.

"He trains almost every day and night, and in the spare moments he has outside of training, he's wandering around in the Woodlands dreaming."

"I think they call that sleep-walking," Oldar kidded.

"That aside, he truly is a unique creature," Irutia continued. "I'm sure Therene is thoroughly enjoying her time with him as he seems well-educated, too."

"Let us hope that is all the princess is enjoying, his education," Oldar sneered.

"Oh hush, you fowl bird!" Irutia blurted out.

The room filled with an uproar of laughter. Then, there was a knock on the door.

"Ashos, is there a new Courter in your party tonight that he does not know the rules of this room?" Bellor teased.

Puzzled, Asho stood and walked to the door as the knocking grew more hectic.

"It is not to my knowledge," Ashos stated, "Perhaps one of the Courtesses has lost her child, one that does not know the ways of our Great Parlor yet."

The knocking grew louder and more rapid.

"I'm coming!" Ashos boomed.

He opened the door and saw, not a child,

but his most supreme Courter, Hoden, dressed in a beige and gold decorated ensemble.

"Hoden, what is it? You know when this room is occupied we are not to be disturbed."

Hoden bowed.

"I am ever so sorry, my Majesty Crown, but I have word that the Magi Order is at the Great Hall's front gates, a little earlier than expected."

"Oh, well bring them in, and have the Great Hall cleared. We will meet them there."

"Yes."

Hoden bowed and went to do his majesty's bidding.

Closing the door, Ashos said to his royal companions, "It's time."

The Head Nobles finished their wine and made their way to the Great Hall.

When they arrived, the Order was already seated on one half of a round table.

The Magi Order lived in the most southern region of Pangea called the Great Crossings. Here, the caves were haunted with spirits, rivers flowed upstream, and the sky was always flowing with magic. Despite its unusual terrain and aura, the Great Crossings was a glorious landscape, filled with bright rainbows and sunshine. It was even said that the weather matched the magical essence of the Great Crossings people, as its inhabitants were of light, nature, and peace.

The Great Crossings also served as the land barrier between the peaceful Neo-inhabited Pangea and the peninsula that had been recently named the Land of Cassum, home of the Anders. They had been banished to the massive cape one year ago, as soon as the most recent war was over.

Upon their exile, the Magi Order created

a magical barricade between the calm Great
Crossings and the Land of Cassum to prevent
the Anders from invading the main lands.
Although a few bandit Ander groups remained
spread across the Noble terrain, they were
hardly a threat. Tranquility was restored, and
the Neos' people rejoiced in their revived
culture and vitalities.

In return for the Order's magical aid in
the second Great War and the enchanted wall,
the Nobles had sent members of their Courts to
become Orderly Helpers in the Crossings' Great
Abbey. It was an honor to be selected, as
young Neos would be blessed with the chance to
learn and practice a high level of
enchantments. Court Soldiers were also sent
and ordered to provide extra protection if
ever there was a breach, for there were few
shamanistic nomads before the war, and now,
many of the younger ones had died valiantly in
battle.

"Erisi," Ashos said cheerfully as he
opened up his arms to embrace the wise old
priest. "It is nice to see you again and so
soon. I'm accustomed to only seeing you every
five years at the Tellings."

Erisi hugged the Majesty Crown and said,
"War will cause unexpected ripples, my dear
friend. Please, sit. We have much to tell."

The Magi Order was comprised of five Neo
priests, each harboring the power to control
one of the five elements.

There was Erisi, Head Councilman, an Owl
by Neo standards, and Priest of the Air. He
was the oldest of the Magi Order, and in his
human form he bore long silver hair on his
head and hanging from his chin. His grayish
blue eyes were always still, like a pond on a
mid summer's night. His words and hands were

as kind as they were mystical, and he always wore a smile on his face.

There was also the Koi Fish, Nysam, Priest of the Water. He was a slick and clever soul and the youngest out of the Magi Order. His light blonde hair would dance around him as he coasted through the water, his slender build making him seem welcomed by his watery domain.

Thirdly, there was the Dragon, Tridor, Priest of the Fire. His rose colored hair whirled about him as he walked. He was strong and middle aged, though wise beyond his years. His temper was as bold as his flames, but he was affectionate to his colleagues. His emerald eyes boasted with equal passion and burned through the night like starlight.

Then there was the Badger, Kuros, Priest of the Earth. His hands were rough because he was always digging up herbs as he also was well-rehearsed in medicinal healing. His portly body would stagger back and forth as he walked, but he was as healthy as Ashos. His large brown eyes matched the dirt in which he loved to plow in.

Lastly, there was the Baboon, Lafore, Priest of the Metal. His long, thin hands were powerfully built but also resilient. His short white hair complemented his tawny colored skin and olive eyes. He was a man of few words, but when he did speak, his words were absolutely transfixing.

"I hope your spells have not worn off already," Oldar joked. "I'm not ready to return to war."

"No, King Oldar," Erisi replied. "But, this Telling for his Majesty Crown may be slightly unnerving."

The Tellings normally occurred after the

Tournaments which decided the Majesty Crown. There was a week of festivities following the victory, but on the first night, the Magi Order would come and share its prophecy for the upcoming five years under the new rule.

The Telling gave the new leader a hint of what darkness or disturbances that lie ahead but rarely a way to resolve it. This is how the Majesty Crown won his or her respect to maintain the Noble status because a Head Noble was not only named through blood but also by proof of character. If a Head Noble had no children, he or she had the faculty to choose a Noble from his or her ranks to serve, as Delver decided for Rysul.

"Erisi, what do you and the Order foresee in my Lionship?" Ashos questioned.

"I fear, my great king, this next period of time will still shed a dark shadow over Pangea and truly be a test of your strength."

"Another war?" Delver asked.

"Not as soon as you might think," Erisi replied. "For war is not King Ashos' first concern."

A wave of disquiet flooded over all five Head Nobles as they stared across the circular table at the five priests.

"Friar Lafore… the prophecy," Erisi continued.

Lafore slowly stood, pulled out a rolled up parchment and read:

"A stir in the winds born from a hidden affair,
Will bring forth a child with wings to spare,
And paws on the ground to carry it so,
Beyond the borders of our world to a realm unknown.

A betrayal within these Noble walls,
Will cause a Head to perish and fall,
As evil sheds its darkness down,
Upon the land comes a new black crown.

Save the child for a star of hope will
see,
A chance to change the course of destiny,
But only when the child finds true love
again,
Will the spirit of all elements
transcend."

With his final words, Lafore sat back down. The Great Hall was dead silent for, what seemed to be, an eternity until Irutia spoke up.

"This cannot be."

"It is the way the universe has spoken to us," Nysam replied.

"But, how can that be? A hybrid of feathers and fur? We all know what cross-breeding leads to… It's not possible."

Irutia's words fell to the ground.

Delver spoke next.

"Order, you mean to tell me that it's possible for two Neo breeds to bear a child… a child that is not-"

"An abomination!" Irutia interrupted.

Erisi nodded his head.

"It is what we have been told."

"Can you imagine it?" Oldar chimed in. "A cross-breed that's not an Ander? It's phenomenal."

"How can you say it's phenomenal when it's so frightening?" Irutia uttered. "Do you not remember what the Anders did to our people over this past century? They slaughtered us, beat us down, imprisoned us-"

"Is that not we have done to them?" Oldar
continued.

An eerie hush fell over the room.

"Listen, I'm not saying we weren't right
in fighting this war. We had the right to be
free, but I imagine they say the same about us
as we have about them."

"But, we have given them land on which to
live on their own," Delver argued. "They are
free to live at their own leisure. Our
ancestors were oppressed. Remember we only
killed until the war was over and for
survival. We tried for peace. We tried
politics, and it failed."

"It's because they are cowards," Irutia
pitched in.

With that, the three voices clashed, and
a loud banter arose. Ashos sat and listened to
their bickering but soon roared over the
noise.

"Quiet!"

Everyone muted.

Calmly, Ashos asked, "What is my duty in
this term, Order?"

"Though we are not accustomed to giving
any sort of advice at the Telling," Tridor
calmly began. "We find this to be an
extraordinary circumstance."

Kuros continued, "The child must be born
in the Great Abbey. Only then can we secure
its safety and protect it long enough for it
to mature and have time to find its power."

"So you do not know from which exact two
species this child will be born of?" Ashos
questioned.

"No, our powers only sense the trend of
good and evil, unfortunately no specifics,"
Erisi continued. "But, it *will* be born of
Noble blood."

"I hope it's one half of my line," Oldar, the Falcon King, exclaimed in attempt to lighten the mood. "But, who shall my child be mated with? Ashos, your lions have great strength, but Delver's wolves consist of high speeds… and Bellor's children boast well of gusto. So many choices!"

"And the betrayal?" Ashos inquired.

"It will lead to one of your deaths, I'm afraid," Erisi softly spoke.

Oldar quieted down, his light-hearted spirit torn at the statement. All Head Nobles sat silently. Then, Ashos stood.

"Thank you, Order, for coming and sharing your Telling with us tonight. My dear Nobles, we must not let our hopes waver now. Now is the time where it is of high importance that we stay focused, understanding, accepting and courageous in order to secure a righteous fate for future generations. At any stage of life, death is possible. It lingers in the shadows, waiting to sweep us away to the afterlife. This, we are aware of, and now is no different. Though the shadow's intent has been brought into light, we must not fear it. We must stand before it with our heads held high and our spirits bold because this is our role. This is why we were chosen to be Head Nobles, to take the road that our people should not, to be valiant and brave for those we love and swear to protect. My brothers and sister, stand with me if you remember your vows, if you remember your trust, and if you remember your honorable love."

With those mighty words, all remaining members stood, filled with the passionate words of their new Majesty Crown.

Erisi smiled and said, "I believe we are in good hands with you at the helm, your highness."

The five priests stood as well and bowed to their Noble Heads.

"Come now," Ashos cheeringly said. "Your feet must be tired from your long travels from the Great Crossings. Let me call Hoden to show you to your chambers. We still have much to celebrate in the next six days."

With that, Hoden escorted the priests upstairs to their rooms, and the Head Nobles followed. Ashos and Bellor followed in the rear.

"Bellor, brother," Ashos started. "You were seemingly quiet in the Telling this year. Is something wrong?"

"No," Bellor smiled. "It was hard to get any word in with the other three squabbling like young maidens."

Ashos laughed.

"Very true! Well, I am glad that you are alright. Sleep well tonight, for I shall meet you in the morning by the Lilac Pond for a round of fishing."

Ashos patted his dear friend on the back and headed down the hallway to his room. Bellor stopped and dropped to his knees. Tears flooded his face as he wept with torment. He knew what fate had in store and what he had to do to stop it.

Darkness Rising

A year and two seasons had passed. The gardens surrounding the Great Hall were now covered in an ivory blanket of snow, but even with the flowers and tall grasses out of bloom, the Great Hall was still majestic.

Its high stone walls would glisten in the morning as the sun rose to mildly melt the thin sheets of ice lingering on its surface while the ponds stayed glazed over with a pale crystal coating, sealing off the aquatic world beneath it. The cool winds sang a lovely winter sonata as it danced through the lush pine needles of the forest and lulled the frosty wonderland to a deep and peaceful slumber when the moon dominated the sky at night.

But, on this particular night, the atmosphere was far from still as the Nobles and their Courts had assembled once again in the Great Hall for their reinstated Winter Ball. It lasted seven days, filled with opulent dinners, recreational sports, and endless laughter and celebration. This being the first Winter Ball since the end of the war, meant that the gathering was to be extra magnificent.

As the third night's dinner carried on inside the Great Hall, outside, two shadows swiftly crossed the front lawn and escaped to a nearby gazebo on the outer rim of the property, just north of the Great Hall's entrance.

When the shadows reached the gazebo, they sat down and smiled.

"You are truly lovely, my darling, Therene," Rysul said through panting breaths.

Therene smiled.

"And so are you, lovely," Therene joked as she playfully nudged Rysul's arm.

"You have Pangea's grandest warrior sitting beside you, to protect you and to love you everyday as long as I live."

"Yes. I am aware of my good fortune and am entirely grateful."

Therene snuggled in closer to Rysul's warm muscular body, soaking in his strong arm's embrace around her. She closed her eyes and let her lungs fall in step with his. The soft palpitations of his heartbeat, pulsing in her ear.

"Rysul?"

"Yes?"

"This is crazy… You and I."

Rysul chuckled.

"Yes. I suppose we are crazy, but I do not regret any decision that has led you to my arms tonight because when I look down at you, under the blessed moon's brilliance, I know this is where I am meant to be."

"You always know how to ease my heart," Therene whispered.

"I hope that is always the case."

Rysul tightened his arm around Therene, and she wrapped her arms around him in return. A steady silence encircled them so all they could hear was the marvelous pine tree choir singing its rich melodies.

Therene interrupted the savory tunes.

"Rysul… I'm with child."

Rysul's breathing stopped.

"I'm so sorry," she continued softly.

Rysul pulled back and propped Therene up so he could look her in the eyes. He still had not said anything.

"I'm so sorry," she repeated. "We have to end it."

"Why?"

"Our child… will not be a Neo. It will be exiled or worse, killed. I'm the Princess of the Mystic Canyons. How could I birth an Ander and look my mother in the face?"

"So you plan on killing it yourself?" Rysul asked puzzled.

"There is no other way," Therene wept, broken heartedly.

Rysul sat quietly for a moment before piping up, "Come away with me."

"What?" Therene asked flabbergasted.

"Come away with me. We can run away and live in the grand nature Mother Pangea has to offer us. Her land is fertile and her waters are nourishing. We are both strong-bodied and strong-willed. With our love we can make it. We can get away from here, and we will raise *our* child… together."

"But-"

"I don't care about anything or anyone else. I will love our child no matter what he or she turns out to be because it's proof of our existing and undying love. There is no way evil can be born from us. We will teach our child to love, universally, and even if he or she ends up being the only Ander that can love the beasts inside us, then at least we can say there was one."

"You speak so poetically, and I love that about you… but, Rysul, this is real life. Poetry does not always save us here. We have to end it."

"Therene-"

"No," Therene said shortly, wiping away her tears. "I have made my decision."

With that, Therene ran off to the Great
Hall entrance and up toward her room. Rysul
sat in the gazebo, stunned.

*Was Therene right? Is there no real place
for my romanticism?* Rysul thought.

He shook his head and his thoughts with
it. Leaning back, he stared up at the starry
sky. Two stars were shining particularly
bright.

Rysul smiled and whispered to himself,
"There will always be love."

When Therene returned to her bedroom,
tears flooded her face once more. Inside her
room, she slammed the door shut.

"What in heaven's name is wrong,
Therene?" a concerned voice echoed behind her.

Surprised, Therene whisked around and
stammered, "Mother?"

The Phoenix Queen stepped forward,
beautiful as always.

"Yes, dear."

"What are you doing here?"

"Dinner ended early as the rambunctious
Oldar challenged Delver to a bow and arrow
contest in the back gardens. You know how
excited everyone gets when a Head Noble
challenges another. It's like reliving the
Tournament all over again. However, I imagine
Oldar will be eating his words by the end of
the night."

Therene slightly smiled and sat on her
bed. Irutia sat down next to her.

"Now, tell me, my darling daughter, what
seems to be the matter? I noticed you were not
at dinner. Is everything alright?"

"I cannot even begin to describe how I
feel."

The tears started again.

Seeing the hurt in her daughter's eyes,

Irutia wrapped her resounding arms around her.

"There, there," Irutia comforted. "Is it about young Rysul?"

Shocked, Therene faltered, "How did you know?"

"A mother knows, Therene. I saw the fire fly at the Tournament's dinner a year and some ago. You need not be ashamed. He is a handsome young fellow, with a strong-able body, and his words are quite fetching. In fact, I cannot hide that I was once taken by another breed prior to my throne."

Therene sniffled, "You did? What happened?"

"Like any adolescent, it was a phase. The thrill of experiencing something different and unique was intriguing to me, but as I matured, I came to know my place and fell in love with a young Phoenix archer, your father. Bless him. He was always there for me. When I was inducted into the Head Nobles, he was not jealous nor did his ego put an end to his love for me. He was quite the opposite, always full of joy and praise, saying how lucky he was to stand by my side."

Irutia sighed.

"I miss him terribly sometimes, and I curse the Ander who slew him, but this is life. We must deal and adapt to the cards we are dealt because in any instant of time, we can lose all that we love. That being said, we must learn to appreciate and love with all our hearts in every case. We culture love through experience, not through people."

Irutia wiped Therene's eyes.

"Let me get you a glass of water," Irutia smiled. "With all these wretched tears you've shed, your body must be thirsty."

Irutia stood up, walked to the door, and

opened it.

"I'm pregnant," Therene whispered.

Irutia stopped dead in her tracks.

"The child is Rysul's," Therene continued.

Irutia slowly shut the door and turned around.

"You are sure?" Irutia questioned.

"Yes."

Therene lowered her head.

"I'm so sorry, Mother," she cried again.

Stunned, Irutia stood wordless.

Finally, after a few minutes, Irutia walked to her daughter's bedside and knelt down in front of her.

"Therene, you must listen closely as to what I tell you next. You and Rysul must leave here and head to the Great Crossings where the Magi Order resides and take residence there. It is the only place where you will be safe."

"I don't understand," Therene stumbled over her words. "You aren't upset?"

"No; however, I am most concerned for your well-being."

"Why? Am I in danger? Will the Head Nobles have me killed if they find out?"

"Just the opposite. They will tell you what I am saying to you now."

"Mother, I don't understand."

"At the Telling last year, the Order's prophecy told us of a cross-bred child, of Neo blood, being born. This child is going to be our savior against an incredible darkness in the future if it manages to live. Though my heart breaks for not being able to be with you during this stressful time, you are not safe here, nor at home, and must retreat to the Great Abbey."

"How are you certain that the child in

the prophecy is mine?"

Irutia whispered the lines of the prophecy, "A stir in the winds born from a hidden affair, will bring forth a child with wings to bear, and paws on the ground to carry it so, beyond the borders of this world to a realm unknown…"

Irutia stood.

Therene, still shocked, muttered, "My baby… A pure Neo hybrid…"

"Make haste and pack your belongings. Then, go to Rysul, and tell him of your plans. If he loves you as much as I hope, then he will go without question."

Therene quickly stood up and wrapped her arms around her mother's waist.

"I love you, mother."

"I love you more, my sweet child. You bring more honor to me than I could ever speak of. I know you are strong and will get through this. Fate could not have picked a better choice to shoulder such a responsibility."

Irutia stepped away.

"I must return downstairs and tell the other Head Nobles about this, as we must prepare for what's to come."

Meanwhile, downstairs, all the guests were filtering back inside from Oldar and Delver's arching match.

"You cheated!" exclaimed Oldar.

"How could I cheat if I was standing a full three arm's length away from you? Do not blame me for your lousy shots," Delver argued back.

"Come now," Ashos chimed in. "Oldar, surely you must blame the winds."

"Yes!" agreed Oldar. "The good Majesty Crown has rightfully defined my loss! You see? It has nothing to do with my lack of skill."

Ashos continued, "And Delver's were much too fast and precise for the wind to command his arrows, so to that, I applaud you, Wolf King."

Delver howled with laughter as did the Ashos and Bellor. Oldar folded his arms across his chest, continuing to act out his childish tantrum.

"By the by," Ashos started mid-laughter. "Where is your son, Ceros, tonight? I'm sure *he* might have put good King Delver in his place at the contest. He seemed quite adamant about accepting challenges two summers ago."

"He is up north in the ocean border's mountains. There was word that an Ander bandit group had been vandalizing a small Neo village. He and a group of our finest soldiers went to take care of the problem."

"Ah, I see. Well, it sounds like he got his challenge anyway."

When the Head Nobles approached the staircase, Irutia stopped them.

"My dear Head Nobles, we must retreat to the Great Parlor as I have much to tell you… The prophecy has started."

The Head Nobles stopped in their tracks and stared at one another.

"To the parlor," Ashos stated calmly.

The Head Nobles nodded and retreated silently to the Great Parlor where the fate of Pangea would be discussed.

Meanwhile, Princess Therene and Rysul had begun their journey south to the Great Crossings while way up north, Ceros was dealing with the group of Anders, but not in the way described to his father, and he was not on the eastern mountains.

Instead, Ceros was at his father's castle, just north of the Savannahs uppermost border, sitting in his own parlor.

Aside from the brightly burning fireplace, the rest of the large room was dark. Ceros sat at a table placed in the middle of the floor. A large fat man with a dirty face covered in a black beard but balding head sat across from the Black Prince.

"And what is it that *we* get from this deal?" the filthy man asked Ceros.

"Insurance that we don't kill you and all of your kind. I know Anders aren't the brightest of breeds, but you can follow that logic. Only the fit survive. Those who are not shall perish or live underneath them. The only reason why we did not exterminate all of you after the war was because that damned King Ashos forbad it. His heart is much more forgiving than mine. The terms for bloodshed are never ending for me. That is why he and the rest of the Head Nobles are weak and why they will fall to me. It is why you are to obey me now, Gelaro."

Displeased but compliant, Gelaro asked, "What is it that you want me to do exactly?"

Ceros leaned forward.

"You are to take your Ander group and search the free land of Pangea. Find any and all coalitions of your people. I know there are more of you in hiding than the Nobles think.

After you have met with each coalition's leader, you will inform them that they are to travel to the border that separates the Savannahs from the Great Crossings where they will make camp. Then, you and *your* mediocre band of thieves will travel along the most western coast of the Great Crossings to the Land of Cassum. You will enter the Land of Cassum and ready an army at the border."

"Isn't there a magical barrier surrounding that place?"

"You can enter the magical barrier, but cannot escape."

"So, we're stuck there?"

"You leave that to me. Just make sure to be ready."

"And my incentive if I obey?" the Ander captive muttered.

"Your incentive?"

Ceros laughed.

"Your incentive is your life and the welfare of your people. My future plans do not have to include you. If you join me though, I can give you revenge on the Neos who banished you, and I shall lift the magical barrier that confines the remaining. If you refuse me, I will carry on with my endeavors, and before you have time to beg and gravel for my forgiveness, I will have killed off your entire family and your species."

Ceros cackled once more as the Ander stranger was finally struck with fear of the crazed beast.

"It will be done," Gelaro replied.

He stood up and bowed.

"Prince Ceros."

"Yes, it will and what a glorious time it will be. Leveel!"

An enormous man opened the door and walked into the room. He was much larger than Ceros and more rugged around the face. Dirt clung to his nails and smile that was filled with yellow and razor-sharp teeth. Leveel also carried an overpowering stench, like that of the rotten fish he consumed daily, and it stung Gelaro's nose so badly he gagged.

Leveel was Ceros' right hand man, another Black Bear Neo, almost like his body guard. He was not very intelligent, but when he was put to the battlefield, every opponent would flee his presence. His mighty fists and fierce bite could butcher many a foe.

"Yes, Prince?" Leveel slowly said.

"Take our new ally down to the dungeon with his other wretched folk. In the morning call upon five of our soldiers to escort them on their journey. If there are any disputes or lack of respect, do not hesitate to punish the offender as you see fit."

"Yes, Prince."

With that, Leveel snatched up the Ander by the collar in one quick swoop and exited the room.

Ceros poured himself a glass of wine, stood up, and walked over to the fireplace where he stared deep into the burning flames.

A soft and eerie voice crept up behind him.

"You see much of yourself in the flames, my prince?"

Ceros did not need to turn around to know who the voice belonged to. He knew it was that of Quar, a snake wizard who was cast out of the Great Crossings for practicing forbidden magic.

Ceros ran across Quar after a battle in the Woodlands and brought him back to his castle without his father's knowledge, for Quar stayed hidden in the shadows and only made his presence known when the Black Prince was alone.

Quar was old and frail but full of magical strength. He hobbled on an old oak cane and recited his incantations through stained black teeth and a musty grey beard that nearly touched the floor. Each decrepit movement resonated in a cracking bone or squeaking joint while his thin and wrinkled skin stretched tightly over his feeble muscles. The years had not been kind to Quar for his body had paid a price for the evil enchantments he provoked.

"You have come to bring me good news, I hope, Quar," Ceros calmly said as he continued to gaze into the fire.

"I do, my liege. Your father shall return home in less than two weeks time from the winter festival."

"That, I am already aware of. Tell me if your potion is ready or not."

"'Tis ready."

Ceros finally turned around and saw Quar's outstretched hand holding a small red vial.

"A drop of this on your blade and you will be able to kill or stab, cut or slice any flesh with no trail or hint of a scar behind."

"But, the damage?"

"Will be just as lethal. No one will be able to tell that he has died at your hands. I assure you that the murder shall sail unnoticed over seas of judgment and suspicion with the clouds I have provided."

Ceros took the vial from Quar's hand and held it to the light of the fire.

"And you are sure he will come to me?"

"Yes. My premonitions do not lie."

"Good. So now… it begins."

Ceros grinned as Quar's body dissipated back into the looming darkness. Little did the land of Pangea know, it would be doing the same.

About two weeks passed before Bellor arrived back to his castle from the Winter Ball, just as Quar said. It was nighttime when he walked through the front gates.

Seeing how tired his followers were after their long trek home, Bellor immediately sent all his Nobles and Courts to bed. He was tired as well but knew there was something he had to take care of before he rested.

Bellor sat on a bench just outside of the front doors. His mind was still marveled at how quickly the prophecy was unfolding. He had hoped that the fates would allow him to prepare a bit longer for, what he knew to be, the most inexcusable and sinful task a father could commit.

He took a huge deep breath in, stood up, and walked inside.

Bellor made his way upstairs to the sleeping quarters and paused at a closed door. His hand was trembling, and his body was fighting back tears that wanted to escape. Finally, after a few moments, Bellor cautiously opened the door.

The room was dark, for its dweller was fast asleep, but Bellor's keen sense of smell and night vision guided him to the bed without making a sound.

When Bellor reached the bedside, he paused again, and a single tear rolled down his cheek as he pulled out a small dagger. Looking up the heavens for exoneration, Bellor raised the dagger high above his head, ready to thrust the blade downward with full force, but before the dagger reached its full plunge, the sleeping figure swiftly erected and lodged its own dagger into the Black Bear King's chest.

Broken hearted, literally and figuratively, the great Bear King dropped to his knees, his face flooded with the tears he fought so hard not to show. Bellor took a few heavy breaths and looked up at his attacker.

"My son…" Bellor wheezed. "I am so sorry."

"You know father," Ceros said wiping the blood from his cursed blade. "Quar told me of your betrayal to me."

"Quar? The Snake Wizard?"

"Yes. I commissioned him to work for me quite some time ago after one of the battles in the Woodlands. Quite a nice surprise, isn't it?"

"Then my intentions for tonight," Bellor stammered and smiled. "Were right."

Enraged by his father's coolness to the situation, Ceros struck Bellor across the face, putting Bellor's entire body to the floor.

"How dare you say that killing your own son was right? I wouldn't have had to kill you if Quar hadn't warned me of your betrayal to me. You see… my hand was forced."

"No, my boy…"

Bellor's voice was down to a whisper now for his life was fleeing him.

"No… It was *my* hand that was forced. You have always been different… darker than the rest of us. I hoped for many years that you would change, but alas, my fears were proven true tonight, and I beg the stars to pardon my actions."

"The stars will not save you tonight, father," Ceros said coldly.

With his son's words echoing in his ears, Bellor's eyes slowly shut as he passed.

Quar emerged from the shadows.

"It is done, my prince."

"I suppose I must send word to the other Head Nobles that one of their own has fallen, dead of old age and a nasty heart failure. A funeral must be prepared as I expect much mourning," Ceros said, staring down at his deceased father.

Quar bowed and left Cero's room.

"Yes, Prince Ceros."

"No," Ceros whispered to himself. "You may call me King."

And So It Begins

Only a handful of months passed before the chilly winds of winter began to settle and waved goodbye to the world while signs of a returning spring resurfaced to all of Pangea.

The Great Crossings was beautiful this time of year. Streams and ponds were filled with salmon and other brilliantly hued fishes as they swam with the upstream current. The air was crisp, yet dampened by the morning dew, and subtle winds blew the long grass back and forth. The flowers and fruits were all in blossom now and speckled each tree and bush with so much more color that one could still close their eyes and feel the stimulating rainbow's caress.

Yes, the land was alive with life as the spring aura warmed the hearts of all the creatures of the Great Crossings.

The Great Abby was no exception. Friars and young maidens swarmed the rolling fields and flocked to the orchards of the grand estate. Many fruits were to be harvested after the anxious waiting in winter.

But, not everyone would spend their spring hours plucking apples and berries from the green wildlife outside.

A particular young soul, Sam'ona, stayed in the library while her friends all scurried to the cool waters to swim or to the tops of leafy hills to play in the sun.

She was an orphan fox Neo. Both parents had been killed in the one of the many battles against the Anders, but she was rescued by King Ashos and placed in the immediate care of the Order.

Only at the age of five, Sam'ona was beyond ahead of her older classmates. She was well read and more focused. Her hazel brown eyes were saturated in excitement, and her long chestnut hair flowed behind her as she ran, tripping on the oversized robe she wore, through the candlelit hallways of the Great Abby with every new discovery she unveiled in the ancient books.

Tonight was no different. Full of eagerness and a bit of clumsiness, she slid into an oak door but quickly recovered and stood pounding heavily on its surface.

"Friar Sulny! Friar Sulny! I found it!" she shouted, waving a tattered red book in the air. "I found the book you asked me to retrieve!"

The large oak door creaked open as an elderly man stepped into the hallway to greet the enthusiastic toddler. His white beard gravitated to the floor, and his long matching white hair was pulled back into a ponytail. Small bifocals rested above his nose and pleasant smile.

"Did you now? That was quite fast. I thought it would take you at least one more day to solve my riddle map."

"I stayed up all night just to figure it out! You know how much I love your riddle maps!"

"More than any other young lad or maiden I've ever taught, my dear," laughed Friar Sulny. "Come in, Sam'ona. You're in luck. I just put on a pot of tea. We can discuss the matters of your treasure over the nice blueberry pie Lady Tanan brought by this afternoon, a belated birthday gift for you. I apologize for missing the actual date last week."

"It's okay! Lady Tanan's blueberry pie is my favorite!"

Sam'ona hurriedly entered the friar's room and sat down at the table.

With anxiousness, she slammed the book down right next to the pie and panted, "Is this the Healer's Mastery?"

Stunned but quickly remembering who his guest was, Friar Sulny replied, "Surely you were not able to read this, Sam'ona. This book is difficult to read for most students three times your age."

Blushing, Sam'ona responded, "I only knew a couple of words, but I guessed from what the pictures showed."

"Ah yes! Pictures. They are quite beautiful."

Friar Sulny sat down across the table from her.

"A single portrait or painting can tell the same story a thousand words can."

"Isn't that because… in a painting, there can be a thousand strokes?" Sam'ona inquired.

Laughing, Friar Sulny responded, "You are truly a clever girl, Sam'ona."

He stood to tend to the whistling teapot and to set the table for their tiny dessert feast.

"Why did you have me find this book, Friar Sulny?"

With his back still turned, Friar Sulny replied, "Because, my child, your task will be to learn it."

"What?" Sam'ona stammered hysterically. "I'm only five! In basic studies, I've only gotten to chapter six of my herbal remedies!"

Friar Sulny returned to the table with two cups of tea.

"The Healer's Mastery extends far beyond that of plants and incantations. The Healer's Mastery is a blessed power that only a handful have been bestowed with since the very beginning of Pangea. Would you be so kind to get the plates and forks from the cabinet?"

Sam'ona obliged.

Still stunned by what the friar had said to her, she whirled around after grabbing two plates and exclaimed, "But, I'm five!"

Friar Sulny laughed.

"My dear child, age is of no importance. What matters is the maturity of your heart. That has always been the true measure of any Healer. Healers are defined by their compassion, their empathy, their understanding, and their connection to others."

Finished setting the table, Sam'ona sat down in her seat once again.

"But, I'm only five…" she repeated calmly. "How do you know all of these things?"

"Because that is *my* job. As the Great Abby's librarian, it is my duty to find the similarities between our history and our present time so that I may help produce a better future. All the grand qualities that bore a Healer worthy of knowing the Healer's Mastery in our ancient past I find in you."

Friar Sulny served Sam'ona a slice of pie.

"You're a very special child, Sam'ona. I believe even King Ashos recognized that in you which is why he brought you to us, here in the Order."

He smiled and took a bite out his blueberry dessert.

"Delicious!" he exclaimed. "Lady Tanan has surely outdone herself this time. I will

have to thank her in the morning, for she must
be busy giving the little ones their baths
now."

Sam'ona laughed and happily dug into her
pie. Another knock sounded at the door.

"Who is it?" Friar Sulny asked.

"It's me, Friar Sulny! Eton!" the voice
yelled.

"Oh! Do come in Eton!"

The door opened, and a young Neo boy,
only a year older than Sam'ona, walked in. His
bright green eyes and wavy blonde hair moved
swiftly with him as he entered the room.

"I gave the Order your message. They said
they are free to meet with you on the back
terrace."

"Thank you," Friar Sulny responded.
"Eton, you remember my star student, Miss
Sam'ona."

"Oh yes, Friar Sulny. How are you doing,
Miss Sam'ona?"

Mouth full of blueberry pie, she
murmured, "I'm… fine."

Eton chuckled.

"Um… you've got some-" he pointed out.

Sam'ona's eyes widened.

"What?"

Eton continued as he walked toward
Sam'ona, "There's pie on your chin."

Embarrassed Sam'ona quickly turned away
from Eton as he sat down beside her. He
laughed.

"It's okay," Eton said, softly putting
his hand on her shoulder. "It happens to me
all the time. I can wipe it off for you."

Feeling the release of tension in
Sam'ona's shoulders, Eton gently turned her
body to face him as he pulled down his rolled
up sleeve to wipe the blue stain on her chin.

After he had finished, Eton said, "There. Good as new!"

"Thank you…" Sam'ona whispered.

Watching the whole event, Friar Sulny smiled.

"Eton, my boy, would you be so kind as to escort Miss Sam'ona to her room. It's approaching *both* your bedtimes."

"Yes, Friar Sulny."

The pair of young Neos stood.

"Thank you for the pie," Sam'ona said cheeringly as she turned to leave.

"Miss Sam'ona?" Friar Sulny called out.

Sam'ona turned around. Friar Sulny was holding the red book she brought in and patted the Healer's Mastery gently on the vintage cover.

"Remember what I told you. The power does not lie in years but in true love."

"Yes, Friar Sulny."

When Eton and Sam'ona left, the old librarian stood at his window gazing up at the night sky. All was calm in the heavens until a star twinkled, almost winking at Friar Sulny. Seeing this, he nodded and made his way to the back terrace.

The night air was chilly as the Magi Order stood at the back entrance to the Great Abby. It was highly decorated with flowers, patio chairs and tables and outlined by a row of lantern light posts. A single fire pit sat in the middle of the brick courtyard where the Order gathered to maintain their warmth. Friar Sulny emerged from within the Great Abby walls and joined them.

"Friar Sulny, how are you this evening?" Erisi greeted.

"Quite well. I just indulged on Lady Tanan's famous blueberry pie."

The Magi Order chuckled.

"Tell me why we have gathered, Friar Sulny," Erisi continued. "Your assistant, Eton, has informed us you bear urgent news."

"The Healer's Mastery has been revealed."

A lulling hush fell over the Order. Erisi spoke up first.

"When?"

"Just this evening. To a young fox maiden named Sam'ona."

"How old is she?" questioned Kuros.

"She is but five years old."

A restless and worried murmur swept across the terrace.

"Are you sure, Friar Sulny?" Nysam replied. "Five years old seems much too young."

"I know, but this child is special. Her intelligence lies far beyond her years, and her heart is innocent and true. I had a feeling she could be the chosen one so I sent her out on one of my riddle quests with her treasure being the book, and it revealed itself to her."

"But, it seems like such a large task for such a small child," Erisi said again, worried. "How aware is she of her responsibilities?"

"I have not yet told her, but I trust her to listen to my advice. There is no doubt she will learn and master the trade. The book would not have let itself be found by her if she wasn't. You know that. I'm just happy it emerged itself within our abbey walls; it could've resurfaced anywhere in Pangea. Perhaps our desperation for it, swayed its decision."

The Magi Order all nodded silently, still trying to assure themselves.

Friar Sulny proceeded.

"We also have to be thankful that the Healer's Mastery found a suitor before the baby's arrival. How is Princess Therene, by the by?"

"She rests more and more each the day," Lafore answered. "We suspect that the baby is to be born soon which does not leave us much time to prepare, but if you are confident in your Sam'ona, then that relieves my spirits greatly."

"I have full faith in her."

The terrace fell silent of voices again, and the singing of the trees pranced about but was soon interrupted by a loud cry from one of the rooms in the upper wing. The Magi Order and Friar Sulny all turned to one another with concerned countenances and ran inside the Great Abby.

As they got closer and closer to the upper wing, their hearts raced because they knew exactly which room the cries of agony were coming from.

When they arrived at Therene's chambers, a group of young maidens had already swarmed the princess' bedside. Therene was wide awake, sweating, and in labor.

"You certainly were not lying when you said soon, eh?" Friar Sulny joked to Lafore. "But, where is Rysul?"

Stopping a passing Bobcat maiden, Friar Sulny asked, "My dear, where is Rysul this evening? Shouldn't a father be present at the birthing of his own child?"

"Rysul is not at the Abby, sir," the maiden responded.

"Where is he then?"

"He had taken some of the boys to the western woods so they can practice their fishing and hunting skills.

"How long will they be gone for?"

"I think the trip is to last five days. Uhhh… travel outward for two, make camp for one… then return. If I remember correctly, Rysul and the boys should be home by tomorrow morning."

"Thank you. Please continue with your task, and I apologize for the inconvenience."

The maiden curtsied and hurried into the room. Therene was still screaming. Seeing that there was nothing they could do, Friar Sulny and the Order headed downstairs to wait.

Several hours passed until the screaming stopped. Slowly, Friar Sulny and the Order headed back upstairs to Therene's room. When they entered the room, all the maidens were in tears, the air within the room weighted down by a despairing heaviness upon the lungs.

The Order surrounded Therene's bed. Erisi laid his hand on her forehead.

"My poor child," he whispered as he swept the damp hair out of her eyes.

Therene did not stir, for her body lie cold and clammy, but her face still glistened peacefully in the candlelight.

As the Magi Order held hands and said a prayer, Friar Sulny walked up to Lady Tanan who was sitting in the corner rocking chair holding a small bundle.

He stood beside her and looked over her shoulder. Inside the blanket bundle was a tiny white wolf pup.

"Isn't she precious?" Lady Tanan cooed.

"She certainly is."

"And look…"

Lady Tanan pulled the blanket slightly back and out popped two small golden tipped-feathered wings.

"A true hybrid," Friar Sulny whispered.

"What's going on?" a tiny voice queried from the doorway.

Friar Sulny turned around and saw Sam'ona standing in her nightgown wiping the sleep from her eyes.

"I heard screaming," she continued.

Friar Sulny smiled and motioned for her to stand beside him.

"Come, Sam'ona. There is someone I'd like you to meet."

Sam'ona slowly staggered over to the friar, and after yawning two more times, she peered into Lady Tanan's arms.

Her eyes widened in wonder.

"Is that a wolf… with wings?"

"Yes it is," Friar Sulny chuckled.

"Wow! But, I thought when two species mate, the magi blood cancels and an Ander was born."

"That is typically the case, but this child is special, just like you."

"Will *I* have wings, *too*?" Sam'ona asked excitedly.

"No, I'm afraid not."

"Aw…" she sighed disappointed.

"But, you have an exceptional trait. Yours just isn't visible to the eye. You remember that book you found earlier?"

"The Healer's Mastery!"

"Yes. I told you the individual chosen by the Mastery will hold a remarkable power."

"What is it?"

"You will have the ability to heal any wound or gash simply through your touch."

"You mean… without herbs?"

"Yes. See this small cut I have on my thumb?"

Friar Sulny held up his thumb to the

light so Sam'ona could see. She nodded.

"You could wrap your tiny hand around it, and it would be brand new, as if I had never been hurt."

"Really?"

Eager to try her power, she grabbed Friar Sulny's thumb and clenched both her hands around it, closing her eyes.

Friar Sulny laughed, "You do not possess these powers yet, I'm afraid."

Sam'ona's shoulders slumped with another wave of childish disappointment.

"Do not worry. It will come to you."

"When?"

Friar Sulny bent over and picked Sam'ona up.

"You see this baby?"

"Mmhmm."

"You and her are going to discover your powers together. In fact, the Mastery has chosen you at this very moment so you can protect her."

"What's her name?" Sam'ona asked.

"Solaris," Lady Tanan whispered.

"So…lar…is…" Sam'ona repeated slowly. "I like it!"

Both Friar Sulny and Lady Tanan chuckled, and the tiny child's innocence lifted the heartbroken spirits.

The Magi Order had just finished saying their prayer when a loud booming noise came from outside the window. Soon following it, shouts from the watch tower echoed through the air.

"We're being attacked! Attacked!"

The maidens ran to the window and screamed at the sight below. A large army was approaching, covered in shiny black armor and carrying a slew of weapons. Brightly burning torches illuminated their golden shields. Burning arrows soared in the night sky towards the Great Abby and fell to the grounds within the high stone walls. More screams from below resonated as more fire arrows flew and silenced their victims.

The Magi Order had not moved from Therene's bedside.

Erisi looked to Friar Sulny and calmly spoke, "It's time."

Friar Sulny nodded and helped Lady Tanan to stand.

"Come Sam'ona, Lady Tanan," rushing them out the door with baby Solaris still in Lady Tanan's arms. "We must take leave to my chambers now."

"What's going on?" cried a worried Sam'ona.

"We have to go and hide. Don't worry, It will be alright."

The quartet rushed downstairs to Friar Sulny's quarters. Inside, Eton was fast asleep.

"Eton, my boy," Friar Sulny asserted. "Eton, wake up."

Eton stirred a little on his cot, still dazed from his unexpected rising.

"What is it, Friar Sulny?"

"Do you remember the bottles the Magi Order gave me and the maps of stars we charted last week? I need you to fetch those, quickly."

Eton nodded and rushed off around the corner to the friar's adjoining bedroom. He reached under the bed and began retrieving all the items Friar Sulny mentioned.

After putting Sam'ona back on the ground to her own feet, Friar Sulny placed a pillow in one of the chairs and helped Lady Tanan to sit down so she could calm Solaris who was howling and whimpering at the commotion.

"Is this the prophecy unfolding, Friar Sulny?" Lady Tanan asked.

"Yes. It is. I don't know why it's happening here. The Order was convinced the attack would be on a Noble land, not on Great Crossings' soil."

"Who's attacking us?" Sam'ona begged.

"A traitor to the Crown, I'm afraid."

"Who would want to do that?"

Friar Sulny knelt down to Sam'ona's height.

"There are some Neos in this world that do not wish for peace and love. There are those who are greedy, selfish, and ruthless. They will do anything for power and glory. It is because they fear the natural order of life so they destroy anything in their way, feeling a necessity to control it instead, but that is an impossible feat."

After a brief pause, Sam'ona whispered, "Are we going to die, Friar Sulny?"

"Oh no, my dear."

He pulled the shaking child into his arms.

"*You* must live. You and this baby must live for all our sakes."

As soon as the words left Friar Sulny's mouth, Eton returned from the bedroom, arms full of scrolls and bottles.

"I think I got them all."

"Good," Friar Sulny said standing. "Put the potion bottles on the table and stretch out the maps on the cot. We must hurry."

Friar Sulny grabbed one of the bottles which was filled with a deep purple colored cloud inside. He threw the bottle at the door; glass shattered to the ground. After the elusive violet smoke faded, Eton, Lady Tanan, and Sam'ona gasped. The door had vanished and had been replaced by stones matching the surrounding walls.

"Did you make the door disappear, Friar Sulny?" Eton asked astonished.

"No. It's just a false image; however, it will buy us more time."

Meanwhile, upstairs, the Great Abby door had been breached. The dark soldiers marched in setting fire to the tapestries and furniture in the main hall while some filtered down the corridors into rooms, pulling out its scared and screaming inhibitors.

When the final line of soldiers walked into the Abby, a single black steed galloped in. On its back was Ceros. He dismounted his saddle and handed the reins to Leveel.

"Tie the horse up inside. It smells like rain, and I don't want my horse to get wet."

Leveel nodded and walked Ceros' horse to a post near the main door, tied it up, and returned to Ceros' side.

"Take men with you, and find the Order, but only tie them up. I need them alive… at least… for awhile."

Leveel rushed off, grabbing three soldiers to accompany him.

"Make sure you wake up every wretched body in this Abby, men!" Ceros shouted over the panic and chaos. "Leave no door unlocked and no Neo in their bed! I want them all brought downstairs to the dining hall!"

A roar of agreement rose from the soldiers' voices over the yelps and frightened voices of Great Abby residents.

At the top of the stairs leading to the west wing, Leveel shouted down to his leader, "We have found them!"

Ceros whispered to himself, "Good."

Ceros marched up the stairs.

When he reached Leveel's side, Leveel slowly stammered, "My King, we found something else when we came across the Order."

"What is it?"

"We found that pretty girl you fought the wolf over."

"Princess Therene?" Ceros questioned puzzled. "What is she doing here?"

Ceros followed Leveel down the hallway and into Princess Therene's room. Five maidens were tied up and lying down on the ground at the foot of Therene's bed, and the Magi Order were tied up kneeling in a line in front of the fire place. The still Therene remained lying in her bed.

Ceros walked up to the bedside.

"Princess, you must forgive my intrusion, but fear not, your life will most definitely be spared, as I have not forgotten your eminent beauty and your dashing smile. If you say the words, you can be mine and I yours."

Silence.

Frustrated by Therene's lack of response, Ceros shook her shoulder.

"Princess, wake up."

He shook her once more.

"Princess Therene?"

Ceros cupped her face in his hands, and his eyes widened at the lifeless skin in his grasp.

Enraged, he bellowed, "What happened here?!?"

The maidens, frightened, just cried even louder.

Ceros spun around to face the Order.

"Did you do this?" Ceros demanded.

All members of the Order remained silent.

"Tell me what happened! Why is she dead?" Ceros continued to dictate.

Still, there was no response.

"Fine. Have it your way."

Ceros unsheathed his blade and walked over to the fireplace. After holding the blade in the fire, he grabbed Erisi by the neck and pressed the smoldering blade to the priest's cheek. Erisi's skin sizzled as the flesh burned away, leaving a bloody mark. Though painful, Erisi kept his mouth closed.

"Well," Ceros replied, dissatisfied by the silence. "If the Order does not feel pain for itself, perhaps they feel differently about their followers."

Sticking the blade back into the fire, Ceros motioned Leveel forward.

"Leveel, bring one of those fine young maidens to me."

Leveel snatched up one the girls and carried her over to Ceros.

"No!" Nysam broke.

"Ah! We have a winner! Or shall I say a loser?" Ceros announced satisfied. "Nysam is it? Tell me what happened to the princess or the girl gets it. I have no problem scolding her more than once. I am deaf to other people's pain."

With pain in his eyes, Nysum successfully fought the urge to speak as his heart swam in the innocent girl's salty tears, still writhing in Leveel's strong grasp.

"Always the hard way," Ceros replied plainly, now taking joy in torturing the Order.

But, just before Ceros laid his blade on the girl's face, Lafore spoke out.

"She died giving birth."

"Birth?"

"Yes."

"Why was she sent here to deliver?"

Lafore said nothing.

Enraged and in a louder voice, Ceros repeated, "Why was she sent-"

Then he paused.

"Wait… Who was this bastard child's father?"

This time, it was Erisi's turn to speak.

"You know him very well, Ceros. Actually, one could say you despise him."

"Rysul!" Ceros screamed infuriated. "How dare he? That insignificant, worthless piece of trash! His pelt is mine. Leveel! Tell all the soldiers downstairs that the wolf is left to me."

"He's not here," Erisi said calmly.

Further perturbed by Erisi's response, Ceros slowly muttered, "Then where is he?"

"Away, but when he arrives here, he will notice that darkness has entered this place and not embark."

"You really believe that he will not enter? The dog may be a poet, but he has a fighter's spirit. If he senses the darkness, he will rush into it without a doubt. His woman and child are here. Speaking of, where is the wretched thing?"

"It was a stillborn," Lafore spoke up. "It was a true sadness that both mother and child did not make it."

"Then poor Rysul will be crushed!" Ceros cackled. "And I will make my mark on his gallant face. Leveel, make sure every prisoner is in the dining hall. When Rysul returns, I want the entire lot of them to watch as I end his life."

"Last I heard, Rysul made a fool out of you at your last duel," Tridor sneered.

"We'll have to do something about that then, won't we? Quar!"

From the darkest corner of the room, Quar, in his ebony python form, slithered his way out of the shadows. After a swelling collection of black smoke engulfed his scaly body, Quar transformed to his decrepit human form and stood by Ceros' side.

"Quar!" Erisi exclaimed. "How dare you show your face here again? What are you thinking, doing business with such an evil? Even when we cast you out from the Great Crossings, your only crime was attempting to resurrect the dead, but this is much worse. Why?"

"King Ceros appreciates my abilities. My magic is far greater than you think."

"Is that why you helped him murder his own father?" Erisi asked.

"How did you know that?" Quar spat back.

"We, the Order, have magic far greater than *you* think," Erisi insulted.

Ceros interrupted the magicians' banter.

"Either way, the Mighty King Bellor is dead, and a new king lives in his place. Our Mountain armies are much too powerful and restless to be kept on the sidelines of peace, and I thirst for blood too much to celebrate winter balls and leap about in the sun. No. Pangea needs chaos, and her people need fear. *That* is how order is kept, through fear of the most powerful creature on this earth, and that creature, my dear Magi Order, will be me."

Ceros threw back his head began laughing hysterically.

"My king," Quar cut in. "We need the blood of each priest in order for the spell to work."

"Not a problem. Leveel?"

Leveel threw the maiden back to the floor
and walked over to the Order. He swiftly
pulled out a knife and cut a deep gash into
each of the priests forearms. Leveel then
pulled out a small glass and let a few drops
of each priest's blood fall into it.

After all the blood was collected, Leveel
held the contents in front of the dark wizard.
Quar pulled out two small vials, one filled
with a dark green liquid and the other
containing tiny charcoal colored beads. First,
he poured the thick green substance into the
bloody concoction.

"Ground up buffalobur nightshade. A
deceptively alluring plant, but it bears
thorns along its stems covered in a substance
that causes excruciating pain to its
predators."

Quar poured out the beads into his hand.

"These are beads saturated with my dark
incantations, damned by the spirits, and born
of the shadows."

Dropping each bead in, a large cloud of
black smoke was released from the glass.
Finally, Quar took the potion from Leveel and
swished the drink around.

"Drink this, King Ceros, and you will
possess that which we dark wizards call, the
Shadow Force."

Quar handed Ceros the glass. The foul
smell filled the room. Even Ceros looked leery
about drinking Quar's mixture.

"You are sure this will work?"

"Yes."

"You said its never been done."

"True. No one has ever successfully
received the *full* Shadow Force, the *Prima
Umbros*, but none before you had killed their
own father. Now that the Princess is gone,

what love do you really have? You, my king, are truly the Black Prince of the Dark. That is why I know the Shadow's ultimate power will come to you. There is no light inside your heart anymore."

Ceros smirked and guzzled down the repugnant smelling drink. The Magi Order knelt quietly in fear, watching the prophecy come true before their very eyes.

Finished with the drink, Ceros threw down the glass and growled. He let out a wild scream before doubling over.

"King Ceros!" Leveel shouted while making an attempt to help.

"No!" Quar exclaimed. "This is supposed to happen."

Leveel halted and stared down at Ceros who was kneeling on the floor, crouched over with his hands clutching each side of his head. Ceros screamed more and more as the Shadow crept inside him and pulsed his veins. His heart was throbbing and racing while his breathing was short and heavy. Then, Ceros stopped screaming and moving.

"Is he-" Leveel started.

"No. Wait," Quar assured.

The Magi Order held their breaths in hopes that the Shadow was indeed too much for Ceros' body to handle, but Ceros slowly lifted his forehead off the cold stone floor.

"My king?" Quar asked.

Suddenly, knees still planted on the floor, Ceros' chest shot upward, and his arms dangled along the sides of his body. His head cocked back as he let out one final deafening scream. His eyes opened only to reveal no pupils, no whiteness, just blackness in each socket. Veins bulged from within Ceros' neck as the screaming continued. More and more voices of darkness, and cries of agony swirled about in the scream. Every ounce of hate, tremble of fear, and tear of pain swelled in Ceros' lungs. The Shadow had completely taken over him.

The screaming finally stopped as the blackness left his eyes, and Ceros' body fell limp to the floor.

The room watched in silence as Ceros grunted and picked himself off the ground to stand to his feet.

"How do you feel, King Ceros?" Quar questioned.

Ceros stared down at his hands as he made each one into a fist. A black smoke swirled around them as he turned them over and over to examine them.

"I feel outstanding. There's so much power in these hands now, and my body… feels a hundred times stronger," Ceros said slowly as he breathed in heavily. "And my lungs feel like fire."

"Then you have achieved it, my king. You have been bestowed the power of the *Primo Umbros*."

Ceros sneered and turned to the Order.

"*Now*, let your Rysul come, and let us see who is the strongest fighter."

The Escape

As Ceros basked in his new magical strength, Friar Sulny was busy working with magic of his own.

"Make sure that the star charts are in the correct order, Eton. We cannot mess this up."

Eton nodded and surveyed his work for a third time.

"Your instructions are in the stars, Friar Sulny?" Sam'ona inquired.

"Yes, my dear. At night, if you are lost in the woods, you look up to the stars for guidance to lead you home, do you not?"

Sam'ona agreed.

"The stars have to be brave in order to live in the dark skies. They must shine brightly in the shadows of the air in order to help those who need it. This is why we must always look to the stars. They exist to all who need them. Remember that, Sam'ona. You will need them again someday."

"Friar Sulny!" Eton called out. "The order is ready."

"Good. Begin."

Eton began reading over the first scroll.

"First, there is earth. Here, the fair maiden rides the bull across vast plains to seek out a mythical creature."

Friar Sulny rummaged through the bottles. After looking several over, he gathered three. Each of them were filled with dirt. He pushed aside a chair and pulled up the rug, exposing the bare stone floor.

"Maiden, bull, mythical creature…" Friar

Sulny muttered to himself.

He uncorked one of the bottles and poured the dirt from it in a curved line from a twelve o'clock position to a nine o'clock one. He took a second bottle and poured its contents from the end of the first line across to a four o'clock position. Finishing with that, Friar Sulny took the last bottle, uncorked it and connected the end of the latest line to where he first began to pour the dirt.

"Very good. What is next, Eton?"

"Next comes powers on high winds. Two children born of the same day weigh their gold in order to pay the water bearer for a drink."

"Mmhmm… Air, of course."

Friar Sulny returned back to the table and grabbed three more bottles. These were not filled with dirt though. Instead, one was filled with tiny gold bits, one was filled with grayish tinted fur, and the last was filled with a suspiciously cerulean blue water.

Following the same pattern but starting at the eight o'clock position and working his way back, Friar Sulny emptied out the three bottles. Eton watched amazed.

"Quickly, Eton," Friar Sulny interjected. "What does the third scroll say?"

"I'm sorry, Friar Sulny," Eton replied, snapping back to his responsibilities. "Um… Water follows the winds as fish and crabs swim deeper into the ocean to escape the scorpion on the shore."

After comprehending Eton's words, Friar Sulny went to the table again to retrieve three more bottles. These were filled with water, but small particles floated in the liquid. Each bottle looked a little different.

Scales floated in one, scraps of crab shell in another, and in the last, there appeared to be bits of an insect.

Now in motion with the ceremony, Friar Sulny started pouring at the three o'clock position and made an identical pattern to the previous two.

"Lastly, the fires will burn as the archer shoots his bow at the fearsome lion with hopes the innocent ram can run free. Only after these stages have been complete shall the fifth one come to be."

Upon collecting the last three bottles on the table, all filled with ashes, Friar Sulny made the last triangular shape on the floor, starting at the eleven o'clock position. With all four elements completed, the lines of the bottles' contents formed a sun with twelve points.

"Solaris," Friar Sulny whispered to himself.

Sam'ona counted on her fingers.

"Earth, air, water, fire… What's the fifth element Friar Sulny?"

"Metal," he calmly said as he walked over to a wooden nightstand.

He opened the top drawer and lifted up a shiny silver necklace. The chain was thin but strong and from its bottom, hung a beautiful pendant in the shape of a moon.

Friar Sulny kissed it compassionately, walked to Sam'ona, and knelt down to her.

"This is for you to wear now," Friar Sulny gently whispered as he fastened the necklace around Sam'ona's neck. "You must keep this safe… And this."

Friar Sulny pulled out the Healer's Mastery book from his cloak.

"These are your tools, my sweet child,

the tools you must use when you look after baby Solaris."

He put the book in a satchel filled with food and a blanket then hung the knapsack on her shoulder.

"Are we going somewhere?" Sam'ona asked confused.

"Yes. I am sending you to another realm."

"Aren't you, Lady Tanan, and Eton coming with me?"

"I'm afraid not."

"Why?"

"Because this is a path only you must take. Eton, Lady Tanan, and I must stay here and keep things in order."

Sam'ona wrapped her tiny hand around the charm suspended from her neck. She turned to look at Lady Tanan who was still rocking Solaris in her arms.

"Don't worry, little one," Lady Tanan assured as she walked to Sam'ona. "We'll be fine here. I promise to make you another blueberry pie when you return. Friar Sulny will make sure everything gets sorted out. Don't you worry."

Lady Tanan stood up, then crouched down, and carefully placed the baby in Sam'ona's trembling arms.

"Eton?" Friar Sulny asked.

"Yes?"

"I believe there is supposed to be one more bottle. It should be smaller than the others and have a clear liquid inside. The cork should also be white."

Eton ran off into the neighboring room again to find the missing bottle.

"Come, Sam'ona," Friar Sulny ushered. "Step into the center of the sun. It'll be alright."

He carefully guided her to the middle of the outlined shape so that the lines were not disturbed by her long nightgown. When Sam'ona reached the shape's core, she looked down into the fidgeting bundle in her arms.

Solaris' fur was as white as snow. Her small paws jabbed upwards, swatting at the air as her hind legs kicked. The golden tips of her wings glistened in the candlelight as they flapped but did not take flight. Her dark brown eyes, though young and naïve, were filled with energy. Sam'ona felt an instant connection with the newborn Neo.

Sam'ona smiled and whispered, "I promise to always be there for you."

Eton returned from Friar Sulny's other room with the miniature bottle in hand.

"I found it!"

"Good," Friar Sulny said. "Bring it here."

Eton obeyed, and Friar Sulny popped off the cork.

"She must drink this."

"What is it?" Sam'ona questioned.

"It's a special potion the Magi Order prepared. It will strip Solaris of her Neo identity."

"But, that will leave her as a-"

"I know, but we must keep her powers hidden as long as possible. We have no idea what kind of darkness will be trying to find her and when it might happen."

A worried expression swept across Sam'ona's face.

"Don't worry," Friar Sulny assured. "The Neo part of her will only be concealed, not removed. It is much like how we masked the door and stayed hidden in this room. No one knows we are here, and yet, we exist. When the time comes, that façade will fall, and all will be revealed again."

Sam'ona took the bottle from the friar and slowly tipped the opening to Solaris' mouth. She drank it ravenously.

"Okay. Now what?" Sam'ona asked.

"Do you remember the lullaby I sing to you every seventh night?"

Sam'ona nodded.

"I need you to sing that now."

Sam'ona blushed as she returned the bottle to Friar Sulny. He put the empty bottle in his cloak pocket and hugged Sam'ona.

He whispered into her ear, "Have no fear, my child."

Friar Sulny pulled away and kissed her on her forehead. Sam'ona nodded her head in determination.

After taking a huge breath in, Sam'ona closed her eyes and sang,

Although it seems like a world beyond my eyes is just a dream,
I know within my heart a place exists, as I sing my sweet vibrations to the wind.
Water falls and fire burns while the air sings to the earth's blessed turns.
So I heed my calling to that unknown place, where I know that you and I survived the chase.

As the song progressed, each outline of the sun began to glow in green, orange, blue, and red. With each word leaving Sam'ona's mouth, the lines burned brighter and brighter, and as the final words of her melody escaped her, the silver moon pendant burst with a blinding white light.

Sam'ona opened her eyes and gasped at

what she saw. A rainbow of lights swirled around her, engulfing her, and combining to make a brilliant crystal colorless blaze. She looked frantically through the radiance. She could barely make out the walls of Friar Sulny's room or the furniture that resided within them.

Lady Tanan was waving and smiling, as she always was. Friar Sulny bowed and smirked, but Eton, in his fox form now, was screaming something. Sam'ona could not hear him. Whatever this light was, began flooding *all* her senses. She squinted as the light continued to grow with intensity. Her ears were filled with silence despite the chaos around her, but her body felt like a feather. There was no weight or tension ; in fact, she felt like she was flying.

Remembering flight and wings, Sam'ona looked down to her arms, worried that Solaris might have been scared and crying, but she was not. Instead, Solaris' mouth was open in awe and eyes full of fascination as the last hints of their world vanished into the sea of white. Sam'ona clung tighter to Solaris and closed her eyes.

Outside of the light, Eton's voice was still audible.

"Sam'ona, I love you! I will come for you! Do you hear me? Sam'ona!"

Tears flooded his furry face.

"Sam'ona!"

Friar Sulny patted the young fox on his back and consoled, "She cannot hear you though I'm sure she knows how much you care for her."

Sobbing, Eton fell to the floor, exhausted from yelling and his youthful heart shattered.

Both Friar Sulny and Lady Tanan sighed as

they looked at Eton's shaking figure on the ground while the light vanished.

"We should clean this up and get rid of the evidence, Lady Tanan," Friar Sulny advised.

Lady Tanan took a nearby broom and started sweeping the outline's makeup into a pile, destroying the image of the sun as Friar Sulny took the star maps and threw them into the fireplace. As soon as he did, a loud pounding started at the stones masking as the door.

"I'm telling you, I heard a yell from behind this wall a minute ago," a muffled voice spoke.

Another voice chimed in, "You idiot! There's nothing but stone here. You mean to tell me there are Neos living in the walls? Oooooo!"

"Stop it!" the first voice yelled back.

Friar Sulny, Lady Tanan, and Eton froze, completely silent, hoping the enemies would press on to another location.

They waited to hear the loud pounding again, but did not.

Just as Eton let out a sigh of relief, the "stone wall" caved in, and two colossal soldiers burst in.

"I knew it!" the first soldier exclaimed. "We'll bring them upstairs with the rest of their Abby weaklings. King Ceros will also be happy to see that we found the friar librarian."

The second soldier grabbed Friar Sulny by the arm and growled, "Don't worry. He doesn't want to kill you. There's a special place the king has reserved for you in his castle."

The two troopers cackled as they tied up their three new prisoners and shoved them upstairs.

When they arrived at the dining hall, all other Abby inhabitants were already bound or chained, crying along the walls. At the head of the room, Ceros sat eating a small feast. The Magi Order stood in chains behind him.

"Your Majesty! We found the librarian!" the proud lackeys yelled out as they entered the dining hall.

"Bring him to me!"

Ceros' two henchmen pushed and shoved the resistant Friar Sulny across the hall to their king.

"Friar Sulny, it is said that you possess the most knowledge of any living creature on Pangea," Ceros said in between bites. "Do you deny it?"

Friar Sulny kept silent.

"You see," Ceros continued regardless. "A beast of my rank might find your kind of power… intimidating. Such a beast would also have you killed on the spot, but I am not most beasts. When I look at you, I see potential. I see a working relationship. With your brain and my strength, we could be unstoppable. Not even the Magi Order could touch you. Doesn't that sound appealing?"

Again, Friar Sulny said nothing.

Aggravated by the friar's lack of response, Ceros quickly stood up and threw his glass at the wall. The sudden shattering of the glass startled all the Orderly Helpers, imprisoned around the hall, as they watched in fear for their beloved friar's life.

"Perhaps you're not as smart as they say. I should have you killed right now. There's no use for you if you won't compromise."

The two guardsmen tensed in anticipation to strike on command, but finally Friar Sulny spoke up confidently.

"If that was truly the case then you would have had me killed when I was discovered in my chambers."

Ceros snarled at the friar's remark, knowing the truth behind it.

"What is it that you want, Ceros? If it is just me you desire, let the others go."

Ceros threw back his head and roared with laughter.

"You idiot! You are just like those Noble fools to think that all may be solved with peacful reasoning. Did the war not prove anything? Chaos *needs* to happen."

"Is that what you wish? For there to be constant chaos and disorder in the world?"

"No. That already exists. You morons try to cover it up with smiles, games, and mindless celebrations. You call that order? Order does not stem from multiple thrones; it is born from one. That one throne shall and will be me."

"So, you wish to rule all of Pangea? Why not wait for the next Tournament? Now that you are King of the Mountains, you may have your time to rule for five years. Despite you murdering your father, I'm sure if his spirit were to appear here, he would tell you the same thing upon his forgiveness."

"Did your Magi Order's visions not uncover more of my father's dying events? *He* tried to kill me! It is *he* that should be target of *my* forgiveness!" Ceros screamed violently.

Friar Sulny stared into Ceros' eyes unflustered.

Regaining his composure, Ceros carried on.

"Either way, the almighty King Bellor is

fallen. He was weak, unlike me, but even I am aware that I am not invincible. That is why you are going to tell me how I can find the Healer's Mastery book."

"The Healer's Mastery seeks out its holder. One does not seek it."

"Then make me its holder."

"That would be impossible."

"And why is that?"

"Because the Healer's Mastery only makes itself known to a spirit of true kindness, of strong integrity, and pure love. You possess none of these. Even if the Healer's Mastery was displayed right in front of you, you would not be able to touch it."

Ceros sat back in his chair quietly and summoned Quar with the snap of his fingers. Quar crept out of the shadows as a snake and bowed.

"Quar, tell me if he speaks true."

Quar bowed once more and slithered over to Friar Sulny. Quar wrapped his scaley body around him and peered deep into Friar Sulny's eyes.

"He lies, my king!"

"About?"

"There is a way for one of impure nature to be a keeper of the Healer's Mastery."

Quar uncoiled his body from Friar Sulny and stood, back to his human form, leaning on his crooked cane.

"You must kill the current possessor of the book. Then, the Healer's Mastery will be soaked with the blood of death, and darkness may take hold of it."

"Ironic, isn't it?" Ceros teased the Magi Order behind him. "I kill for a book that will give me the power to heal any wound or ailment my body encounters. Well, Quar… *is* there a current holder?"

Quar returned his glaring eyes back to Friar Sulny's.

"Yes. It is a young fox maiden, but the friar's mind has blocked my visions from seeing further."

"Is there no more information you can reap from him?"

"It appears not at the moment, but give him as a prisoner to me, and I will be able to discover more in his fear with time. You shall have your answer."

"Fine," Ceros said disappointedly. "Onto the next order of business. Leveel! Bring forth the Order and my sword."

Friar Sulny, Lady Tanan, and Eton were lead into a dark corner of the room where Quar sealed them into a shadow and disappeared with them. Leveel dragged the chained priests in front of the prisoner crowd and handed Ceros' long sword to him, the single golden line shimmering in the faint torch light.

"My dear Order," Ceros began. "There comes a time when a sacrifice for the greater good must be made. Surely, you understand the weight of this, as you have made sacrifices to become members of the Order, so, it won't be entirely vicious when one of you give yourself to my greater cause."

Ceros smirked and licked his teeth.

"Spilled blood tastes so sweet when power is the reward, don't you think?"

The Order remained wordless as Ceros paced in front of them, joggling his sword back and forth in the air.

"Well, whether or not you agree with me, a sacrifice will be made tonight. The real question is, 'Which one of you will be willing to give yourself up for the others?'"

Erisi quickly spoke up, "Me."
Ceros laughed.

"I figured it would be you, Erisi! Such a bold owl. Soft feathers but razor sharp talons. Leveel, unchain the good Air Priest."

Leveel unlocked the metal cuffs around Erisi's ankles and wrists and shoved him to the floor in front of Ceros' feet. Ceros turned around to face the audience in the Great Abbey dining hall. Everyone was crying, overwhelmed with fear and heartbreak. Ceros smiled at the sight.

"Good people of the Abbey, be prepared to witness," Ceros announced as he turned around to face Erisi lying on the floor and raised his sword high above his head. "Greatness!"

Just before Ceros' sword landed its fatal blow to Erisi's back, a deafening howl echoed through the hall. The howl was deep and long, sending shivers down everyone's spine, for every spine knew the owner of such a noise.

Ceros lowered his sword to his side and called out, "I've been waiting for you, old friend! Step out of the shadows and show yourself!"

At that instant, the dining hall doors swung open and out stepped a silver-colored wolf. Rysul's fur seemed to glow on its own with a smooth silkiness, quite uncommon for most wolves, but despite his elegant hide, Rysul's broad shoulders and perfectly sculpted body swelled as he let out another booming howl. His profound brown eyes aimed at Ceros like an arrow prepped for launching.

"Ceros! How dare you invade and massacre such a sacred place! These are peaceful people who know nothing of war, nothing of blood. They only know a world full of mystic and wonder. What kind of Neo are you to put harm to such innocent victims?"

"Well, my dear Rysul, I suppose I am the kind of Neo who doesn't care, but if you're so concerned with the differences in rank, then why don't you and I have another go? I must say, I am supremely excited to see how much you've grown since last we fought."

Saying nothing, Rysul slowly started to walk forward towards Ceros. Ceros dropped his sword and ripped off his shirt, showing off the Shadow Force's strength in his pumping muscles. He cracked his neck to each side and clenched his fists as he walked towards his opponent. All eyes, even those filled with tears, were fixed on the center of the hall.

"I should warn you, Rysul," Ceros stated cockily. "I'm not as I was two years ago. You might say, I've embraced more darkness since then."

"Then let me show you the light," Rysul growled.

With that, Rysul was back to his human state and lunged forward at Ceros, muscles flexed. He swung his right fist around to hit Ceros in the face, but Ceros quickly ducked and landed his own punch into Rysul's chest. Rysul coughed up blood and staggered backward.

After regaining his balance, Rysul rushed forward again but jumped this time, aiming to pounce on Ceros, but Ceros, once again, swiftly dodged the attack and threw a powerful elbow downward on Rysul's back. Rysul fell to the ground.

"This is pathetic!" Ceros yelled mockingly. "Abbey, is this your greatest fighter?!?"

Rysul slowly stood and faced the laughing Ceros' back. He charged again, but Ceros spun around and kicked him in the face, bringing

Rysul right back down to the floor. Ceros towered over him, the Shadow Force filling his eyes once more.

"Dark magic," Rysul whispered as he stared into the black holes of Ceros' eyes.

"Yes, dear Rysul. It is dark magic, and it feels outstanding."

Ceros bent over and picked up Rysul by his hair.

"The light means nothing to me," Ceros whispered. "And soon, it will mean nothing to the people of Pangea when I rule over this entire land."

Still holding Rysul up, Ceros kneed him in the stomach. Rysul doubled over and spit up more blood on the floor.

"Why is it that the light is so important to you? Hope leads you to disappointment. Happiness leads you to pain. And love," Ceros paused then smiled slyly. "Love leads you to the deepest shadows of your soul, but I suppose you would disagree with me, eh poet?"

Rysul gathered his strength and stumbled to his feet.

"Yes. I would have to disagree with you. Love is magnificent. It is the one true light that can pierce any shadow's darkness and penetrate any fear."

"Ah… I see," Ceros replied sarcastically. "So, you're saying that there is no way that love can make you… wicked?"

Rysul stood, holding his side, saying nothing.

"I would have to prove you wrong, Rysul. You may know the presence of love, but have you ever felt the loss of it?"

"What are you talking about?"

"I'm talking about the lovely Princess Therene."

Enraged, Rysul reverted to his wolf shape and charged forward, letting a massive howl escape his lungs once more. Ceros, now fully saturated with the swirling Shadow Force around his body, simply stretched out his arm, grabbed hold of Rysul's neck, and effortlessly lifted Rysul's paws off the ground.

"I'm talking about the death of her," Ceros coldly stated.

Then he brought Rysul's pointy ear close to his mouth and whispered, "And your bastard child."

Hearing the gasps for air from Rysul, Ceros threw him down to the ground and kicked him over. Then, he stepped and rested one foot on Rysul's heaving chest.

"There it is," Ceros taunted. "There's that shadow I was talking about."

Rysul's eyes were flooded with tears as his breathing became heavier and darker.

Ceros continued, "But, it wasn't me who killed them, though you'd prefer it that way. You'd have someone to blame, someone to seek revenge on, but you don't. No, the universe stole your love from you."

Rysul writhed underneath Ceros' foot. He attempted to rise, but Ceros immediately slammed Rysul's body back to the ground.

"Who do you blame now? Who do you punish for the crime? What do you do with all that anger? With all that pain? All that hate?"

Rysul screamed in pain as Ceros's Shadow Force spirals started revolving around the both of them.

"It isn't fair, is it?" Ceros continued maliciously. "You were gone. You should've been here for her, but you weren't. How does that make you feel? Regret? Self-loathing? Yes. Of course, it does. I see it in your face; you want to welcome this surge of power. Let yourself."

"No!" Rysul screamed.

"Yes! Let it consume you! What do you have in this world anymore? You have nothing! Your lover, your child… Gone! Be something from that. Embrace the Shadow!"

Ceros cackled as a shuddering boom of thunder exploded outside. Terrified screams attempted to escape the dining hall, but a possessing evil clung ruthlessly to their dismay and hurled the bawling back to their mouths, shoving helplessness down their throats like a gag.

Ceros' cackle soared over the top of the chaos as he stared down at Rysul's still body. Ceros sneered and stared down at his new servant.

"Rise," Ceros whispered as he lifted his foot off of Rysul's chest.

Rysul's eyes shot open. His once kind brown eyes had turned blood red. He rose slowly and bowed to Ceros.

"My king," he ghostly stated.

"That's better… Now, kill the owl."

Rysul briskly turned around and ran towards Erisi, who was still lying on the ground in shock from the horrid scene.

Rysul leaped up high and landed all four paws on Erisi's back, smashing Erisi's head into the stone floor. The old priest's body went limp as Rysul hurled back his head and howled, but his cry was cut short as Rysul felt a cool metal sting cut neatly through his own back. The red hue left his eyes as he peered down at the blood pooling around a black blade protruding from his cavity.

"Easy," Ceros said, withdrawing his sword.

Rysul fell off Erisi's body and stared up at Ceros who was licking his blade. The blade's sable hue slowly defaulted to its silver polish and golden accent.

"Why?" Rysul muttered.

"Like I said before, love leads you to the deepest shadows of your soul. What's the point of love if I feel darkness already?"

"You're wrong-"

"No! You're wrong! Power is the only thing I need to survive this world, and I've got it. It is a shame though. You won't be here to witness it."

Kneeling down beside Rysul, Ceros whispered, "Give Therene the last remaining parts of my love."

Then, before anyone could blink, Ceros thrust his sword into Rysul's back a second time. Rysul's breathing ceased, and he quietly drifted off into the afterlife smiling, hoping to see his beloved and child on the other side.

Little did Rysul know, that he would only be meeting the lovely princess at the Lighted Gates of Afterlife as Solaris cried, very much alive, in Sam'ona's arms only a world away.

The shimmering light had stopped, and Sam'ona's vision came back into focus. After a few blinks, she began to walk forward, scared about the new world she had been transported to.

There were two brick walls on each side of her, covered in the evening's misty fog as she made her way toward a flickering illumination across, what seemed to be, a cemented path.

She began crossing it, and as she did, the illumination became clearer. It was a lit up neon blue sign reading, "Open."

Just before she stepped off the street, a large metal box on wheels rushed by, making a loud honking noise. Sam'ona screamed with surprise as she stumbled and ran to the blue light, still clutching onto Solaris. Sam'ona had closed her eyes due to fright, so she did not see the man exiting the building.

Sam'ona bumped into the stranger and exclaimed, "I'm so sorry, sir!"

She looked up at the man. He was very tall and slender with a jet-black mustache and hair to match, neatly slicked back. He was wearing a bright red coat and ivory pants, finished with shiny black boots and a tall satin top hat.

Sam'ona gasped and whispered to herself, "An Ander…"

The man smiled through his bushy mustache and said, "What do we have here? It's much too late for a young girl like you to be out here so late and in this weather!"

The man laughed, and Sam'ona couldn't help but snicker, as the man's laugh was at a much higher pitch than his voice. Suddenly, Sam'ona felt at ease. She sensed the good-natured heart within the man.

"My name is Sam'ona," she said kindly.

"It's nice to meet you, Sam'ona. That's a very pretty name."

"Thank you."

Sam'ona curtsied.

"I'll be darned," the stranger said astonished. "Such manners! It surely is a pleasure then, Miss Sam'ona. My name is Simon."

He took off his top hat and bowed.

Now at Sam'ona's level, the man noticed the small blanket-bundle in her arms and the satchel hanging at her side.

"What's this? A traveler?"

"I guess you can call me that. Though… I don't know where I'm traveling to."

"Well, for starters, a blanket, Miss Sam'ona, on a dreary night like this, is not to be carried. It is to be draped across the shoulders. Let me demonstrate."

Simon started to peel the blanket from Sam'ona's arms when the blanket moved on its own.

Simon gasped.

"Another surprise?"

Simon peered into the blanket, one eyebrow cocked.

The blanket moved again but this time exposing a tiny fleshy arm, then a small baby girl's face.

"My word!" Simon exclaimed. "So precious! And who is this?"

"This is…" Sam'ona started but remembering Friar Sulny's stress on secrecy for Solaris' safety, she said, "Chase."

"Ah! Sam'ona and Chase. Beeeeaut-i-ful names! And traveling orphans with no destination at such a young age? This will not do. No. Miss Sam'ona, I know we have just met, but rest assured, my heart is pure. I live but two blocks from here in a large old Victorian house, and there you may rest your feet for the night, at the very least. Perhaps you may also enjoy a hot meal. I surely would not agree with myself if I let you tread these awful streets alone with such a darling treasure in your arms."

Simon bowed once more. Sam'ona touched the top of his head, and a warming light filled her heart. Something about this odd stranger, Sam'ona felt like she could trust.

"Your kindness is greatly appreciated.

Thank you very much."

Simon leaned back upward and put his top hat back in place.

"And your thanks is quite welcome," he said cheerily.

Simon laughed again as Sam'ona and Chase accompanied Simon down the street into the fog, now, with a place to go.

The Circus is in Town

The doorbell rang.

"Sam! It's for you!" a voice yelled from upstairs.

A young woman in denim jeans and a light green tee shirt emerged from the back sitting room.

Twenty years had passed, and age had treated Sam'ona nicely, for she had blossomed into a remarkable and beautiful sight. She was of average height and her once long nut-brown hair was cut to medium length, gracefully sitting on her slim shoulders. Her softly tinted skin glowed, as when she was a child, but the air around her was more mature. She stood taller in poise than before, and her equally elegant eyes sparkled in the morning's innocence.

She walked to the door and opened it.

"Hi, Conner."

The man's hand shook as he handed over the bundle of letters.

"Umm… Hi, Sam. Here's today's mail."

The timid man's sandy, overgrown bangs kept blowing in his face as he nervously tried to brush them back behind his ears. His pale skin glistened in the afternoon sun as his lanky body sweat through his gray mail-carrier uniform, result of the day's heat and the young man's anxiety.

"Thank you, Conner. Have a great day."

Sam closed the door and turned around, filtering through the mail.

"He likes you, you know," the voice from above teased.

Sam looked up and saw a grown-up Chase leaning over the upstairs banister that overlooked the foyer.

Chase's skin had tanned to a darker tint over the years, and her hair was a dark brown, much shorter than Sam's, styled closed to her face and layered. Her almond shaped eyes reflected that of her Phoenix mother, and her broad shoulders bore much resemblance to her father's Wolf genes. She had an array of tattoos on her hands and arms, as well as hidden under her white short sleeve shirt and black basketball shorts that only added to her roguish charm. There was a mischievous mien to Chase's words as she made her way down the creaky wooden staircase.

"He doesn't like me," Sam protested.

"How can you say that? If you can tell me of any other person on this block that gets their mail *hand*-delivered to their doorstep every day, *in* the city of Chicago, then you might have a case. Until then, you can keep deluding yourself of the obvious."

Chase continued into the kitchen, and Sam followed.

"You should ask him to go out with us this Friday night when we celebrate your birthday," Chase continued stubbornly.

"No! He wouldn't say yes anyway."

"You know, for someone as smart as you are, you're really dumb."

"That doesn't make any sense."

"Course it does. Crystal clear sense."

Chase smiled as she raised a small glass of whiskey up and took a sip.

"I can't wait," Chase carried on. "Your birthday means *my* birthday is coming up in a week, and I'll be able to drink legally. It's going to be awesome."

"It's one o'clock in the afternoon. Why on earth are you drinking?"

"It's Wednesday. More importantly, it's the third Wednesday of March, meaning Pierre leaves for his monthly poker game to Indiana after dinner tonight and won't be back home until Saturday afternoon… meaning I get to be with Cia. This is my early celebration."

"I still don't get why you're with her. She's married. It's not right."

"I know. Sometimes, I feel horrible."

"Sometimes?"

"Yeah, but then I remember how he doesn't have time for her, how he's too busy and so caught up in improving his magic act that he pays no attention to her. And Cia… is too beautiful of a woman to not be appreciated."

"She's also almost twice your age."

"But, when she looks at me, I just feel… like it's we're supposed to be with each other."

"It's still wrong."

"Well, until I've learned my lesson the hard way, I think I'm okay with being a little misbehaved."

Chase winked.

"And you, Sam, need to be a little more risky."

"I'm not dating a married man," Sam said sternly.

"I'm not talking about that. I'm talking about getting out and living life up a little. You spend so much time in your room reading; I hardly think there's a book out there you haven't read yet, and that's a lot of books."

Sam laughed.

"I just enjoy being by myself. Plus, you don't know what goes on in my room at night."

"That sounds mysterious and mildly

suggestive, not like you at all. I'm proud of you," Chase joked.

"What are you proud of Sam for?" two voices inquired in harmony.

A ten year old boy and girl walked into the kitchen. Their names were Ray and Sydney. Both had bright red hair and faces full of freckles. Their pale skin and bright goofy smiles contrasted greatly with the dark blue spandex suits they were wearing.

"I think Sam is getting a little bit too sensual for her usual manner," Chase said bluntly.

"Eew!" the twins shrieked. "That's gross."

"I am not," Sam defended. "And why are we always talking about me? What have you two been up to? The birthday party we're working isn't for another three hours, and you're already in your uniforms."

"But, they're new! We had to put them on right away!" exclaimed Ray. "Look how shiny they are!"

Sydney spun around in dance.

"And when we juggle our light-up balls, they look like tiny stars shimmering around us. It's so pretty. We've been practicing all morning."

"That's the kind of spirit I like to hear!" a friendly voice shouted from the kitchen back door, leading to the outside.

Simon stood tall as he did twenty years ago, holding three brown bags full of groceries. A thin streak of silver hair had grown on the left side of his slicked back hair, a small marker for his age.

"A great show has performers who not only act their part but become them. Bravo, kids!"

Simon's shrilly high laugh rang in the

kitchen. The twins giggled as Simon walked
over to the round kitchen table, which was
covered in old newspapers and magazines, and
set down his load.

"But, we mustn't ruin those beautiful
costumes that the lovely Sam made for you.
They are much too exquisite, are they not?"

Ray and Sydney nodded furiously.

"So, why don't the two of you head
upstairs to your rooms, settle down, and
polish up those juggling balls for this
afternoon's performance? You really do want
those stars to sparkle today! I can feel it in
my bones that today Simon's Golden Circus is
going to have a spectacular show!"

He laughed again.

Ray and Sydney yelled out in chorus,
"Yes, Sir!"

With that, they raced upstairs and
retreated to their bedroom, slamming the door
shut.

"Ah, to be young again," Simon sighed as
he began unloading the bags. "And how are my
very own once nomadic stars doing today?"

"Great!" Chase declared. "Simon, I was
wondering…"

"Yes?"

"Would it be possible for Sam and I to
have this Friday night off? I know we're
supposed to work on the sets and the new
costumes for that fair on Sunday, but Sam's
birthday is that night, and I'd like to take
her out to dinner, a treat from Cia and me.
I'm even going to ask Conner to accompany us."

"She is not!" Sam shouted.

"Who is this Conner fellow?"

"Our mailman," Chase quickly replied.
"He's got the hots for Sam, though she doesn't
think so."

Sam slapped her forehead and rolled her eyes.

"I see. Well, who am I to deprive one of hotness?" Simon questioned happily while he tossed an apple up and over his head, catching it neatly in his hand behind his back.

"You are! You're the ringmaster," Sam stated hoping Simon would demand they stay in to finish their work.

"Of course you may indulge for Miss Sam's birthday," Simon continued despite Sam's disapproval. "Even if the new set and costumes aren't ready for Sunday, the gift of Sam's presence in our lives makes it a grand exception."

"Thanks, Simon! You're the man," Chase chuckled.

"Not just a man, but *the* man… I like it!" Simon laughed again. "Now, why don't the two of you start loading up the truck? That way, when Leo gets back from the doctor's office, we can all eat as a big happy family."

"You got it," Chase said as she grabbed Sam by the arm and guided her out the door to the small yard that separated the house from the garage.

"I can't believe he agreed," Sam muttered as Chase unlocked and lifted the old garage door.

"I have an amazing amount of woo," Chase bragged. "Besides, you know you'll have a fun time… Especially if Conner goes."

"I told you before, he's not interested."

"You keep saying that, but, are you? This sounds more and more like denial if I ever heard it."

"I'm not interested. I'm too busy-"

"Reading? C'mon, Sam, you deserve to be happy."

"Oh? Like you?"

"I am happy. Cia's breathtaking," Chase paused and rested her elbow on the box she was about to lift. "I'm telling you, Sam, I think I'm in love."

"Goodness…"

Playing offended, Chase retorted, "I would think after all those books you've read that somewhere in the mix, you've come across some great romance novels."

"I have…" Sam whispered.

"So, why not have some for yourself?"

Sam did not answer while she started packaging up a set of colored banners and flags. Chase walked over to her friend and took Sam's hand in hers.

"Sam, look at me."

Sam took a breath in and reluctantly looked at Chase's smiling face.

"What?"

"You've taken care of me all my life, or at least, that's what Simon tells me."

Sam chuckled slightly.

"I know you've always wanted what's best for me," Chase continued. "I'm grateful for that. I really am because I know I can be an idiot sometimes, or a lot of times, but I also want you to know that I want what's best for you, too. It's a two-way street of happiness for us, okay? That means a lot to me. So, please? Please come out with us Friday. You might have more fun than you think."

Sam averted her eyes away from Chase's pleading face and sighed, "Fine."

Chase grinned.

"Sweet! I can't wait!"

"Can't wait for what?" a soft woman's voice queried from behind.

Sam and Chase turned around.

A tall fair-skinned woman stood at the garage opening. A large sparkling necklace glittered in the sunlight and bounced off her electric blue eyes. Her lips were thin, but the shape of them secured her illustrious and sultry mouth. Long mahogany hair suspended over her narrow frame and fell into the deep v-neck cut of her silk gray shirt, and the tall black stilettos only helped show off her long denim covered legs.

"Hello, Cia," Sam said politely.

Chase quickly let go of Sam's hand and casually walked to Cia's side.

"She's excited for her birthday dinner this Friday night," Chase announced.

Cia gently stroked the side of Chase's face and softly spoke, her British accent alluring with every syllable.

"As happy as I am to have a girl's night out, I'm more excited for the alone time you and I have planned afterward."

"I'm one-hundred percent with you on that one," Chase echoed back slyly.

Cia smiled sweetly and looked at Sam.

"I'm sorry, Sam. I didn't mean to make your birthday any less important. I actually was out shopping today for your gift. I'm bursting at the seams to give it you."

"I'm sure I'll love it."

"Hey, guess what?" Chase interrupted. "It looks like we'll have our first double date, too. Sam caved and is letting me invite Conner. It should be fun."

"Conner? Our postman? I've always wondered why he brought our mail directly to our door every morning. So much for girl's night."

"I told you!" Chase exclaimed, chest full of satisfaction.

Sam leered at Chase and said, "I'm just happy that I will be able to share my birthday with friends."

"And potentially a new lover!" Chase cracked.

"Sweetheart, stop being so vicious," Cia teased as Chase went back to loading the truck. "Sam, I know I'm not the best example for the proper kind of love, but I do know what it feels like and what kind of happiness it can bring someone. Despite my deceptive situation, one thing stays consistent, and that is what I feel for Chase. Besides, I think by this point, Pierre knows what's going on."

"He what?" Chase blurted.

"Did he say something?" Sam calmly asked.

"Not particularly, but this morning he looked at me and said, 'My precious Felicia, it makes me smile knowing that you have found your happiness again.' Then, he kissed me on the forehead and told me that he still loves me."

"Wow…" Chase whispered to herself.

"Where is Pierre now?" Sam questioned.

"He's out looking at a new antique store. He's in search of a more vintage looking box for our disappearing trick. Any way, I should get inside and start lunch. We all know what happens when Simon tries his hand at cooking."

Cia walked over to, the still stunned, Chase and kissed her on the cheek.

"Pierre's decided to leave right after today's show so my door will be open when we get back."

After Cia left the garage, Sam and Chase sat in an unsettling silence.

Sam decided to speak up first.

"I suppose we should finish loading these

into the truck?"

"You know what? Cia just reminded me that I have to go pick up your gift. I should probably do that now seeing how we have the show today and two more tomorrow. Can you finish up here? I owe you one. Thanks."

"Sure," Sam said slowly as Chase shot around the corner of the house and sped down the street on her bicycle.

About thirty minutes later, Sam finished loading the truck up, closed the garage, and headed inside to the kitchen. The house smelled of spaghetti and garlic bread. The table had been cleared, and everyone was already seated, chatting about their day so far.

It was lunches like these Sam loved so much. Outside of the performances, everyone had busy schedules so downtime together was rare, but when they were lucky enough to meet, the air was filled with loving high spirits and infectious laughter. Most days, Sam either ate at the park, alone, or with Chase.

"Hurry and wash up, Sam. I'm starving!"

A small, scrawny middle-aged man pounded his fork on the table in jest. He was wearing a red baseball cap, hiding his bald head, and a set of navy blue scrubs that looked two sizes too big for him.

"Long day at the office, Leo?" Sam inquired.

"Doctor Matthews had me scanning all his old paper charts to the computer and organizing them overnight so they would be done by today. Needless to say, I didn't get much of a break or time to eat."

"That sounds terrible. I'm sorry. If Cia has lunch ready, you can start without me."

"Nonsense!" Simon shouted. "We have

manners in this house, and no one eats until we are all seated at this table."

Leo groaned in disappointment.

"Well, you may have to break that rule today, Simon," Sam replied. "Chase left, and I don't think she'll be back until we leave for the show."

"In that case, Felicia, we are more than ready to fill our stomachs with this mouthwatering pasta you have prepared for us. Wait! Where is Pierre?"

"For God's sake!" Leo shouted just as he was about to stab his fork into a large piece of garlic bread.

"He's out, as well," Cia responded as she rinsed her hands of marinara sauce. "I'm not sure when he will be back."

"So, we can eat now?" Ray and Sydney chimed in with Leo's begging.

"Might as well! Can't let a good meal get cold," Simon caved.

"I'll be right down," Sam said as she rushed upstairs to the bathroom to wash her own hands.

The cool water ran over Sam's soft hands. It felt nice considering the unusual heat of the spring day. She turned the faucet off and dabbed tiny beads of sweat off her forehead before she exited the bathroom.

As Sam started her way back downstairs, she noticed the door to Pierre and Cia's room was open when it usually remained shut. Intrigued, Sam walked over to the room and gasped as she saw Pierre standing there, holding a framed wedding photo.

"Pierre, when did you get here? Cia thought you were still out at the new antique store."

"I just recently arrived home."

Pierre had a thick French accent and a coordinating thick head of shiny, but graying hair. His tan skin complimented his crumbling facial features, and his slumped over shoulders barely held up his tan sports coat. One could tell through his eyes that he was tired, but tonight's fatigue was accompanied by a fragile sadness.

"Is everything alright?" Sam said as she inched forward.

Pierre lifted up the photo of Cia and himself.

"This was twelve years ago. Where has the time gone?"

"I'm so sorry."

"I remember when I first saw her. I was in Paris looking for a new assistant. One day, I was taking a break from casting girls when from across the street, I saw her. She was sitting at a table by herself drinking a cup of coffee. I was instantly drawn to the way her lips caressed the cup and how her ponytail danced in the wind. She was the most beautiful girl I had ever seen. I surprised myself when I mustered up the courage to approach her. Sparks flew. How could they not? There I was, a talented magician willing to share my secrets with an eager girl. Maybe… the magic in our early shows was mistaken for love."

He smiled faintly.

"I asked her to marry me, and she said yes. I was the happiest man alive, and now…"

Pierre sighed.

"I don't blame her though. I became obsessed with perfecting my show, constantly traveling around the world looking for new tricks, new feats, new challenges to face. I had hoped she would follow me and be as excited as I was, but she did not. I wonder, sometimes, if I was attempting to recreate the spark we shared upon our first meeting."

Sam continued to stare at Pierre, eyes full of sympathy.

"Chase is a good person, and their love is real, this I know," Pierre proceeded. "She is full of energy, and I think that is what Felicia needs. It is what I can no longer do. That is why after Sunday's fair, I will be leaving the house."

"You can't!"

"Don't worry about me, Sam. I'm quite alright. I love Cia and because of that, I am able to look at this decision with clarity. I want what's best for her. If that isn't me, then what kind of man would I be? Remember that. Love is a recognition. It is the bond that creates unspoken understanding and reflection of oneself through the eyes of another. That no longer exists for me here. Maybe it's time for me to discover that again, as well."

Surging with emotion, Sam lunged at Pierre and gave him a hug. Pierre graciously returned the embrace.

"We'll miss you," she whispered.

"And I will miss everyone, too. You have all become my family."

"Hey Sam!" Leo's yelled from the kitchen. "Chase is back! Are you coming down or what? I swear I'll eat your share!"

"Coming!" Sam shouted back.

"Let's eat and not worry about this matter," Pierre comforted. "We must eat if we are to do well at the private show today."

Sam nodded, and the pair made their way to the kitchen to join everyone else.

Simon exclaimed, "Pierre! When did you arrive here? Using your magic outside of the performance to sneak your way in?"

His soprano laugh resonated.

"If I told you, I'd have to kill you,"
Pierre joked.

Simon cackled again.

"Such humor! Perhaps you should add
'comedian' to your resume."

Sam sat down and began dishing spaghetti
in her plate. She smiled across the table at
Chase, but Chase did not look up from her food
as she ate.

"As much as I enjoy our quality time
together at meals, we should try to hurry
along," Simon suggested. "I know the party
isn't far from here, but with traffic, we will
have to leave within the next hour or so to
have enough time to set up."

Leo burped and leaned back into his
chair.

"That was delicious, Cia! I'm so full."

"Thank you. Hopefully you're not *too* full
or you won't be able to do your act," she
replied.

Ray snorted.

"Yeah! Can you imagine a contortionist
who's so full of food that he can't even fit
into his uniform?"

His sister joined in with the wisecrack.

"We'd have to label him 'The Human
Balloon' instead!"

"Oh shut up," Leo barked. "Keep on
talking like that, I'll shove you in my tiny
glass box and lock you up."

The entire group laughed, except for
Chase who was busy stuffing food down her
throat. Only Sam noticed but did not say
anything.

When lunch was over, everyone went to
their rooms, changed into their uniforms, and

returned downstairs where they piled into the black truck Sam loaded and a red minivan that wore the Golden Circus brand on the door. The logo was a bright goldenrod sun with a portrait of Simon's face in the middle of it, smiling with a navy blue ribbon streaming underneath saying "The Circus is in Town!".

Chase drove the cargo truck, Leo as her passenger, and lead the crew out of the driveway. Sam revved up the van and followed with the remaining members.

The traveling circus drove only about twenty minutes until they came to a small park.

A dozen or so young children were running around and jumping on a newly modeled swing-set and playground area, screaming at the tops of their lungs. Just to the right of the play area, there was a large gazebo. Smoke from two grills clouded the air as a group of adults swam in conversation, music, and beer.

After Sam parked, Simon adjusted his top hat and grinned.

"Well, I suppose I should go find whoever is in charge of this festivity."

He surveyed the park and pointed to a large empty grassy region.

"That looks like a prime spot to set up."

"I'll tell her!" Sydney yelled as she rushed out the van.

"No, I will!" Ray challenged as he jumped out after her.

Simon continued his instructions, "Sam, tell Chase to use the old velvet curtains today. If my nose is correct," Simon said while sniffing the air. "Then it might rain on us before the show's over. What a birthday surprise that would be, eh?"

Simon laughed hysterically as he exited

the van and walked over to the gazebo. Sam hesitantly sat in the van, afraid that she had said something to offend Chase earlier while packing the truck.

The others were already out of the vehicles when Sam finally decided to get out of the van. Leo was stretching, and the twins were practicing their juggling tricks. Next to them, Pierre and Cia were quietly discussing the last minute details of their performance. Chase had unloaded some of the set boxes and was busy setting up the stage and curtains in the area Simon had picked out. She had already finished constructing the green and white striped holding-tent, so Sam picked up a box of pink balloons and the helium tank, and walked over to join Chase.

"Do you need a hand with anything, or can I start blowing up the balloons?" Sam asked tentatively.

"I should be fine. Not like I haven't done it before."

"Okay."

Sam set the box down and started filling each one up with helium, tying the ends with a long piece of purple ribbon.

The awkward silence between the two of them was ironically deafening. Luckily enough, Simon had finished talking with the birthday girl's father and made his way over to where Sam and Chase worked soundlessly.

"Good news, you two. In the case that it rains, Tracey's father said that he is still going to pay us in full. My heart smiles knowing that there are still decent people in this world."

"That's great," Chase replied. "We need the money especially since two shows got cancelled last month."

"True, true," Simon said surprisingly cheeringly. "But, at least Leo has that new doctor's assistant job, Cia's paintings have been selling pretty well, and I hear you landed a job at the bagel shop down the street!"

"Yup. I start on Friday."

"Excellent! And if all fails, Pierre and I have a little money set aside for such a rainy day. Ah! Rainy day! Today! I crack myself up."

Simon walked away to give a pep talk to his performers who were finishing getting ready by the parking lot. Chase completed the last part of the stage and stood up.

"I've got to grab the curtains from the truck. Be right back."

Sam nodded and watched Chase trudge over to the trunk of the truck. Simon lead everyone back to where Sam sat.

"Everything ready, my dear Sam?"

"Almost. Chase just has to hang up the curtains."

"Velvet, right?" Simon reminded.

"Oh! Right! I'll go tell her."

Sam quickly stood and ran over to Chase.

"I almost forgot to tell you," Sam panted. "Simon said to use the velvet ones today because it might rain. He doesn't want to ruin the nice silk ones."

"Okay. Thanks."

Chase replaced the silk curtains in their box and pulled out an older and more rugged wooden box. She opened it, pulled out a deep red velvet set of curtains, and jumped down from the cargo area after shutting the hatch.

Sam followed Chase back to the stage where the parents had corralled the kids to sit down in front. The circus performers were waiting in the holding tent for Simon to start the show.

Chase walked up to the set, carefully attached the curtains to each side of the stage, and pulled the rope to shut them. The young chatter settled as Simon stepped onto the stage.

"Welcome little ladies and gents to Simon's Golden Circus! I'm Simon, the ringmaster of our traveling show. Now, where is the birthday girl, Tracey?"

A small round blonde girl eagerly raised her hand, chocolate cake smeared all over her cheeks.

"Me! I'm Tracey!"

"Ah! Well, Tracey, Happy Birthday! I have a special surprise for you."

Simon looked at the audience then felt around his coat- pockets confused as if searching for something.

"That's strange. I know I brought it here with me. Where could it be?"

Simon continued to fumble around as the kids laughed. Acting upset, he put his hands on his waist and tapped his foot.

"Where… where could it be?"

Simon took off his top hat and scratched his head. Sitting on top of his head was a shiny silver tiara with an emerald gem in the center front. The crowd shouted crazily at Simon.

"It's on your head! Your head! Look!"

Simon stared at the kids flabbergasted.

"My head? What's on my head? Is it a bird?"

"No!" voices shouted unanimously.

"Then what is it?"

"A crown! A crown!" the anxious crowd cried out.

"A crown?"

Simon reached for the top of his head and grabbed the shiny tiara.

"Ah, yes! A crown for the birthday girl, for today you are a princess!"

Tracey rushed to the stage, and Simon steadily placed the crown on her head.

"I dub thee, Princess Tracey of the park!"

The crowd cheered as Tracey turned around and curtsied.

Simon continued, "Now that the royal ceremony is over, let the show begin!"

The kids cheered once more.

"For our first act, you will see a man twist and turn into shapes you never thought possible for a man to be in… He can fit into the smallest boxes. You could even put him in your suitcase if you wanted to! My dear royal court of Princess Tracey, I give you… Leo, the Great Bendmaster!"

Simon bowed and slid off stage as Chase pulled the curtain open revealing Leo in a glittery golden spandex suit. The audience clapped.

A techno beat started to play as Leo began his act. Simon walked to the back of the stage and stood next to Sam who was propped up against the pillar opposite of Chase.

"Well I think it's off to a fantastic start, don't you think? The costumes look beautiful."

"Thank you, Simon," Sam replied. "I enjoy making them. Maybe I can find a job that can utilize my skills so Leo, Cia, and Chase won't have to work so hard."

"Don't worry, love," Simon consoled. "Monetary problems aren't really the problems I'm concerned with. Besides, I think this bagel job might keep our Miss Chase out of a certain kind of trouble, hmm?"

"You know about that?" Sam said astonished.

"I'm the ringmaster. It's my duty to know what happens under my tent… or I suppose my roof."

He laughed.

"But, Pierre is thinking about leaving."

"Yes, which is why I said that we might have more concerning problems that money can't solve. What's the point of a heart if we do not listen to it?"

Sam looked over at Chase who was watching Leo perform but appeared to be lost in her thoughts.

"My dear, life isn't always fair," Simon continued. "We are hardly given directions. We are, however, given minds and hearts to help guide us to our destination. Sure, it's messy and chaotic, but that's what makes life so exciting and engaging, don't you think?"

Sam silently nodded.

Simon proceeded, "Life has certainly surprised me in many a ways, flinging me into worlds and experiences unknown, but I look at the amazing people I've met and the amazing events that have taken place, and I laugh at how awesome my life turned out to be, rather, how I made it be. Pierre's a strong man. He wouldn't be leaving if he wasn't sure that it was the best move for him and Felicia."

Sam's gaze drifted from Chase to the ground.

"But," Simon hinted. "Perhaps that's not the *real* problem you're facing."

Sam shook her head and knocked herself out of her trance.

"What do you mean?"

Simon cupped a hand to his ear and leaned toward to the stage. The kids were cheering and applauding.

"That sounds like my cue. Don't worry, Sam. People always end up doing what they want to do, whether they're conscious of it or not."

He grinned and popped back onto the stage to interject a short comedic act and then, to introduce Ray and Sydney. Leo walked up to Sam and nudged her in the arm.

"I love making those kids smile. Don't know what I'd do if I didn't have this. Oh and the costume bent really well, lots of room. Nice job."

"Thanks, Leo. I packed your change of clothes in the back of the van so you can leave straight from here to your date."

"I almost forgot! Phew! Thanks, Sam. You're a lifesaver. For some odd reason I thought it was Saturday. Man, this new job has got my head all messed up."

"It's not a problem, Leo. I hope you have fun."

"Oh, you know I always do. The ladies can't say 'no' to me. I'm too irresistible."

Chase walked by Sam and Leo and grabbed a water bottle from a small cooler.

"You know if you were taller, you wouldn't be able to get away with half the stuff you say," Chase said coolly.

"I know. That's what makes me so lucky. Well, I've got to go change and head out. Tell Simon not to expect me back until tomorrow morning."

Leo winked and casually strutted off to the van to change.

Chase shook her head and rolled her eyes as she took a sip of water.

Just as Chase was about to return to her post at the curtains, Sam reached out and grabbed her by the arm.

"Hey. Are we okay?"

"Yeah. Why wouldn't we be?" Chase asked puzzled.

"I'm not sure. I can't help but feel like you're upset. Is it about Cia?"

Chase stared down into her water bottle.

"Chase?"

Chase looked up and smiled.

"I'm fine, honestly. You worry too much, but thanks for your concern. I've got to get back to the ropes. Gotta be ready for when the twins are done, and I never know how long or short they'll take, the game changers."

Sam nodded as Chase walked back to the stage.

"Pst!"

Sam turned around. Pierre was peeking out the holding-tent.

"Sam! I think one of Felicia's snaps came undone."

Sam rushed over to the tent and stepped inside. Cia was holding up the sequined one piece suit, the back was undone. A snap was hanging off the seam by a thread.

"This is an easy fix. I'll have you fixed up in a second," Sam said confidently.

Sam pulled a small sewing kit from her back jean pocket. She threaded a needle and began reattaching the snap in place.

Seeing that Sam had everything under control, Pierre said, "I have to go and finish preparing our tricks. Felicia, I'll see you on stage."

He exited the tent as Sam continued working on Cia's suit.

"He told me he's leaving me," Cia

announced.

Knowing she could not reveal her previous knowledge, Sam whispered, "I'm so sorry, Cia."

"He said he wants to find his spark again, like I've found mine in Chase. He's such a good man. As awful as I feel, I can't tell you how relieved I am to not keep this a secret anymore. I just hope Chase feels the same."

"Why wouldn't she?"

"When we kept it a secret, it was almost unreal, like a fantasy being played out, but now, what we have is in the light. I'm not sure she'll be able to handle it. She's wonderful, don't get me wrong, but she still has a lot of growing to do."

"She loves you, Cia. You can see it in her eyes, and she told me today that she did."

Sam knotted off the stitch and cut the thread.

"All done."

Cia turned around and wrapped her arms around Sam.

"Thank you, Sam."

Cia straightened up and made her way to the tent opening. She paused and faced Sam one more time.

"I really am looking forward to celebrating your birthday this Friday. I think it will be a nice time for us all."

"I'm sure it will," Sam replied.

Cia left the tent and met Pierre at the back of the stage. Chase pulled the curtains closed as Ray and Sydney made their way offstage, and Simon sang out his introduction for the final act.

Sam opened the tent flap and watched the twins walk in front of the set to watch the Pierre's show with the rest of the audience.

Simon announced Pierre's name as the magician joined the flamboyant ringmaster onstage. The kids whooped and hollered for the magic show. Pierre was always the longest and best, closing act.

As Pierre performed card tricks and optical illusions, Cia remained backstage and walked over to Chase's side.

Sam could see Cia was trying to comfort Chase. Cia caressed Chase's shoulders and rested her hand on Chase's back. Chase was not saying a word though.

Pierre called for his assistant to join him, so Cia gently kissed Chase on the lips and emerged from the curtains. The crowd's cheer rose once more.

But, just as Pierre was about to start his "Saw in Half" trick, a rumbling thunder roared in the sky. The kids screamed as rain started to pour down.

Parents rushed to gather the kids and bring them under the gazebo's shelter. Ray and Sydney joined Sam and Simon behind the set.

"I was right! Rain! Isn't it glorious?" Simon shouted over the heavy beat of raindrops. "Such magic!"

"We need to take the set down!" Sam yelled back.

"Ah! Yes! Where is Chase?"

Chase had already begun ripping down the set, piece by piece as Pierre covered Cia in his cape and ushered her to the group.

"Sam," Pierre called out. "Take Felicia and the twins back to the house. Simon, Chase, and I will finish up here. There's no use in having us all stay in this weather and catch colds."

"Agreed!" Simon chimed in. "Just be sure to have a nice pot of tea ready for us when we get home. If that's not too much trouble."

"Not at all," Sam replied. "C'mon Ray, Sydney. Let's get you inside."

Sam and Cia rushed the twins to the van as Simon and Pierre ran to help Chase disassemble the stage.

There was only an hour difference in between the two group's arrival home.

The doorbell rang, and Sam rushed to the front door. Sam opened it and let Chase and Simon inside.

"Where is Pierre?" Sam asked, not surprised by her friend's absence.

Chase entered the house and shook the excess water from her coat.

"He had brought his suitcase with him. He took a taxi to the airport to leave for Indiana."

"I see. Well, the tea is hot and ready if you would like some."

"I definitely would!" exclaimed Simon as he sloshed his way into the kitchen, not even removing his wet clothing.

"I made a rooibos blend, your favorite," Sam said as she helped peel off Chase's drenched coat.

"I'd love some," Chase sighed.

"Glad to see you made it back in one piece," Cia's voice echoed from the second floor.

Sam and Chase turned and saw Cia leaning on the banister dressed in a silk lilac-colored robe.

"Always," Chase replied.

"If you're interested," Cia offered. "I've got an idea on how to warm you up."

Chase smiled and turned to Sam.

"Can I take a rain check? I promise I'll make it up to you Friday."

Sam smiled.

"Sure. Have a great night."

"You, too."

Chase hung her wet coat on the lower railing and made her way up to Cia. They kissed and retreated back into Cia's room. The door shut behind them. Sam returned to the kitchen but did not see Simon.

"Simon?"

"I'm over here!"

Sam walked over to the adjoining room. It was a small parlor room, moderately furnished with a cozy antique couch, two sofa chairs, and a rustic standup piano. Simon was crouched down in front of the fireplace, throwing logs into the warming fire.

"Twins are off in bed, I assume," Simon said. "It seems like a stellar night to just sit and enjoy a nice fire, a good cup of tea, and great company, don't you think?"

Sam sat down on the couch and sank into the old cushions. Simon joined her.

"It really was a spectacular show today," Simon sighed.

"Yes. It was," Sam agreed.

They both sat in silence as the flames flickered back and forth to the sounds of the raindrops on the roof. The melodies of their pattering melted into the mild crackling of the fire.

Sam leaned her head back and closed her eyes.

It was the most soothing song any ear could listen to.

A Birthday Surprise

Friday morning came faster than anyone had counted on.

Sam hit her alarm clock as it beeped annoyingly in her ear. Trying to return to her sleep, she stuffed her head underneath her pillow and curled up even tighter within her blankets.

There was a subtle rumbling on the floor outside her room, and it gradually got louder until the twins burst through Sam's door and pounced on the bed.

"Wake up, sleepyhead!" Ray shouted.

"Yeah! It's your birthday! You can't sleep all day!" Sydney joined in.

Sam reluctantly emerged from her pillow's safety and playfully swatted it at the twins.

"If it's my birthday, then I have the power to do as I please, and I choose to sleep."

"But, Chase helped us make you pancakes! They're gonna get cold if you don't hurry," pleaded Sydney.

"Are they blueberry pancakes?" Sam interrogated jokingly.

"They're the *only* kind of pancakes!" Ray shouted.

"Fine. For blueberry pancakes, I suppose I can make an exception."

"Yay!" they both cheered.

Each twin grabbed one of Sam's hand and pulled her out of bed and down the stairs.

"Hurry, Sam!" they both rushed.

"If you pull me any harder, I'll fall down the stairs!"

Sam entered the kitchen.

"Surprise!"

Everyone was standing around the table, save for Leo who was seated with his head hanging down.

Upon the table, there was blueberry pie and a large stack of blueberry pancakes next to it, both glowing with candles.

"I couldn't figure out which you'd prefer to eat first, so I just covered them both with candles," Chase said, wearing a large smile.

"Thank you, everyone. It's lovely."

"You've got to blow out the candles before they melt all over everything, and we won't be able to eat it!" Ray screamed.

"Enough with the screaming, Ray," Leo moaned as he lifted his head off the table.

As Sam pulled out a chair to sit, she laughed, "Too much partying for one night, Leo?"

"You can say that. The girl was crazy. That's the last time I date younger than thirty years old. I'm too old for this crap."

His head dropped back to where it was resting.

"Darling Sam," Simon interrupted. "I beg your pardon, but you really should blow out these candles so we can eat!"

"Right."

Sam sat, eyes closed, as she made a wish. After a brief pause, she opened her eyes and blew out all the candles in one breath.

"Wow!" the twins exclaimed.

"Quite impressive!" Simon cheered. "Well, onward with eating!"

"Yay!" the twins shouted again.

Cia picked up a spatula, dished a load of pancakes onto a plate, and handed it to Sam.

"Sam, after we eat, I'm going to take you

shopping. It'll go well with the rest of my gift to you, but I'll give you the finale when we go out to dinner tonight."

"That sounds delightful. Thank you, Cia."

"Why can't we go out with you guys tonight?" Sydney whined.

"Because you're not old enough," Chase teased as Cia handed the twins a heaping pile of pancakes.

"That's not fair! We wanna go!"

Through chewing, Simon piped up, "But, if you two go to dinner with them, then who will accompany me to the Music and Lights Concert at Millennium Park tonight? I don't think Leo will be up for it…"

"Oo we'll go with you, Simon!"

The twins turned around and stuck out their tongues at Chase, who defensively returned the favor.

After breakfast, Leo retreated back to his bed and shut the door. Simon stood up and began clearing the table.

"Well, I'd love to stay and help, but I've got to head off to work," Chase stated begrudgingly.

"The first day of work! Splendid!" Simon shouted excitedly.

"Yeah," Chase replied. "At least I'll get paid to clear off the table."

"Brilliant. Always have a positive attitude, Chase."

Just before Chase left the kitchen, Chase turned around and said, "I almost forgot! I told Conner about tonight's plans, and he's really excited to go. He was a little bummed I answered the door today for the mail, but I think the offer I presented him cleared that right up."

Not waiting too long, Chase ran up the

stairs before Sam could get a word in.

"Don't worry, Sam," Cia said in her gentle voice. "You can vent about her actions when we go shopping. Simon, do you have the rest of this? I'd like to get an early start; we've got a lot of places to visit today. I even booked an appointment at the day spa and salon so we can get all dolled up for the evening."

"Cia, you really shouldn't have," Sam said bashfully at the extravagant proposal.

"I sold two paintings yesterday at a much higher price than I thought so this is nothing at all, and we deserve some real pampering. Conner will be even more blown away by you. I guarantee it."

"Yes," Simon cut in. "Don't fret about me, here. The twins will help me clean up."

"We will?" Ray and Sydney stammered in harmony.

"No complaining, you two, especially if you want to see that show tonight."

"Awwww man."

"Now, you two lovely ladies head on up and get dressed for your fun filled day!"

"Thanks, Simon," Sam replied.

Cia and Sam both exited the kitchen and headed upstairs just as Chase was running down them to get to work. She was dressed in a khaki colored hat, a forest green polo shirt and dark wash jeans.

"Don't you dare judge me on what I'm wearing," Chase shouted as she raced by. "I know how stupid I look. I'll see you later!"

Chase ran out the front door, hopped on her bike, and peddled down the street.

Cia turned to Sam, "Let's hope she doesn't wear that to dinner tonight, or I really will have to pretend like there's nothing going on between us."

Sam laughed as the two women returned to their rooms to change their clothes before their outing.

When Cia and Sam arrived at the mall, the stores were empty. Although schools were on spring break, it was much too early for kids to be up and out, and it was just late enough to miss all the elderly mall-walkers.

"Where do you want to start?" Cia asked.

"I'm not sure. Are we looking for anything in particular? It's been awhile since I went shopping for fun."

"Why don't we start off with choosing an outfit to wear out to dinner tonight?"

"Where are we going?"

"Chase won't tell me," Cia said, rolling her eyes. "She wants to surprise all of us. She said she saved up a sum of money from when she shoveled snow this past winter."

"I hope she doesn't spend all of it on me," Sam said worriedly.

"Oh sweetheart, you really need to stop worrying so much. You'll give yourself wrinkles before you thirty. Oo! Let's stop in here. I see a sign for a shoe sale, and that's always a good sign."

Cia and Sam walked into the first store and started looking around. As timid and unsure Sam was at the beginning of the trip, she soon relaxed and began to have fun trying on all the different types of shoes and dresses that Cia picked out for her. The shopping spree and hair appointments lasted until early evening.

Cia and Sam walked through the front door laughing and smiling. Both were carrying over half a dozen bags from different stores, satisfied with their findings. Simon came to greet them.

"I see you had an excellent time, ladies!"

"Yes, we did," Sam answered.

"Is Chase back from work yet?" Cia questioned.

"She is. She returned just before you did actually. I think she has passed out in her room."

Cia sat her bags down on the floor and gave Sam a hug.

"I'm going to go say 'hello' to Chase, but I'll meet you in your room in about an hour to get ready. I've really enjoyed our day together. I'm certain the night will be just as splendid."

"I have, as well. Thank you so very much for everything. I couldn't have asked for a better way to spend my birthday."

Cia gathered her purchases and gracefully sprinted up the stairs and into Chase's bedroom.

"Do you need help bringing up any of your bags?" Simon asked.

"Oh no, I'm fine, but thank you."

Sam trudged upstairs with all of her bags banging at her knees making it difficult to walk.

I don't know how Cia does it, Sam wondered to herself.

Sam set her bags on her bed and began unloading them into her closet and dresser drawers. After she finished, she collapsed on her bed, and while staring at the ceiling, she fell asleep.

She dozed for about forty-five minutes. When she woke up, she pulled out the tiny silver moon necklace from under her shirt and held it up as far as the chain would let her.

The pendant sparkled in the dim lighting of her room.

Sam was just about to cry, her mind filled with distant memories, but she stopped herself when she heard a knock at her door.

"Who is it?" Sam asked.

"It's me, Cia!"

"Come in."

Sam sat up in her bed as Cia opened the door.

"It's time to give you the rest of your gift."

Cia gasped as she saw that Sam's hair was slightly messed up from napping.

"Oh no! Your hair! Don't worry, we'll fix it after this."

Cia sat next to Sam on the bed and handed her a flat black box.

"Here you go. I think it will go well with the dress you bought for tonight."

Sam took the box and opened it cautiously. Inside there was a beautiful set of silver earrings with princess cut diamonds hanging from each center.

"I always see you with that silver moon on, so I tried to find something that shined just as nicely to match."

"They're beautiful. Thank you, Cia."

Sam lunged forward and gave Cia a huge hug.

"You really have outdone yourself today. I can't thank you enough."

"We still have quite the night ahead of us, too," Cia replied. "Chase finally caved and told me that we're going to that new Italian restaurant downtown. She rented a really nice black SUV for it, too."

"What? Why?"

"She really does love you, and how could

she not? You're always there for her, and you're literally the nicest person I've ever met."

Sam looked back down at her shimmering new earrings.

"Now," Cia continued as she stood and locked the door. "Let's get ready."

Another hour passed when the doorbell rang.

"I got it!" Chase yelled as she ran downstairs. She was wearing slim black slacks, a matching black button up collared shirt, and a white and gray striped tie. Her short, dark brown bangs flew in her eyes as she jumped the last three steps and hurdled into the door.

After regaining her composure, she fixed her hair and opened the door.

"Hey there, Conner."

Chase stepped aside and let Conner in. He was wearing a baby blue polo shirt underneath a tan colored sports coat. His black slacks looked a bit too baggy as they fell a little longer than the heels of his black loafers, and his blonde hair was slicked back behind his big ears.

A stray piece of hair popped from behind his ear to which Conner reacted swiftly, nervously tucking it back in place.

"Thanks again, Chase, for inviting me tonight. You have no idea how long I've been trying to muster up the courage to ask Sam out."

"Oh, I've actually got a pretty good idea. I don't know when she'll be down though. I swear Cia and Sam have been locked up in Sam's room for over an hour. Who knows how much longer they'll take."

"I'd wait forever for her," Conner said with a smitten sigh.

Chase patted him on the back.

"Steady there, Romeo. Don't want to show all your cards at once."

"Right. Cards, not all at once."

"Let me see if I can get them down here. Cia!" Chase yelled. "Conner's here! How long do you plan on making us wait? We *do* have reservations!"

"Out in a second!" Cia shouted back.

Chase looked at Conner.

"I'm a girl, and I *still* don't know or question why she takes so long to get ready. Remember that. Don't question the makeup rituals."

"Gotcha. Allow makeup rituals."

"Dude, loosen up," Chase joked as she slapped Conner on the back again. "You're not taking out a princess, you're taking out a regular down-to-earth girl."

Conner nodded furiously.

"We're ready!" Cia shouted from the top of the stairs.

"Finally!" Chase yelled back.

The door to Sam's room swung open. Cia stepped out first. She was elegant, as always, dressed in a long silky halter black gown with a low v-cut front, stemming down just below her breast line. Her long coffee-colored hair lay perfectly down her back so that her slender shoulders gleamed in the hallway light. With a toss of her hair she glided downstairs.

"Hi, sweetheart. You look beautiful as ever. I'm glad you're wearing my favorite tie," Cia said, kissing Chase on the cheek then turning her attention to Conner. "You must be Conner. It's wonderful to meet you."

Conner stuck out a shaky hand and shook Cia's steady and soft one.

"It's… um nice to meet you, too Mrs…"

"You can call me Cia."

"It's nice to meet you, Cia. You look amazing."

"Thank you, but you should save your compliments for your own date. Sam?" Cia yelled upstairs. "Come on out and show everyone just how gorgeous you look."

Sam peeked her head from her door and protested, "This isn't what I'm used to wearing. I'm not sure if I look okay in it."

"Darling, you look absolutely fine," Cia reassured.

Still uneasy, Sam timidly stepped out from the confines of her room. Chase and Conner's mouths dropped open.

Sam was wearing a floor-length maroon colored strapless dress with a small train behind her. The simple frame of her dress contrasted with her dashing hairstyle which was pinned up in a bun, decorated with tiny, diamond floral-shaped embellishments. This only helped define her slender neckline, bringing out her shy smile. The diamond earrings Cia gave her hung delicately from her ears and shined like tiny chandeliers.

Conner unknowingly approached the staircase as she descended down them.

"You… look… like a princess, Sam."

"Really?" Sam blushed.

A cheesy grin expanded across Conner's face as he nodded furiously.

Sam walked down the last few steps to join Conner who immediately kissed the back of her hand when she stood beside him. He offered her his arm, and the pair made their way to the door where Cia and Chase were smiling.

"My, what a lovely pair you two make," Cia complimented.

"Wow," Chase started. "Sam, you look stunning. Honestly, I can't get over how great you look."

"Thank you. Thank you to all of you. Your kind words are really helping me feel more comfortable in this dress."

"Well then, champ," Chase aimed at Conner. "You better keep those compliments going all night."

"I don't think I'll have a problem with that," Conner said dreamily, still caught up in Sam's beauty.

"We should get going though," Chase insisted. "We don't want to lose our reservations, and this SUV is by the hour."

The two couples made their way to their vehicle and on to dinner.

Dinner went very well. The new Italian restaurant was just as magnificent as the reviews had described. They each ordered dishes that were filled to the brim with succulent pasta.

Their stomachs full, the couples made their way back home laughing in the evening's joyous air.

Chase pulled up in front of the house and turned down the music.

"As much as I'd like to keep joy-riding in this set of wheels, I really should return this thing before I get charged extra for keeping it out late."

Chase reached around and shook Conner's hand.

"Conner, thanks for making it out with us tonight. I hope you had a nice time."

"An excellent time. Thanks again for inviting me."

"Never a problem. Now, I hate to rush you, but get out my car," Chase joked.

Conner rushed out of SUV and ran to open Sam's door.

Chase took Cia's hand and kissed it.

"I'll make up not opening your door when I get back."

Chase winked.

"You better," Cia replied in jest. "Drive safe, darling."

Cia leaned over the armrest and kissed Chase before leaving the SUV. She shut the door and blew one more kiss. Chase mocked catching it and slammed it on her heart. Then, she drove off.

Conner whispered into Sam's ear, "Those two are breathtaking. I want what they have, all that chemistry."

Cia walked up the house's creaky front steps and turned around.

"Conner, it was very nice to spend the evening with you. I hope we can all do this again soon."

"I hope so too, Mrs- oops. I mean Cia. Have a great night!"

"You, too. Sam, I'll see you in the morning."

"Goodnight, Cia," Sam said waving.

Cia entered the house closing the door behind her. Conner shifted his weight back and forth nervously.

"Sam, I had a really fantastic time tonight. I hope I didn't ruin your birthday by honing in on you and your friends."

"No, you didn't. This was all a surprise to me, too. I'm glad you came actually. It might've been really awkward if it was just the two of them and myself."

Conner laughed.

"Yeah, I guess you're right."

He rubbed his hands as he continued to

sway back and forth anxiously.

Deciding to break the uncomfortable silence, Sam started up, "Okay, have a great night, Conner."

But, as soon as Sam tried to retreat inside, Conner grabbed her by the hand and said, "Wait."

Sam paused as Conner turned her body to face him.

"Sam, I've been dying to ask you this since I saw you come down the stairs earlier."

"What is it?"

Conner's eyes blinked rapidly.

"Can I… umm… Would I be able to… I'd very much like to kiss you, now."

"What?"

"I've been dying to since the first time I delivered the mail to your house. I thought you were the prettiest girl I'd ever seen, and I still think that. And… I see a lot of faces, you know… delivering a lot of mail and whatnot. I'm sorry. I think I'm rambling."

Sam giggled.

"It's okay. It's cute."

Conner took a deep breath in and gently pulled Sam's body into his. His hands were still a little shaky as he rested them on each side of her waist. Sam could feel his panting on her flushed cheeks as their faces neared each other, and as they did, *she* also started to get nervous.

Sam had never kissed anyone before. Thoughts began to fill her head.

What does my breath smell and taste like? Did I eat too much garlic bread at dinner? I wonder if I'll be any good at kissing. I wonder how many girls Conner has kissed. What if I'm not any good? Will he laugh?

The wait until his lips met hers was

moving painstakingly slow as Sam's thoughts rapidly swarmed her mind. Remembering what she had seen in movies, Sam slowly lifted her arms and wrapped them around Conner's skinny neck. She ran her fingers through his short bristly hair, the stubble just under his hairline tickling the palms of her hands, and closed her eyes waiting for the impact.

Finally, she felt a slight wetness touch her lips. She briefly opened her eyes and saw Conner's face, his eyes were tightly closed, and his eyebrows showed that his head was flocked with the same insecurities. Seeing this, Sam relaxed as she kissed him a little longer.

Sam pulled away slowly.

"That was very nice."

"Was it?" Conner asked shocked. "Thank God. I mean… Thanks. I didn't know what to get you for your birthday so I decided to make a bold move instead."

"Well, it was a very thoughtful gift."

Another wide goofy grin spread across Conner's face.

"I really should head inside now," Sam said kindly.

"Right. Of course. Have a great night, and don't let the bed bugs bite!"

Sam turned around at the doorstep and laughed. Embarrassed, Conner whipped around and hurried down the street, yelling at himself for how stupid he sounded. Sam smiled once more and headed inside.

It was about midnight when Chase finally arrived back home. She hopped out of the cab with her shirt hanging half out of her pants, her tie undone, and the faint smell of a couple beers she had sneakily bought on her breath.

Noticing this, Chase popped in a piece of gum and headed inside. Quietly, she crept up the stairs and slowly opened Sam's door.

Tip-toeing to Sam's bed, Chase whispered, "Sam. Sam? Are you awake?"

Sam did not answer for she was fast asleep.

At her bedside, Chase gently shook Sam's body, and Sam awoke startled, but Chase slipped her hand over Sam's mouth to keep her from screaming.

"It's just me. C'mon. I have to give you your birthday gift now."

"Chase, it must be twelve o'clock in the morning. Can't it wait?"

"No. It has to be now. It won't make much sense if I give it to you in daylight. Grab a jacket. It got a little chilly outside."

Chase inched slowly back to the door as Sam got out of bed, still half asleep and put on her jacket.

Before they walked out the front door, Chase grabbed a long narrow box covered in yellow wrapping paper, topped with a neon green bow, and a blue backpack that were lying by the front door.

"Can't forget these," Chase joked as she locked up. "C'mon."

Sam tried to wipe the lingering sleep from her eyes.

"Where are we going?"

"To the van. We have to drive somewhere for you to get the full effect of the gift."

"You're kidding me."

"Surprisingly, this time I'm not."

Sam unwillingly climbed into the van as Chase started the engine. They drove back to the park where Tracey's birthday party was a couple days ago.

Chase parked and said, "Okay. Let's go."

Chase climbed out of the van, opened Sam's door, and helped her out.

"This way."

"You're crazy," Sam muttered.

"Yes, but it's why you love me. C'mon."

Chase lead Sam to the open grassy space where they had set up their stage and pulled a blanket out of her backpack.

"Blanket? Check. Now, for some music."

Chase pulled out a set of small speakers hooked up to an ipod and pressed play. The misty night air was then blessed with the sounds of a smooth bossa nova tune.

"What in heaven's sake are you doing?" Sam asked confused.

"Shh… I'm prepping your gift ambiance."

Chase took Sam's hand and guided her to the blanket to sit down. After she did, Chase knelt down in front of her and handed her the brightly wrapped gift.

"Happy Birthday, Sam."

Sam gulped, joining her friend on the cold ground, and took Chase's present. She unloosened the bow and tore the yellow paper until a plain brown box was revealed.

"Go on. Open it," Chase urged.

Sam crumpled the wrapping paper into a ball and tossed it aside. Then, she slowly lifted the box-lid and gasped. Chase smiled at the reaction.

"I know that your favorite books are the ones about stars and constellations so I thought that maybe you could use this to get a closer look."

Sam sat in astonishment at the sight of the vibrant orange telescope that lie so peacefully in the box.

"I love it," Sam whispered.

"Really?"

"I love it so much," Sam repeated.

She set the box down and sprung forward, giving Chase a strong hug then kissed her on the cheek.

After Sam let go, she leaned back and carefully pulled the telescope out of the box.

Sam set it up, and as she started gazing up at the night sky, Chase fell back off her knees and sat, leaning on her hands watching Sam glow with happiness.

The bossa nova song had ended, and a slow jazzy ballad came on next. Chase stood up and reached out her hand.

"Sam?"

"Yes?" Sam said, still looking through her telescope.

"This may sound incredibly cheesy, but would you like to dance? You know I'm a sucker for a good jazz ballad."

Sam sat back from stargazing and taking Chases' hand, gradually stood up.

Chase pulled Sam's body into hers and wrapped her hand around her waist, letting it rest on the arch of Sam's lower back.

Chase began to sway back and forth to the beating pulse of the music, taking Sam with her subtle rocking.

"Sam, you really looked spectacular at dinner. I've never seen you so dressed up."

Sam blushed.

"Thanks. You were quite charming yourself, and Cia… she always looks so classy and beautiful."

"She sure does. Conner didn't look too bad either."

"Yes. He was very handsome outside of his mailman uniform. I was pleasantly surprised."

Chase did not respond, but the increasing

swinging rhythms carried them to the next part of their conversation.

"I want to apologize for how I acted on Wednesday at the show. I was a huge jerk, and I'm sorry," Chase whispered.

"It's okay. I know that must have been a lot to take in, what Cia told you."

"And now Pierre's leaving? It's all my fault. You were right. All of this was so wrong."

"It wasn't entirely your fault. Pierre and Cia weren't happy. They made decisions that would give them their happiness back. You were just caught in the crossfire."

"Do you think that Cia really loves me?"

"Yes. We talked about it earlier when she was telling me how worried she was that *you* didn't love her. I suppose the both of you have nothing to fear now."

"Maybe…" Chase's voice trailed off as she pulled Sam's body closer to hers. "It's just that, when Cia told me that Pierre knew, everything became so real to me. How am I going to match up to him? I work part-time at a bagel shop, and I can't even drink a whiskey and coke in a bar yet."

Sam laughed.

"I'm sure if those were the reasons not to love you, Cia would have called it off a long time ago. Chase, you have to trust what you've done up to this point. Stop and listen to what your heart has been telling you all along. You have to ask yourself, 'Am I happy with who I am in this very instant?' If the answer is 'yes,' then how can you regret anything, good or bad? You can't. You're a good person with a very kind spirit. That's what matters."

"You know… No one talks like you," Chase

smiled.

"I'm… um… sorry?" Sam asked puzzled by the comment.

"It's a good thing. You always know what to say, and it always feels so genuine and pure. Sometimes, I swear there's no ounce of anger or cruelty in your body. It's always refreshing."

Chase leaned closer to Sam and rested the side of her temple on Sam's while Sam let go of Chase's hand and put her arms around Chase's warm neck, allowing both of Chase's hands to lie on her own waist.

Sam felt nervous again, but it was not the same kind of nervous that she felt when she was with Conner. Sam breathed out heavily, watching the air fog in front of her. The ballad seemed to be playing forever to immortalize the moment. Her body moved back and forth along with Chase's guidance. Sam hugged Chase's neck a little tighter and closed her eyes making her notice the chills running up and down her spine as they danced in the starlight.

Chase pulled away slightly and looked into Sam's eyes.

"Sam, you're the most phenomenal person in this world. I'm so happy that I have you in my life."

Chase smiled that oh-so-endearing smile that Sam wanted to hate but could not.

Choked up, Sam managed to whisper, "I told you that I'd always be here for you."

Chase leaned in just enough for their noses to touch and peered down at Sam's mouth then back to her eyes.

"Even your mouth… seems so refined."

"Thank… you," Sam stuttered.

They each moved in slowly, Sam feeling

compelled to kiss her best friend, but just as she was about to make a decision, Sam noticed a tall built man stumbling from the bushes. He was bleeding profusely from a what looked to be a stab wound on his left upper pectoral.

Realizing who it was, Sam broke away from Chase's hold and ran to the man.

"Eton!"

The man collapsed to the ground wheezing heavily.

Chase turned around and saw Sam crouched down next to, not a man, but a brawny looking fox. Its coat was covered in a rusted blood color.

"You named a fox?" Chase asked confused.

"No… I mean yes… I mean… it's complicated," Sam stammered. "Eton? Talk to me. Are you okay?"

The fox slowly moved its head to look up at Sam and spoke softly, "Sam'ona… I found you."

"Yes, I'm here. Shhh… don't worry."

Sam cradled the injured fox in her arms.

Chase's mouth was wide open in shock.

"Did I just hear that fox speak? Did I even drink that much?"

"You're not crazy," Sam replied, still tending to Eton's wound. "He did speak."

"He's a fox! I can't speak fox. *You* can't speak fox! Foxes don't speak!"

Eton jokingly whispered, "I see she inherited her father's quick wit."

"What the hell is going on?" Chase yelled as she threw up her hands.

"I promise I will explain everything to you later, but right now he needs my help. All of my bandages and herbs are in my room. We need to bring him back home with us," Sam rushed.

"The talking fox? We're bringing the talking fox back with us?"

"I'm not joking. He needs serious medical attention."

"Then we'll bring him to a vet. Maybe talking is just a symptom of some strange disease."

"They can't help him there," Sam argued. "This stab wound was made from a cursed blade, and he needs the proper spellbound medicine to heal it properly, or he'll die."

Chase stood still, dumbfounded as Sam struggled to hold up Eton's heavy body by herself. To Sam, Eton was still in human form though Chase could not see it.

"Eton, you're going to have to allow her to see you fully now. I can't carry you by myself."

Eton sighed and let out a heavy stubborn sigh. Within a blink of her eye, Chase immediately saw Eton in his manlike form.

"What the-"

Chase rubbed her eyes furiously.

"This is not happening," she repeated.

"Chase! I need you to help me bring him to the van."

Still stunned but obliging her friend's command, Chase positioned herself under Eton's other arm and helped lead him to the backseat of the van. After putting him in the back, Sam ran back to the open grassy area at the park.

"Where are you going?" Chase yelled.

"The telescope! I have to go get it."

"You're leaving me alone with Fox-Man?!?"

Sam disappeared into the darkness.

Sitting in the driver's seat, Chase turned around and looked at Eton.

Still a man. Maybe he was always a man, and for some crazy reason I thought I saw a fox first. That's not ludicrous at all…

Eton was curled up on the seat in the fetal position shaking. Chase turned to face out the front windshield and waited for Sam to return.

A couple minutes passed before Chase saw Sam running into the parking lot, the lampposts' light guiding her back. Out of breath, she climbed in the van and buckled up.

"Okay. I got everything. Let's go."

Chase turned the car on, backed out and sped out of the parking lot back home.

They pulled up to the garage and parked.

"Let's bring him through the kitchen, and we'll put him in the parlor room. I'll run upstairs and grab what I need. Chase, can you start a fire up for him? He looks like he's freezing."

"Umm… yeah."

Chase opened up the back door and helped Eton out. Sam ran underneath his other side when he fully emerged, and the trio made their way to the back kitchen door.

Inside, Sam flicked on the light switch, and they carried Eton to the back room attached to the kitchen.

"Can you hang onto him for one second?" Sam asked. "I'm going to run back out to the van and grab that blanket for him to lie on. It's bad enough we already ruined the backseat of the van with his blood."

Sam freed herself, dashed back outside and retrieved the blanket. When she came back in, she spread it out over the couch and helped Chase carefully lay Eton's weak body down.

"Okay. I'll go get my things."

Sam sprinted as quietly as she could up to her room. Chase walked over to the fireplace and started getting the dry logs ready.

Sam returned with a beat-up looking, red book and a bag filled with clanging vials and herbs. She knelt down beside Eton and flipped open the book while organizing the contents of her bag on the table.

Then, Sam stopped what she was doing and looked longingly at Eton.

Who is this guy? Chase thought as she threw a lit match into the fire igniting the logs.

Sam put both her hands on Eton's arm and closed her eyes. She inhaled deeply. After the fifth inhalation, she peeked open one eye to see what Eton's condition was, hoping it had changed, but it had not.

Sam's shoulders slumped with disappointment as she returned to thumbing through the book's pages.

Chase stood and shook her head.

"I need a drink."

She walked into the kitchen, poured herself a glass of whiskey, and chugged the entire thing. She poured another and sat down at the kitchen table.

Sam tended to Eton for about an hour. Chase could hear Sam chanting and mumbling words but could not make them out.

Keep drinking, Chase.

Another thirty minutes went by before Sam joined Chase in the kitchen. She sat down quietly.

"I'm sorry you had to find out this way," she whispered.

"I'm still trying to figure out exactly what I found," Chase joked while taking another sip of whiskey.

Sam reached out and took Chase's hand in

hers.

"Please, listen. I have so much to tell you."

Chase finished her drink and pushed the glass aside.

"Okay. Shoot."

"Have you ever wondered if there was another world, beyond this one?"

"I considered the possibility, but I left the thought to the sci-fi movies."

"Well, they do exist, at least one anyway. That's where Eton is from. It's where… you and I are from as well."

"Us?" Chase asked flabbergasted.

"You wouldn't remember. You were just a baby when we came here, and I was only five years old. I ran into Simon at a bar the night we entered this realm, and he took us in."

"What…" Chase slouched in her chair in disbelief.

A long silence passed before Chase could put her words together.

"So… where *did* we come from?"

Sam continued, "Based on my understandings of the knowledge and facts in this dimension, we came from a parallel world. Both our Earths have the same resources and same atmosphere, but they've differed in how their inhabitants evolved. Here, there was a definitive evolutionary curve that separated humans from your more basic animals versus our home world."

"What's this place called?"

"Pangea. The continents have not split yet, and the technology is far less advanced than it is here. You can say, Pangea is at the Medieval era."

"How did animals evolve on this medieval *Pangea*?"

"Thousands of years ago, some animals started to evolve into more sophisticated versions of their predecessors. These dominate species transformed into what we call Neos, the 'New Breed.' You see, where this Earth thrives in technology, Pangea flourishes in the supernatural. The Neos are actually just animals who are able to possess the full human form through the help of magic."

"Did someone cast a spell on the Neos that allowed them to progress farther along?"

"No. Since the beginning of time, magic was in all matter that lived. The soon-to-be Neos grew in accordance to the Great Crossings magical lands. It was like developing another trait that exists in your DNA as a result of your environment. For example, look at how humans here developed the thumb, a single trait that, over time, made you unique to any other animal on Earth."

"And what about the animals that didn't evolve?"

"The much lower species that were consistently hunted as food, like chickens, deer, and cattle, stayed in their pure animal form. They're known as Devoluts, the 'De-Evolved,' but there are some Devoluts that weren't ever a source of food. They just didn't develop magically."

"How many kinds of animals did… er… do the Neos consist of?"

"In respect to how many different kinds of animals there are on Pangea, there aren't that many. Foxes, for example are a type of Neo, like Eton and myself."

"You're a fox? And I mean that in a non-flirtatious way, obviously."

Sam laughed.

"Yes, I am."

Chase sat quietly and spun her glass on the table.

"And you're saying I'm a Neo, too?"

Sam nodded.

"So… what am I? Why haven't I ever noticed anything? Like a tail or fuzzy pointy ears?"

"You're a special Neo, Chase."

"I'm scared to know what that means."

"Before I answer that, I think it will help you to know why I've kept your identity a secret for so long."

"Not sure if anything can help clear up what's in my head right now, but you can try," Chase sighed.

"When the Neos became more reformed, they initiated the Noble Royal Organization and built the Great Hall in the middle of Pangea to act as a central base of yearly activities and celebrations.

There are five Head Nobles, the five strongest of the Neo race. They consist of a lion, a phoenix, a wolf, a black bear, and a falcon, while the rest of their perspective families remain part of the Noble line. Each Head Noble governs a region of the land while the lesser of the Neo species became part of the Noble Court. Each Noble line has a corresponding Court species. The Lionship has gazelles."

"That's odd," Chase interrupted. "Don't lions eat gazelles?"

"Here, yes. In Pangea, gazelles aren't that tasty according to the majority of lions I've talked to."

"Uh huh. If you say so."

"But, to continue, the Phoenix Clan has us, the foxes. The Wolf's Reign has bobcats. The Black Bear Sovereignty has snakes, and the

Falcon Order has peacocks. There are five other forms of Neos, too, but they continued to roam free as Mystical Nomads and did not join the Organization."

"You're not a slave, are you?"

"Goodness, no. The bond between a Noble line and its Court is a sacred one. The Court serves the Nobles, and in turn, the Court is guaranteed protection from any evil, if that is ever the case, but majority of the Neos are quite peaceful and respectful. Pangea was born a calm and serene land. That is… up until the Great War broke out about hundred years ago when every Neo was fighting for their life."

Sam fidgeted in her seat.

"Species, like here, in their animal form never found others outside of their own attractive, so mating stayed within, but after the Noble Royal Organization came to be, the Neos became more and more accustomed to staying in their human form. This lead to cross-breeding due to the overall attractiveness to the human form.

The babies were alive and healthy but were born without the Neo genes; they were simply… human. At first, the Neos raised their human babies, and everyone continued to grow in peace. There was no hate, no jealous nor thirst for power, but that didn't last very long.

The human population exploded over Pangea and was increasing much faster than the purebred Neos. When this happened, the Neos thought that peace would still be possible, but the humans were so afraid that the Neos would overthrow them that they turned against the Neos first.

They enslaved them, kept them as laborers and entertainment pieces. The first Great War broke out as Neos fought for their freedom, but many did not survive. The ones that did fled to the Great Crossings because it was a safe haven. The humans never dared to go there. The magic-soaked lands scared them because they viewed its powers as evil.

Soon, the pure Neo population began to rise again and with it, the Noble Royal Organization was reinstated, but this time, there was a strict policy that no two different species could ever mate. The Head Nobles also inducted another form of power into the Organization called the Magi Order.

The Order was made up five priests. These priests were the eldest of the Mystical Nomadic clans. There was one for each element: earth, air, water, fire and metal."

"What kind of animals, oops I mean, Neos were they?"

"There was Kuros, a badger and Priest of the Earth, Erisi or the Head Councilman, an owl and Priest of the Air, Nysam, a koi fish and Priest of the Water, Tridor, a dragon and Priest of the Fire and finally, Lafore, a baboon and Priest of the Metals. Together, the Head Nobles and the Magi Order built the Great Abbey to house the growing Neo population.

Another fifty or so years passed, and the Neos' traditional peaceful lives took shape again. The Great Abbey was filled with song and laughter, and the Tournaments to decide which Head Noble would be the Majesty Crown, leader of all Head Nobles, for the next five year term took place once more. Soon, the Neos forgot about the troubled and wretched lives resisting the Anders."

"Anders?"

"Oh. Yes. The humans of Pangea. It's short for-"

"Neanderthals?" Chase guessed.

Sam nodded.

"What about the other Neos that were still enslaved by the Anders, outside the Great Crossings? Did the Head Nobles just forget about them?"

"No. That was the heated topic of debate at every Head Noble meeting. The Head Nobles argued about sending out rescue squads to complete covert missions to free the remaining Neos, but the risk of another war was too great.

Some refugees had migrated to the safety of the Great Crossings, but most remained prisoners. It wasn't until the Wolf King, King Delver, won the Tournament about five years before you were born. As Majesty Crown and with the help of his head commanding officer, Hydo, he made the final decision to send his best men out to search for any Neo prisoners and bring them all back to the Great Crossings.

They were successful for the first two years until word spread throughout the Anders that the Neos were stealing the slaves. King Delver declared war on the Anders, and sent out all of the Great Crossings' troops to save any Neo they came across.

This time the Neo armies were properly prepared with weapons and armor that matched with the Anders, but they were better because the Neo apparatuses were enchanted with the Magi Order's spells. The Order even had apprentices who traveled with the Neo armies to help heal the wounded and breech enemy lines.

Neo armies swept across Pangea taking back what was rightfully theirs. The battling raged on for a fast two years of King Delver's

Reign, but he was successful. The surviving Anders were banished to a peninsula, known as the Land of Cassum, separated from the mainland Pangea by the Great Crossings, and none were taken as slaves."

"What's to stop them from revolting and starting another war?"

"The Magi Order sealed the Anders to the Land of Cassum with a powerful spell surrounding the entire peninsula. The Nobles and their Court returned to their respective kingdoms, and the Great Hall was reopened. The Great Abbey remained open and housed the Magi Order and many other Neos who wished to learn conjuring arts. The year before you were born was the first year the Great Hall was used for the Tournament since the two wars while I was studying at the Great Abbey to be a healer in case of another crusade."

"But, if the Anders are banished to the Land of Cassum, do the Neos even have any enemies?"

"Unfortunately, yes. With war there are always consequences. There are small groups of Anders that linger in the mainland, and many of the Neos that had been kept in captivity right after the first Great War held a harsh bitterness to the Head Nobles for not coming to retrieve them sooner. They formed their own deviant groups. Some Nobles even left the Organization because of it and joined their forces, but all groups usually keep to themselves. If they ever do cause trouble, the Nobles take care of it."

"Okay," Chase said as she shook her head. "I think I understand the majority of it, but you still never said where I fit in to all of this."

Sam turned to Chase and put her hand on

Chase's shoulder.

"Chase, you are special because you are the first true Neo hybrid ever to be born. You mother was Princess Therene, princess of the Phoenixes, and your father was Rysul, King Delver's most prized wolf soldier. The Magi Order foresaw your birth as a part of a prophecy to save Pangea from a dreadful evil. That's why the Order sent me to this world with you, to raise you and make sure you grew up safe until the time for your return came. I'm positive Eton's presence here is no accident. I believe he is a sign that we must return home."

"Wait, wait, wait. You mean to tell me that I'm not really human, but I'm actually part phoenix and part wolf?"

"Yes."

"Where the hell are my wings? Or my wolf-like fangs?"

"Right before we came here, you were given a special potion that sealed your Neo traits in your blood to prevent your detection if any evil tried to find you, but the power still exists inside."

"What kind of power?"

"I'm not sure. Friar Sulny never told me that, as he did not tell me a lot of things."

"Who's Friar Sulny?"

"He was the librarian at the Great Abbey and one of my teachers. He was the only hare that transcended into a Neo. His knowledge was great, and he was the Magi Order's finest mind, though he bore no elemental ties. He preferred being with his students and helping us learn to become great enchanters, so he never officially joined the Magi Order's circle."

Sam sighed and wiped the cluster of water

developing at the corners of her eyes.

"Friar Sulny was like a father to me, and he was the one that helped send us here."

"Your parents sent you there from the Noble life?"

"No…" Sam's voice trailed off. "They were killed in a raid during the second Great War. Kings Ashos, the Lion King, saved me and brought me to the Great Abbey."

"Sam," Chase comforted. "I'm so sorry."

"It was a long time ago."

Sam grabbed the bottle of whiskey on the table and took a heavy swig. Chase watched, speechless, before speaking up.

"I want to ask you something, but please don't take offense to it," Chase piped up.

"Sure. What is it, Chase?"

"Why you? The Magi Order and this Friar Sulny guy chose you, out of all Neos, but you were only five. Might be me, but that seems like a pretty big task for such a little girl."

"I thought exactly that when I first arrived here. I've been trying to piece it all together which is why I spend so much time reading. There are a lot of parallels in this world that link us to Pangea."

She took another swig.

"I've been trying to figure out, 'Why me?', so your guess is as good as mine."

"Well, whatever the reason is," Chase said, reaching across for the whiskey bottle. "I'm really happy that it was you."

Chase finished off the bottle and put it on the table. Sam smiled.

A tired voice spoke from behind them.

"It's because you found the Healer's Mastery."

Sam and Chase spun around and saw Eton,

wrapped up in his blanket, staggering by the door that connected the sitting room to the dining room.

"Eton! Sit down, or you'll pass out!"

Sam leapt out of her chair and helped Eton to sit.

"Got another bottle of that, mate?" Eton said wearily, pointing to the empty bottle of whiskey.

"Yeah. Let me grab it."

Chase walked over to the cabinet under the sink and pulled out another bottle of whiskey. She grabbed a glass from the dishwasher and poured Eton a drink.

"Here you go."

Chase handed Eton the glass and sat back down. Eton guzzled it and sighed.

"Sam," Eton started. "The book, the Healer's Mastery?"

"Yes. I still have it. I used one of the healing ointments from it to cover your stab wound."

"That book is why you were chosen to bring Solaris here."

"Solaris? What's that?" Chase asked.

"It's your name, Solaris," Eton replied. "Your birth name anyway."

"Right…"

Chase leaned back in her chair.

"Sam," Eton said, coming back to the Healer's Mastery topic. "You have the power to be the Ultimate Healer. The Healer's Mastery isn't just a book. It bestows its finder the ability to heal any body with the mere touch of his or her hand. That kind of healing potential is essential to keeping Solaris safe."

Sam looked at Chase and then back to Eton.

"I know what the full Healer's Mastery is, but I tried it with you, and it didn't work," Sam said disappointedly.

"Friar Sulny said that might be the case."

"Is he alright? Where is he?" Sam asked eagerly.

Eton opened his mouth to speak, but a gruesome pain from his wound surged through him. He moaned in agony as cursed gash glowed red.

"Chase, is it? How 'bout another drink?"

Chase looked puzzled at the luminous laceration but rushed and grabbed the bottle, then poured Eton another glass. Eton took a small sip as the tear in his chest settled down.

Sam sighed at her inability to completely cure the cursed wound.

"He's fine," Eton comforted. "But, he told me that you and Solaris might not have come into your full powers yet."

"Does he know how to summon them?" Sam asked eagerly.

"He said, 'When the mind caves under the weight of the heart, will one experience the miracle of a prism, and a power will rise upon this naked truth, bringing forth a light of altruism.'"

"See?" Chase intervened. "That's what I've always hated about fantasy movies. Always a riddle, never a statement."

Sam swatted at Chase to be quiet.

Before Eton could speak again, he doubled over in more pain as the cut began to glow again.

"That's it," Sam ordered. "You're going back to sleep. C'mon, Eton. I'll tuck you in."

Sam guided Eton back to the couch and

applied a new bandage.

When Sam was done, and Eton was fast asleep, she walked back into the kitchen to sit with Chase, but the bottle of whiskey was gone, and the two glasses were washed and left out to dry in the dish rack.

She must have went to bed which doesn't sound like a bad idea.

Sam trudged up the stairs and stopped at the closed door to Chase's bedroom. With Eton's surprise visit, she had never gotten the chance to talk to Chase about what happened between them when they were dancing in the park.

She knocked quietly but heard no reply. Sam carefully opened the door and peeked inside. It was dark.

"Chase? Chase, are you still up?"

Still, there was no response so Sam turned on the light and saw that Chase's bed was empty.

She flicked the lights back off and shut the door. Then, a hushed giggle escaped Cia's room.

Sam slowly walked over to Cia's door and rested her ear on it.

"I've been waiting for you to come back," Cia whispered from inside. "Did Sam like the telescope?"

"Yeah," Chase's voice responded back. "I'll tell you about it in the morning. Right now, I really just need to sleep."

Sam pulled away from the door and returned secretly to her room. She shut the door and lied down on her bed.

Staring up into the darkness of her room, she pulled out the moon pendant from under her shirt and caressed it wondering what tomorrow might bring.

Disbelief

Chase opened her eyes. The new morning sun seeped through the blinds and danced on the floor of Cia's room. Each thin bar of light stroked Chase's cheeks, supplying a smooth blanket of heat upon her skin.

She turned over to put her arm around Cia, but Cia had already gotten up. Chase rubbed the empty space on the bed beside her and buried her face in the pillow.

Did last night really happen?

Chase lifted her head up and muttered to herself, "I *did* have a lot to drink. Maybe it was just a long nightmare."

She stubbornly got out of bed, fixed her hair, and made her way down to the kitchen. When she entered, her jaw dropped.

"Morning, dear," Cia said smiling as she walked from the oven to the doorway and kissed Chase on the cheek. "Have you met Sam's friend, Eton? Eton, right?"

Eton nodded as he bit into a piece of toast.

In the sunlight and with a sober view, Chase could clearly make out what Eton looked like.

He had sandy-blonde hair that had straightened out since he was a boy and energetic green eyes that sparkled in the light along with his naked light-toned skin. His bandage was freshly changed and clung to his smooth left pectoral. His light hair even sparkled on his dirty but muscular calves. In fact, all of Eton was completely buffed out, almost threatening, but his sweet aura permeated the room like Christmas morning.

Stunned, Chase walked over to the table and sat down next to Eton. Simon walked in waving a white shirt in his hand.

"I sure hope this is big enough for our guest here!" Simon said cheerily.

Simon tossed Eton the shirt.

Eton smiled.

"Thank you very much, sir."

"Don't worry about it, my friend! And you can call me Simon. 'Sir' is much too serious for someone like me."

"Okay. Thank you very much, Simon."

"Ah! Much better! Now," Simon wondered as he sat down at the table. "What is Miss Cia preparing today for breakfast? Looks like eggs, sausage, toast, and fruit? Lovely. Absolutely lovely!"

Simon picked up his plate and started filling it with food as Eton poked his head through the shirt.

His sculpted biceps ripped through the seams of the sleeves as he tried to pull the white cloth over his toned chest and abdomens.

Simon laughed in between bites of his apple at the sight.

"Perhaps I should have found a bigger shirt for our brawny friend here."

"It'll do until we go buy him another one after breakfast," Sam chimed in.

"You'll have to buy him pants, too," Cia stated as she leaned against the counter and sipped her coffee. "Those pants look like he came out of a Renaissance fair."

Eton squirmed in his seat and looked down at his tattered and dirty hide-pants.

"The fair!" Simon exclaimed. "Oh Eton, I hope you are staying with us for Sunday's fair. I'm sure Chase will be more than happy to have some extra hands building our stage. It's going to be a long day, and I'm sure the two of you combined will have everything set up in a jiffy, leaving you some leisure time to explore and enjoy the other booths and events."

"Yeah, that'd be great," Chase replied semi-enthusiastically.

"I am honored to help out as a thank you for allowing me to take rest in your home."

"So, tell us a little more about yourself, Eton," Cia coaxed. "Where has Sam been hiding you? No wonder she didn't want to go out with the mailboy."

Sam's eyes dropped to the floor in embarrassment.

"Well," Eton began. "I met Sam when I was six or seven. We were born in the same area and raised by the same set of friars."

"Friars? Where exactly did the two of you come from?" Cia continued to question. "Sam never told us anything."

Sam stood up quickly and grabbed Eton's arm.

"I don't like to talk about it. It was a rough time in my life. Eton, could you come with me?"

"Where are we going?"

"We umm… need to wash you up so we can shopping for some your clothes."

"As you wish, Sam."

Eton stood and bowed to Cia, Simon, and Chase.

"Miss Cia, your breakfast was absolutely delightful. It was a wonderful way to start my morning."

"You flatter me," Cia replied as she walked over to join Simon and Chase at the table. "Have fun shopping today."

Sam lead Eton out of the kitchen to the upstairs bathroom. Cia put her arm around Chase's shoulders.

"I really do wonder about that girl's history. And you don't remember anything?"

"I was just a baby. Not much to remember," Chase responded.

Dissatisfied with Chase's response, Cia directed her conversation to Simon who was sitting back in his chair, patting his full belly.

"Simon? You swear you don't remember anything else about her when you first took them in?"

"I don't suppose I do. It probably didn't help that I was just leaving a bar. I must have had too many drinks, but I do remember how sweet and trusting tiny Sam was when we first met, and I remember how cute baby Chase was, as well."

Chase rolled her eyes and smirked.

"They were both so pure and helpless looking," Simon continued. "For I myself, was an orphan. How could I *not* take them under my wing and show them the life of a circus?!"

He threw back his head and his, always high-pitched, laugh soared throughout the kitchen.

"But, I'm glad I did. They've made great assets to the show as well as our little family we have here, for fate has always been a good friend of mine."

Cia combed her fingers through Chases short locks and smiled.

"Yes, absolutely wonderful assets."

Chase stood up.

"I'm going to take a shower and get ready. I told Sam that I'd go with her and Eton."

"Want some company in the shower?" Cia asked slyly.

Cia stood, wrapped her arms around Chase, and nuzzled her chin onto Chase's shoulder. Simon quickly covered his eyes with his hands.

"Take it upstairs! What will the kids say?" Simon joked.

Holding Chase's hand, Cia lead the way upstairs into her bedroom. Besides Simon's room in the basement, Cia and Pierre's room was the only other bedroom in the house that had its own bathroom with a shower.

The couple passed in front of the community bathroom as Eton was leaving. His golden hair was wet and plastered to his shiny clean face. Some droplets of water had leaked onto his shirt from washing his face and so, the shirt clung even tighter to his ripped muscles. He smiled as Chase and Cia rushed by him and retreated to Cia's room. Eton tousled his wet mane and walked to Sam's room.

The door was shut, but without thinking, Eton opened the door and caught a half-naked Sam off guard. She screamed with surprise, as did Eton, which was immediately followed by him stepping out into the hallway and slamming the door shut.

"I'm so sorry, Sam! I wasn't thinking. I promise I didn't see anything!" Eton insisted.

After a few moments of silence, Sam's door slowly creaked open, and she stepped from behind it fully clothed.

"It's okay, Eton. I forgive you. You can come in now."

Sam opened the door even wider and let Eton in. She walked over to her bed and picked up a pair of dark gray sweatpants.

"We used to have a body builder in our circus line up. He got married, so he left about two years ago. I found this in a box of some things he left behind. They should fit you."

Eton took the pair of sweatpants and held them up to his waist.

"The style of clothing is very different from Pangea," Eton replied bewildered. "Your clothing is much too tight."

Sam laughed.

"Well, I think we can find some clothes that are more suited to your build when we go shopping. I think you'll find the sweatpants a lot more comfortable."

"I trust your judgment."

Eton hesitated to switch pants and just stared at Sam without saying a word.

"Right!" she exclaimed. "I'll step outside and give you some privacy."

Blushing, Sam rushed to the door and stepped outside, closing it shut behind her. She went to the railing of the balcony overlooking the entryway and hummed as she waited.

Cia's door opened before Sam's did.

"Sam, you never told me how cute your boyfriend is!" Cia teased. "And what a body he has."

"He's not my boyfriend. He's just a friend who happens to be a boy."

"That's a cliché if I ever heard one."

"Where's Chase?"

"Ugh. She's still showering. She said I was crowding her space. I don't know what's with her this morning. Did something happen last night when she gave you your birthday gift?"

"No. I positively loved the telescope. It was the perfect gift."

"That's what I said when she told me she

bought it. Perhaps she's just jealous that her best friend has gotten a new buddy to play with. I can see her getting worried over something like that."

"She really has nothing to worry about."

"I know how much the two of you mean to one another," Cia continued. "But, Sam, you're young, smart, and incredibly beautiful. It wouldn't surprise me if you chose not to stick around in Simon's circus for much longer."

"What do you mean?"

"I mean, it'd be perfectly normal for you to indulge a little with this Eton, move out ,and start a life of your own. No one would hate you for it. In fact, I think everyone here would applaud you for it."

"Do you feel that way?"

Cia chuckled.

"Oh no. I lived a lot of exciting tales in my youth with Pierre. We toured all of Europe without a plan in mind. Then, we came here and did the same. We settled down with Simon when we realized that our time for adventure was over."

Cia's cheerful demeanor then changed to something more solemn.

"As much as I love Chase, I can't help but fear that sometimes that I'm robbing her of her adventures. I suppose I'm being a tad bit selfish by loving her. Is that a bad thing?"

"I don't think so. You know Chase. If she wasn't really happy with you, she would have let it go by now. She finds her own adventures even if they're not all over the country."

"I suppose you're right. Thank you, Sam. I needed that."

Cia turned and gave Sam a hug.

"You are truly wise beyond your years."

As soon as Cia's words left her mouth, Eton and Chase stepped out of their perspective rooms at the same time.

"Looks like you two are ready," Chase determined. "Let's go. I have work at three so we have to be back here by two."

Cia gave Sam one more squeeze before she let go.

"Have fun, you three," Cia yelled over her shoulder as she walked into her room.

Sam, Eton, and Chase made their way out the back kitchen door and climbed into the van.

The trio stayed out shopping for four hours and arrived back home with plenty of time to spare before Chase had to bike to work.

When they walked in, Leo was sitting on the staircase playing with his cell phone when they returned.

"So, it is true?" Leo exclaimed, jumping up. "We have a new body builder for the fair on Sunday."

Leo walked up to Eton and waved his phone in Eton's face.

"Listen, buddy, don't think your good looks are going to swindle their way into my time slot. You may be all muscles, but I'm clever."

Leo tapped his forehead with his index finger.

"Really clever."

Eton silently nodded his head stupefied. Chase patted Eton on the back and jokingly pushed Leo away.

"Don't worry about Leo. He's just cocky. Likes to think he's a stud, but I'm pretty sure girls just get with him out of pity rather than actual interest."

Frustrated that he could not think of a come back, Leo stormed off into the sitting room.

"I'll go put your clothes upstairs in my room," Sam said as she hurried off.

The front door opened behind Eton and Chase. Simon and the twins entered.

"Hi!" Ray and Sydney sang out simultaneously.

"Hello," Eton returned.

"My name's Ray!"

"And I'm Sydney, the better twin."

Eton laughed.

"It's nice to meet both of you. My name is Eton."

"Eton?" Ray echoed. "That's a funny name. Where are you from?"

Simon knocked Ray on the back of his head.

"That is no way to treat a guest, Raymond. Apologize."

"Sorry, Mr. Eton."

"Now, the two of you are in charge of lunch today," Simon said satisfied with Ray's apologies. "Let's try to have something other than just peanut butter and jelly. Cia said she was going to buy groceries this morning so I'm sure you can make some nice deli sandwiches for everyone."

"Yes sir!"

The twins saluted and ran into the kitchen.

"I suppose I should help them. You never know with those two. Last time, we had an explosion of chicken noodle soup all over the place. Or was that me? Anyway, it took forever to clean up. Excuse me."

Simon followed the twins into the kitchen.

"Hey, Eton, do you want to sit awhile outside?" Chase questioned. "I'm going to be stuck inside all day at work so I like to get as much fresh air beforehand as possible."

"Sure."

Eton and Chase stepped outside and sat on the small white wooden bench just to the right of entrance.

"So… I wasn't dreaming last night when I saw you change from a fox to a man, right? I know I had a little to drink, but I've never hallucinated like that before."

Eton chuckled.

"What you saw last night was no illusion."

Chase blinked and in that instant, she no longer saw Eton in his human form but as a fox.

"Dude! What the hell?"

She blinked again, and Eton was back with his blonde hair and wearing his newly purchased teal and white striped shirt and khaki pants.

"You've got to stop doing that."

"My apologies, Chase."

"Man, I don't know what to think about any of this. Sam told me a lot of crazy stuff last night."

"I know it must be scary and abnormal to think that another world exists, but I am proof that it does."

"Sam said that you coming here was a sign that we have to return to Pangea. Was she right?"

Eton stared up into the blue sky and watched the fluffy clouds roll by.

"She was, but this is a topic I must discuss with both you and Sam present."

"Okay. New topic. What *is* the deal with

you and Sam?"

"Deal? We have made no deal."

"Right… Lingo's probably a little different where you come from. I mean, do you like her?"

"I love her," Eton quickly responded.

"Wow. That was fast."

"I'm sorry."

"Didn't you say that you met her when you guys were only kids? You knew what love was way back then?"

"Maybe I didn't know what to call it, but as I grew up, I later knew that my feelings were that of love. They have stayed that way ever since she left Pangea. She's been the only light I've been able to see these past twenty years. She's been my only hope for good to reign over Pangea once again."

"That's deep… Go with that if you ever decide to ask her out."

"But, you know of love, don't you? With Miss Cia? I saw the way she kisses you. She is also quite beautiful."

"That she is, and I do love her. I'm not sure I'd say that she's my only light of hope, but I definitely care about her. That's something, right?"

Eton smiled, and his emerald green eyes sparkled.

"Yes. Yes, it is."

Sam opened the front door and peeked her head outside.

"There you are. Chase, Simon needs you to help manage the twins. They decided to crush two full bags of chips to sprinkle on the sandwiches. It's a mess."

"Duty calls," Chase moaned as she went inside.

Eton remained seated on the bench.

"Are you coming in soon?" Sam questioned.
"I was wondering if you could help me with
some set work. Chase and I were supposed to do
it yesterday, but she insisted we take the
night off. I need to have it finished by the
show tomorrow."

Eton got off the bench, walked up to Sam,
and took both her hands in his.

"Anything for you, Sam."

Sam gazed deep into Eton's vibrant stare.

"Thank you," she stammered as they
returned back inside.

The rest of the day was taken up by work.
Chase headed off to the bagel shop until
closing, Cia locked herself up in her room to
finish a painting, Simon sat in his room in
the basement making phone calls for future
shows, Leo was off at the doctor's office,
filing more annoying paperwork, and the twins
were busy catching up on the homework they had
procrastinated on for the week of their spring
break.

Meanwhile, Sam and Eton were out in the
backyard working on the set. Sam was busy
sewing a frayed seam on one of the nicer silk
curtains, and Eton was hammering away at a
wooden beam.

"It really is nice to see you," Sam
announced. "I don't know if I told you that
since you came here."

"It's always nice to see you, Sam. It's
been much too long."

Eton wiped the sweat from his brow and
continued hammering.

"Sam? I must ask… Why had you not told
Chase of her powers? Of who she is and where
she came from?"

"I'm not sure. As much as it broke my
heart to think of never returning home, a part

of me hoped that the Order was wrong about the Prophecy and that her and I could just remain here. We've made a great life and been loved by a great family."

"But, could you honestly be happy here? I've seen dogs on leashes, birds in cages, and I even saw a lion being whipped in a painting on the wall in this house. How does that not remind you of the terrible things the Anders did to our kind?"

"Simon and everyone else have been nothing but kind to us," Sam defended.

"I'm not saying that your Anders are bad people. From what I have gathered, they seem quite nice and good-natured, but I fear that when we return to Pangea, your judgment may be clouded. It's not the same there. Things have significantly changed. Anders aren't the only evil these days. I should know-"

Before Eton could finish his sentence, he dropped the hammer and clutched his injured chest.

"Eton! Are you okay?"

Stunned, Eton replied, "Yes. I'm fine. I probably just irritated the wound with all this hammering."

He looked down at his left pectoral and saw the burning redness for the third time. Eton covered it with his hand so Sam would not notice.

"I'm so sorry! I don't know what I was thinking," Sam apologized.

"Don't worry. I wanted to help."

"Why don't we take a quick break, and I'll make us a nice lemonade. I think we deserve one."

Sam and Eton went into the kitchen to freshen up before finishing the last repairs outside.

When they were done, everyone was home
but had retired to their beds. Tomorrow would
be a long day, and everyone needed their rest.

Sam retrieved clean linens from the
hallway closet and changed the sheets on
Chase's bed.

"Chase said that you could sleep in her
bed tonight. She's staying in Cia's room. That
couch is so lumpy; I'm surprised you fell
asleep on it last night."

"I'm sure your soothing ointments helped
me find peace in slumber," Eton replied.

Sam finished tucking in the corner of a
navy blue blanket under the end of the
mattress.

"There. All done. You can probably use
the mesh shorts to sleep in. You remember
where the bathroom is… I think that should be
it."

Sam tapped her foot anxiously and put her
hands on her waist. Eton walked up to her and
rested his hands on her shoulders.

"Relax, Sam. I'll be fine tonight. I will
see you in the morning."

Sam nodded and left the room.

After she had changed into her pajamas,
Sam went to the bathroom to clean her face.
She splashed cold water over her shut eyes and
mouth and let the liquid beads fall to the
sink. She opened her eyes slowly and stared
into her reflection.

Tomorrow is a new day.

Sam dabbed her face dry with a hand towel
and went to her room to sleep.

The next morning was just as sunny as the
day before, setting the perfect mood for the
day's fair.

The tenants were awakened just after the
crack of dawn to the sound of Simon banging a

wooden spoon on a pan as he paced the halls.

"Rise and shine everyone! I know it's early, but today is an important day! We've got to get the fair grounds early to claim a prime spot! You remember last year, don't you? We were beat by that ridiculous 'Guess Your Weight' booth! Can't have that again!"

Simon continued to march up and down the hallways until everyone was standing outside of their rooms, sleep still occupying their eyes and yawns escaping their mouths.

"Is that racket really necessary?" Leo groaned.

"Why of course not!" Simon shouted. "But, it sure is fun!"

He cackled as he walked downstairs and made one final bang on the metal pan.

"We'll pick up some to-go breakfast on our way to the grounds. Chop, chop, lazy heads! We've still got to load the truck and the van!"

Begrudgingly, everyone returned to their rooms to change and get ready for the fair.

By the time the crew arrived at the fairgrounds, everyone had had their coffee-fix and hunger fulfilled. The twins' faces were plastered to the windows as they "ooed" and "ahhed" at the flashing lights, brightly colored balloons, and musical rides that composed the fair. It was their first time performing at such a huge venue.

They pulled up to a portly man standing in a neon yellow reflective jacket who motioned Simon to roll the passenger window down.

"Which one of you is in charge?"

"That would be me, my fine gentleman," Simon introduced exuberantly. "I am Simon of the infamous Simon's Golden Circus."

"That's nice," the fair worker said grumpily. "You know what site you want?"

"Yes, of course I do! Is site 14A available?"

"14A?"

The crabby man flipped through a stack of papers on a clipboard.

"Yup. 14A's available. You want that one?"

"Perfecto! Yes. We'd *love* to occupy site 14A."

"Okay. You take this gravel path to the left, the site will be at the first fork on the right hand side of the path."

"Thank you, my kind sir!" Simon replied.

Simon rolled up the window and looked at Leo who was driving.

"Well, that was not a very nice man. How could he not be excited about today?"

The truck and the van made their way to the site. When they parked, everyone climbed out and started unloading the set.

It took about an hour for the stage and the holding-tent to be set up. At that point, the majority of other fair spectacles started to show up.

"See?" Simon boasted. "Aren't you glad we came early? Why don't the lot of you take a walk around. Scout the place out for any competition and where we can get the best food for lunch."

Cia took the excited twins to look at the all the rides as they planned which ones they were going to ride first. Simon and Leo went to talk to an old friend who happened to be running the ferris wheel while Sam, Chase, and Eton went to sit in the grass by a nearby pond to talk in private.

"What will Cia do now that Pierre isn't

here to perform his magic tricks?" Sam
inquired.

"She performed with him for a little over
ten years and knows the big parlor tricks.
Plus, she asked Simon to help her perform some
of the two person stunts. He was more than
happy to help and learn Pierre's secrets of
the trade," Chase replied.

The trio sat in silence and stared out
into the restless water in the pond.

"Well," Chase began. "I guess I'll be the
first to break the awkward silence and ask,
'Eton, why are you here?'"

"An eminent evil has taken over the land
of Pangea," Eton responded softly.

"How so?" Sam asked. "Did the Anders
manage to escape the Land of Cassum? Is there
another war between the Neos and the Anders?"

"I'm afraid it's much more complicated
than that. The night the two of you traveled
to this world, Prince Ceros invaded the Great
Abbey."

"Who's that?" Chase interrogated.

"Prince Ceros is the son of King Bellor,
the brave black bear king, one of our Head
Nobles," Eton answered.

"But, King Bellor was found dead in his
chambers one night due to a heart failure so
Ceros took over his crown," Sam continued.

"Yes, but the night that Ceros
infiltrated our Great Abbey walls, it was
announced that *he* killed King Bellor, using a
cursed dagger."

"That's horrible!" Sam exclaimed.

"It gets worse. Friar Sulny, Lady Tanan,
and I were taken upstairs by Ceros' henchmen.
Everyone had been gathered into the dining
hall to watch Ceros unveil his master plan,
but just as Ceros was about to kill Erisi,

Rysul stormed in."

"Rysul? My father?" Chase stuttered.

"Yes. He fought valiantly against Ceros, but Ceros had a secret weapon. He had drank the blood of the Magi Order, and with Quar's dark magic, he was in possession of the Shadow Force's *Prima Umbros*. It's the most evil form of magic. Ceros used the death of Princess Therene and the supposed death of Chase to fill Rysul's heart with darkness. After manipulating him, Ceros commanded Rysul to kill Erisi, and Rysul obeyed. As soon as the deed was done, Ceros killed Rysul with his sword, and at that instant, we all knew hope was lost."

Chase moved restlessly in the grass.

"Both my parent's are dead?"

"I'm afraid so," Eton replied.

Seeing the pain and shock in Chase's eyes, Sam scooted over to her and put a comforting arm around her.

"Continue, Eton," Sam said calmly.

"Ceros also knew that if a member of the Order was slain that the barrier confining the Anders to the Land of Cassum would be broken. An army of Anders stood at the ready when Erisi's death was secure and stormed the Great Crossings within weeks. Even small bands of rogue Ander groups had gathered at the northern border of the Great Crossings. All innocent Neos were either taken prisoner or killed. Fear of the enchanted lands had no longer lived in the Anders, for the Shadow Force had consumed them and their conscious thoughts.

After the Great Abbey was subdued, Ceros turned as many Neos into his servants or warriors, using the Shadow Force magic to fill the gaps in their spirits with fear and hatred. The Nobles had no idea that any of this was going on at the time, so Ceros used it to his advantage and built an immense army full of both Ander and Neo kind.

He forced his troops into the Savannahs first, taking over King Ashos castle, turning the weak and fearful into his own followers. The ones who would not embrace the darkness, were taken prisoner. Ceros continued this rampage until he had penetrated all five kingdoms' defenses successfully."

"Were all the Head Nobles killed?" Sam asked worriedly.

"No. Ceros wanted too much to humiliate them, so he did not kill them. He keeps them as his personal prisoners at the Great Hall which he has coined his main location.

But, like any new regime, complete and utter power does not stay consistent for very long.

The Shadow Force can only consume a body if there is no hope within. With all the fear and chaos that Ceros had stirred up, it was easy for him to possess everyone's minds at first, but about five years into his tyranny, a small band of Neos, not turned by Ceros' magic and named the Light Mafia, managed to escape one of the prisons in the Woodlands.

They came across other prisoners, mainly kept under traveling branches of the main Shadow Force authority, and freed them. Some were freed through broken chains and shattered shackles, and others were freed by restoring hope and light back into their hearts.

Bit by bit, villages of good Neos sprouted but… the lines of what used to be defined as good and evil became blurred."

"What do you mean?" Sam asked curiously.

"In the past ten years, it has no longer

been a matter of Anders being the sign of evil
and Neos being the bearers of all which is
good. Anders and Neos alike banded together on
either side of the spectrum. It truly became a
constant battle between Light and Darkness.

Ceros could feel the strength of his
Shadow Force diminishing over the entire land,
so he remained in control of only the truest
Shadow Force believers. Other evil alliances
formed outside his rule and outside of the
Shadow Force. Even so, Ceros' reign still
remains to be the most powerful and fearing in
both number and strength.

Those that bear the Light, are
regrettably still the minority and remain
mostly in hiding, but they are hopeful, and
the Light Mafia and others roam the lands
leading as many Neos and Anders back to the
Light as possible, but due to the lasting
unstable nature of the environment, it's been
much harder to convert them.

Friar Sulny and I were given to Quar as
his very own special prisoners. Since Ceros'
raid of the Great Abbey, we we've been held
prisoners there. Quar made the Great Abbey his
own fortress, living on the soil that would
provide him the most magical strength."

"Why were you and the friar so special to
this guy?" Chase finally spoke up.

"As I'm sure Sam informed you, Friar
Sulny's mind is a great treasure. Using all
his skills and tricks, Quar has been
attempting to break into Friar Sulny's mind
and learn all that he knows."

The immense burning returned to Eton's
wound, but he ignored it.

Sam took a deep breath in.

"Is Friar Sulny still alive?"

"When I left, yes. Quar still had not

been able to crack Friar Sulny's mind. Ceros demanded that Quar find out who the Ultimate Healer is because…" Eton's voice quieted as the flaming in his chest increased.

"Because why?" Sam asked anxiously.

"Because if Ceros manages to kill you, he will be in possession of the Healer's Mastery's powers. Then, he would be unstoppable, able to heal himself while maintaining the Shadow Force's detrimental capabilities."

The smoldering sting in Eton's laceration climaxed and Eton bit his tongue silently to keep from screaming in pain. He did not want to worry Sam.

Sam stared off into the pond for a few moments before asking, "Is Ceros or Quar aware of Chase's existence and how she plays a role into the Order's prophecy?"

Eton took a deep breath in and focused his attention on speaking. The pain on his chest was settling down.

"Not that I'm aware of. When Ceros discovered Princess Therene, the Order told him that the baby was a stillbirth. Ceros has no motivation to believe that any thing or any body could have the capacity to stop him."

"How did you manage to escape Quar?" Sam inquired eagerly.

"I was able to free myself of my shackles one night. Friar Sulny had been removed from our cell so I decided to sneak around to find him, hoping that I could break him free as well.

I was snooping around the left wing corridors when I was spotted by Quar himself. I charged into him, thinking I could force him down the stairs, but he was too quick for me. He moved swiftly out my way, and I ran into the wall.

With the momentum of my charge, I was slightly stunned. Quar spun me around and stabbed me through the chest. Just before he was about to deliver the fatal blow, I shoved him aside and ran back down the corridor. When I turned around to see if Quar was chasing after me, a large cloud of black smoke surrounded me. I had heard the sound of glass breaking just before the cloud engulfed my body. I think it was a potion of some sort that sent me out of Pangea's realm."

"So, Quar knows of this realm?" Sam exclaimed.

"I don't think so. Quar was experimenting with a new Death Casting elixir, a potion that sends one directly to the afterlife, but he was failing miserably. Most of his unsuccessful attempts turned out to simply transport a subject somewhere else either in the castle or on the Great Abbey grounds somewhere. He probably still has men searching for me."

Sam unwrapped her arm from Chase's shoulder, put her hand gracefully under Chase's chin and turned Chase's face toward hers.

"Chase, I know all of this is really intense and almost unbelievable, but we have to go back. It's in our destiny to do so."

Chase's eyes did not meet Sam's. She kept her gaze locked on the ground and said nothing.

"There you wandering wanderers are!" Simon's voice shouted from behind them.

He was standing quite a distance from the trio and was waving his top hat furiously.

"The gates open in twenty minutes and we need to go over some last minute details before we are bombarded with cheering and adoring fans!"

Chase gently pushed Sam's hand aside, stood up, and started making her way back to their site.

Eton took Sam's hand and whispered, "She'll come around. Give her a little time. If someone told me I was born to save the world, I'd want to be alone for awhile, too."

Sam forced a smile as her and Eton joined the others at the circus stage.

The gates opened and a mad rush of people swarmed in.

Simon clenched the bill of his hat.

"Get ready, folks. It's going to be one hell of a ride."

Sam, Chase, and Eton all looked at each other knowing how Simon's words sang true in more ways than one.

The Quest

For the next two days, Chase mainly kept to herself. She went quietly off to work and even took a double shift on Monday to avoid being home.

When she was at home, Chase sat in her room listening to music or sat with Cia as she painted.

"Is everything alright?" Cia asked worried. "You've been acting distant since the fair on Sunday. Did something happen?"

"Just trying to organize my thoughts. I'm okay though," Chase said plainly as she flipped through a magazine.

"You're not making me believe you. You've hardly said a word to Sam since Saturday."

"I'm just giving her space and time to catch up with an old friend. They've missed out on twenty years of each other's lives."

"Well, I'm sure Sam's worried. You should at least tell her that you're okay," Cia said firmly as she brushed a purple outline onto the canvas.

"Where is she?"

"She took Eton out to the beach, I think."

Chase stood up and walked to the door.

Without turning around, Chase paused and said, "I'm going for a walk."

"Will you be back by lunchtime?"

"I think I'll grab something while I'm out so don't wait for me."

Chase opened the door and walked downstairs.

Cia sighed as she returned to her

painting.

A couple hours passed by, and Sam and Eton had returned from the beach. They met up with everyone in the kitchen as Cia pulled two rotisserie chickens out of the oven. The twins were setting up the table, and Simon and Leo were standing by the back window drinking beer.

"How was the beach you two?" Cia smiled as Sam and Eton entered the kitchen.

"It was excellent," Eton answered. "It reminded me much of the beaches we have at home."

"And where did you say that was again?" Cia prodded.

"Just somewhere far from here," Sam interjected.

Eton mouthed, "I'm sorry" to Sam before running to the bathroom to wash up.

Sam was about to follow him when Cia stopped Sam.

"Can I talk to you for a minute?" Cia asked politely.

"Sure."

Sam and Cia stepped just outside the kitchen by the front door.

"Chase has been really distant. I know you're worried, too, but do you know why she's so upset? Did something happen between the two of you?"

"Kind of… Eton gave her some bad news about her parents. They both died when Chase and I left home."

Cia covered her mouth with her hand in shock.

"Oh no! That's horrible."

"I guess a part of her wished that they were still alive so when she had the means to, she could go find them," Sam replied.

"My poor girl," Cia whimpered.

"She'll be alright. Let's not worry about it now. Ray and Sydney will be whining by now for their food."

Cia wiped away a small tear and nodded before returning to the kitchen. Sam stared blankly at the floor, knowing that she had not revealed the entire truth to Cia. It was times like these, especially now upon Eton's return, that Sam hated, lying to her friends.

Eton jogged downstairs to meet Sam.

"Today has been amazing, Sam. I can see why you'd want to stay here. You know, if you're here, I'd stay here for you."

Eton kissed her on the cheek and walked into the kitchen.

Sam gently touched the spot where Eton's kiss lingered. She turned to gaze out the front window at a couple walking by outside, hand in hand. She smiled as she remembered what Cia had said about making a life for herself before walking into the kitchen to join the others.

It was not until late after dinner that Chase returned home. Everyone but Eton had fallen asleep. He stood by the window in Chase's room, staring out at the night sky. He sighed softly and was startled when the door opened. Chase walked in.

"Chase, it's nice to see you," Eton whispered.

Chase stepped aside to reveal Sam standing behind her.

"We need to talk," Chase replied.

"Sure. What about?"

Chase and Sam entered the room. Eton and Sam sat on the bed while Chase paced frantically in front of them.

"How do we get back to Pangea?" Chase

finally uttered.

"We'd have to recreate the portal that brought us here twenty years ago," Sam answered slowly, as she was startled by Chase's choice to return to Pangea.

"How do we do that?" Chase responded.

"Eton? Do you remember anything from the star maps?" Sam inquired as she rushed to a desk in corner and grabbed a pen and a piece of paper.

"Um… I only remember fragments," Eton started. "There were four steps that Friar Sulny poured the vials out in. I think the first had to do with earth and something about a maiden and a bull and something else…"

Sam wrote down Eton's words.

Eton winced in pain as his cut flared up again. He rubbed it gently and played it off as nothing was wrong.

"Okay. What about the second step?" Sam asked, not noticing.

Eton closed his eyes to try and visualize the night he read the star maps aloud to Friar Sulny.

"Then there was air and something about a pair of siblings, twins maybe?"

"Air and twins," Sam whispered to herself as she continued to write.

"Then there was water and fire and a variety of animals like a fish, a scorpion and a lion, I think?"

Eton opened his eyes.

"It was such a long time ago. That's all I remember. I'm sorry."

"It's okay. Hopefully we can figure it out with what you gave us. If you think of anything else-"

"I'll be sure to tell you."

Sam looked down at the piece of paper

under the moonlight peering in through the window.

"Earth, air, water, fire…" she muttered to herself.

Sam laid the paper on the desk and stared at the stars in the sky.

"Friar Sulny always told me that if I was ever lost to look up to the stars, and they would always guide me home, but this… I'm not sure what it means."

At that instant, Chase ran to the desk and picked up the piece of paper, shouting, "That's it!"

Catching the loudness of her voice, Chase winced and returned to whispering, "The stars. That's the answer. A maiden, a bull, a pair of twins, a fish, a scorpion and a lion? They're all Zodiac symbols."

"Zodiac?" Eton asked puzzled.

Sam slapped her forehead.

"Of course! The Zodiacs are a set of twelve constellations in the stars that represent the twelve calendar months of the year. It has to do with the relationship between our earth's revolution and our sun."

"And I remember a little clearer now," Eton chimed in. "When Friar Sulny poured the contents of the vials on the floor, the concluding outline looked like a sun."

"He must have poured each line in reference to the hours of a clock. Twelve and twelve. It makes perfect sense!" Sam said excitedly.

Sam stroked her chin.

"And the four steps each contained an element that manipulates the fifth, metal. The vials must have contained pieces of each Zodiac within each form of element. Chase, you figured it out!"

Sam hugged Chase.

"All we have to do now is find pieces of each Zodiac, combine it with earth, air, water, and fire, then lay it all out in the ecliptic order, and we should be fine," Sam said excitedly.

"I hate to be the bearer of bad news," Chase started as Sam let her embrace relax. "Not sure exactly what kind of animals you have in your world, but where the hell are we going to find a mer-goat here?"

"What do you mean?" Sam asked.

"Isn't Capricorn a sea-goat? Do those exist in Pangea? Because they certainly don't exist here."

"That's right," Sam realized. "But, we didn't have sea-goats in Pangea either, so what did Friar Sulny and the Order use?"

"Maybe we should just sleep on it," Eton suggested. "Now that we have a plan, we at least have something to start on. I'm sure the solution will come to us when we least expect it. I will also try to tap into my memories and see if I can recover any hints that will help us."

"Eton's right," Sam agreed. "Chase, do you work tomorrow?"

"Nope. I don't think I'm scheduled to work until Friday. Go figure, on my birthday."

"Okay. Well, you won't have to worry about work for much longer. We'll start tomorrow on gathering everything that we need," Sam ordered. "Then when night falls, we'll make the portal."

Eton and Chase nodded.

"Goodnight, Eton," Sam whispered. "Sleep well."

"Goodnight, Sam. Goodnight, Chase."

Sam and Chase exited the room, closed the

door, and stood in the hallway.

Before Sam turned to go to her room, Chase grabbed Sam's hand and said, "Do you think that we'll ever come back here? I know Pangea is where we were born, but we've made this our home, Sam."

Sam faced Chase and wrapped her best friend in another embrace.

"I'm not sure of anything right now, but I do know that I won't leave you. I swore on the day we left Pangea that I'd keep you safe and be with you, always."

Chase lifted her arms and hugged Sam back.

Sam let go, smiled, and returned to her room. Chase stood there for a moment staring at Sam's closed door. Then, she stretched out her back, yawned, and went into Cia's room to sleep as well.

Right before she opened the door, Chase noticed, what appeared to be, a shadow that crept from the kitchen and out the front door.

"Man, it must be late. No whiskey and I'm imagining things."

Chase chuckled to herself and walked in Cia's room, ready to face the unexpectedness excitement of tomorrow, and excitement Chase certainly got.

Wednesday morning rolled around with dark rain clouds and a suspicious chill, not entirely unusual for late March weather, but the vivid sparks of lightning streaked the sky like vicious shooting stars.

Chase pulled on her heavy black peacoat and stepped outside. She shivered, the cold plucking her nerves like strings of a harp, each vibration rippling down to her fingertips. She pulled the hood from her sweatshirt over her head, and squinted up at the looming gray blankets sweeping through the skies.

"Well isn't this perfect?" Chase muttered to herself.

With a clash of thunder, a light rain started to shower down over the gray city.

"Even better," Chase said sarcastically.

She turned around and yelled inside the house.

"Are you two ready yet? We need to hurry. I don't know how bad this weather is going to get."

Another five minutes passed before Sam and Eton met up with Chase outside.

"Well, it's about time," Chase joked. "Not like we have to save the world and all."

Sam playfully hit Chase in the arm.

"Let's take the van."

Chase climbed into the driver's seat, Sam sat passenger, and Eton buckled up in the back.

"Okay, let's go over what we know we need to get," Sam started. "We already pulled hair from Ray and Sydney's hairbrushes, that covers Gemini, and Eton scraped some metal pieces off of that old weighing scale in Simon's office so that covers Libra."

"And I snatched a feather from our old fire-archer's set of arrows from the attic," Chase boasted.

"Good. We've got nine more. I guess we'll start at the fresh market and get a fish and a crab."

"Piscus and Cancer," Chase replied. "Ugh. I hate fish."

Chase started the van and pulled out of the driveway and onto the street.

"They smell weird, they don't blink, and they're slimy."

Eton spoke up from the back, "Will we be able to find a water bearer in the same vicinity that we locate the fish and crab? It seems logical with the water connection."

"Not sure," Sam replied. "They'd be fishermen and not necessarily bringers of water. We need to think of someone who would distribute water as a mean of life."

"What about a firefighter?" Chase asked as she stopped at the corner stoplight.

"That might work!" Sam exclaimed. "You can drop Eton and me by the firehouse before you go to the market. This is great! We can cross Aquarius off the list, too."

Chase's jaw dropped open in disapproval.

"Wait! Why do I have to go get the fish?"

"You need to get over your irrational fear at some point, Chase," Sam teased.

Chase grunted as she pulled over in front of the firehouse and put on her hazards. Sam and Eton jumped out of the van.

"I put a cooler in the back," Sam advised. "There's enough ice in there to last the time we are out today. Eton and I will meet back up with you at the market. There's a church on our way there that we can stop by and get something from one of the nuns for Virgo."

Sam shut the door and made her way to the firehouse with Eton. Chase turned off her hazards and drove off another five minutes down the street to the fresh market.

The rain had stopped temporarily as Chase jumped out of the van and splashed through the shallow puddles to the store.

Inside, it smelled like salty water and, to much of Chase's dismay, like fish. The putrid odors pierced her nostrils like tiny daggers stabbing her airways. Chase coughed as the stench reworked itself and sat on her taste-buds with a foul tang.

"God, I hate it in here," Chase complained as she plugged her nose and walked over to the fresh seafood section.

She pulled a ticket stub and waited for her number to be called.

"Number twenty-two!" a portly man behind the icy glass display case shouted. "Number twenty-two!"

Chase looked down at her ticket and walked up to the counter.

"What can I get for you, Miss?" the man said cheerfully.

"Um… I'd like one king crab leg and a fish."

"Are you sure you only want one leg? We've got a special going on for anything over four pounds. Won't get a deal like this again anytime soon."

"No. I just need one leg," Chase argued.

"Suit yourself," the stout grocer man replied. "Just as well, I don't have much to sell."

Chase raised a quizzical eyebrow at the grocer's response.

"We were robbed yesterday. Some of it was left, half eaten, mind you. Must have been a raccoon… a very hungry raccoon though. I have a lot fish here. Luckily, I had pre-cut some of it and stored it in the mini cooler. Weird, right?"

Chase took the wrapped crab leg the flustered grocer gave her.

"Yeah… Weird."

That really is weird. I wonder- Chase began to ponder.

"For your fish selection, I'm afraid we don't have much, of course. Salmon alright?"

Chase peered through the glass and shivered at the open eyes and scaly bodies of the some of the other fish.

"Yeah. Just one filet is perfect," Chase muttered.

The fish dealer pulled out a bright pink filet and wrapped it up in foil and paper. He handed it to Chase.

"Thanks, man. Umm… Hope things get better for you."

Chase walked towards the front of the store to pay.

Wow. We lucked out there. Is it a coincidence that this fish robbing happened when we needed it? Chase wondered.

Chase shook off the thought and paid. She scurried to the van as the rain started up again. She opened the trunk of the van and put the fish and the crab leg inside the small cooler. After slamming the trunk down, Chase rushed to the driver's side and climbed in.

Maybe it's nothing. Besides, I'm still not even sure if I believe everything that's going on.

"Then again, I'm out in the rain buying fish and not caring that we're stealing from nuns," Chase said aloud, crazily to herself.

Chase sat in deep in wonder. She was startled when Sam and Eton arrived at the van banging on the window. Chase unlocked the doors, and they rushed in.

"Did you get the fish and the crab?" Sam asked.

"Yup. Hey, Eton?"

"Yes?"

"Did you see anyone else come out of the portal when Quar sent you here?"

"No. Why?"

"It's nothing. Just wondering."

Eton stared blankly at Chase.

"Where to next?" Chase said, changing the topic.

"The zoo," Sam answered. "That's where we'll find the remaining Zodiacs. There's the ram, the bull, the lion, and the scorpion."

"With all this rain," Chase reasoned. "I don't think the zoo will be open. Looks like it's going to get worse before it gets better."

A bright bolt of lightning cracked the darkness like a whip to the untamed skies.

"Leave that to Eton and me," Sam assured as Chase began driving toward the zoo.

The storm grew darker and darker as the rain fell more furiously. The old red minivan pulled into the empty parking lot. Chase parked and turned the engine off.

"Looks like it's closed. Not a surprise though. What's the game plan?"

"Eton and I could sneak in much easier if we were in our fox form. Chase, it'd be much to risky if you came with."

"Fine by me. I'll just be the getaway driver if you guys get in trouble."

"Sam, I think she should come with us," Eton argued. "I'm still new to this world, and it would be helpful to have two bodies that are familiar with this place rather than just one."

"You have a point," Sam caved. "Do you have any ideas on how to get her in though?"

"I do. Follow me," Eton replied confidentally.

Chase and Sam followed Eton out of the van and ran to the maintenance entrance of the zoo. This particular part of the gate was heavily surrounded by trees and bushes so the three of them were easily concealed as they stayed low and inconspicuous.

Eton closed his eyes and wrapped both hands around two of the metal posts.

"*Vaniso proncius,*" Eton whispered.

As soon as the words left Eton's lips, the two metal posts began to quiver. Then, in a blink of an eye, the posts disappeared. Chase's eyes widened in awe.

"You know, I really shouldn't be shocked," Chase stated. "After the whole talking fox bit and realizing that I'm half canine and bird, you'd think the disappearing gate trick wouldn't affect me so much."

Eton opened his eyes and smiled.

"Let's go."

One by one, each of them slid through. Sam unfolded a crumpled paper from her back pocket.

"I printed the zoo map before we left. According to this, the Lion's Den exhibit should be to our right."

Just when Sam and Eton were about to take off, Chase yelled, "Wait!"

They stopped and turned around.

"I'm pretty sure there are cameras around the park. If surveillance catches us, we're through. Not to mention, we'd probably face arrests for breaking and entering."

"I can fix that," Eton assured.

He walked behind Sam and Chase, laid a hand on each of their backs, and whispered, "*Granti Inviso.*"

A strange tingling feeling surged through Sam and Chase's bodies. It was a subtle wave of tremors within their bodies, almost like a playful stream of electricity coursing their veins.

"What just happened?" Chase asked.

"I made us invisible. It might slow us

down a bit because you will have to stay in contact with me as we move, but does this solve our surveillance problem?"

"Yeah," Chase said stunned.

They moved cautiously toward to Lion's Den exhibit.

"How were you not able to escape Quar with all this fancy magic stuff?" Chase interrogated. "Seems to me like it would've been a walk in the park for you."

"Quar's chains were more than shackles around my wrists and ankles. They were cursed with his own dark magic. I tried using my spells, but my Illusion incantations are no match for his sorcery level."

They reached the back wall of the interior holding cell of the lions. Eton shook his head.

"This is not right. Those lions should be free."

"But, this is the way *this* world operates," Sam responded. "The Anders here actually do care for their animals."

Eton sighed, still displeased.

Chase looked around the area.

"Okay. I don't see any cameras here. Eton, got any spells that can get us in?"

Eton nodded.

"Perhaps I should do this one alone. We're not sure how many lions are in there."

"Please be careful," Sam pleaded.

Eton removed his hands from Sam and Chase's backs. Another weird shiver moved throughout their bodies, like Eton vacuumed some sort of energy from their spines, as they became visible again.

Eton pressed his hands and forehead against the wall and closed his eyes once more.

"Meldus ma-trium."

Keeping his eyes closed, Eton walked forward and vanished into the wall.

"I can't tell if I'm really impressed or really freaked out right now," Chase joked. "Did you know he could do all of this?"

"I knew he wanted to specialize in Illusion and Manipulation Arts back at the Great Abbey, but we were only children. I don't know how he learned to master all of those techniques when he was captured by Quar."

"Maybe the good friar taught him while they were captured."

"Maybe…"

"Who cares how he learned it, Sam? He's here now, and he's helping us to get back. You trust the guy, right?"

"Yes, of course."

"Then that's all I need."

Chase smiled, and Sam felt instantly at ease.

Eton emerged from the wall holding a small clump of matted hair.

"Got it."

Chase pulled out a small sandwich bag from her coat pocket, and Eton carefully placed the hair inside.

"One down, three to go," Chase celebrated.

The Mountaintop Stop was next to the Lion's Den. Eton repeated the phasing spell while Sam and Chase waited once more. Eton emerged from within the building with a much smaller clump of grey hair from a mountain ram.

"And that's Aries," Sam said folding the sandwich bag top down and returning the bag to her jacket. "Next we have the Insect House then the Kid's Play Farm."

Eton put his hands on Sam and Chase's backs for the third time as they made their way to the Insect House.

When Eton was inside, Chase said joyfully, "I'm glad your boyfriend is taking care of all this. How very sweet of him."

"He's not my boyfriend," Sam protested. "We're friends."

"Tell *him* that."

Eton came back out of the Insect House holding a plastic tupperware container with a fidgety scorpion inside.

"You're good hanging onto that?" Chase asked Eton.

"You're going to have to hold it as we walk to the farm. I need both my hands free."

Chase moaned as she took the scorpion from Eton.

When they arrived at the white fence surrounding the Play Farm, Sam pointed to the open stable.

"Look! There's a male cow in there. Technically, you can call it a bull."

"I'll go get the hair," Eton said.

He climbed the fence and made his way over to the stables.

Chase leaned over the white fence. She shook the scorpion in the container and looked up. She saw something dash from behind a water trough to a wooden box. She squinted through the rain to see what it was.

"What is that?" Chase asked.

Sam peered out into the direction where Chase was looking.

"I think it's a goat."

She looked a little longer.

"Yes. It's a baby goat."

Chase's eyes widened. Quickly, she jumped

over the fence.

Alarmed and confused by Chase's actions, Sam climbed over the fence and followed Chase as she ran to where the goat was hiding.

"What are you doing?" Sam yelled over a booming clap of thunder.

"It's a goat!"

"Yes! I see that!"

Chase ran to the goat and knelt down beside it. It was shaking in its shiny brown coat. Chase pet its head gently.

"It's raining, and there just *happens* to be a runaway goat in the middle of it? That has to be a sign," Chase said proudly.

Sam started blankly into Chase's clever grin.

"It's Capricorn!" Chase exclaimed as she picked the goat up in her arms still managing to hold the scorpion container. "You can't get any closer than this."

"It just might work," Sam said anxiously as she pulled a few hairs from the baby goat's tail.

It whined and thrashed its body around.

"We should bring it back to its shed," Sam replied. "I can see this storm only getting worse."

The rain started to fall even harder as Chase and Sam walked over to the shed where the goats were being kept. Sam tried to open the door.

"It's locked."

"Great. Where's Wonder Boy when you need him?"

"I think I can handle this one."

Sam grasped the lock in her hand and whispered, "*Finicki Solvo.*"

The lock clicked and snapped open.

"You've got to be kidding me," Chase

muttered.

Sam removed the lock from the door and smiled.

"I was never into Manipulation Spells, but I remember forcing Eton to teach me this one. I liked to sneak into the library after hours."

"So you *do* have a bad side?" Chase teased as Sam opened the door.

Sam chuckled as Chase returned the baby goat in place.

Eton ran up to meet them as Sam replaced the lock on the closed shed door.

"I have it," Eton panted.

They put the two new hair samples into bags and made their way back to the fence. After they scrambled over it and started making their way out of the zoo, two security guards spotted them before Eton could put up his invisible shield.

"Run!" Chase screamed as the guards began chasing after them.

"I've got an idea," Eton shouted. "You two continue making your way to the opening at the gate."

Sam and Chase nodded as Eton ceased running and turned to face the guards.

"Stop right there!" one of the guards demanded.

Eton smirked and stared each security guard in the eye. Their bodies froze as they felt the density of the air around them intensify.

Before the guards could pull out their tazers, Eton spread out his arms and called out, "*Illuso!*"

With a howling roar, an image of a gigantic black bear with blazing red eyes appeared between Eton and the guards.

Both guards shrieked as Eton turned and made his way to his escape. The mirage he left behind began to pursue the petrified guards.

Seeing his trick work, Eton slid quickly through the opening in the gate, which magically reformed afterward, and ran to meet Sam and Chase at the van.

He jumped quickly in, and Chase sped off.

"What did you do?" Sam questioned.

"Just gave them a little scare. An Illusion trick," Eton chuckled in between breaths as Chase sped off down the street.

Chase pulled into the garage when they arrived back home.

The rain, though much lighter now, was still falling. Leaving all of their findings in the trunk of the van, they closed the garage door and rushed inside. Simon was reading a newspaper at the table.

His left sleeve was rolled up, and Sam saw, what looked to be, a long, recently bleeding scar on Simon's forearm. Simon quickly but casually rolled the cuff of his shirt back down to his wrist. Sam started to say something to Chase and Eton, but they had not noticed.

"Why salutations!" Simon cried out as he picked up his paper again. "My oh my! Look at the sight of you. All three of you mush upstairs and take warm showers before you catch a cold. One of you can use the bathroom in my room downstairs. Hurry now! Dinner will be here soon. We ordered a pizza."

Sam, Chase, and Eton followed Simon's orders and went to shower. When the trio left the kitchen, Simon rubbed his arm gently, feeling the faint sting of his wound. He sighed and picked up his paper again to read.

Just a few moments later, Cia opened the

back kitchen door, shaking her umbrella out before stepping fully in.

"Hello, Miss Felicia. How did your selling go?"

"He bought the painting for one hundred and fifty."

"Bravo! A sincere congratulations, dear. We'll have to open a bottle of champagne tonight with dinner."

"Thank you, Simon. Is Chase back yet?"

"She actually just arrived minutes before you. She's currently upstairs, most likely in your bathroom, showering."

"Okay. Thanks."

Cia propped her dripping umbrella by the door and walked up to her room. She peeled off her wet black trench coat and hung it on the back of the door. She heard the shower turn off.

After drying off and throwing on her typical white tee shirt and athletic pants, Chase stepped out of the steamy bathroom.

"Oh, hey. I hope you don't mind I used your shower," she stated as she sat on the foot of Cia's bed and shook out the excess water from her short hair.

"Not at all. I want to talk to you though."

Cia sat down next to Chase and softly caressed the side of Chase's moist face.

"Sweetheart, I love you," Cia started.

"I love you, too," Chase replied.

"I used to think that you did, but lately it seems like you're afraid of something. Is it us?"

"No…"

"I don't know what to do. I know that you and I came out of a secret, and I hope you know that I don't regret my decision. Pierre and I, we lost our magic together. I'm a coward for not ending things properly with him, but I hope you can forgive me for that."

"I don't blame you for anything," Chase defended. "I promise that you're doing nothing wrong. I've just had a lot on my mind lately."

"Sam told me about your parents. I'm so sorry."

Chase sighed.

"Yeah. A part of me hoped that I could meet them one day, but I had to be realistic."

"I'm here for you if you need it."

Chase sat silently for awhile as the raindrops beat rhythmically on the window.

"Cia," Chase finally whispered. "I have to go somewhere. I'm not sure how long I'll be gone, but I have to leave."

Cia pulled away from Chase and walked over to the window watching the grayness swell in the sky until she muttered, "Where are you going?"

"I'm not really sure. It's all really complicated, and to be honest, I'm not even sure I can explain it to myself."

Cia folded her arms, gazed out the window, and continued, "Is Sam going with you?"

"Yeah. Her and Eton… Please don't be upset."

Cia brushed her hair to one side of her head and turned around to face Chase. A lump in her throat swelled as she swallowed her throbbing heartache. It sat reluctantly in her chest like an anchor.

After a long silence, Cia mustered up her words.

"Are you ever coming back?"

Chase averted Cia's look and stared at the floor.

"It kills me to say that I don't know."

Cia unfolded her arms and gracefully walked over to the bed and stood in front of Chase who reflexively wrapped her arms around Cia's slender body and buried her face in her lover's stomach.

Cia gently pushed Chase back on the bed. Chase slowly inched her way upward, closer to the pillows. Cia gracefully climbed on top of the bed and lied down next to Chase. She lifted Chase's arm and nuzzled underneath it.

"Can we just lie here then?" Cia begged but knowinf that this would be the best for Chase.

Chase hugged Cia's body a little closer to hers. They kissed, and Cia rested her head lightly on Chase's chest.

They did not come downstairs for dinner as they continued to lie on the soft mattress, listening to the rain fall and the echoing laughter of their friends. It was the most intimate music they could have wished for in their last moments together.

It was two o'clock in the morning before Sam, Chase and Eton reconvened at the garage. They entered discreetly through the regular side door and gathered all the Zodiac items before returning to the backyard.

Luckily, the rain had stopped around midnight so they were able to prepare the portal under the clear moonlight.

"We have to be sure not to bring anything that makes us stand out too much," Eton warned. "Once we are at Pangea, we can find a Light village and change into something more appropriate. Until then, I think these dark clothes were a good call to help keep us hidden as we travel."

As Sam poured the mixtures from the vials

on the ground while reading from a Zodiac Circle she had made, Chase and Eton finished packing blankets and food into their backpacks.

"Sam, you made sure to bring the Healer's Mastery?" Eton reminded.

"Yes," Sam acknowledged as she finished pouring the last vial. "We're ready to go."

Eton handed Chase her backpack, put his on, and stepped inside the outlined sun next to Sam.

Chase put on her backpack, turned around, and looked back at the house.

"I'll miss them, too," Sam echoed Chase's silent thoughts behind her.

Chase took a deep breath in and stood alongside Sam and Eton.

Sam revealed the silver moon pendant from under her black long-sleeve shirt and kissed it. It shined miraculously under the real moon hanging in the sky.

Closing her eyes, Sam began to sing the lullaby that sung her to sleep so many years ago.

Although it seems like a world beyond my eyes is just a dream,
I know within my heart a place exists,
as I sing my sweet vibrations to the wind.
Water falls and fire burns while the air sings to the earth's blessed turns.
So I heed my calling to that unknown place, where I know that you and I survived the chase.

Sam's beautiful voice floated in the chilly night air as a bright light began to shimmer from her necklace.

Chase frantically looked around as the

light became brighter and brighter. Colored light waves shot off in every direction as it swelled around her. She turned and looked at Sam who was holding out her hand. Chase took it.

A strange feeling started to possess Chase's body, similar to how she felt when Eton cast his invisibility spell on them, but this was uplifting. She felt like gravity no longer existed and like she was flying. Chase peeked over to Sam to see her reaction.

Although Sam appeared to be relaxed, in reality, she was highly stressed.

This was the second time that Sam had experienced the fusing of a rainbow, and once again, as beautiful as the integration sounded, the uncertainty of what lay beyond the rebirth of her vision frightened Sam.

The illumination was so intense now, Sam, Chase, and Eton all had to close their eyes. The sounds of straggler cars whizzing by, a distant clatter of the el train, and the chirping crickets left them as well. The white bubble they were in was absolutely noiseless.

When the brilliant gleam ended, the city sounds returned to the night air, but the backyard was empty, save for a sun, outlined on the grass waiting for morning, and a secretive spectator, smiling at the best disappearing act ever witnessed.

Sam placed her hand on Chase's shoulder.

"Chase, open your eyes."

Chase slightly peeked through her half squinted eyes.

"We're not dead?" she joked.

"Of course, not," Sam insisted. "We're home. Welcome to Pangea."

Chase opened her eyes fully and saw that she was no longer standing in her city-backyard but in a heavily dense forest.

The trees loomed overhead blocking the sunlight from getting in so Chase could not tell if it was day or night. A soft fog just lingered just above the long blades of grass, and an eerie, lonely feeling choked the moist cold air.

Chase shivered.

"Where are we?"

Eton walked up to an old pine tree and placed his hand gently on the trunk.

"We're in a part of the Woodlands, most likely the southern portion. The wetness on the ground and in the winds tell me so."

"Right. That helps," Chase murmured.

"The Woodlands make up what our Earth calls South America," Sam answered.

Chase looked around at the wooded forest puzzled.

"Umm… I may not be too good with geography, but these don't look like forests that would be in South America. Other than this world's continents not being split up yet, Sam, I thought you said that our worlds are the same."

"I said that there were the same resources. We breath oxygen, and all life is sustained by water, but here, our climate regions work a little differently. The climate patterns aren't in relation to how the sun hits the land. It more or less has to do with…"

A soft howl from afar interrupted Sam's clarification.

Chase waved up her hands in surrendering.

"You know what. Don't worry about explaining the details. I think I get the gist of it. Why don't we start moving before that howl gets any closer."

"Agreed," Eton said. "Let's move."

The trio made their way in the opposite direction of the threatening howl. The lack of sunlight in the forest was making it difficult for Chase to see where they were going. Sam and Eton walked easily through the darkness, using their fox Neo instincts to guide them.

"I can't see anything," Chase complained as she tripped over a jutted out rock. "This should help."

Chase pulled out a small flashlight from her backpack and turned it on. Eton turned swiftly around and angrily grabbed Chase by the shirt.

"What do you think you're doing?!?"

"Lighting the way. Not all of us have night vision. Let me go!"

Chase struggled and pushed Eton off her. Sam walked over and stood by Chase's side. She looked sternly at Eton.

"What's wrong with you?" Sam confronted.

"I told you not to bring anything that would raise unnecessary attention! With odd tools like that, whatever cover we *might* have will surely be blown!"

"That may be true, but she's right. You and I can see perfectly fine in the dark. You have to remember that she doesn't have her Neo powers back yet."

Eton's tense shoulders relaxed as he apologized, "I'm sorry, Chase. I should have been more considerate."

"It's okay, Wonder Boy," Chase replied as she adjusted her shirt.

"Good," Sam interjected. "Now, we really should keep moving."

With Eton in the lead, they continued deep into what seemed like a never-ending cluster of trees.

There was a reigning gloominess Sam did not remember in the Woodlands. The dingy foliage sat quietly, staring down at her as if she were being watched by the leaves' suspicious eyes. A sense of uneasiness tingled Sam's bones.

"How do we know we're going the right way?" Chase inquired. "God, this place creeps me out."

"We don't," Eton replied.

"That's comforting," Chase jeered, equally uncomfortable as Sam.

They walked for another two hours before they decided to rest and eat a snack.

Sam sat on a cold boulder and bit into her sandwich.

"Eton? Now that we're back, what's our first goal?"

Eton leaned against a tree and tossed his apple up and down.

"I think our best move is to go to the Great Abbey and free Friar Sulny. Friar Sulny has a strong mind, but twenty years of attempted psychic infiltration from Quar has really taken a toll on him, body and spirit."

Sam's head lowered as she stared at the ground. She felt a lump in her throat, and tears began to gather in her eyes.

"Oh Friar Sulny…" Sam whispered.

Eton continued, "If we're where I think we are in the Woodlands, then the Great Abbey is only about a month's travel away."

"A month?" Chase exclaimed, springing up from lying on the grass. "I don't think I can walk that much."

"We have to," Eton explained. "The trip may be shorter if we get lucky enough to find Light Alliances along the way with faster transportation, but a month is a pretty accurate estimate."

Chase moaned as her body fell back down on the ground.

"Man! What is up with place? No cars, weird vibes from trees, magic, and who knows what else? Maybe this wasn't such a good idea… Chase, what were you thinking?" Chase argued with herself.

"That you must save your world," Eton said plainly.

"Oh yeah. That, too," Chase sighed smart-alecky.

"What should we do after we save Friar Sulny?" Sam interrupted.

"We start our journey to the Great Hall and gather as many Light allies as we can on the way, forming an army to stop Ceros and free the Nobles and the Magi Order. Then we reestablish order and goodness in Pangea."

Sam nodded in assurance.

"No big deal, right?" Chase commented one last time before Sam playfully kicked a pile of dry leaves at her.

Sam knew that Chase's sarcasm was her best friend's way of coping with unbelievable or intense circumstances. This was definitely one of them.

After their short break, the three comrades started walking again, darkness still prevailing around them like surreptitious assassins.

Chase pointed her flashlight up to the tops of the trees.

"Man, those trees really don't want light getting in."

"You're not mistaken," Eton replied. "Since the earth and soils feed off the reigning aura of the world, Ceros' corrupt rule has severely disrupted nature. The Shadow Force has caused the trees to block out more sun, making the lands drier and the rivers flowing less and less, but the Great Crossings is much worse. I overheard some prisoners talk of how the land turned on them, fighting the innocent as if Quar was pulling the strings."

A worried look washed over Sam's face. Chase saw this and decided to enter the conversation again even though she, herself, was scared witless about the entire state of affairs she was quickly thrown into.

"So, Eton? What are we looking for exactly?"

"Like I said, despite Ceros' attempt for complete rule of darkness, there are some areas where the Light shines through. We need to search for a break in the treetops. It will be a good sign that a Light Alliance village is there with good company."

Suddenly, Eton stopped. He halted Sam and Chase with his hand and then, turned around to motion them to stay silent.

Barely speaking, Eton whispered to Chase, "Turn your flashlight off and slowly get as low to the ground as you can."

Chase obeyed and slowly lied down on the ground, not knowing what to expect.

Standing, Sam remained motionless as Eton changed into a fox. He looked back at Sam once more before steadily creeping forward.

Sam saw him disappear into the darkness and waited.

Silence.

Sam changed into her delicate fox form and lied down beside Chase.

"What the-" Chase whispered in shock as she felt Sam's soft fur coat brush against her arm."

"It's just me," Sam mumbled.

"Umm…" Chase stuttered, shocked at Sam's fox introduction. "Where… uh… where did Eton go?"

Before Sam could answer, Sam and Chase heard a loud rustling from the bushed ahead of them. They both held their breaths.

Still as a fox, Eton leapt out of the bushes screaming, "Run!"

Quickly, Sam and Chase got up and started running with Eton closely behind them.

Chase fumbled around to turn her flashlight back on. There was a thundering rumble following Eton.

Chase finally managed to get her flashlight on as she pointed the beaming light out in front of her. Sam and Eton, remainging in their fox forms, ran beside her.

The rumbling started to surround them as they continued to run. Low growls and the sound of heavy thumping became audible from both sides of the fleeing group as well as behind them. The sounds were closing in. Fast.

Chase kept her flashlight pointed forward but kept looking all around to try and catch a glimpse of their assailants.

When her stare returned to the aim of her
flashlight, Chase's eyes widened as she saw a
monstrous black bear standing on its hind legs
before her.

Shocked by the animal, Chase did not
notice a tree root sticking out of the ground.
She tripped and fell with a loud thump. She
looked up at the roaring beast.

The black bear stood at an overwhelming
height and pounded on its chest with its
powerful claws, outlined with long sharp
nails. Its mouth was heavily saturated in
drool as it bore its fierce teeth.

"Oh… my… God…" Chase stammered in
disbelief.

All of a sudden, Eton jumped in between
the large black bear and the stunned Chase.
Eton snarled at the bear, but the bear just
laughed.

"You've got to be kidding me!" the black
bear sneered. "Fellas! Look at this pathetic
fox. He thinks he can take me, the mighty
Boull!"

A steady rising of chuckles emerged from
the surrounding darkness as mangy-looking
bobcats and more black bears emerged. Some
morphed into humans once the circle around the
trio closed.

An ashy looking bobcat with a wild fur
coat and one glass eye hopped beside Boull and
laughed.

"You're ri…ri…right, Boss! Loo… look at
him! He's so puny! You can ta… take him!"

Boull patted his bobcat friend on the
back and walked forward to Eton as a human.

Boull was still large in size, and his
thick black hair remained but it looked much
courser than his fur coat. Dirt clung to every
inch of his skin, and his musty smell

saturated the night air along with the grubby-looking leather outfit he wore.

"You know something, Queech? I just might."

Boull unveiled a spike-ended club and lifted it high above his head, preparing to strike, when Sam joined Eton at his side. Surprised, Boull let his club drop back down to his side.

"Well, isn't this a nice treat? A lady fox? Is this your girlfriend?" Boull mocked. "No matter. I've always liked an audience when I put out a Light."

Boull pointed at Sam.

"I've got something special planned for you afterward."

Eton leapt up at Boull and bit him on the arm, but Boull simply thrashed his arm and hurled Eton into a tree. As he came downward, Eton hit his head on a rock, knocking him unconscious.

"So much for that one!" Boull yelled. "Now, as promised, little lady, I believe you and I have a date."

Boull's crew snickered as he made his way toward Sam, but just before Boull grabbed Sam by her bushy tail, a mud-covered stone flew in and struck him on the head.

Infuriated, Boull cried out, "Who threw that?"

He glanced back and forth into the darkness to see who his attacker was.

Chase was crouched behind the bush whose root had caused her to fall.

"I can't believe I hit him," Chase whispered to herself.

Then, unexpectedly, Chase felt a large set of hands grab her by the neck.

Chase writhed under the grip as she

gasped for air.

"Chase!" Sam screamed, returning to her human form, as she started to run to Chase's aid.

But, Boull reached out and held Sam by the waist.

"No! Let me go!" Sam resisted.

Chase pounded at the mighty hands wrapped around her throat. Beginning to feel light-headed, Chase felt around in the darkness for the assaulter's fingertips. Finally feeling the index finger, she pressed deeply into the cuticle using her own nail.

The chokehold released as the lackey yelped at the pressure point pain.

Still dizzy, Chase stumbled around a bit before two of Boull's men grabbed each one her arms. A third jumped in and punched Chase across the face.

The blow did not help Chase's already faint state. The blackness in her vision was only lit up by fuzzy looking torches. Sam's scream started to fade out as Chase's head dropped to her chest, knocked out.

When Chase finally came to, she felt a rope tightly wrapped around each one of her wrists. She blinked a few times and looked around.

She could see her surroundings now, as the previous blurry torchlight was clear and lit up the dark area of the forest. There was a dozen or so burly and dirty-looking men around her.

Eton lie motionless on a wooden flatbed cart. He was also tied up in ropes.

"Sam?" Chase croaked hoarsely.

"Is that her name?" Boull shouted as he steadily plowed his way in front of his crew.

Boull laughed.

Despite the throbbing of her head, Chase gathered her strength and tried to lunge forward at Boull but was restricted by her ropes. She winced as her arms strained back. Chase turned around and saw that even though her hands were tied separately, they were bound by one single rope wrapped around a tree.

"Where is she?" Chase demanded.

"Feisty," Boull mocked.

Boull motioned for one of his men to bring Sam forth. Sam was held captive in a set of shackles.

"Chase!"

Sam tried to rush to Chase but was swiftly stopped by her guard.

"Let her go!" Chase screamed.

"I don't think so," Boull smoothly replied. "You see, I have special plans for this one, and they are oh-so-very special plans indeed. I thought about killing the other one, but I figured I might have a use for him after all."

Boull stepped closer to Chase.

"But, you… I actually don't have any use for an Ander, so I've decided to just dispose of you."

"No!" Sam protested.

Boull continued, "I wanted to kill you myself, nice and quick with my spiky club here, but Queech persuaded me otherwise."

Chase breathed heavily, anticipating the ensuing comment.

"Instead, I'm going to let my boys beat you death… slowly."

Boull reached forward and grabbed Chase under the chin.

"Nobody embarrasses, Boull. Nobody."

Chase jerked her chin away from Boull's

hold.

Boull smirked and shouted, "Who's first?"

Two men stepped forward and started the beating. Chase winced as punches landed in her stomach, chest, cheek, and ribs. Boull's men laughed at the sight.

"Stop it! No!" Sam continued to yell as she squirmed, trying to break free of the large man's embrace.

Boull's group continued to get riled up as Chase took more beatings, until she was kneeling on the ground barely alive, coughing and wheezing. Boull's men hooted and cheered as the two attackers cracked their knuckles, ready for round two.

Seeing this, Sam quickly jabbed her elbow into her holder's juggler. He choked and let his release go. Sam pushed him aside and ran to Chase.

Slipping right between the two large men, Sam slid to the ground, grabbed Chase's face, and kissed her.

Sam had no idea what she was doing or why she was doing it, but it felt like the right thing to do. Then, there was a warm tingling in her hands as she continued to kiss the dying Chase.

Suddenly, with a quick heave, Boull pulled Sam away from Chase. Sam rolled to the ground.

Boull stepped in front of Chase and glared down at her as her head wavered back and forth.

"You're tougher than I thought," Boull stated.

He withdrew a jagged dagger and thrust it into Chase's heart. Chase coughed, and in two more gasp for air, her body went limp.

"Nooooo!" Sam cried out.

She tried to return to Chase, but two men subdued her.

Boull wiggled his blade free of Chase's body and returned it to a small sheath on his belt. Chase's body fell over to the ground.

"We're done here. To the Sector!"

Boull's men hurrahed and followed their leader into the Woodlands forest.

When the last gleam from the bandits' torches left the scene, a shadow moved around Chase's limp body. It crept in to take a closer look.

When the shadow reached Chase, it knelt down and rested its hand on the top of her head. It quickly withdrew its hand and pulled out a small knife. The shadow cut through the rope and picked Chase's body up in its arms.

Chase had no clue of the actions outside her body. She was too busy roaming, what she thought to be, the Afterlife.

There were lights all around Chase as she walked through the white realm. Each one of her footsteps sounded like an echo in a canyon, but she felt light as a feather.

"Am I dead?" Chase wondered aloud.

Her voice reverberated just as much as her footsteps. There was no reply so she continued to walk into the infinite colorless abyss.

"If this is heaven, it sucks. Where are all the people?!?" she yelled.

Suddenly, a green beam of light shot down from above and landed directly in front if Chase's face. Floating in the air was a tiny glowing orb. Its emerald shade swirled inside like mercury in water.

"Whoa," Chase said as she squinted at it to get a closer look. "What the heck is this?"

Then, a genderless voice boomed from all

around, "Take it."

Caught off guard, Chase stumbled backwards a bit.

"Who's there?"

There was a brief pause until the voice repeated, "Take it."

"The little ball of light?" Chase asked.

"You must take it."

Chase inched back closer to the green orb and took it in her hand.

"Um…Okay, what do I now?"

Another silent pause.

"Hello?" Chase questioned.

"Become one with it," the mysterious voice replied.

"How do I do that? Do I eat it?"

"Become one with it."

"You know, for an almighty being, or whatever you are, you're not very good at giving directions," Chase barked back.

She turned the orb over in her hands then tossed it up and down.

"Become one with it," the voice reiterated.

"Alright, alright. Calm down."

Chase tapped on the orb. It was hard yet fragile like glass.

"I guess that means I can't eat it," Chase said disappointedly.

She held the orb above her head and peered through it. Not seeing anything, she sighed and brought it back down to chest level where she felt a strange pull from her lungs to the orb.

Feels like a magnet, Chase realized.

As she brought the orb closer to her sternum, she looked down and saw the orb fusing to her body.

Even though she was freaked out by the

sight, Chase continued to push the green light ball into her chest until it was fully submerged inside of her. Much to Chase's surprise, the fusing felt like a tickle.

"There!" Chase yelled at the whiteness. "I became one with it."

But, the voice did not respond.

"Figures. What the-"

Chase grabbed her chest as a burning sensation arose from within. The burning grew stronger and stronger. It felt like Chase's lungs were filled with a toxic air she could not breath. She fell to the ground clutching her chest as the green fire blazed in her lungs. She screamed in pain as she threw her head back.

Then, Chase felt someone shaking her.

"Hey, wake up! Wake up! You're having a bad dream!"

Chase's eyes shot open as she caught herself panting heavily in a cold sweat. She turned to her left and saw a man sitting on the edge of where she lied.

He had dark brown eyes, a full head of short curly black hair and stubble on his sturdy chin. His wide shoulders were covered in tribal looking tattoos and his bare chest was quite hairy.

"Where am I?" Chase asked warily.

"You're safe. My name is Taidyn, but you can call me Tai."

Chase wearily looked around.

She was covered in a wool blanket warming her cold body. Small snippets of light snuck in through the cracks of the poorly constructed twig roof. The floor was bare dirt and held almost no furniture save for a beaten down eating table and two hand crafted stools. There was a tin tub in the far most corner of

the rustic hut filled with water, and a few
pots and pans were displayed next to it, lying
neatly on a ratty towel.

"That beautiful woman over there cooking
by the fire is my wife, Kalough," Tai
continued.

The woman that Tai pointed out waved to
Chase. Her white hair and dazzling blue eyes
sparkled in the firelight. She was wearing a
long beige dress with frayed edges at the hem
line. She was barefoot and held a navy blue
shawl around her shoulders as she stirred the
contents of the pot.

"Good morning. It's so nice to see you
up. For a moment last night, we weren't sure
if you were going to make it."

"Sam…" Chase coughed then sprung up in
bed. "Sam! I have to go find her!"

Chase felt a large pain in her chest
again. Tai eased her back down.

"You need to rest before you go find
anyone. Go back to sleep. We'll be sure to
leave enough breakfast for you when you come
to again."

Feeling weak and tired, Chase nodded and
dozed off again for the rest of the day until
nighttime melted into the sky she had not seen
yet.

When she woke up again, the single-room
hut was empty. Chase slowly and achingly got
out of bed and walked outside.

What a great way to spend my birthday,
she thought sarcastically to herself.

There were several other crafted huts
around, all of similar shape and size. They
appeared to be made of sticks and a brown
clay, and all around the tiny village, tall
stakes with torches illuminated the dim forest
gloom.

As unusual as the scene was, Chase was more distressed by the condition of the small town's inhabitants.

A group of elderly women sat around an outdoor fire pit, knitting and rocking back and forth in creaky rocking chairs. One of them chanted an ancient hymn, but instead of being filled with hope her refrain was blemished by despair and resignation. The years of darkness and unmerited suffering had taken a toll on the historic ladies.

The young children in the village were a nice contrast, though it was not the usual form of play Chase was used to in the city. Covered in filth, three girls took turns braiding a rag doll's dusty locks while a group of young boys sword-played with thin sticks of fallen branches.

Although the games were rudimentary, the juveniles smiled, their budding spirits not yet tarnished by the harsh reality of their future upbringing.

Watchful parents stayed closed to guard against any unwarranted surprises from the neighboring forest. Disappointment hung from their eyelids like drapes, masking the tears that wanted so much to break free.

Chase tried to find something, anything, to keep from crying at the strange and devastating sight. She looked up and was further shocked when she saw the stars shining so brightly in the sky.

"They are beautiful aren't they?" a soft female voice questioned from behind.

Chase spun around and saw Kalough.

"Kalough, right?"

The slender woman nodded.

"Yes, my name is Kalough, but I'm afraid I do not know what to call you."

"Oh! My name's Chase. Um… thank you for taking me in. I really thought I died back there."

"Yes, the dark forests can be very scary at night, especially in these parts if you're alone."

"But, I wasn't alone. I was with two friends, and they were captured."

"That's horrible," Kalough replied as she led Chase back into her hut. "But, there is nothing you can do right now if you don't have the proper strength."

Kalough sat Chase down at the table where there was a plate of meat slathered in gravy and a stale piece of bread.

"I'm sorry we can't offer you anything better," Kalough said gently.

"Oh don't worry about it."

Chase picked up a two-pronged fork and stabbed a piece of meat with it. She raised it slowly to her mouth.

This could be interesting, Chase thought as she stared at the native grub.

Hunger heavily guiding Chase, she popped the meat in. She chewed a bit then swallowed.

"Do you like it?" Kalough asked curiously.

"This is great!" Chase exclaimed, surprising both herself and Kalough.

"Really?"

"Yeah! If my taste buds are correct, this is chicken? It's really tender from all this gravy which is really good by the way."

Kalough laughed at her guest's liking to the rationed food.

"I'm happy you enjoy it. I have more in the pot over the fireplace if you'd like seconds."

"I'm sure I will. I eat anything and

everything. Not picky at all," Chase replied in between bites. "Even stale bread doesn't bother me. I finish all the left over bread where I work."

Kalough laughed once more at Chase's refreshing upbeat attitude.

"You certainly are strange. This includes your clothes. I've never seen materials like these before."

Chase stopped eating as she looked down at her black polyester tee shirt, lightweight cargo pants, and hiking boots.

She chuckled nervously.

"They're imports," Chase joked.

Before Kalough could ask another question, the sound of galloping horses came from outside. Kalough rushed to the door and flung it open.

"Thank goodness he's back," Kalough sighed with relief. "As trained as he is, I'm always worried until he returns home."

Kalough walked outside to meet Tai as he and five other men got off their horses. Chase finished up the last bit of her dinner and joined them.

"You've awaken, I see," Tai said cheerfully as Chase approached him.

"Yes. Thank you for taking me in," Chase replied.

"This is Chase, honey," Kalough introduced.

"Chase. It's a strong name, like your body. I'm surprised you're up and moving already considering how beaten up your were when I found you. How's that stab wound?"

Chase put her hand on her chest.

"When I first woke up, it felt like it was burning, but it feels much better now."

"That's good to hear," Tai said as he

tossed the reins of his horse to a husky man beside him.

"Did you find anyone tonight, dear?" Kalough questioned.

"Not tonight but we caught a trail. Tomorrow we head further south to investigate it. I might be gone for two or three days."

Kalough bit her lip and briskly walked inside a neighboring hut.

"Is she alright?" Chase asked.

"She'll be fine. Always worried, that one. Come, Chase. Let's head to my hut. I can already smell my wife's famous Gravy Special."

Tai put a hand on Chase's back and walked back to his home.

"Where are you going?" Chase inquired as she sat down on one of the wooden stools.

Tai stood over the fire and dished his plate full.

"As you probably saw, these forests are dangerous. Those cursed trees are filled with not only Shadow Force followers but other dark magic groups. For the few of us that still follow the lighted path, we band together in order to survive. We have to look out for one another. That's where my crew and I go. We head out into those forests looking for any lone and or wounded travelers and bring them to safety here. You are proof of our good work."

Tai sat down across from Chase and started eating but continued, "When this village was first established two years ago, we were just made of Anders, and we had the mindset of keeping it that way. You know, there are more risks to us if a Neo turns to the Shadow Force, but as time passed, we realized that we needed more protection. We took in Neos to help keep the village safe and to aid us as trackers."

"How many do you have?"

"Only three. Two are falcons, and the other is a badger. The badger is our doctor. Apparently, he was a traveling Healer for the Great Abbey before the war."

Tai coughed.

"I need water. Are you thirsty?"

Chase nodded so Tai walked over to the bin of water, dipped two clay cups inside and returned to the table.

"There you go."

"Thanks."

Not realizing how thirsty she was, Chase chugged the entire cup of water down. The liquid was gritty from the poor filtration, but Chase kept quiet and licked her teeth clean, another thing to get accustomed to.

After wiping her mouth, Chase asserted, "I have to go find my friends."

Tai licked his plate clean and replied, "I don't think that's going to be possible."

"Why not?"

"You said your friends were captured?"

"Yes. By a black bear named Ball… Boll…"

"Boull?"

"Yeah, that's it!"

"Then you really have no possibility of seeing your friends again."

"Why not?" Chase repeated.

"If Boull took your friends, then he is bringing them to the Sector, just over the border in the Savannahs."

"The Sector? What's that?"

"It's a fighting arena where Boull and other sick freaks reside. His gang actually isn't a part of the Shadow Force regime, but they're evil nonetheless.

The Sector only has one goal and that is

to kill innocents, but they thrive on fighting and spilled blood no matter where it comes from. Boull has even had some of his own men fight to the death when he runs out of Light innocents."

"There has to be some way to get them out!" Chase demanded.

"No. The Sector is heavily guarded with fifty or more Shadow Forcers. You'd die before you'd even get in. No Ander would ever survive going there, and our Falcon Neos are much to valuable to risk losing in such a scheme."

Chase slammed a fist on the table and stormed out. Tai sat silently, upset that he could not help the newcomer.

Chase walked up to a tree and leaned a hand on it, breathing in heavily. Frustrated, she let out a wild yell and closing her teary eyes, threw her fist forward, punching the tree.

She expected for her knuckle to explode with pain as her fist met the hard surface, but Chase did not feel anything.

Confused, she slowly opened her eyes and shrieked when she saw what was before her.

She had punched clear through the tree's solid surface and into its cavity. She could not see her hand as it was buried deep inside the trunk.

Chase tried to pull her fist out but struggled. Putting her entire body into it, she pushed outward from the base of the tree with her feet and finally yanked her arm free.

She stumbled back a bit. After regaining her balance she staggered over to the tree and peered inside the hole she had apparently made. The hole had to be a least a foot deep.

But how did I? Chase wondered.

She looked down at her clenched fist.

"What the hell?!?"

Keeping her fist closed, Chase brought her hand up from the side of her body.

Her hand and forearm looked normal except they were no longer made of flesh and skin. Instead, Chase's distal part of her upper extremity was composed of, what appeared to be, solid rock.

She rotated her arm in astonishment. The torchlight from the village background reflected playfully on the sandy gray tint of her fist. Chase ran her left hand over her right arm. It was smooth and cool, like granite.

After examining all views of her rocky arm, she released her fist and relaxed her clench. As soon as she did, her arm transformed back into its normal fleshy state.

Astounded again, Chase wiggled her fingers. Then, she made another fist, and it changed back into its stony appearance. She let go once more, and her skin was back.

This just keeps getting weirder and weirder.

Breathing heavy to make sure she was awake, Chase lifted both her hands and made fists. She was sure both had morphed into stone but wanted to see better in the torch lights.

Chase turned and walked closer to the village, keeping her fists tight. As she did, she noticed there was a ripple of dirt that lied directly underneath the shadows of her arms.

Chase crouched down and moved her fists in circular motions just inches above the ground. As expected, the earth moved with her fists, following the pattern Chase had traced in the air.

"There might be a way for you to get your friends back after all."

Chase looked up and saw Tai standing with his hands on his waist, smiling.

She looked back down at her hands as she relaxed her fingers, and the soft surface of her skin returned.

Meanwhile, not too far away from the Ander camp, Sam shook fervently in her sleep.

She started to mumble, twisting and shouting, "No!"

Eton rushed to her side and woke her up.

"Sam! Wake up! You were having a nightmare."

Sam wiped a tear from her eye, sat up, and looked around at the grim walls and the cast iron bars that confined them to a dark adobe cell.

With Boull and his gang, they had traveled for almost two days over the Woodland border and into the Savannahs. The climate had drastically changed as the Savannahs were mainly composed of dry flatlands with a few scattered oases, but this was no oasis.

The Sector was a colossal stadium made out of a deep orange clay. Its high walls were stacked with long rows of benches for its grotesque spectators. The stage was a barren dirt center, allowing plenty of room for competitors to fight. The air was dry and dusty, a result of the sun's fierce rays and relentless heat.

Sam and Eton had been taken underground to the prison cells which were split up into two sides.

On one side, innocent Neos had been badly beaten and stayed crumpled up on their straw beds. On the other, Boull's men had enslaved a particular type of creature Eton and Sam did not know of. They paced eagerly in their cells waiting for their call to fight.

These Neos were not normal. They were untamable monsters created by some unknown dark magic. Their human and animal-Neo forms collided and contrived a frightful creature. Features from both sides melted into their final appearance. They were savage-like, primal, and no longer spoke words, for the noises they made were their battle cries, a mixture of grunts and roars. Boull and his followers referred to these beasts as Bolics.

"How long have I been sleeping?" Sam wondered aloud.

"A long time," Eton replied. "Understandable though, seeing how you had to walk for the entire two days while I was carried on that cart. What was your dream about?"

Sam scratched her head.

"I was standing in an ocean when suddenly, lightning struck its surface. My body was instantly paralyzed as my body was carried away by the waves. I must have drifted for hours because when I opened my eyes, there was no land in sight as floated, and the sky was completely white, like it was saturated with clouds. Then, I heard Chase's voice. I couldn't understand what she was saying though."

"Chase?"

"Yes. I started to shout to find out where she was, but I still couldn't figure out what she was saying. My moon pendant started to glow, and a beam of green light shot from it.

The power of the beam was so great I was thrust underwater. It was so dark there I couldn't see a thing until my pendant glowed

again. This time, it was yellow, but then my
lungs started to fill with water, and I
started drowning. That's when you woke me."

"I'm glad I did. That sounds horrible. Do
you think your dream means something?"

"I'm not sure…"

Just then, a large hairy man swung open
their prison cell door.

"Okay, you two," he demanded. "Come with
me."

Sam and Eton walked slowly behind the
guard as he led them upstairs to Boull's
chambers.

When they walked in, Boull was lying on a
large bed decorated with purple velvet pillows
and golden tassels. A fine white silk swam
over the tall bed posts like the curtains of a
theater stage. Looming savannah plants reached
high toward the ceiling, waving back and forth
from the slight breeze that snuck through the
open door leading to a balcony that oversaw
the fighting center. A sumptuous feast was
deliciously laid out on a long bronze table,
and two maidens, dressed in sheer green robes
and bedazzled golden sandals, were preparing a
plate for their vile captor.

"Ah! Welcome mutts," Boull chuckled as
the guard pushed Sam and Eton forward, closer
to the foot of Boull's bed. "Welcome to… the
Sector."

Sam did not look up at Boull but kept her
stare glued to the sandy floor.

"I see the young lady has yet to forgive
me for killing your friend," Boull stated
coldly. "Sorry, love, but there's not much use
for an Ander here. They die much too quickly
in the fight. You understand, don't you?"

Sam finally looked up and spit, "You're
disgusting."

Boull's chest swelled up as fury began to run through his veins, but he stopped himself from an outburst of rage, coolly walked up to Sam, and grabbed her by the throat. Eton made move to stop Boull, but Boull was much too strong for Eton. Without a flinch, Boull knocked Eton directly to the ground. The guard drew his sword and held it at Eton's throat before another strike could be made.

Boull laughed.

"Look's like your boyfriend is in need of learning some manners. Don't worry… I'll make sure he's taught some. Guard, take him to Cage One."

"Who should I put in the other, sir?"

"Hmmm… Surprise me."

The guard bowed and shoved Eton out of the room.

"Where are you taking him?" Sam coughed through Boull's grip.

"You'll soon find out, but first," Boull licked his lips and looked Sam up and down. "We need to get you into something different. Oh ladies?"

The two maidens glided smoothly across the sand and stood at Boull's side.

"My liege," they chanted in harmony.

"Get her changed into something more… comfortable. If she tries anything," Boull sneered as he tightened his hold around Sam's neck. "Kill her. As much as I like her, she can easily be replaced."

Boull pushed Sam away from him. She bent over heaving and gasping for air. The servants grabbed each one of Sam's arms and dragged her out of Boull's room.

Boull snickered as the door shut behind them.

"She'll learn her place, too."

Earthquake

"This is truly a fascinating tool you have, Chase," Tai stated as he shined the flashlight at a tree in the distance. "Are you sure you don't need it? The Woodlands nowadays are very dark."

"Yeah I'm sure," Chase replied.

Tai had agreed to accompany Chase to the Sector after witnessing her new ability. They had been walking for a day and a half in the dark forest, and Chase could now see in the dark.

I guess my wolf skills are kicking in, Chase concluded.

"It will be about another day's time until we reach the Sector. If she behaves, your female companion will most likely be alive as one of Boull's personal servants, but the other… Is he a strong fighter?"

"I'm not sure exactly," Chase answered as she ducked under a low hanging branch. "I don't know him very well, but he did practice umm… Illusion magic at the Great Abbey twenty years ago, and he's pretty built."

"Illusion magic might help keep him alive a little longer than most. Those Bolic beasts are wild and vicious, but they're not too bright."

"Was Kalough upset when you told her that you were taking me to the Sector?"

"Not as much as I thought," Tai responded. "I think she cared more that I was helping you out rather than running off on some blind chase. At least with you, we have a plan."

"What is that plan exactly? You said they have fifty guards? There's only two of us."

"I may just be an Ander, but I can hold my own against a Neo. I've fought hard and well to stay alive this long and keep a village of good people protected. I'm more concerned about you. Have you ever engaged in battle before?"

"No, I haven't," Chase realized. "Where I come from, battles are on a totally different playing field. Combat's usually from a distance."

"Well, you'll have to come back down to this one if you wish to survive. The clashing of swords, the pounding from knuckle bones, the heat of your opponent's breath, and the sweat of their fear are all parts of what deems an encounter as a battle."

"More major adjusting to do. I've never even used a sword before let alone punch someone."

"I can guide you in how to use a sword. It's more about grace and precision and not power."

"That's good because I'm not that strong," Chase laughed.

"But, when I saw you out at the border of the village last night… You had punched a hole clear through a tree without even breaking the skin of your hand."

"Yeah, I'm not sure what that was, but my fist turned into stone when I threw the punch."

"I also saw the earth move underneath you as if you guided it, as well."

Chase stopped walking.

"Listen, Tai, I'm not from here, and I'm not talking about not being from the Woodlands."

Tai stopped walking as well, turned around, and pointed the flashlight at Chase. She squinted at the direct brightness.

"I had a feeling from the time I rescued you that you were no ordinary Ander. For starters, no one could have survived a beating *and* a stab like you endured, and secondly, no Ander, in the history of Pangea, has been able to master any form of magic. It's not in our blood."

"That actually still holds true," Chase explained. "I'm not an Ander. I'm a Neo."

"Really? A Neo?"

Chase nodded.

"I didn't sense it…" Tai said puzzled. "What breed are you?"

"I'm part wolf, part phoenix."

"I suppose that explains why you don't need this magic light stick, but I've never heard of a hybrid Neo. When two breeds cross, the magic blood is cancelled, and an Ander, a pure human, is born."

"I know. It's complicated."

"Sounds like it," Tai said intrigued as he scratched his head. "I'm sure we will have plenty of time to discuss it after we find your friends though. Let's go. It's never a good idea to stay in one place too long here."

Chase nodded another time and followed Tai through the Woodlands trees.

Further east, at the Sector, Eton was in his second Sector fight. His muscular body was covered in bruises and cuts from the dangerous and violent fights from the day before.

Today's fight was against a vicious Dragon Bolic. Though its form was primarily in the shape of an Ander, its mangled body was half covered in rough carmine scales that glinted in the bright Savannah sunlight while the other half was composed of dark brown skin that was heavily scarred and dirty. His right arm was in the form of a dragon's with a deadly poisonous claw hanging from the deranged looking limb.

The Bolic also had vibrant yellow eyes that pierced the air with its apathetic stare. Drool dangled from its partly opened mouth as it heaved in the dust, created from circling Eton's weak body in the middle of the arena.

The crowd cheered with excitement and anticipation of death as the Bolic kicked Eton in the ribs and sent him hurdling into the air.

"Stop it!" Sam screamed as she lunged at Boull, but the chains that confined her to the floor of Boull's balcony made her charge fall short of a successful attack.

Boull threw his head back and cackled.

"My girl, I cannot stop what the people desire. There is a lust for blood at the Sector, and as a leader, I must pay homage to that. What kind of leader would I be if I didn't?"

Boull roared in laughter once more.

"Besides, he might even survive this. He's managed to beat one of my Bolics and is fighting again in just one day of healing."

Sam looked over the balcony's barrier and down below as Eton slowly started to rise. The Bolic snapped its disapproving mouth at its enemy's ability to still stand.

Desperate to help her friend, Sam glanced around the balcony for some sort of escape plan.

The maidens were standing on either side of Boull's large brass-framed chair as he leaned into the large cushions and stuffed his face with a juicy chicken leg. They held huge leaf fans and gently cooled Boull off.

The day was extremely hot as there were no clouds in the sky that afternoon. This made the fight even more treacherous.

Eton brushed a trail of blood off from his forehead and clapped his hands together screaming, "*Illuso!*"

Instead of a large black bear appearing before him, like he did at the zoo, ten more images of Eton appeared around him.

The Dragon Bolic's eyes skirted back and forth from each figure trying to determine which one was real. Fuming with rage and confusion, the Bolic sounded a blood-curdling cry and launched itself at the nearest figure.

The crowd went into an upset as multiple Etons ran around the Bolic. The creature became more confused as it pounced from each illusion to the next, depleting only an image with its attack.

Finally, when only three figures remained, they encircled the savage beast. The Bolic stood peering suspiciously at each character debating which to attack next, but before it could decide, one of the three assailants leaped out of the circle and wrapped his arms around the Bolic's neck in a chokehold making sure to avoid the poisonous claw.

The Dragon Bolic howled as it tried to fight Eton's squeeze, but with each struggled attempt, Eton held on even tighter. The Bolic dropped to its knees, and only a few seconds after, it dropped to the ground motionless.

After Eton was sure that the creature would stay down, he released his arms and stood up and faced the condemning wave of hostile comments and disapproving shouts from the arena seats.

Boull signaled the maids to stop fanning, turned to Sam, and said, "You see? He's alright after all."

Boull stood, directed the guards on the Sector ground floor to dispose of the Bolic, and to take Eton back to the Cage where he would be held until his next fight.

"You can't send him back to the Cage! He's too weak to fight. He hasn't had a decent recovery from these two fights!"

"That's the consequence of war, darling," Boull retorted. "You can't always pick and choose your downtime. He'll fight first thing in the morning. After a fight like today, the people will want to see a brawl as soon as the sun rises."

As Boull predicted, when the next morning came around, an enormous crowd of dark beasts, from the neighboring Woodlands and nearby villages in the Savannahs, came storming into the Sector.

In his animal form, Eton sat in the Cage licking his tired paws as he listened to the heavy sounds of anxious and electrified pounding of feet and voices above him. Even the guards to the Cage were conversing of bets that had been placed the night before.

Eton had surprised himself that he had made it this far. He had never fought or had any form of combat training and chalked up his winnings to luck and instinctual reflexes.

"I'm lucky those Bolics are pretty dumb," Eton whispered to himself. "It makes my illusions that much more powerful and effective."

Just outside the Sector walls, in a brush of tall grass, Chase and Tai crouched low and hid to discuss the last details of their plan.

"Wait," Chase argued in misunderstanding.

"You just plan to walk in there? There's no covert mission or hidden passageways to the dungeons?"

"That is correct."

"Then this really is a suicide mission. I thought you said that Boull only takes Neos to fight, and like I showed you just before we left the Woodlands, I don't know how to change myself into my Neo form yet. I'm still just a human… I mean Ander, in that respect."

"I know, but Boull never backs down from a challenge. He has such an inflated image of himself; if anything poses a threat to his reputation as the strongest force in this region, he will not stop until he is back on top with one hundred percent certainty. Trust me, he'll take the bait."

With that, Tai brushed the dry earth from his knees, wiped the sweat from his brow, and walked over to the open Sector gate.

Queech, the henchman Chase had seen on the night of their attack, and another guard ran up to meet him and drew their swords.

Queech demanded, "What do you…ou…ou want, An… Ander?"

"I wish to speak to Boull. I have an interesting proposal for him."

"I find that un…likely," Queech snorted back. "How could a weak A…A…A…nder like you have such bus…s…iness with a great Ne…o."

"I wish to take some part in a fight in the Sector."

Queech and the guardsman looked at one another and broke out into a wild laughing frenzy.

"A fight? You'd die in a ma…ah…ah…tter of seconds!"

"Well, I wouldn't be the one fighting. You see, I have a very special fighter that's stronger than your mighty Boull."

"How dare you?!" shouted Queech.

He made a swift move to slice through Tai's chest, but Tai keenly stepped out of harm's way and drew a small dagger. Before the second guard could blink, Tai had already made his way behind Queech and pressed the blade against the pulsating throat.

"Oh. I dare," Tai whispered snidely in Queech's ear. "Now, drop your weapon and tell your friend here to do the same."

Queech gulped at the dagger's cool presence against his skin, dropped his sword and directed the other guard to follow. The assisting guard raised up his left hand as he gently laid the sword on the ground and kicked it away from him.

"Okay, boys," Tai continued. "It's time for you to set up a meeting with your boss."

Chase watched intensely from the bushes. After Tai, Queech, and the guard walked into the gate, she sat on the warm, sandy dirt bed that housed her leafy refuge and waited for his return.

Inside, Tai had safely made his way up to Boull's chambers without any disturbances from the other guards.

Still using Queech as a shield, Tai ordered the guard, "Knock."

The guard obliged and pounded on Boull's door. A few moments later, the maiden opened it and stepped aside, allowing the guests to enter the room.

Boull was seated at his eating table sipping a glass of wine and shoving a fistful of berries in his mouth. Seeing the shimmering reflection of the morning's light off Tai's blade, Boull quickly stood up and reached to the wall where his spiky club was leaning.

"I wouldn't do that if I were you."

Tai pressed the dagger in just enough for a small drop of blood to emerge from Queech's skin. Queech squealed in pain.

Disgruntled and vexed, Boull retracted his attempt and sat back down.

"What is it that you want, Ander?"

"You have a couple of Neos that I want."

"It appears an Ander like you doesn't need the assist of Neos," Boull snorted.

"These two have a particular value."

"Well, I'm sorry, but I'd have to decline your demands. I have a tight reign to hold here, and if I start letting prisoners free, what will my people say about me?"

Boull reached to the table and grabbed an apple. He wiped it on his shirt and took a large bite of it.

"You're no king, Boull," Tai said bluntly. "You're a coward who uses lower Neos to fight because you're too damn scared to."

Enraged by Tai's words, Boull squeezed the apple until it burst, and he was left holding a tiny remain of the core.

"You insolent piece of Ander trash!" Boull yelled.

"It's true. You're no king at all. All those people in the seats aren't *your* people. They're spectators or travelers who aren't here for you but for the entertainment. You don't even govern a village. By that standard, I'm more of a king than you."

Boull roared with anger.

"What's stopping any one of your guards or prisoners to realize that they're stronger than you?" Tai progressed. "Nothing. Even those Bolics, dumb as they are, can see that you never get your hands dirty. They could overthrow you in a heartbeat."

Fuming with irritation, Boull squeezed both of his fists so tight that his nails drew blood from his own palms.

"What do you propose then?" Boull snarled between clenched teeth.

"A test of your diplomacy as a leader. I have an Ander that could do battle with any one of your fiercest Bolic fighters, and she wouldn't need one of your low-life henchmen as a shield. If she wins against one of your beasts, you will free the two prisoners I have come here for."

"And which two prisoners would that be?"

"The two foxes you captured in the Woodlands a few days ago."

"Ahh… they truly are prized pieces," Boull said coolly as he settled back into his chair. "Pieces like that are worth far more than a simple dual."

Tai paused for a moment worried that he might have gotten Chase into a fight she could not win. After all, she had never fought an Bolic before, let alone fight in any hand on hand combat.

I need to get back in control of the bargain, Tai reasoned in his head.

"I'm glad to see you've finally stepped up, Boull," Tai finally stated. "Taking on the second fight against my Ander if your first challenger is beaten."

Boull's eyes widened for he about to propose Chase fight three Bolics instead of just one.

"I… I…" Boull stammered.

Seeing this, Tai directed in Queech's ear.

"Look at how brave your *leader* is being. This is why you could never be on top of the food chain. *He* will show everyone once and for all that no one can beat him. Imagine the impression when Boull comes out and strikes down an Ander who beat out a Bolic with her bare hands. How much stronger will Boull look then?"

Boull's ears perked at Tai's words.

Tai continued, "He'll show all of those fools out there that he should be in command of more than a fighting prison. He'll be…"

Tai redirected his voice and stared at Boull.

"The greatest warrior and leader this part of the Savannahs has ever seen. Your henchman said it himself that I'm crazy for suggesting an Ander fight you in the first place. What do you say, Boull?"

Boull leaned back contemplating Tai's statements about showing the Sector inhabitants of his true strength. After all, he would only be facing off against an Ander…

"Fine!" Boull shouted. "Bring the Ander to the Sector, and we shall have ourselves a grand fight. Be here by midday. Now, let my man go."

"I'll let him go when I depart from the gate. I need insurance. It's been nice doing business with you. I shall see you soon."

Still holding onto Queech with his blade, Tai backed out of the room and down to the main entrance of the Sector. When he cleared the gate, Tai flung Queech forward.

Finally free and comfortable speaking, Queech yelled, "Don't you for…fo…forget me! No one ma…a…kes Queech a f…f…fool!"

"I'll hold you to that, cat," Tai remarked nonchalantly.

Queech turned around and retreated back into the Sector walls.

Tai returned to the region of grass where

Chase was lying down waiting.

"Good news, friend," Tai stated as he approached. "Boull has accepted the terms."

Chase took a deep breath in.

"Do not worry," Tai assured. "We have until noon. In that time, keep drinking water. With this sun, you might dry up faster than you might get beaten. Come, I will teach you a few tricks for the fight. It won't be much, but it will be something."

Chase nodded as they walked to a small area of thin trees to practice in the tiny bit of shade their narrow leaves provided.

When noontime came, the seats were just as full as they were when Eton's fight was scheduled in the morning. Boull was seated on his regular balcony, overseeing the entire arena.

Eton was brought up to his side and chained down to the ground with Sam.

"Eton!" Sam exclaimed as Queech secured Eton's chains to the ground hook. "But, I thought you were supposed to fight this morning?"

"I was," Eton coughed. "But, the guards came and sent me back to my dungeon cell and told me that Boull accepted some deal from a mysterious Ander. Something about fighting for possession of prisoners."

Boull walked up to the edge of the balcony and raised his hands. The people in the stadium silenced as he made his announcement.

"My guests, today we have a special treat for you! Earlier today, I was presented an intriguing offer. Tell me folks, have you ever heard of an Ander with the physical abilities to beat a Bolic with his bare hands?"

The crowd roared, "No!"

"Apparently one exists! Don't believe me? See for yourself!"

Boull motioned Cage One's door to open. From the blackness within, a brown hooded figure stepped out. The crowd booed as the mysterious character made its way to the middle of the arena.

"Don't even wish to show your face?" Boull ridiculed.

The hooded figure revealed an arm and slowly pulled back the hood. Boull's heart raced when he saw who was standing before him on the Sector floor.

"But… but…" Boull whispered to himself, his face as white as the ghost that haunted his Sector floor. "You're supposed to be dead."

Sam and Eton looked at each other then walked to the edge of the balcony and peered over to see what surprised Boull so much. They both gasped in disbelief.

Chase removed the cloak completely and threw it to the ground. Tai had given her a change of clothes, and she was now dressed in something more fitting to Pangea's style. She wore black leather hide boots, tan cloth pants, and a dirty white tunic shirt.

"But, how…?" Sam whispered to Eton.

"I'm not sure," Eton replied back.

He grabbed his chest as the burning of his wound returned. This was the first time it had flared up since he returned to Pangea. Eton rubbed it until the pain stopped. He was becoming accustomed to the glowing sensation. He looked at Sam to see if she noticed, but she was preoccupied with watching Chase below.

When Boull's shock had fled him, a hot temper and wrath took its place.

"Open the Cage! Open the Cage!" he

screamed wildly.

As Boull's chants echoed in the arena, the sound of creaky old wood gates being reeled up chimed in. The crowd hushed as the remaining the gate to Cage Two opened.

Chase turned around when she heard a loud beating noise echo from the Cage behind her. She gulped, waiting to see what her opponent would look like.

A golden paw covered in dried up blood emerged from the shadow. Then another one stepped beside it. With one more step, the figure was fully revealed. The paws resembled that of a lion's but the rest of the body was that of a towering woman with untamed dirty orange hair. She was covered in filthy tattered rags and had a long tail whipping behind her, but instead of the tail ending with a cluster of hair, there was a tiny ball with spikes protruding from all sides. Her fierce green eyes glistened in the sun as she licked her sharp fangs and cracked her neck.

"Damn it," Chase muttered to herself.

Sam turned to Boull and yelled, "That's cheating! What is that metal attachment?"

"Not cheating, darling," Boull replied viciously. "Modifying."

The Lioness Bolic began to slowly circle Chase.

"I'm done for," Chase muttered hopelessly as she put up her fists convincing herself she was ready to fight.

The Bolic crouched down low, and almost instantaneously, leaped back up, soared through the air and landed a punch right across Chase's face. The spiked tail-end also managed to scrape Chase's leg. Chase fell to the ground immediately.

The crowd regained its delirium and

bellowed in cheers.

Chase staggered but managed to find her
stance as the Bolic began circling her once
more.

The Lioness Bolic smirked and cut through
the air once more with just as much grace, but
this time, she flung open her fists and
revealed razor sharp claws. Chase took a few
quick steps back, but the Bolic was still able
to make a deep gash on the side of Chase's
face.

Quickly recovering from her sail in the
air, the Lioness Bolic planted her feet and
threw a straight jab into Chase's stomach.
Chase doubled over and coughed up blood.

Up on the balcony, Boull had relaxed in
his chair.

"She might be back from the dead once,
but she definitely won't survive today. This
time, I'll make sure she stays down. Finish
her off!"

Chase heaved in and out trying to catch
her breath. The Bolic spit to the side and
cranked back her arm, readying her slash
attack once more. The crazed beast flung her
arm down, bearing her honed nails, but Chase
closed her eyes, tightened her fists, and
crossed arms to block the blow from cutting
open the rest of her face.

Chase expected to feel the warm rush of
blood seep out of burning flesh wounds as the
Lioness Bolic finished following through with
her offensive strike, but all Chase felt was a
slight tickle.

Confused, Chase slowly opened her eyes.

Right in front of her, the Lioness Bolic
was savagely hashing away at Chase's arms, but
instead of seeing skin, Chase once again saw
her forearms were composed of hard sediment.

Though the substance was now tinted and contrived more to the Sector's sediment, Chase's arms were impenetrable.

As if on a new instinct, Chase flung her arms down and threw a punch into the Bolic's face. The beast instantly flew back and slid across the sandy ground. The crowd hushed again at the sight.

Upstairs, Boull had spit out his wine after seeing Chase's arms turn to the same red stone clay that constructed the Sector walls. Sam and Eton were in just as much shock.

"She did it," Eton whispered.

"Her powers…" Sam chimed in softly. "She can control the elements."

Watching the Lioness Bolic fumble at standing up, Chase looked at her stony clay forearms. Fueled with a surprising confidence, Chase charged forward at the Bolic, ducked slightly and rammed her rocky fist into the creature's chest. There was a loud cracking of ribs just before the Bolic let out one final holler while falling to the ground, eyes shut and unmoving.

Chase's hands were shaking. She had never been filled with so much energy and fear at the same time. She stood over the Bolic panting.

The singing of exotic birds from the grassy region outside the Sector complex hummed through the still air as the crowd stared in awe at the sight. Boull looked around at his spectators' faces. Their shock matched his.

Then, out of the blue, the audience shouted and rumbled with applause and acclamation.

Sam and Eton looked at one another and smiled.

Meanwhile, Tai had been secretly and easily making his way back to Boull's chambers. The guards were too busy watching the fight and neglected their watch duties.

After creeping past two cheering guards and around the corner, Tai whispered to himself, "That's it, Chase."

In that instant, everyone in the Sector became supporters of the mysterious Ander fighter.

"No!" Boull roared as he slammed his glass to the floor.

Boull did not want to face Chase nor humiliation so he stood and walked to the edge of the balcony.

"Open Cage Three!" Boull yelled over the crazed fans.

From Cage Three, a whirlwind of dust shot out of the opening and within seconds, out flew a Falcon Bolic. It flapped its immense wings and returned to the ground. The Falcon Bolic mainly represented a normal man, wearing just ripped black pants, except its hands were shaped in the form of jagged talons covered by a thin sheet of metal and the set of immense wings protruding from his back.

"You've got to be kidding me," Chase whispered to herself.

Chase looked at her right arm which was completely made of earthy clay. She extended her left arm and tightened her muscles. Just as she predicted, the rest of her left arm filled out just as her right did.

"Nice," she smiled.

The Falcon Bolic spread its wings, jumped, and flew up into the sky. It circled overhead, casting a colossal shadow on the ground below. A loud screech broke the sounds of chaotic cheering as the Bolic dove from the sky at Chase.

Chase put up both her arms to deflect the metallic talons that shined brightly in the air.

The Falcon Bolic's first dive was unsuccessful as the metal talons just merely scraped the solid surface of Chase's arms.

The Bolic circled around and made another attempt. This time, instead of trying to scratch Chase, the talons opened up and clutched onto Chase's right arm, lifting her off the high off the ground before releasing her and dropping Chase flat on her back.

Chase winced at the sharp pain that raced up and down her spine. The Falcon Bolic remained well out of Chase's reach. Chase sat up and rubbed the back of her throbbing head. She stood up and gathered her thoughts.

I've got to find a way to land a blow to his body.

Chase's thoughts were interrupted as another screech pierced her ears, and the Falcon Bolic came plummeting downward for his third attack.

Chase lifted up her left arm to block the lustrous talons again hoping the Bolic would make the same move to pick her up and drop her on the ground.

The unintelligent beast did exactly as Chase anticipated, but before the it could fly much higher, Chase thrust her right fist directly into the Bolic's stomach. It cried out in pain as it let Chase's arm go to try and escape before another blow could land, but Chase managed to grab hold of the Falcon Bolic's arm and yanked the bird creature to the ground in front of her as her arm turned to flesh.

The Bolic quickly recovered, and with one

gigantic flap of his feathers, he hit Chase on
both sides with his powerful wings and sprung
backwards well on the other side of the arena.

The force of the hit, as well as the
overwhelming gust of wind that nearly sucked
the breath from her lungs, brought Chase to
her knees. She tiled her head up and saw the
Falcon Bolic swelling his chest singing out a
battle cry.

"I can control the earth…" Chase reminded
herself. "Right. Time to get creative and hope
to God it works."

Chase clutched her right fist again and
pounded it to the ground. She closed her eyes
and envisioned a long rope.

Opening her eyes, she briskly stood up
and keeping her fist tight, she lifted what
seemed to be a whip made out of sand from the
ground. The long line of sand continued to
rise all the way to the Falcon Bolic's feet,
where the end wrapped around both of them.

Noticing this, the Bolic flapped its
wings and tried to flee, but Chase maintained
her hold and used her sandy whip to forcefully
bring the Bolic back down to the ground face
first.

"Okay. Let's see what these powers can
really do."

Chase continued to bring down the
thrashing Falcon Bolic as Tai continued to
make his way up to Boull's room.

When he reached the final hallway to
Boull's chambers, there were two husky guards
standing watch at the door.

Tai drew his sword, as did the guards,
and charged forward. Swords clashed as Tai
blocked each shot with ease. He really was a
fine swordsman as he moved swiftly from side
to side, ducked down, and jumped up.

He cast down his blade and sliced into one of the guard's thigh. The guard howled in pain. Seeing his open mark, Tai flipped the sword and knocked the guard unconscious with the butt of the sword handle.

The other guard lunged forward from behind Tai, but Tai threw back his elbow and hit the guard in his nose and mouth. The guard dropped his sword at the immense amount of pain and blood rippling from the hit spot. Tai turned and grabbed hold of the guard's torso and pushed him back into Boull's door with a loud thump.

On the other side of the door, Boull was too engaged in his Bolic's losing battle to notice the sound, but Queech's keen bobcat ears picked it up.

He put the keys to the chains that bound Sam and Eton on Boull's eating table and walked to the door.

After Queech opened the door, a quick hand reached out pulled Queech into the hallway.

Queech staggered forward from the surprising tug and turned around.

"Yo…you."

"I think you and I have a score to settle," Tai said coolly.

Tai tossed Queech a sword.

"Let's make things fair."

Queech snarled and stormed his frontal attack on Tai, but Tai slid past the attack and slashed at Queech's back. Queech yelled in agony but turned around jumping right back into an offensive position.

"I'm going to hang your hide in my room, Ander," Queech growled.

"You'll have to defeat me first," Tai replied.

A series of attacks found their way to Tai's blade, but they were no match for his exemplary skills.

Finally, Tai dove and thrust his sword forward right into Queech's chest. Queech choked on the blood beginning to gather in the back of his throat.

"Sorry, pal," Tai stated as he withdrew his sword from Queech's cavity. "This skin doesn't go well with red walls."

A tidal wave of shouting swept through the Sector again, vibrating the entire stadium as Chase delivered the Falcon Bolic to the ground for the last time. He passed out from excessive throw-downs and fatigue from trying to escape the sandy vine enveloping his legs.

Boull slammed both fists on the balcony rail and screamed, "Open the last Cage! Open the last Cage!"

From the final Cage, a dark skinned man covered in tribal tattoos and scars leaped out and onto the Sector floor. He screamed and ranted unrecognizable garble as he ran about on his furry knuckles and beat his chest. The Baboon Bolic's disheveled black hair twirled in the dusty wind as he threw back his head and let out a cackling screech. Inside his mouth was a set of metal sharpened fangs that almost resembled a line of spikes.

"Will somebody please kill that damned Ander?!?" Boull shouted at the top of his lungs.

Tai had snuck into Boull's room and saw the keys on the eating table. He crawled up to the table and quietly grabbed the keys.

Below, the Baboon Bolic bounded forward, on all fours, from across the stadium towards Chase.

Chase closed her fists tight and knelt

down keeping her knuckles firmly planted on the ground. She looked up and stared at the beast surging for her.

Boull was practically falling over the edge of the balcony as he watched in anticipation. He was so involved with the events below him that he did not notice Tai had crawled up to Sam and Eton and unlocked their chains. Tai motioned Sam and Eton to remain quiet and still until his signal.

The Baboon Bolic had gathered a grand amount of momentum by the time he leaped off the ground preparing to pounce, but while the Bolic was mid-air, Chase whipped her arms up and lifted a large thick wall of hard sandy earth up from the ground directly in front of the soaring beast.

The Baboon Bolic smacked right into the wall instantly cracking its skull.

Chase stood up, loosened her fists, and wiggled her fingers. The immense wall immediately dissipated and crumbled to a small pile of dust over the unconscious creature.

The spectators went wild with frenzy as Boull roared with fury. He turned to face his prisoners and saw Tai standing with them.

"What the-" Boull began.

"Now!" Tai screamed as loud as he could.

He grabbed Sam and Eton by the arms and ran toward the door.

Boull turned around and looked back down at Chase. She was standing directly in front of the balcony with her hands closed in fists again and her clay arms pointed at an angle aimed at Boull.

Chase closed her eyes and thought back to when Tai and Chase had first entered the Sector together.

"But, I'm not even sure how I control

this power," she had said.

"I think it relies on your instinct and your mind," Tai had answered. "When I saw you wield the Earth power at the village, you were filled with such passion for your friends' welfare. Focus on that when you step into the fighting arena today. Follow what your mind and will tell you. Trust it. Trust yourself that you can do it."

Chase opened her eyes and refocused her stare from Boull to the clay foundation supporting the balcony up.

Breathing heavily, Chase's clay muscles flexed as she concentrated on the wall underneath Boull's perch. She let out aloud yell as she began to slowly bend her arms with struggle controlling the balcony's composition.

This is the only way, Chase assured herself. *This is the only way we can get out of here. For Eton. For Tai. For Sam.*

With each tiny movement of Chase's command, the wall supporting the balcony began to crack and shake.

Boull looked down at the floor under his feet as it began to split. He fell back, caught off balance. The furniture in his room fell over and the food on his eating table gravitated to the ground. Glasses were breaking, plates were crashing and a candle fell off into a draped curtain starting a small fire.

Chase continued to pull the wall out from under Boull, each one of her arm muscles straining.

The crowd watched in amazement, too stunned to move.

Then, with one final yell and pull, Chase jerked her arms back causing a massive earthquake in the Sector as the wall came tumbling down.

Now realizing that the whole place was going to collapse, the spectators and the guards flew into chaos as they scrambled to get to lower ground before they were buried under the blizzard of falling rocks.

The balcony caved in on itself and drifted downward into a massive pile of rubble. Boull was nowhere to be seen.

Drained from the surge of power she had to muster, Chase collapsed on the ground dazed.

Tai came running out from Cage Two's entrance and lifted her up.

"Come on, champ," Tai said cheeringly. "You've got friends that wish to say, 'thanks.'"

Leaning on Tai's support, Chase rushed back to the Cage holding, down the hallway, and out a side door.

The pair hobbled to their previous hiding place in the tall grasses where Sam and Eton were waiting.

Sam threw her arms around Chase.

"Chase! But, how did you-?"

"There will be plenty of time for that later, Miss," Tai stated. "Right now, we need to get back to the Woodlands. We don't stand a chance of staying hidden in these thin patches of grass. I can assure you, after that last stunt, whatever survivors escape from the Sector ruins will be hot on our trails."

Eton scooped under Chase's other arm and helped her walk, along with Tai, back to the Woodlands border which was about twenty minutes away.

Luckily, the Sector was still caught in a state of confusion by the time the group reached the Woodlands. They continued walking for another thirty minutes before crossing a stream and entering a small cave covered in moss.

Eton and Tai laid Chase on the damp ground.

"Sir?" Eton directed toward Tai.

"Yes? Oh, my name is Taidyn, by the by, but you can call me Tai. You are Chase's friends, I presume."

"Yes. My name is Eton, and this is Sam. Tai, I see you have a sword. Will you come help me cut down and gather some branches with leaves on them? If we can lay enough of them across the entrance of the cave, I can use an Illusion spell that will keep us hidden from the enemies while we rest."

"I most certainly can," Tai answered. "Ladies, we will be right back."

Tai followed Eton out of the cave while Sam sat down beside Chase.

"I don't understand how you're alive," Sam whispered soothingly.

"I don't either, but I am," Chase replied. "Are you okay?"

"Yes. I'm fine. I just need to change out of these ridiculous clothes. I feel so foolish in them."

"I don't know. I like them," Chase joked.

"Oh shush," Sam said sternly as she playfully hit Chase's shoulder.

"Ow!"

Chase winced mockingly as she closed her eyes smiling.

"Be careful. You're hitting someone that just saved your life."

But, Sam was not paying attention to Chase's remark for she had noticed a pale blue light emitting from her hand when she touched

Chase.

Sam overlooked her hand then looked at Chase. She spotted the gash on Chase's cheek from her fight with the Lioness Bolic. Without hesitating, Sam slowly set her hand down over the open wound. Her hand glowed the bright blue light again, and a strange tingling feeling flowed down her arm and through her fingertips.

Chase felt the warming sensation, too, and opened her eyes. Beyond the shimmering light coming from Sam's hand and her own face, Chase could see the amazement in Sam's glistening eyes.

When the glowing stopped, Sam removed her hand and saw that the gash on Chase's face had completely vanished.

Sam's eyes widened as she gasped and covered her mouth with surprise.

"What is it?" Chase questioned curiously.

"Your… cheek. It's healed."

Chase sat up and felt her cheek. She did not feel any blood or sting.

Behind Chase, Sam sat in wonderment.

Weight of the heart… the mind… Sam wondered.

Sam gently traced her lips with her index finger.

"Oh…" she started.

"Sam! This is great!" Chase exclaimed. "You and I both have our powers now. I don't know how because that old guy's 'wise words' still don't make sense to me, but who cares about how we got them? We have them!"

Sam snapped out of her daze and back to Chase's elatedness.

"Right. This will definitely make things easier."

"Or harder," Chase refuted. "That's how

it is in the movies. Once a superhero gains a new power or something, everything goes downhill."

"Well, let's hope that doesn't happen," Sam replied.

Eton and Tai returned dragging several branches of full leafy bushes behind them. They stepped inside the cave and started propping them up to block the entrance with Eton's magic.

After they were done, Tai pulled out Chase's flashlight and turned it on.

"That's better," Tai stated.

"How long will we be staying hidden here?" Eton asked.

"Hopefully not too long," Tai answered. "But, we need to be sure that we aren't being followed back to my village. With the condition Chase is in, we won't be able to fight all those survivors off by ourselves, especially with only one sword. You don't look too good yourself, Eton. Did Boull have you fight?"

"Twice," Eton replied. "But, I'm okay."

Eton walked over to the wall of the cave and whispered, "*Vaniso proncius.*"

The cave shook a little.

"What was that?" Tai asked.

Eton sat down next to Sam.

"It's the Illusion spell. It will make the cave, the leaf barrier, and anything within it invisible. As long as I remain inside the cave, it will look like the cave isn't here."

"Now *that* is my kind of camouflage," Tai smirked. "To be safe we should spend the night. We'll take shifts keeping watch."

Tai pointed the flashlight at Chase.

"That gash on your face… It's gone!"

Chase rubbed her cheek again. Eton looked at Sam who nervously fidgeting with her hair.

"Sam? Did you powers come to you?" Eton asked softly.

"You have powers, too? Go figure," Tai stated. "I *am* in a cave with three Neos."

"Sam?" Eton repeated.

"Yes, they did, but…" Sam hesitated. "But, I'm not sure how they came to be. The important thing is, like Chase mentioned, that I have them though. I can fully heal both you and Chase before we head to Tai's village tomorrow. It will raise our chance of success if we encounter anything."

Eton nodded and smiled. He rested his hand on hers.

"I knew you could do it. You are absolutely lovely."

Tai grinned at the young love.

"Why don't I take the first shift? Sam, you can heal our brave fighters here."

Sam looked at Chase.

"You can take care of Eton first," Chase piped up. "He looks worse than I feel."

Chase stood up and limped over to join Tai at the entrance of the cave. They peered outside at the rain that began to fall.

Sam cleared her throat as she scooted over to Eton. His black shirt was tattered and torn up.

"I need to… umm… touch the skin directly," Sam stuttered blushing.

"Sure. Let me just take off the shirt."

Eton stood up and pulled the raggedy shirt off of him.

"Is that better?"

Sam stood up to his level and nodded nervously. She slowly inched forward and placed her hands on his bruised but still very muscular chest. Though covered in dirt and dried blood, Eton's skin was still smooth and warm to the touch.

Sam's hands quivered as she closed her eyes and the blue healing light returned. The strange buzzing feeling coursed her nerves like a steady electric pulse as she healed Eton's wounds.

When she was done Eton softly said, "You can open your eyes, Sam'ona."

Sam opened her eyes to see Eton's smiling face. She looked him over, and all his bruises and cut marks were gone except for the Quar's stab wound.

"I don't understand. Why didn't this heal as well?"

"Quar's blade was probably cursed. The Healer's Mastery might not heal it, but it's okay. It doesn't hurt," he lied.

Eton took Sam's hands in his.

"Your powers… Remember what I told you that Friar Sulny said to me? He said that you would gain your full Healer's Mastery powers when 'her mind caves under the weight of her heart.' Sam, I hope that the appearance of your powers is a sign that you have finally realized that what you feel for me is the exactly how I feel for you."

Before Sam could answer, Tai turned around and hushed them.

"Quiet. I think I hear something."

The four of them stood silently as they listened to the steady rain fall and crooning breeze sift through the treetops.

Two wolfs appeared on the other side of the stream. Their charcoal coats were matted down by the rain as they sniffed around a few bushes.

Chase watched intently through the leafy

covering.

"This damned rain," one wolf growled.
"It's making the scent hard to follow."

"They probably tread with the path of the
stream to further throw us off," the other
wolf hunter replied.

The wolves howled and ran following the
course of the stream away from the hideout.

"Phew. That was close," Chase sighed with
relief.

When Eton saw Chase relax, he turned to
Sam and said, "Sam, you never answered me on
how you feel."

Sam's eyes shifted from side to side.

"I have to go heal Chase in case we get
discovered, and she has to fight."

Sam withdrew her hands from Eton's
repaired chest and walked to the entrance of
the cave by Tai and Chase.

Eton sighed, picked up his raggedy shirt
and put it back on.

Sam stood behind Chase and said, "I'm
ready to heal you now."

Chase turned around.

"Awesome. I don't have to take my shirt
off, do I?"

"I'll leave you two to your business.
Just come get me when you're done," Tai
lightly stated as he walked to the back of the
cave by Eton. "Maybe Eton can explain to me
exactly what's going on with the three of
you,"

Sam took a deep breath in and gently laid
the palm of her soft hand in the curvature of
Chase's neck. She stroked Chase's cheek with
her thumb as the Healing process began again.

Chase's eyes were always so alive yet
calm. The soft dark coffee color swirled in
them as Chase's gaze silently calmed Sam's.

With each inhalation, Chase took a little
more of Sam's warming blue light in. Chase
raised her hand and turned it over and watched
as the tiny cuts on her knuckles disappeared.

When Chase's body recovered, Chase put
both her hands on Sam's shoulders and smiled.

"I've said it before, and I'll say it
again. Sam, you are absolutely amazing."

Chase pulled Sam in, kissed her on the
cheek, and threw her arms around her, wrapping
Sam in a tight embrace.

Chase whispered, "Thank you, Sam."

Sam returned Chase's hug.

"Well," Chase began as she released Sam
from the hug. "I should grab Tai. Despite your
incredible healing powers, I'm still pretty
tired. Maybe you can find a way to inject
caffeine into those caring hands of yours.
That way, I'll be totally alert when I take
the second shift."

Chase laughed as she walked back to Eton
and Tai.

The rain was falling harder as Sam
crossed her arms and rubbed out the last
shivers in her body while she stared through
the brush of leaves into the dark forest.

Weight of the heart… the mind… she no
longer wondered.

She knew.

Traveling Shadows

Back at the Sector, the clay rubble lied still as the dusty winds swirled around it. The once grand stadium now stood like an ancient ruin in the sand. The eerie echoes of cheers and applause still haunted the crushed hallways and arena seats. The only thing that was still prominent about the titanic relic was the sun beating down with its violent rays of heat and light during the day.

The surviving spectators had fled back to their villages in the Woodlands and Savannahs. What was left of the guards remained at the Sector's fallen site. They had constructed a small tent out of Savannah plant leaves and pieces of wood to shield themselves from the horrible hot streams of sunshine that had been scolding their tired backs.

Another nighttime had fallen, and the heat sank into the horizon with the sun so the air was chilled by a refreshing breeze and a comforting starlight. The guards discussed what to do next around a small fire.

"I told you we should have gone to the Ghondro Village with that group of Gazelles. I hear that their oasis is filled with good-looking women. I'd kill for that right now. It's better than being stuck in this place with the lot of you," a grizzly wolf muttered.

"I don't know," a dirty, bald, young man with facial piercings replied back. "I still think we should look for Boull."

"Boull's dead!" the wolf shot back angered. "You saw what that Ander did. There's no way that he's alive. His cocky bones are now the foundation to that massive pile of rocks over there."

The weary group looked over to where Boull's balcony once sat proudly over the arena floor. All that remained was a heaping pile of stone barely shining under the moon's subtle glow.

The wolf continued, "All we have left is ourselves. Without Boull, a new leader needs to be elected. I think because I have had the most fighting experience, I should be it."

A loud debate rose from the crew as they began to bicker about who should be the new rightful commander.

The fighting drew their attention away from Boull's grave as a few rocks began to wiggle and shake. A powerful fist broke through the clay mess and frantically pushed more and more boulders from the pile. After a few moments, a beaten down, angry Boull crawled out from his dusty tomb.

With only the upper half of his body revealed, Boull collapsed on the pile coughing. His henchmen were still too busy arguing over Boull's position to notice that their leader had risen back from the supposed dead.

Heaving in and out, Boull saw a shadow appear on the rocky surface he took rest on.

"I was wondering when you'd show your ugly face again," Boull panted.

He looked up and before him stood a tall figure dressed in a black cloak holding a black iron staff with a ruby seated at its pinnicle. A hood covered the stranger's face.

"What happened here, Boull? When I endowed the Sector to you, I had a certain set of expectations from you. From the look of things, you seem to have not met them."

Boull coughed again.

"Listen, you old bag, this wasn't my fault. I did as I was told. I kept every damned Bolic beast you sent here and put them to fight. I don't know why you even spend time making those vile things. They're uncontrollable."

"That may be true," the hooded stranger hissed. "But, they are necessary for the grander goal."

"Is that why you outsourced your experiment's results to a legion not in the Shadow Force?" Boull questioned as he started pulling his legs out from the rocks' heavy weight. "Why *are* you keeping this off the grid, away from that King Ceros of yours?"

"I needed to know that they worked before I unveiled the project to the good king, but seeing the damage they have caused here, I think now would be a good time to exhibit the product. I suppose your actions weren't a complete failure after all, Boull."

The shadowy figure turned and started to leave.

"The Bolics didn't do this," Boull grunted as he freed himself completely and sat cracking his neck. "I know you'd like to think those insane creatures had the capability to conjure a destructive plan like this, but I have to burst your elatedness."

The figure stopped.

"Then who, pray tell, did?"

Boull smiled slyly.

"What do you have to offer me in return? I *am* the mighty Boull, and no one gets anything from me for free."

Boull smiled again, cockily, as the cloaked figure turned back around and pointed its staff at Boull's face.

"Adurosi cutonif," the figure whispered.

In an instant, Boull felt his the right side of his face begin to burn. He immediately grabbed his scolding face but felt no flames. His flesh was simply searing away by the second. He gritted his teeth in pain and curled up in the fetal position.

The stranger lowered his staff and walked up to Boull who was wallowing on the pile of rocks in agony. The tip of the scepter made its way to Boull's tender and scarred cheek. Boull whimpered at the very touch of it.

"I don't think you're in a position to make any demands, Boull," the cloaked figure stated coolly. "Let me ask again. If the Bolics didn't do this, then who or what did?"

Boull cringed as the staff pressed deeper into his open wound.

"It was some damned girl. An Ander with magical powers. I've never seen anything like it."

"An Ander?"

"Yeah! She could control the rocks with her hands. The Sector fell like the walls were her slaves."

"Was she alone?"

"No. She came here looking for two fox prisoners that I had captured from the Woodlands. I don't know why though. Seemed like the male fox could take care of himself. He was using Illusion magic, and the girl was just as annoying."

The stranger eased its magical stave up from Boull's face, and Boull sighed in relief.

"Now, that wasn't so hard was it, Boull?"

Boull sat back up and winced as he touched his sore and inflamed eyebrow. The burn had extended to all parts of the right side of his face. Even his right eye was so badly burned that Boull could no longer see out of it.

"Is that all you want, Quar?" Boull retorted.

The figure drew back its hood revealing Quar's face, but it was not the long, wrinkly face most others knew him by. His drab beard remained; however, his stature was taller and much younger. His thin frame was now fuller with sculpted muscles, and his blackened teeth were instead a pearly white. He stared up at the silvery moon.

"The foxes… Are they still alive?"

"Yeah. They managed to escape before this place crumbled to the ground. They're probably with that Ander, or whatever you call it."

"Do you know where they went?"

"I have a feeling, but I'm not going after them if that's what you're implying."

"The Mighty Boull's afraid?" Quar mocked.

Surprisingly, Boull laughed.

"I *am* mighty, but I'm not stupid. If you want them, you can go get them yourself."

"I would, but I have other things I need to attend to which is why I have a new proposal for you."

Quar put forth his staff again, but this time jabbed the ruby end into Boull's chest. Boull hacked up blood as his body began to fill with a heavy dark feeling. The swirling smoke of the Shadow Force slowly wrapped its greedy and probing spirals around Boull's body.

Boull's muscles pulsed and grew larger with every breath he took in. The moon's light tried to penetrate Boull's eyes as he geared his head back, eyes wide open in shock, but the swelling blackness that consumed his dilated pupils swallowed any light that tried to shine.

Quar removed his cane again and turned away for the final time to retreat to the shadows behind a cracked clay wall.

Before leaving, Quar whispered, "Find them."

Quar disappeared into the darkness as Boull rose, chest fuller and wider, and his stature more looming than ever. He smiled, licked his elongated fangs, and made his way to the quarreling congregation in the distance.

Much further north in the Savannahs, Ceros had summoned Ashos up to the Great Hall's dining area.

The Great Hall was no longer a place filled with merriment and cheer. Ceros and his Shadow Force presence had created a dreary and gloomy atmosphere around the quarters. The marble floors no longer shined but was marked with grime from the mud-covered feet of guards, who did not care about the beautiful art of the building, and trodden prisoners. Even the walls were soaked in darkness as they lie quiet in the morning sun instead of shimmering with dew. The tall grasses barely moved in the wind's presence, and the ponds' once clear waters had been poisoned by a dull murkiness.

Despite the dramatic downfall in the loveliness of the Great Hall's resources, the lands still provided Ceros with bountiful meals and luxuries fit for a king.

Ashos walked wearily into the dining hall.

He was no longer lavished in bright colored robes and brilliant exquisite clothes but was covered in old, musty, and tattered rags. Ceros laughed at the sight of the once magnificent Lion King as he was chained down to the floor in front of Ceros' tall black iron throne at the head of the room.

"Twenty years later and the sight of you as a slave still makes me smile," Ceros sneered.

Ashos spoke up, "You will pay for your crimes, Ceros, whether it be here or in the afterlife."

Ceros cackled again.

"Do you really believe that to be so? Look around you, Ashos! What do you see? I see *my* reign, *my* rule, *my* way. You're as delirious as you are kind if you think that I will ever fall."

"Everyone has a weakness," Ashos continued. "Even you."

"We'll see about that."

"You're bored, aren't you?" Ashos insulted.

"What?"

"Why else would you bring me up here? Just to trade words with? Your reign is starting to fall, Ceros. I hear the conversations that roam the prison cells. That Shadow Force you claim to be undefeatable is slowly falling. More and more coalitions rise by the day. Eventually, one, or maybe more, will gain the senses to go against you."

Ceros stood up and cast a black sphere of Shadow Force power at Ashos. The dark orb struck Ashos in the chest, knocking the good man to his knees.

Ashos just snickered and wheezed, "You may be able to possess fear and anger, Ceros, but you cannot possess free will. In time, you will lose."

Enraged by Ashos' smooth and collected comeback, Ceros launched himself up from his throne and landed directly in front of Ashos, who remained on his knees. Ceros made a clean jab across Ashos' face which delivered him fully to the ground.

With the power of the *Prima Umbros* driving Ceros' attack, Ashos lay stunned on the ground with the wind knocked out of him. Pleased, Ceros brushed his hands and returned to his throne. He sat down and picked up a wine glass.

"No… I just won," Ceros whispered to himself.

Just as Ceros took a confident sip of his wine, Quar emerged from the shadows behind some gray curtains next to the throne, back in his elderly disguise.

"Your highness," Quar stated respectfully as he bowed.

"Quar, you've come at an excellent time. I was just about to give Ashos a whipping in attempt to knock some sense into him. Leveel!"

Leveel walked into the dining hall from around a corner wearing the Bear Sovereignty armor. As he continued to walk to the fallen Ashos, Leveel pulled a long leather whip from his belt and snapped it harshly on the tarnished floor.

"King Ceros, before you put Ashos completely out, perhaps you will be interested in what I have to show you. I think Ashos will be equally delighted in my display," Quar said snidely.

Curious about his magician's scheme, Ceros raised up his hand to halt Leveel from striking Ashos.

"Proceed, Quar."

Quar bowed again and ordered Leveel, "Go to the dungeons and bring me back an innocent Neo and an innocent Ander. Any will do."

Leveel looked to Ceros for approval. Ceros nodded, and Leveel went back around the corner and down the stairs to the dungeons to carry out Quar's demands.

"What great discovery have you made, Quar, that I need to sacrifice *two* potential servants for?"

Limping on the, now, rugged cane, Quar made his way down the small flight of stairs that held Ceros' throne above the rest of the dining hall floor to Ashos who had regained his strength and was standing.

"My king," Quar started. "For years, I have been working on creating the perfect soldier."

"That's absurd. Everyone in Pangea knows that I am the strongest and most feared creature that walks this earth."

"That may be true, King Ceros, but you know as well as I do that there is always room for improvement. I don't mean to offend by speaking the truth, but I heard what Ashos said to you moments ago, and I am afraid that he is right. As powerful as the Shadow Force is, it, like all forces in nature, is in a constant state of chaos trying to find order. That being said, there will be those that fight against us, and I'm not just talking about the Light Alliances, for those who share a common enemy may become friends even if light and dark must blend together. For that, we must be ready. Better yet, we must strike first."

"And these so called 'perfect soldiers' you have created are the solution to this?"

"I would not call them perfect yet, my king, but I have made much improvement since when I first began."

At that moment, Leveel returned leading

two prisoners behind him. One was a dark red male phoenix whose wing was badly broken as it dragged the floor. The other was a male Ander. He was a teenager and scraggly thin from malnourishment. Leveel pushed them down to the ground in between Ceros' throne and where Quar stood, hunched over next to Ashos.

Quar continued, "In battle, your strength is irrefutable. When you take your Neo form, your mighty paws and immaculate punches make all before you tremble, and when you are in your human form your swiftness and skills with a sword are majestic as well as victorious."

Ceros sipped his wine graciously accepting Quar's flattering words.

"But, what if you had the ability to take both forms as once?" Quar carried on. "What if you were able to control when and what parts of each form you wished to use at the same time? Then, you would truly be unstoppable."

"Interesting idea, Quar."

"Let me show you the reality of such an idea."

Quar drew a small knife from his heavy black cloak and hobbled behind the wounded phoenix. He cut a deep gash into its back. The phoenix flinched in pain but was too wounded to fight back. Instead, it lie quietly on the ground.

Quar then placed a small vial next to the bleeding laceration and let a sufficient amount of phoenix blood pool into the vial before removing it.

Leveel was busy restraining the young Ander. The poor boy was fighting helplessly against Leveel's steady hold and the chains that bound his hands and feet.

"Pull back his head," Quar ordered Leveel.

Leveel obeyed and forcefully pulled back the Ander's head to reveal a smooth clean patch of skin under his jaw line. Quar slowly made an incision. A rush of blood oozed from the mark and flowed down the Ander's neck. The excessive amount of dirt that clung to his skin governed the bloody drip like rocks in a surging river.

Before the Ander could lose too much blood, Quar held the vial next to the Ander's neck and poured the phoenix blood into the jaw line cut.

"Apply pressure to the wound," Quar further demanded.

Leveel once again obeyed and held his large hand over the Ander's neck, pressing hard. The Ander tried to scream, but blood curdled in the back of his throat, so all he could do was spit up the thick red fluid.

Ashos stood, appalled by the sight that was being presented before him. He stared helplessly into the Ander's eyes. Tears began to descend down the lad's bruised cheeks and the saltiness of his weeping stung the lesion under Leveel's hand.

Quar put the emptied vial back into the hidden pockets of his mangy cloak and pulled out another vial with a muddy blue liquid inside. Quar moved Leveel's hand aside and poured the mysterious content into the gash. The Ander squirmed as his flesh sizzled. Then, Quar raised his old oak cane high into the air.

"*Inclinio ferra tu nox et silentu luxcio*!" Quar shouted.

The Ander pulled away and shoved Leveel so forcefully that Leveel flew into the air, slamming his back against the stony wall. The Ander screamed in writhing pain as he began to pull the hair from his head, muttering a slew of nonsensical jabber. His eyes shook in their sockets while he twitched his head from left to right as if he were no longer controlled by his brain. His arms flew outward as he began to flap them up and down. As he did so, tiny dark crimson feathers began to sprout through the surface of his skin and became a full set of wings in a matter of seconds. The morphing continued as the Ander's eyes changed from a somber brown to a neon green, and sharp talons replaced his bare feet.

Luckily, the chains that bound the Ander's feet were still intact as the newly formed Bolic tried to fly away.

By this time, Leveel had recovered from the surprising blow and grabbed the chains. The Phoenix Bolic cried out with a shrill screech as Leveel pulled it back to the ground and thrust his sword into the crazed beast's viscera. The Bolic snorted and stopped flapping its wings as its head crashed to the marble floor defeated.

Ceros and Ashos watched completely stunned.

Quar broke the silence.

"Granted, there are still improvements to be made, rest assured, my king, that I can give you the most defining power there is. We can create an army of Bolics that will sweep over Pangea and put it completely back into your hands."

"Bolics? Is that what you call them?" Ceros responded.

"Yes."

"Are they tamable?"

"They're rambunctious when they first change, but with enough discipline, the Bolics tend to listen better."

"And you know this how?" Ceros further interrogated.

"I've been working on this for some time. I wanted to make my presentation the best it could be for your highness."

"Though the transformation is impressive, Quar," Ceros continued. "The lack of formality and control of these… Bolics is quite alarming. How are you sure that you can cure the dysfunctions in your enchantments?"

"Every tweak I make has brought me progress. Trust me, my king. The Bolics have come a long way since the beginning of my trials. The Shadow Force takes time to win over a subject, and even then, the possibility of returning to the Light remains. With this potion and spell I've made, you will have the ability to create Darkness in an instant… forever and unchangeable. I only have one more concern though."

"And what is that?" Ceros demanded.

"I have only been able to bind the blood in one direction. For a reason unknown, when I try to combine the blood of an *Ander* to a Neo under the Shadow Force, the subject always…"

"Spit it out, Quar."

"Dies within hours, my king."

"Well then, I hope that you find a solution to the problem as fast as possible, Quar. You know once my palate for power is tempted, I have very little patience for its satisfaction."

"Yes, King Ceros," Quar said as he bowed. "Once I have the perfected Fusioning potion for Neos, I will bless only your lips with it, and you shall become the divine. It will be beyond magic, beyond the *Prima Umbros,* and beyond life itself."

"You're a monster!" Ashos loudly

interjected. "How dare you dominate the spirit's will?"

Remembering Ashos' rude comments to him earlier, Ceros spoke with much relish.

"Quar, your discovery is bewitching indeed. I condone your actions. Feel free to access any means necessary to complete the task. You will keep me informed of any new progress?"

"Of course, your majesty," Quar said humbly as he bowed before his king.

"You're both mad!" Ashos shouted in fury. "You cannot do this!"

Annoyed with Ashos presence, Ceros motioned for Leveel to take Ashos back down to the prisoner cells.

As Leveel unlocked Ashos' chains from the hook in the ground, Quar leaned over to Ashos' ear and whispered, "Don't be coy, Ashos. You know very well that the mixing of bloods *is* possible. Your prophecy's presence here proves it so."

Ashos' eyes widened at the news but was shoved away before he could organize his thoughts and respond to Quar's remark.

Quar returned to Ceros' side as Ceros poured himself another round of wine.

"You must not tell the Council about this, my king."

"You're right. Such power will pose a threat to them. I feel that they are not to be trusted, for they might have their own aim in mind. I don't want anyone else securing the power before me. Let me handle the Council and continue to report directly to me."

"Yes, your majesty. I will disclose any new findings from my trials as soon as they happen. Is there anything else you need from me?"

"Not for the moment, Quar," Ceros replied as he swirled the dark cardinal colored wine in his glass. "You may leave me."

Quar bowed and backed into the shadows of the curtains from whence he made his entrance.

When he reemerged from the gloomy shadows, he was no longer standing in the Great Hall's dining area. Instead, he materialized in Friar Sulny's old chambers.

Quar had changed the friar's room into his own conjuring chambers. The cabinets, where hundreds of ancient history books were once stored, had now been stacked with a variety of potion bottles, jars of fermented organs, exotic plants, and tons of dried up herbs. The table that held many a tutoring sessions and sampled blueberry pies was covered with black ashes as Quar's mixing pot sat in the middle of it surrounded by dusty dark magic books.

A set of prisoner chains had been installed on the side wall across from the fireplace for anchoring down the tested Bolic subjects. Large claw and nail marks had been carved into the dark stony walls and the floor, markings of the shackled prisoners.

Nearby, a set of poisonous knives lay quietly in a cherry wood box waiting for a misbehaved Bolic so they could sail the air and administer their lethal toxins into the creature's veins.

Tonight, though, Quar had a much calmer Neo in his possession.

Quar sat, pulled out a jug of aged rum from a cabinet, and took a large swig from it.

"You know something Friar Sulny? You have been quite the headache to me these past years."

Quar turned around and glared at the old

friar.

Friar Sulny's age was definitely prominent in his surface features. His eyes looked as tired and weak as his fragile body felt. His once distinguished white beard was knotted and filthy from the poor living conditions of his cell, and his back was badly scarred from the countless whippings Quar had cursed him with. The only thing Friar Sulny had managed to keep control over was his mind. Quar had continuously tried to penetrate Friar Sulny's mind to discover his secret. Twenty years had passed, but Quar was unsuccessful.

"I should be saying the same to you, Quar," Friar Sulny shot back calmly as he leaned his back against the wall. "With all that prying you have done in my head, no wonder the very sight of you makes me nauseated."

Quar simply chuckled and took another drink from his rum.

"I truly have enjoyed this game you and I have been playing, but I hate to say that the game is over. I know that the Healer's Mastery has returned to Pangea."

Friar Sulny had no rally to counter Quar's statement.

"I knew you'd be speechless," Quar hissed, pleased by the friar's reaction. "Even though I would have preferred to obtain the knowledge by cracking that lovely head of yours, I'll still take the win graciously."

Quar waited for Friar Sulny to speak, but he did not. Friar Sulny sat silently on the floor.

"Playing ignorant won't throw me off course, but perhaps I shall throw you a bone that will surely dumbfound you. I also know about the Ander."

"What Ander?" Friar Sulny finally responded.

"The Ander that can control the earth."

Friar Sulny shut his eyes realizing that Quar had discovered Chase's existence, yet a wave of comfort washed over him as he was consoled that the prophecy's child had returned safely to Pangea. A tiny flare of hope began to sprout in Friar Sulny's heart, but Quar did not notice.

"Ah! There's the response I was looking for," Quar said proudly. "I'm surprised you managed to hide that so well from me, but I suppose that it is harder to find a door that one does not know exists."

Quar set the jug of rum on the table, rested his cane against a chair and limped over to the shackled yet calm Friar Sulny. His eyes were still closed as he began to meditate knowing what Quar was about to do next.

Quar stood over Friar Sulny, reached out his hands and chanted, *"Eximus mensana."*

Friar Sulny's body shot upward from the floor in a quick violent reaction as his head stopped neatly in between Quar's hands. As soon as Quar's hands touched Friar Sulny's temples, Quar's eyes became clouded by a ghostly whiteness as he began to sort through the friar's mind once more.

Friar Sulny had had twenty years of practice at avoiding Quar's metal attacks, but tonight, the rejuvenated promise of Solaris' return guided Friar Sulny's cognitive defense to be stronger than ever before.

After minutes of psychological pummeling, Quar released Friar Sulny disappointedly. Friar Sulny's body dropped to the cold hard ground with a thud. His hip hit the ground first.

Rubbing his stricken hip, Friar Sulny asked unnerved, "Couldn't find what you were looking for, Quar?"

Quar hobbled back to the table and grabbed his cane.

"Maybe not now, but don't get too confident, Friar. I have eyes everywhere on Pangea. Even when you think you're not being watched, you are."

Quar picked up his rum and took a third swill of the biting liquid.

"Because no one can escape their shadow."

"You should be one to talk, Quar. How many years has it been? And your heart has not yet forgiven that night-"

"Silence!" Quar demanded as he struck Friar Sulny across the face.

"It is what keeps you from passing," Friar Sulny continued after licking blood from his cut lip. "You will never find what you *truly* seek if you do not exonerate your spirit. Discontinue the obsession with these Bolic creatures. They will not save you."

"I don't need saving, Friar. You know exactly what I need, what your mind needs to give me."

"I shall die before I do so."

Quar inched forward and raised his hands again.

"Don't make requests that I enjoy fulfilling so much, Friar. All in good time, anyway."

Eton stared across the fire at Sam and Chase. The two young ladies laughed with Kalough and some of the other women who were busy mashing potatoes in large stone bowls.

The four comrades had made their way back to Tai's village without being seen. A large dinner feast was set into motion with the word that Boull, his gang, and the Sector had been taken down.

Eton sat on a log sharpening a sword that Tai had given him.

"Yup. Those two are beautiful ladies in their own special way, aren't they mate?" Tai asked cheerily as he sat down beside Eton. "They're so different from one another yet, I can't help but feel a sense of similarity between them. It's almost like they're one person… that connected, yes?"

Eton replied curtly, "They're good friends. Sam has taken care of Chase her entire life."

Just then, a twinge of flaming pain pulsed in Eton's wound. He looked down and peeled back his shirt to look at it. Just like before, the unhealed cut blazed red. Eton massaged it until it stopped.

"True, but what I'm talking about is something more, and it's catching. Can't put my finger upon it. To be honest, I'm not sure they even know it exists, but those around them can feel it. Look at my Kalough talking with them. I've never seen her so relaxed."

"Couldn't it be because Boull is no longer a threat?" Eton examined.

Tai chuckled.

"I suppose. Perhaps I am thinking too much into things. Kalough has always said that I overanalyze situations."

Tai nudged Eton in the side.

"But, it doesn't take a wizard to see that *you* hold a particular set of feelings for the young Sam."

Eton held up his sword in front of the firelight. The bold flames reflected gallantly on the blade. Then he set the weapon on his lap.

"I've been in love with Sam all my life."

"Does she know?"

"I told her when we were in the cave, after we escaped the Sector. Those healing powers she has… We were told that they would only develop when she realized a true love in her heart."

"And you think this love is for you?"

"I don't see how it couldn't be," Eton replied confidently. "I've felt a stronger spark between us ever since we were reunited some days ago. I've felt her body flutter in my arms as my heart quakes in her stare. It's indisputable that she feels the same way for me. I just don't know why she denies it so when I confront her about it."

"Take it from a man of my age, Eton," Tai reassured. "Women, Neo and Ander alike, are complicated creatures. There's an endless network of mayhem in those brains of theirs. You think you figure out one thing, but in a blink of an eye, you'll realize that you were completely wrong.

I made over a dozen attempts in asking Kalough's hand in marriage before she finally said 'yes.' Maybe it was because my good looks and undying charm won her over or because she was sick of my whining. I don't know. I don't ask. I won the girl, and that, my dear friend, is what matters. Give Sam time. Maybe that's all she really needs."

Tai patted Eton on the back and stood up.

"Well, Eton, if you're finished with your sword, I need help gathering more wood for the cooking pit. We have a large pig to roast for the special occasion."

Eton stood up, as well, and followed Tai into the dense Woodlands forests as Sam and Chase finished mashing the last of their potatoes.

"That's the last of mine," Sam said proudly. "Thank you again for allowing us to stay here before we leave. Your village is lovely."

Kalough smiled as she continued to grind at the potato in her stone bowl with a heavy smooth rock.

"It's not a problem. It's the least we can do for you after you rid this part of the land of such an immense evil. I'm sure the people of our village will sleep easier now, and my husband will have less to worry about when he roams the forests for loners. That, in turn, makes me worry less."

"Is there anything else you need us to do for dinner?" Chase chimed in as she wiped her hands on the legs of her pants.

"Chase! Don't wipe your hands on your clean pants," Sam scolded. "Kalough was gracious enough to give us a new set of clothes when we arrived here."

"Sorry, Kalough," Chase apologized.

Kalough laughed.

"Do not worry, Chase. Why don't the two of you go into my hut and check on the gravy? Chase, the tub should be filled with clean water. You can rub out the potato grub with one of the rags."

Chase nodded.

Sam and Chase stood up and made their way into Tai and Kalough's single room hut. The fireplace was burning at a steady low height, and Kalough's famous simmering gravy infused its robust aroma with the smells of other cooking dishes in the village.

Sam walked over to the pot and stirred the gravy slowly. Chase dragged one of the wooden stools over to the tub and sat down. She picked up a thin orange rag and dabbed it in the water.

"So, when do we plan on leaving?" Chase questioned as she began rubbing the potato out of her pants.

"Early tomorrow morning," Sam replied. "Tai said that he would lead us south to a ship that can take us across the Brevi Ocean. It's a small body of water that hooks to a channel in the Great Crossings. It might be a safer way to travel. Tai said that there are less Shadow Force enemies on the waters, and it'll make our journey quicker."

"By how much?"

"A week and a couple days, if we're lucky."

"Great," Chase muttered unenthusiastically.

Sam finished stirring the gravy and tapped the spoon on the edge of the iron pot as the last drippings of gravy fell back into the steaming mixture. She walked over to the wall next to Chase and leaned against it. Chase was still cleaning off the last bit of potato off her pants.

"Chase?"

"Yeah, Sam?"

Sam rubbed her arm nervously. She did not want to discuss the matter which had been an unsettling thought for the past few days.

"Do you remember what happened back when Boull first attacked us?"

"In the woods?"

"Yes."

Chase dropped the rag back into the tub of water and swiveled around on the stool to face Sam.

"There! It was like it never happened," Chase said proudly, showing off her cleaned pants.

Sam smiled and knelt down in front of Chase. She plunged her hand into the tub of water, retrieved the rag, and rung it out.

"There's a small beet stain on your shirt as well."

Sam began to dab at Chase's shirt neckline with the wet rag.

"You know what, Sam?" Chase continued. "I actually have been thinking about that night."

Sam paused and took a deep but subtle breath in before replying, "You have?"

"Yeah. Granted, I was pretty much out of it, I know you kissed me right before Boull stabbed me."

Chase stopped Sam's hand from cleaning and held it. Sam felt her heart beating faster, so she diverted her eyes to the floor.

Chase proceeded, "Sam, I've been thinking about that kiss a lot."

Sam felt her face become as hot as the flames flickering under the pot of gravy. She prayed that Chase could not see the sudden redness that washed over her cheeks.

"At first, I was really confused. I mean, I've never seen you act so impulsively," Chase started.

"Me too," Sam replied hesitantly. "I don't know what I was thinking."

"Don't apologize. I'm really glad you did it."

Sam removed her eyes' stare from the ground and met Chase's easy-going gaze.

"Really?"

"Yeah, because without that kiss I really don't think I would have gained my powers. You know how Eton said something about realizing the truth of the heart?"

Sam slowly nodded. She swallowed the choked up silence in the back of her throat as she attempted to settle her panicked breathing.

"I've been thinking a lot about it, and I think when you kissed me, I was instantly reminded of Cia and the love that I have with her even though we're literally worlds apart now. That, and maybe the fact that it was my birthday must have triggered my Neo self to reactivate."

Sam's heart dropped to the pit of her stomach.

Was it relief? Or was it disappointment?

Sam was not sure, but she removed her hand from Chase's and finished wiping the stain out of Chase's shirt.

Chase continued, "You told me right before we came to Pangea that Cia really did love me. I must have been in denial, but I guess I'm not anymore. Guess you really don't know what you have until it's gone. How cliché!"

"That must have been it," Sam whispered. "I'm glad you figured it out, and… Happy Birthday, Chase."

"Thanks. I hope you can figure out how your powers came to be, too. It had to have

been before you kissed me because I think
that's when you first healed me. Speaking of,
do you think that your Healer's Mastery could
have 'healed' the stain out of my clothes?"
Chase joked.

Sam forced a smile and wiped off the
final remain of smudged beet juice.

"I highly doubt it."

Just then, a loud cluster of screams rose
from outside. Sam and Chase looked at each
other worriedly and stood up to peer through
the small window at the commotion outside.

"You're kidding me," Chase whispered to
herself.

Boull was standing in the middle of the
village behind the central fire. He was in his
Neo black bear form which had also grown
exponentially larger after Quar's Shadow Force
enhancement. His pearly white fangs glistened
in the spasms of the fire, and his claws
looked to be composed of a dark titanium
metal. His sturdy hind legs supported his
tall, matted, and muscular body. Chest stuck
out, Boull was standing at an incredible ten
feet or more.

"How is he alive?" Chase softly wondered
aloud.

"I'm not sure," Sam whispered back. "But,
he looks bigger."

Boull roared loudly as the Ander women
and children ran into their huts to hide. A
handful of the male Anders and the two Falcon
Neos came rushing out to face Boull, holding
long spears and sharpened swords out in front
of them. Boull just laughed.

"You think those measly tools will harm
me? I am the mighty Boull! Your protectors are
pathetic."

Despite Boull's announcement, the Ander

men threw their spears at Boull, but Boull neatly blocked every shot with his enormous paws. They charged him with swords, but the blades' cuts only provided microscopic pain to Boull's thick skin as he thwarted them off before too much damage could be inflicted. Even when the Neos changed into their Falcon forms and tried to claw at Boull, his tough skin made the attacks feel like mild irritations.

After knocking the Anders and the Neos to the ground, Boull yelled, "I know you're here! You know I didn't come all this way to fight weaklings like these! Come out, and fight me, Ander!"

Chase looked at Sam and whispered, "Sam, I have to go out there."

"You can't," she argued. "It wasn't that long ago that you fought. Even though your wounds were healed, we don't even know if your powers have been fully charged back. Plus, you're skills are still raw. Something's not right. Look at him. You can't go out there. He'll kill you."

"If I don't, how many more villagers will get hurt or die? I can't risk that. If this is the kind of evil I have to prepare for, I have to start somewhere."

Chase snuck another look outside at Boull and took a deep breath in.

"Sam, stay in here."

"No-" Sam started, but it was too late.

Chase had opened up the hut door and walked outside to confront Boull. Sam sat petrified, staring out the small window. Chase has always been bold; it was one of the things Sam loved about her, but even this was startling. Chase had been cast into a new world, developed strange powers, and told that she was meant to save the world.

How does she do it? The confidence… Sam thought as she focused in on the soon-to-be battle outside.

"Ah! There she is!" Boull presented. "You know what? I never got your name."

"Chase."

"Chase, eh? That's what I'll be doing to all your Ander friends when I take care of you. I'm always hungry after a dual."

"I would think you learned your lesson the first time," Chase jested. "Or maybe all the rocks that hit your head really made you think that you can fight me."

Boull roared with laughter. The thick black bristles on his back rose with amusement.

"And what hit *your* head to make you think that you can talk to the mighty Boull like that? I can smell the fear on you even though you talk tough. Admit it. That stunt you pulled back at the Sector was pure luck."

Chase clenched both her hands into fists, immediately transforming her upper extremities into stone.

"Why don't we find out?" Chase retorted, somewhat taken aback by her belief in Boull's last comment.

She really was not sure if she could conjure up that kind of focus, let alone strength, to command another move like that.

Chase tried to stall the fight a little longer and said, "What happened to your guards? They left you after your defeat?"

"They were sacrificed for the greater good," Boull replied. "This Shadow Force raging inside of me demands a lot more fuel than I'm used to consuming."

Chase's eyes widened at the realization

of Boull's actions.

"That's disgusting," Chase muttered.

"Necessary," Boull snarled back.

With that, Boull reached down into the large fire pit and picked up a bunch of the burning logs in his massive paws as if they were feathers. In a single heave, he cast the logs onto the huts' wooden roofs. The roofs instantly went up into flames as the resulting smoke propelled the inhabitants to flee from within.

Chase turned around to look at the horrid scene. A fire log had landed on Tai and Kalough's hut.

"Sam!" Chase shouted as she released the form of her fists, changing her arms back to flesh and bone.

But, Boull would not allow Chase to rescue her friend. He abruptly transformed back into his human form and leapt across what was left of the burning fire. He touched down right behind Chase, grabbed her shirt, and flung her backwards into a tree.

Chase hit the tree with such force that several branches and leaves were set free and fell to the ground. Chase slid down to the ground feeling splinters enter her back.

Chase thought the assault should have killed her or at least knock her unconscious, but it did not. She recovered and stood back up. She closed her hands again, allowing her fists to turn her arms into the granite weapons she used before. Boull slowly strutted her way.

"Like I said," Boull repeated. "Pure luck. Now, I'm going to make you wish that you never insulted or embarrassed the mighty Boull in the first place!"

Boull lunged forward to make his second

attack but stopped midway and let out a terribly growl.

He winced as he pulled out an arrow from his right shoulder blade. Fuming, he snapped it in half and turned around.

Standing in front of his burning hut, Tai stood holding a long bow. He had already repositioned himself for another sailing attack. Tai let the arrow fly, but now that Boull was aware of his offender, he keenly snatched the whizzing arrow as it flew toward his face and swatted it as if it were a tiny insect.

Seeing that Tai could be in trouble, Chase slammed her fists into the ground and closed her eyes.

Think, think, think… be creative. Focus.

As Boull started to walk toward Tai, he noticed that the earth beneath his feet was slowly sinking. The more he struggled to raise his foot out of the descending dirt, the more his legs were engulfed.

Boull continued to sink until his legs were completely submerged into the ground. Chase lifted her fists out of the ground and opened her eyes.

Seeing that her quicksand idea had worked, Chase ran over to Tai.

"We don't have much time," Tai said quickly. "You, Sam, and Eton must go. Eton has already gotten Sam and is waiting for you at the stable in back."

"I can't leave you and the others," Chase refuted. "Boull said that he was filled with the Shadow Force now. He could be unstoppable."

Everywhere around them, fiery roofs were caving in as the Ander women and children ran around helping the elderly to the outskirts of the village which were untouched by the vigorous flames. The Ander guards were assisting them, while three ran to Tai's side awaiting orders. They each had a bow and their own set of arrows.

"Don't worry about us," Tai reassured. "I've got enough help now to take care of Boull, but you need to get out of here so you can save us from the eminent darkness that reigns over Pangea. Without you and without Sam, nothing will be worthwhile. You have to go."

Chase looked over Tai's shoulder at Boull. Boull was roaring with irritation and outrage. A possessing blackness began to swell in his eyes as he started to change back into his black bear self again. The heavy earth started to crack around the sudden transformation.

Chase shook Tai's hand and said, "Thank you. I won't forget this. You're the bravest guy I've ever met, Tai."

"And you will be the bravest Neo this world has ever seen," Tai replied back, a smile smeared across his face.

Chase turned around and ran to the back of the village to meet up with Sam and Eton.

Tai faced Boull and loaded another arrow into his bow.

"Okay boys, we've got to give this one all we've got. The future of Pangea depends on it."

Tai let the first arrow free, and it nailed Boull square in the left arm. Boull roared as the final changes to his Neo self had emerged.

Boull ripped through the earth's surface and pulled himself out of Chase's trap.

"Keep him distracted while I make my

move!" Tai commanded as he fired another arrow at Boull.

This time, he hit Boull's right back paw. Boull growled at the annoyance.

Tai's fellow archers began shooting arrows at Boull as the angry black bear made his charge toward them on all four. Tai unloaded his arrows to his friends, unsheathed his sword, and ran forward.

Boull was too busy knocking away the rainstorm of arrows that he was not able to react quick enough to Tai's slide under him and the jabbing of his sword upward into Boull's left shoulder capsule, just barely missing his heart.

Boull roared and knocked Tai aside like a piece of meat. Tai rolled on the ground gathering a collection of cuts and bruises on his body.

Tai managed to stand back up, but as he did, he realized that he had collected more than just tiny cuts and bruises from Boull's toss. Tai winced and stared down at his chest. A vast amount of blood was escaping four gash marks and dripped down the front of his white shirt.

With Tai's sword still lodged in his shoulder capsule, Boull continued to thwart off the remaining arrows that attempted to pierce his hide.

After the hailing arrows stopped, Boull changed back into his human form once more and extracted Tai's sword. He pointed it up in the air and yelled madly.

Black rings of the billowing Shadow Force formed around the blade as the smoke of the burning village converged above it like the beginning of a lightning storm.

The three Ander fighters stood in awe at

the sight. Tai screamed a warning to them, but it was too late. Boull had already boomeranged the sword at the three shocked Anders. They died instantly.

When the sword returned to Boull's hand, he threw it to the ground.

"From the look of things, I won't even need this."

Boull walked up to the slowly dying Tai, laughing.

"I'm going to enjoy watching you die," Boull snickered.

Just as Boull was about to deliver one last blow to Tai, Tai whipped out his small dagger and drove it through Boull's heart. This time, he made sure not to miss.

Boull bellowed with pain, and his ferocious noise rumbled the earth and sky as he fell to his knees, passing into the Afterlife.

Not soon after, Tai's body succumbed to the weight of his death as well, and a hero fell with pride in his chest, breathing hope until his last breath.

Boull's enormous cry sifted through the Woodlands like a knife through butter. Sam, Chase, and Eton were already on their way to the Brevi Ocean. Their horses carried them swiftly through the dark forests. Tai had trained these horses to ride efficiently and successfully in the dense canopies.

Sam fought back tears as she heard Boull's death cry. She could feel deep in her heart that Tai was no longer alive.

Sam looked at Chase whose eyes were also filled with sadness, for she had come to the same realization. Chase gently smiled, and that soothed Sam's mind.

The trio continued to ride into the night

as they silently said their goodbyes to the
burning embers of their quest's first chapters
while the moon, they could not see, shined
brightly in the night sky, glimmering with
conviction and promise of a chance their
fallen friend had died for.

Talking Shadows

A severe storm brewed in the skies above
the Great Hall. It was the scariest storm that
Pangea had seen in a decades. The already
gloomy air was sanctified with more darkness,
and the heavy weight of the winds knocked on
the unique forest foliage that occupied the
Savannahs' grand oasis. Traces of the
bordering desert sands had snuck their way
into the lush green nature and lied elegantly
upon the grass like sprinkles to a cake, but
there was nothing sweet about the forecast.

Corpulent raindrops plunged from the gray
looming abyss and crashed onto every surface
of the Great Hall castle. The stone walls were
drenched in tiny water shows, each gigantic
liquid bead exploding into a watery firework.
The remnants of these fireworks soothed their
course as they slid down the towering walls
and fell slowly to the soaked ground like a
glazed drizzle.

Ceros' ruthless guards were stationed on
the tops of the walls. Their brilliant black
armor clung tightly to their scarred and
muscular chests as they ignored the noisy
squall and incessant whirlwinds while pacing
the tall stony trim.

The guards were not the only ones
subduing the chaotic storm. Even the prisoners
were facing the blustery effects. The musty
air hung persistently as the prisoners inhaled
the unfortunate dampness through tired lungs.
Their poor excuses for clothing did not shield
the coldness nor keep them dry as rain leaked
through the poorly constructed windows. The

prisoners clung closely to the thick wooden doors of their perspective cells to avoid the water gathering underneath their only view of the outside world, a view they tended to cling to.

One cell was immensely larger than any other cell in the stale dungeon because it held the defeated Head Nobles and Magi Order. Each one was bound by chains, damned by Quar's magic so that if any magic was used, Quar would instantly be alerted.

Leveel threw Ashos into the wall and secured the chains back to ex-king's dirty hands and bare feet. Then, Leveel exited the cell and locked the door behind him.

"Ashos! Are you alright?" Irutia whispered.

Though the years of confinement had polluted Itrutia's soft skin with dirt and grime, her beauty still shined through. Her soft voice and soothing presence nonetheless radiated out from her small body.

"Yes, I'm fine."

"I don't understand why you were taken. You hadn't even said anything this time," Irutia responded.

"Yes, if anything, it should have been me in the torture room with that dumb Leveel," Oldar chimed in.

Oldar's features were aging faster now that he was no longer able to soar through the sunny skies. His silver hair was cut very short but still shined gloriously in the torches' firelight. Though a prisoner, his humor and witty remarks remained and had gotten him many whippings from Leveel.

"So, what *did* Ceros want with you?" Irutia asked.

"It started off with Ceros being bored

and wanting to take a beating to me, but Quar came and made a horrible display."

Ashos sat silently and listened to the pattering raindrops clash heavily to the confining walls. He shuddered at remembering the awful sight he witnessed above.

"Is it *that* horrible?" Irutia continued to question.

"I'm afraid it is," Ashos finally replied. "Quar has found a way to merge the blood of Anders with that of Neos. What he has created is a monstrous beast called a Bolic. I saw him take the blood of two innocents and combine them into one body. The result was an uncontrollable and savage creation. The Ander had no capability to speak or think logically... It was possessed by madness, lost to an insanity Quar forced into its spirit. From the sound of Quar's presentation to Ceros, he wishes to build an army of these Bolics to sweep over the land in order to have complete control. This new spell that Quar has conjured can instill darkness in anyone... even one that still embraces the Light, and once Quar perfects his incantation, he will use just one spell to allow Ceros the dual control over his Neo and human form. He will be indomitable."

Oldar leaned back against the wall that held the orgin of his chains and sighed.

"Then, there really is no hope for Pangea," he muttered in defeat.

"I thought that to be true as well, but just before I was brought back down here, Quar whispered something into my ear. He said that the binding of bloods can be completely successful as he knows it to be true. The child has returned."

"You do not think he lies, do you, Ashos?" Irutia began as a tear formed in her eye.

"I believe he speaks truthfully, dear Irutia. I believe your grandchild is alive and has returned to Pangea. She has come back to save us all."

Tears in Irutia's eyes flooded down her cheeks like waterfalls. After the long twenty years in Ceros' prison, she was on the brink of losing hope that she would ever meet her daughter's last gift on Pangea.

Through her tears, Irutia looked over at an empty set of shackles that hung from the wall beside her.

"I only wish Delver was here to see our persistent hope's delivery," she cried. "He would have been proud to know that his most elite soldier's blood still coursed the land."

Ashos' chest swelled as he took a deep breath in remembering the final days of his beloved friend.

"I could not agree more, Irutia," he said softly. "But, at least Delver died at the will of his own sickened body rather than at the tip of Ceros' ruthless sword."

The three remaining Head Nobles bowed their heads with respect to their deceased comrade.

Irutia cleared her throat, managing to pose the question, "What do we do now?"

Up until that point, the Magi Order had remained silent as they soaked in all of Ashos' information. Tridor, the Priest of Fire, was the first to answer the Phoenix Queen's inquiry.

His once bold, red body had been diminished to a rusted look, and his eyes were tired like the worn down temper he had contained long ago.

"There's not much we can do from inside

these walls, I'm afraid," Tridor explained.
"We have to trust that if Solaris has managed
to survive this long that she can continue to
do so. Ashos, did Quar tell you anything of a
young fox maiden as an accomplice?"

"No, he did not."

"The Healer's Mastery child?" Oldar
questioned.

"Yes," Tridor answered. "We can only
assume that she, too, is alive if the Prophecy
child has returned safely. Let us hope that
their powers will continue to grow into their
full potential before Ceros and Quar's plans
come into full circle."

"Surely there must be something we can
do!" Irutia blurted out as she started to cry
again.

"There, there, Irutia," Tridor said
soothingly, trying to comfort the worried
queen. "I know your heart aches to see your
grandchild, and I believe there may be a way
to do so."

Irutia eyes widened with happiness.
Tridor turned his attention to Nysam.

Nysam's youth was callously robbed. His
thin and handsome body was now covered with a
slew of cuts, bruises, and dirt, but his eyes
still sparkled whenever it rained. In the
midst of the night's illustrious storm, they
were particularly alive this evening.

"Nysam, do you think this storm is
extensive enough for your Tracking spell to
work?"

Nysam gazed out the window at the
everlasting rain and the large puddle growing
underneath the sill on their rocky cell floor.
He nodded.

"All we need is a host body," he replied.

Fate responded as a plump black rat

scurried into their cell and nibbled at a piece of dried bread in the corner. Tridor motioned to Kuros, who was the closest to it, to grab it.

With a quick reflex, Kuros reached out and seized the rodent in his still rough hands. He had lost a substantial bit of weight as their meals were presented in small rations, but his immensity still remained.

Kuros threw it to Lafore who was sitting right next to the growing puddle under the window. With his long but firm hands, Lafore held the rat in the pool of water but still allowed it to breath.

Lafore was still a Neo of little words, and most of his white hair had left him, but he still managed to possess quick reflexes and a increments of wisdom.

"What are you doing?" Ashos asked the magical priests.

"We are going to send a Tracker to Solaris," Nysam responded. "With the magnitude of this storm, my spell will be able to send the Tracker much farther away from here without being detected from Quar when he comes to see what magic I have used. My Tracker will remain in any form of water and will travel that way until it reaches Solaris. That way, even if Quar is able to decipher what spell I have used, the Tracker will be long gone for him to find it."

"But, if you use your magic," Irutia whispered concerned. "Then who knows what punishment you'll face. No, it's not worth it."

"Quite the contrary, Irutia," Lafore interjected as he continued to hold the rat in the watery puddle. "Once the Tracker has located Solaris, we will then have eyes and ears on her throughout her journey. This will be very useful to us beyond your personal reasons. It should and must be done either way."

"Do not worry," Nysam reassured. "I am aware of the consequences, but like King Ashos said to us twenty years ago, it is the risks that we take for our people that separates us as leaders. If I am to choose my sacrifice, then it shall be for this purpose."

Irutia looked at Ashos and Oldar with a troubled stare. They both nodded in agreement with Nysam's claim. Irutia sighed and looked back at Nysam.

"Be safe," Irutia breathed.

Nysam smiled and looked to Lafore.

"Remember to keep the Devolut in the water until the incantation has been completely recited."

Lafore nodded and held the rat steady as it squirmed in his grip.

Nysam closed his eyes and tilted his head back. Just as he did, the rain outside seemed to fall heavier and louder. More and more water seeped in through the barred window spraying Lafore and the rat.

"*Marinu aquafinorai, tu invenut una avu, occulari et auricliam.*"

As Nysam's soft chant sang in the prisoners' ears, the pooling water began to dance around the rat. Lafore's steady hold did not budge as the rat began to wriggle violently. Water rushed into its mouth and down is throat, but the rat did not drown. The swirling crystal blue tornado pulsed as the rat's long pink tail turned into a flowing orange fin. Then, its feet followed the same transformation as the rat's fur smoothed out into a connected network of orange scales, and the thin whiskers twisted into protracted barbels. When the twirling movement of the water settled, Lafore was no longer holding a rat firm in the puddle but a small koi fish.

"Go my little friend," Nysam ushered to his new creation. "Let rain, waterfalls, lakes, and rivers guide you. Keep to the waters that birthed you, and find Solaris. Let *us* become your senses."

Lafore released his hold of the tiny koi fish. The fish squirmed back and forth then plunged into the puddle. Though the puddle was only a centimeter deep, it appeared that Nysam's tracker dove in much deeper, as the Head Nobles could no longer see its body.

"It will use the dense rainfall to swim to the outskirts of the storm. Then, it will find another body of water to travel by."

"It should only be a matter of seconds until Quar arrives," Kuros muttered cautiously.

Just as the badger priest predicted, Quar emerged from the shadows inside of the cell. His black hood covered the majority of his old and furrowed face as he limped with his cane into the center of the chamber.

"Well, you're all accounted for," Quar began. "So, the question now is… 'What kind of magical disobedience took place here?'"

Quar slowly looked around at each Head Noble and priest, but none of them spoke.

"You royal swine never learn, do you? No matter…"

Quar raised his crooked oak cane and pointed it at Nysam.

"*Recludsio.*"

The long chain that held Nysam unlocked itself from the wall and quickly wrapped around Nysam's slim body only leaving his legs exposed.

"Come with me, fish," Quar ordered as he forced Nysam out of the cell commanding the spellbound chains.

Quar followed his possessed prisoner up the long flight of stairs leading out of the dungeon and up to Ceros who was busy tending a meeting of his own.

Ceros had called the Council up to the dining hall. A handful of his servants had set up the table that had been used for the Tellings, but now, instead of the table being surrounded by joy and hope, it was now encircled by hatred and evil.

The Council was composed of twelve leaders. Each had control over the six different regions of Pangea and helped Ceros maintain the dominating Shadow Force reign. The Council's members were all dressed in sleek black robes, outlined with golden trimming, much like the Shadow Force armor.

These twelve beings had displayed infinite wickedness and no remorse so the Shadow Force clung tighter to their souls than any of the lower followers.

Two leaders remained at the each of the five Head Nobles' castles, and a sixth was built in the Land of Cassum.

At Ceros' old castle up in the Mountains, there were Tajera and Romados. They were sister and brother, both having dark skin and vivid yellow eyes. They had a considerable amount of tribal tattoos plastered to their arms and faces. All of the markings were done in a vibrant red color and during battles, looked like the blood of their opponents. They had torn off the sleeves of their Council robes in order to show them off as they were proud of their brandings. Both were also medium build and extremely tall, and when they changed into their snake forms, they were the most sly and cunning attackers.

To the west, at the Mystic Canyons castle, there was a zany dragon and owl duo named Perone and Strass. Aside from Quar, the pair was Ceros' leading wizard power. They spent most of their days locked up in their respective chambers coming up with new spells and potions that would ignite fires, freeze rivers, fashion a tornado, or any other kind of dark magic that would inflict damage. Their latest invention was a potion that allowed teleportation across Pangea. This had greatly helped the Council to meet in a quicker fashion.

Perone was a deep cobalt color with olive claws and underbelly in his dragon form, and when human, his wispy white hair clashed with his tanned skin, but his fingernails remained green.

Strass was the exact opposite. He was quite fat and robust. His feathers would easily get ruffled whenever he discovered something new in his shamanistic laboratory. His portliness stayed consistent as a human, and he barely fit his silky robe. He sat at the table snacking on a chicken leg.

The Woodlands' castle was inhabited by a bobcat named Verkel and a baboon named Luxec. Verkel and Luxec were known for their surprising patience in the group of anxious and rash councilmen. They provided the voice of reason when debates began to teeter on the edge of a physical confrontation but were still as ruthless as Ceros. Their smooth personalities even showed as they walked. Their black robes floated and glided across the floor though neither one of them carried wings on their backs. Both of them had jet black hair and pale white skin that contrasted deeply with the dense and dark forests of their terrain.

In the Savannahs castle, miles south of the Great Hall, there was another set of siblings. Together the lion brothers were known as "The Barbarian Brothers" but separately as Ark and Anjeer. Both were extremely muscular and fairly large. Their robes draped easily over their broad shoulders and strong backs, but their manes were like night and day. Ark had a thick blonde head of hair while Anjeer bore thinner but just as distinguished black locks. Their deep brown eyes helped camouflage their attack stance as they lie covertly in the desert brush. Both quick and brawny, these two were not to be fooled with.

Just below the Savannahs' southern coast lied the large island known as the Clifftops. This was King Oldar's previous home and was primarily made of rocky shores and towering ridges with rampant waves crashing against them. The castle was found on the Clifftops' highest ledge, and within its walls, there lived the Council's seers of the skies, two female falcons named Susida and Isumo. Though they were not related, they both had long flowing silver hair that stayed tied up in braids and piercing azure eyes that blended in nicely with their ashen faces. They were astoundingly beautiful. Their scheming charm allured their victims to them as they shocked them with their vicious assaults.

Finally, in the Land of Cassum, Gelaro, the reluctant Ander from twenty years ago, ruled over the enormous peninsula with his recent wife, Yura. Most of the Anders had remained there after Ceros broke the barrier with Erisi's death, and it remained to be the region where the least amount of Shadow Force followers resided.

After Ceros endowed Gelaro with the Shadow Force, Gelaro's body changed dramatically. He was no longer a portly man but was burlesque and toned. His shiny bald head remained, but he had shaved his once unkept beard down to a bushy black goatee. His eyes were mixed with royal blue and jade green and glared more brightly in his new frame. His temper was short, and when agitated, he would strike down any opponent with his curved sword. It was a trait that first sparked Ceros interests years ago when capturing him.

Gelaro's wife, Yura, had an equally matched fury. She had short fire-red curls and emerald green eyes. Her pale skin looked ghostly, and her frail limbs looked as if they were about to break at any moment, but the Ander governess was not weak at all. Within her black dressings, she wore a belt with, what seemed to be, an infinite amount of tiny metal arrow tips. Her agile reflexes could easily take down ten or more assailants in a matter of seconds. With her husband, any and all innocent Anders cowered in their presence.

"None of you know how much work I put in to keep my lands running smoothly and under Shadow order," Gelaro protested. "While the rest of you relax and enjoy peace and quiet in your chambers, my wife and I are out on the battle field almost every day to maintain our dominance. Many of the Anders have yet to be turned to our influence, and we face countless attacks from rebel groups."

"Perhaps you need a Neo presence in the Land of Cassum to help you get your rule straight, Gelaro," Anjeer retorted. "Maybe then you will have your peace."

"How dare you insult my husband?" Yura fought back. "You and your brother are nothing but tactless and unintelligent brutes."

"If that's so, then why do the Savannahs have the highest number of turned innocents each month?" Ark argued with his brother.

"Because you share the terrain with the King," Yura continued. "If Ceros did not reside in the same land as you, I'm sure your region would be lost in chaos."

"This fighting will not solve your problems," Luxec chimed in.

"I agree," Verkel voiced. "Surely, there must be a way to increase the number of Shadow Force presence on the peninsula."

"Susida and I are more than inclined to send some of our finest matrons to your aide, Gelaro," Isumo interjected with her fetching speech.

"We don't need your seductive wenches," Gelaro shot back. "We all know they're only good for one thing."

Strass giggled at Gelaro's derogatory remark.

"Yes, yes. We *all* know what they're good for," Strass snickered madly. "So, while we're on the topic, Susida and Isumo are more than welcome to send their aid to the Mysitc Canyons anytime, anytime."

"Ooooo new toys to play with?" Perone asked wildly as his eyes opened widely. "What fun. Great fun."

The crazed pair laughed manically.

Tajera and Romados stayed silent as they usually were. Their secretive personalities and intents stayed protected that way, but they rolled their eyes at the mad duo's exchange.

"Quiet!" Ceros yelled above the quarrelling Council.

The Shadow Force leaders instantly hushed at the booming sound of their king's annoyance.

"Tell me," Ceros proceeded but in a much calmer manner. "Gelaro, how do you think all these Anders are remaining faithful to the Light? It has been my experience that Anders are usually the easiest to turn."

Ark and Anjeer snickered but stopped immediately after facing an unamused and deathly stare from Ceros.

Gelaro cleared his throat and answered, "It seems that because the Land of Cassum is cut off to the mainland by the Great Crossings, which few Shadow Force Neo and Ander beings tend to range over these days -damn that Quar for keeping those lands so enchanted- the Light Anders' confidence in their own strength seems to be growing. We have managed to keep the retaliations to a minimum, but they continue to swarm our claimed Shadow territory like flies."

"Then, perhaps an increased Neo presence in the Land of Cassum is not a bad idea," Ceros responded. "If you will not take Susida and Isumo's help, then perhaps you have a request for a different set of Neos to beg aid from?"

Ark and Anjeer tried to hold back their pleased smiles but could not.

Seeing this, Ceros replied, "It seems that Ark and Anjeer are eager to assist your troubles, Gelaro."

The lion brothers jerked up straight at their majesty's suggestion. Both were disturbed at the remedial task.

Before either brother could speak a word, Ceros ordered, "And if they fuss about it to you, speak to me. I will be more than happy to promote one of their soldiers to their position, a soldier that is able to take a command obediently."

Ark and Anjeer slouched in their chairs and bowed their heads.

"Your demands shall be fulfilled," they said disappointedly.

"Good," Ceros declared. "Now, what is the next order of business?"

"I believe I know, my king," Quar echoed behind the Council's table.

All the members turned around to see Quar leaning on his cane smiling through his charcoal-stained teeth. Nysam was still bound by Quar's cursed chains and stood next to him.

"Back so soon?" Ceros questioned as he leaned forward in his chair. "I hope you bring good news of our last conversation."

Ceros heart began to race with excitement thinking Quar had made the finishing touches to the Bolic potion and was ready to bestow him with indefinite strength.

"Unfortunately, I do not, King Ceros," Quar pronounced. "But, the news I carry on my tongue still has much weight."

Ceros rested his body back onto his chair and motioned Quar to continue though his hopes had been let down.

"My king, this prisoner is Nysam, the Priest of Water from the Magi Order."

"This we know, Quar. Why have you removed him from his cell?"

"As you know, when the Head Nobles and Magi Order first became your prisoners, I bound their bodies with enchanted chains that would alert me if they were ever to escape or practice magic."

"And which of these crimes did the koi fish Priest commit?" Ceros interrogated.

"It was a Tracking spell. He was tracking an Ander."

"An Ander?" Ceros exclaimed, taken aback.

"This is no ordinary Ander, King Ceros," Quar carried on. "This particular Ander, alone, has taken down a rogue fighting ring."

Ceros' nostrils flared at Quar's response. He was both enraged and confused that a being with matching potential and strength existed.

"How long have you known about this?" Ceros asked coldly.

"Since the last time I visited you," Quar replied calmly.

"Why did you not tell me of this sooner?!?" Ceros roared.

The dining halls shook with fright. The Council silently stared at the old decrepit wizard for his reaction, but Quar was unaffected by his king's outburst.

"Because I did not see it as an immense threat, King Ceros," Quar smoothly continued. "But, when I filtered through Nysam's mind, I discovered that the Ander he sought to track was the same Ander I had heard of. It was only then did I come to the conclusion that if one of the Magi Orders was willing to sacrifice his life for this mysterious Ander, then it is topic that should be discussed. I wanted to be sure before I worried you, your highness."

Ceros strained his neck and clenched his teeth to keep from shouting again.

"Where has this Ander been hiding all these years?" Ceros gritted.

"In a different realm, and it is my assumption that the Healer's Mastery has traveled back to Pangea with it."

Ceros enthusiasm was regained as he stroked his chin and repeated, "The Healer's Mastery? Are you sure?"

"The description of the Ander's accomplice matches that of the features I pulled from Friar Sulny's mind some time ago. This Ander may be its protector."

"Well, this surely is intriguing," Ceros whispered, at first, but then rose his voice back up. "Where is this fighting arena that you speak of, Quar? We will send all forces there to find both the Ander and the Healer's Mastery."

"They were last seen at the most southern and western border of the Savannahs, but who knows what kind of other mystical powers the Ander and Healer's Mastery possess together? We must not presume that they travel by foot. They could be enduring aid from Light Alliances."

"Can't we use the fish's Tracker to pinpoint their exact location then?"

"No," Quar responded to his king. "By the time I arrived, the Tracker had already left and this wretched storm's intensity only increased the speed and extension of the Water priest's spell. I could not locate it, and even if I conjured up the same Tracking spell, I do not know the exact bodies I am looking for."

Frustrated by Quar's words, Ceros muttered, "So what do you propose we do?"

"Keep the Council members at their rightful castles, and initiate their armies to keep a keen eye for the both of them. I believe we will have the most luck with that strategy. We do not know what their plans are or where they wish to strike. In the meantime,

I will take Nysam back to the Great Crossings to further investigate his mind. Any new information, rest assured, I will send to all commanding powers."

"You best do so, Quar and do so fast. Your responsibilities seem to be piling high and fast in the last few days. Are you certain you can handle it all?"

"Quite confident, your majesty," Quar stated as he began to retreat with his new prisoner to the shadows of large tapestry hanging on one of the walls. "You can trust me. I would hide nothing from you."

Quar took a final bow before completely submerging himself in the shadows, but he was indeed withholding a large bit of knowledge. For Quar knew exactly where the holder of the Healer's Mastery *and* the mystical Ander would be heading. They would be in dire need of the Friar's expertise and that would lead them right to Quar's gates.

Quar threw back his head and cackled as the looming darkness swirled around, devouring and digesting him and Nysam into its deepest pit.

Nysam could feel the eerie blackness slide over his skin and behind his body like slime as the dim light from Quar's chambers began to emerge in front of him. Nysam took a huge breath in and closed his eyes, ready to accept his fate.

From Sea to Land

Sam sat on a deck bench at the bow of the ship. She stared off into the faraway horizon as the melting sun slid carefully beneath the ocean brim to rest for another day.

The skies of the ocean were very different from the dark gloominess of the Woodlands and from the relentlessly dry atmosphere in the bright Savannahs. The sherbet colored atmosphere twirled with thin wispy clouds as the hint of navy blue and speckled stars crept slowly in to become the clouds' new dance partner. The sight was absolutely stunning. *This* was the sky that Sam had remembered from her youth.

She took in a deep breath of sea air, the saltiness biting at her nostrils, as she stared down at the Healer's Mastery book in her lap. Boull had not bothered to take their bags when they were captured, and they were lucky enough that Tai had brought back all of their belongings to his village when he saved Chase.

Sam flipped through the dusty, cinnamon-colored pages and ran her fingers over the delicate words and pictures that lied peacefully within the binding. They took her back to when she was at the Great Abbey. She smiled as she smelled Lady Tanan's famous blueberry pies cooking in the kitchens and saw Friar Sulny at his librarian's desk with a new stack of books, ready for Sam to read outside of her normal studies.

Back to reality, Sam pulled the small moon pendant from under her shirt and gently rubbed it between her thumb and forefinger. Sam sighed at her memories and began to cry.

"Oi, me lady, why are ya sobbin' like that fer?"

Sam quickly wiped her teary eyes and turned around.

A tall woman dressed in pirate's clothing stood before her. She was wearing loose black Capri pants whose ragged trims flew lightly in the breeze along with her tan baggy-sleeved shirt. Her long russet hair was pulled back into a pony tail and was highlighted by streaks of goldenrod, most likely from her elongated exposure to the gorgeous ocean sun, but the eyes were the pirate lady's most distinguishing feature. Day and night, they dazzled with a swarming blue and green like the brilliant ocean waves striking the algae-covered coastlines she ported and swam in as the exquisite yet rugged koi fish she was.

"Oh Julissa," Sam sniffled. "It's nothing. This view is just so beautiful. I couldn't help but be reminded of Pangea before all the evil and darkness came about."

"Aye," Julissa agreed as she crossed her arms in front of her chest. "The beauty of bein' at sea is that Ceros and his dark magic dare not cross it. They be fools if they think they can control her. The land maybe, but not the sea. Oh, no. Lucky for me, I've got ole *Ourna* here to guide us."

Ourna was the name was of the colossal ship that Tai had told Sam about. It picked her, Chase, and Eton up at a hidden dock at the southern tip of the Woodlands and had been carrying them for two weeks across the Brevi Ocean toward the Great Crossings coast.

Sam remembered how much awe had struck her when the rustic *Ourna* pulled into the harbor. She was made of white oak and locust wood nails. The sturdiness was only further complimented by the lovely furnished surface and engaging artwork painted on the outside of the captain's cabin at the stern of the ship. The *Ourna* also bore large ivory sails supported by tall looming masts which held bold maroon colored flags that fluttered gracefully in the winds as the ship cut through raging rapids and sailed over lulling currents.

The crew on the *Ourna* was quite the opposite though. Julissa's mates were rough-looking characters but had the kindest and most gentle hearts. Their rugged features and tattered clothes would cause anyone to fear them at first glance, but their greasy hands, smudged faces, and sooty rags were only signs of their loyalty to working hard on the ship.

"How much longer do we have until we reach the Great Crossings?" Sam inquired as she turned her attention back out to the rolling waves before her.

"If the winds carry on like they are now, then we be at the Great Crossins' river openin' by tomorrow night. Then we'll be handin' ya off to the Light Mafia. They be takin' you and your friends the rest of the way by land."

"Thanks again for all your help, Julissa."

"Not a problem marm! Anything fer a friend of Tai's. Rest his soul."

Julissa bowed her head in reverence for her fallen comrade. Then, she looked back up and let her gaze sift through the night sky's starry spectacles.

"Ya know I fell in love with her the first time I seen her," she said proudly.

"Who?" Sam asked curiously as she fiddled with the Healer's Mastery's old pages.

"The sea. Aye, she was a beauty. The first time me dad took me out on this ship -this was his ship ya know- I knew that she'd have me heart forever. It was different than the love I have fer me husband; that's a land kind of love. The ground be firm under ya feet, and ya just know in your soul that it won't give. I don't know what I'd do without him, but the sea… The sea is a whole other story. She's a collection of uncertainty. She moves where she pleases, rages when she wants ta, calms down when she's feelin' tired, and takes no orders from the many ships that sail her. She's a free spirit, but it ain't like she don't love. She may not say it the way we do, but she does. Ya can feel it somehow. Ya know what I mean?"

Julissa looked back down at Sam who was holding the Healer's Mastery book close to her chest and was crying softly to herself. Julissa walked up to her and patted her gently on the shoulder.

"Yes, I suppose ya do, Miss Sam. I suppose you do."

On the stern side of the *Ourna*, Chase was practicing sword fighting with Julissa's husband, Rio.

Rio, like the entire *Ourna* crew, was a Koi Fish Neo. He had a medium build with short chocolate colored hair. His particularly shiny white teeth glistened in the prowling moonlight against his tan bronzed skin. Rio was also the only member of the crew, wife included, that did not have greasy hands or a dirt-smudged face. In fact, he was always prestigiously clean.

Rio smacked Chase's back with the wooden

training sword as she charged forward to strike Rio first, but Rio had keenly avoided the attack.

"You're too rigid in your motions," Rio explained. "You must be fluid in order to change at any given moment. Battles are unpredictable like that. Be as if you were water."

Chase regained her stance and rubbed her back.

Turning around she replied, "Easy for you to say, you're a fish."

Rio laughed as he set his training sword down and picked up a mug of water off a table.

"Break time? Fine by me," Chase said happily as she pulled out a wooden crate from underneath the table and sat down. "So, tell me. How did you and Julissa meet anyway? I wouldn't have expected it."

Rio took a sip of water and asked in return, "Why do you say that?"

"I guess it's just the way that you two talk. It's… really different."

"Ah, yes," Rio smiled. "Well, before Ceros took over, I was a young teen practicing Defense Arts at the Great Abbey. It just so happened that I was away on a Survival Trip when Ceros came and invaded our home. When we returned, your father, Rysul, ordered us to flee into the safety of the Great Crossings' mystical woods. He sensed the immense evil that had taken over the Abbey."

Chase's eyes dropped to the table surface with sadness.

"Your father was a noble fighter, Chase," Rio consoled. "What made him great was his even more noble and loving heart. Without him and without his teachings I would have never survived as long as I did. I would have never met Julissa. Rysul was truly a great and caring man."

Still keeping her eyes down at the table, Chase smiled at the kind words Rio spoke about the father she would never meet.

After seeing Chase's spirit lift, Rio continued, "I was the only survivor from a small battle about seven years after we fled the Great Abbey. I voyaged through the darkness alone for another two before I came to the eastern coast of the Mystic Canyons. I hadn't eaten for weeks and was near my death as I stumbled across the rocky beaches. I blacked out on the shore. When I came to, I was covered in warm blankets and shared the heat of several candles. I felt the rocking of waves underneath my tired body and knew that I was on a ship. Julissa's father, the first captain of the *Ourna*, had just passed. Julissa and the crew had stopped ashore to burn the body to ashes and spread his remains to the glorious sea he loved so much. They came across me in the process and decided to take me aboard."

Rio took a long sip of his water and wiped his mouth.

"I fell in love with her the instant I saw her. I was still in bed when she walked into my room. She was wiping her hands on an old rag because, just having fixed the rudder, and informed me of where I was then left the cabin.

It was just a second really, but I was stunned by a form of energy I cannot define, some force of attraction. I could sense that our backgrounds had stemmed from two completely different worlds, but still, I knew I had to make her fall in love with me."

Now involved with Rio's story, Chase

looked up from the table and asked eagerly, "How did you?"

Rio chuckled.

"I was inducted as a deck worker the moment I regained my strength so it was hard for me to obtain any alone time with her."

Rio paused. Chase was sitting at the edge of the wooden crate, resting her chin in both her hands with her elbows pressed into the table. Her eyes silently begged for Rio to put an end to both her curiosity and anxiousness.

"I did what any man in love would do. I acted like a complete fool in front of her just to attract her attention. I wasn't too picky on what attention it was," Rio chuckled. "I decided to pick a fight and tackle one of the other deck mates for no apparent reason as she made her morning rounds to each section of the ship, and later that night, I formally introduced myself and apologized.

I don't recall exactly what lead us from that point to where we shared our first kiss, but I do know one thing. It was subtlety magical and more delicate than any form of magic I learned at the Great Abbey. I felt it in my bones, in my blood, and in my heart… that comfort and sense of peace only love can bring. It's unexplainable by words but clarified through actions. It just felt right… effortless and like I belonged."

Rio shook his head and looked down to Chase.

"But, you should know all of this, am I correct? Your Miss Cia has created the same spell over you as Julissa has over me?"

Chase sighed and shrugged her shoulders.

"I keep trying to figure that out, and I keep coming to an answer," she replied in a defeated manner. "But, then, I hear someone new talk about love, and I don't know anymore. Isn't love supposed to be consistent? And surely, I *know* what the 'truth of my heart' is if I gained my powers back, right?"

Rio placed a caring hand on Chase's shoulder.

"Your father told me something back at the Abbey that I will never forget. He said, 'Only the affinity sparked by our most adverse feebleness can create the kind of love that I admire and am drawn to the most.' Do you know what he meant by that?"

Chase shook her head.

"Love is born of intimacy, but intimacy is not as extreme or impassioned as many believe. Intimacy is simply the recognition of our vulnerability. Once we become aware of these weaknesses, we are instantly blessed with the ability to change and grow. Within the most condemned regions of our spirits lie the greatest potential to adhere. It's almost as if our hearts are saying, 'We'll be scared together, but let us flourish together, too.'"

Rio patted Chase on the shoulder then picked up the practice sword.

"Not everything distinctly manifests when or how it should, but 'should' is negligible. Everything *will* be pronounced when the pieces fall into place as the universe allows it."

"Like fate?" Chase asked inquisitively.

"Nope. Just natural appreciation and insight salted with a dash of time and peppered with the courage to make a bold move every now and then."

"Oi? Did I hear ya mention salt 'n pepper?" Julissa shouted from behind them.

She was standing on the stairs leading down from the stern quarter to the main ship deck.

"I hope fer both ya sakes that ya ain't be eatin' ya own fancy feast without me!" Julissa jested. "Or I might have to throw ya overboard."

"No, my love," Rio replied in turn. "Just giving Chase some advice."

"Well you best be finishin' that bit up 'cause *real* dinner's bein' served now. Then, we best be headin' off to bed. We've got a long day tomorrow, so put down those twigs and get down here, or I'll drink yer share of the ale."

Julissa turned around and joined her crew on the main deck. The two weeks at sea had been gentle thus far so their fruits were still fresh, their vegetables still crisp, and their meat still tender.

The crew was high in merriment and laughter as Julissa poured herself a mug of ale, picked up a handful of candied nuts, and stuffed them into her mouth. Though the sight should have been appalling, the sparkle in Julissa's eyes, prompted by such great company, made the unappetizing act appealing.

Also, on the deck below, Eton clinked glasses with some of the gun deck workers and was involved in an intense game of dice while Sam helped the ship's cook make sure that everyone had a bowl full of warm vegetable stew.

A young lad sat on the edge of the rail and started to play a small wooden flute. Its hallow sound danced upon the sea winds and circled the lively atmosphere.

Chase stood up and looked down at the festive and lighthearted scene below her as she digested Rio's wise words.

"I still don't get it," she said confoundedly.

Rio stood alongside Chase and whispered as he pointed to her head, "You may not see it here."

Then, he pointed to Chase's heart.

"But, that earth power of yours is proof that you understand it here."

Chase touched her heart at the echoing of Rio's words.

"Salt and pepper, huh?" she joked.

Rio laughed and patted Chase on the back, escorting her down to dinner. Sam walked up to Chase and handed her a bowl of stew.

"Here, Chase, you need to eat this before it gets cold. Julissa said that the nights get near freezing closer to the Great Crossings' coast."

Sam rubbed her hands together and blew her warm breath into them. Tiny hints of her exhalation formed in the night air as a small foggy cloud.

"I should have packed gloves," Sam kidded. "You would think after handling all this hot stew, my hands would be warmer."

"Here, let me help," Chase replied as she set down her untouched broth and wrapped her hands around Sam's.

"Better?"

Chase looked up at Sam's face. As the fogginess of Sam's breath cleared, a slight icy dew formed on the tip of her nose. The fetching starlight from the dark blanket above shimmered on the facial frosty sheet and animated every agreeable feature on Sam's face.

Chase gulped and shifted her fascinated inspection down to Sam's shivering hands within her grasp. The memories of the gentle touch of Sam's healing powers flooded Chase's mind, but before Chase could reminisce her compliments out loud, Sam pulled her hands away and hid them under her arms. She smiled nervously.

"How was your lesson with Rio tonight? Learn anything?" Sam inquired.

Chase picked up her bowl of stew and responded, "Um yeah… I think so."

Just as Julissa had ordered, and not long after the jubilant dinner was over, most of the ship workers retired to the crew deck to sleep while a handful roamed the surface of the ship for the first shift of the evening. The cool night winds poured into the *Ourna's* mighty sails as the gorgeous ship glided through the still waters of the Brevi Ocean.

Chase was part of the first shift. She stood staring out over the starboard side of the ship. The dark waters sparkled with the reflections of the stars. Eton came up from behind her and handed Chase a thick wool blanket.

"I brought this for you in case you get cold," Eton said kindly.

Chase took the fuzzy blanket and smiled. "Thanks Eton."

Her stare returned back to the sea.

"Are you alright?" Eton asked concerned.

"Yeah. I'm just thinking."

Eton leaned over the railing and let his eyes wander to where Chase's were fixed, out to the infinite horizon.

"Do you think Sam loves me?" Eton whispered.

Startled by Eton's bluntness, Chase stammered, "Um… I don't kno- Why are you asking me?"

"Although I knew everything about her when we were younger, it was only through longing and such a long time ago. You know her best now. I can't seem to read what she's thinking."

"Uh…" Chase stuttered. "Did you… did you tell her how you feel?"

"Yes, when we were hiding in the cave. After she healed my wounds, I held her in my arms and told her."

Chase stayed silent for a few moments before finally asking, "What did she say?"

"She didn't say anything."

"That doesn't necessarily mean she doesn't feel the same way. I mean, you can't just drop a bomb like that after all she just went through and expect her to be a hundred percent happy-go-lucky about it."

"Happy-go-lucky?"

Chase sighed as she remembered the differentiating lingo between herself and Eton.

She adjusted her words and continued, "It must have been a lot to take in considering the events of your impeccable timing."

"I suppose you're right," Eton murmured. "After all, I could feel it… in my bones, in my blood, in my heart that she felt the same way when I made my confession. She was practically shaking, but I'm not sure if I should make a second attempt."

Chase stood silently as Eton repeated the exact words Rio had spoken to her earlier. She rolled her eyes jokingly and shook Eton by the shoulder.

"C'mon, Wonder Boy," she teased. "What's life without a little risk? You beat out *two* Bolics. You can't tell me that Sam scares you more than those beasts did. Besides, don't you think she's worth it?"

Eton turned to Chase and smiled.

"You are most certainly correct. Thank

you, Chase."

He stood back up and started walking to the stairs, but just as he was about to descend to the sleeping quarters below, Eton clutched his left pectoral as a sting rose to his skin.

Chase called out behind him, "Hey, Eton!"

Eton stopped and turned around, ignoring the emerging hotness in his cavity.

"You're a good guy, and you've been through a lot. You deserve to be happy."

Eton nodded and replied, "So do you."

With that, Eton disappeared to the deck below, and Chase walked over to help one of the crewmen fix a loose board on the deck floor as the majestic vessel persevered toward the Great Crossings.

The next day's sailing had, once again, progressed smoothly, and nighttime had fallen once more over the *Ourna* and her crew.

The Great Crossings' coastline was a mere shadow not too far off ahead, and Julissa had commanded that they drop anchor before they got any closer.

Every member of the crew had assembled on the main deck in a large circle around Julissa, Rio, and the traveling trio. The dirty and raggedy-clothed crew were unusually quiet as most of the their time awake was filled with swearing, jesting, and shouts of liveliness.

Julissa paced back and forth in the middle of the noiseless ring as she flipped a gold coin up and down in the air. Finally, after several seconds, she stopped.

"Mates!" she shouted. "We have had the greatest of times these past two decades as we sailed right under Ceros' dark rule. We have enjoyed better times than most of the land critters can even imagine possible, and it's been one hell of a ride with the lot of ya."

The crew cheered at their captain's speech, but immediately quieted down when Julissa rose her hand.

She continued, "But, as I said, few Pangeans remember the freedom we taste everyday in this salty air. It's about time we do somethin' about that."

Julissa turned and pointed at Sam, Chase, and Eton.

"These folks here have been our guests for the past two weeks, but in the next few months, they will be much more than that…"

Julissa paused and turned her attention to the three boarders.

"It is our honor to have helped you so far, and it will forever be our duty to extend the same gratitude to you for as long as you need it. I believe Rio has taught Eton a Summoning spell that will call us whenever you need us."

Rio nodded and replied, "Just whisper the words to a body of water, and I will hear you."

Julissa walked up to Sam and dropped a gold coin into the tiny shirt pocket just above Sam's breast.

"For good luck," Julissa whispered. "For every acre of uncertain ocean, there's always something beautiful lying within."

Julissa winked at Sam then unsheathed her sword and raised it up in the air.

"Okay mates! It's about that time, so get yer lazy arses overboard, and let's start singin'!"

The *Ourna* crew whooped and hurrahed as they whipped their leather hats and colored bandanas into the air and jumped over the rails, plunging into the watery depths below.

Some of the crew changed into koi fish while still in the air, jumping over the rail, or during their plummet, while others stayed human to the end of their fall, and after kicking around in the water for a bit, transformed into their aquatic bodies. Within minutes, the *Ourna* was surrounded by a multicolored school of koi fish. Their shiny orange, white, silver, and black fins twinkling in the night.

Chase closed her eyes and started to breath in heavily.

"What's wrong with her?" Julissa directed toward Sam.

Sam chuckled and explained, "She has a weird fear of fish."

"Well then, how the hell were ya able to stay with us so long?" Julissa mocked Chase.

Still with her eyes closed, Chase replied, "You were always in your human form so I guess I ignored it or forgot."

Julissa roared with laughter, "First, an Ander that has magic blood and now, a fear of fish? Chase, trust me when I say you won't want to miss this."

Sam rubbed Chase's back, and Chase slowly opened her eyes.

Julissa had walked over to the starboard rail and was standing next to Rio who was holding out his hand. Julissa took it, and Rio brought her hand up to his lips and kissed it.

Rio turned to the curious trio and said, "I find the best view to be from the bow."

Then, Julissa and Rio jumped over the railing and joined the rest of their crew in the water.

Sam, Chase, and Eton did as Rio suggested and made their way to the front of the ship.

"I wonder what we're looking for," Chase wondered aloud.

"Look!" Sam exclaimed.

In the distance ahead, a tiny glow was spotted in the vast dark waters. Then, in just another second, another small flickering light emerged a few feet away from the first.

In a matter of minutes, more and more spots of the sea in front of them began to glow, and soon, a swirling neon blue and green pool of luminescence formed along the Great Crossings' coast. The starlight was even in awe and envy as the vibrant mass grew and grew until one could see the entire shoreline clearly, lit by the natural light energy of the hidden phytoplankton swarm.

"Oh… my… god…" Chase muttered in shock and disbelief.

"It's beautiful!" Sam yelled out excitedly.

Eton hesitantly grabbed Sam's hand and held it in his. To his surprise, Sam did not let go but looked up at his nervous face and smiled. Eton smiled back and looked at Chase behind Sam's head. Chase winked then returned her stare out to the glowing ocean wonder.

The steady beating of the waves sounded a soft percussion in the chilly night as the soft notes of the koi fish below began to rise.

This was more than the singing Julissa had warranted. The resonance of the rowdy crew was not as rough or course as Sam, Chase, nor Eton would have predicted. Instead, each crewmember's voice floated lightly into the air perfectly pitched and harmonized faultlessly with its neighbor until the *Ourna* was enclosed by a dome of sweet and possessing melodies. There were no words, just heavenly tones like those of an instrument.

As the strange but alluring song progressed, the glowing phytoplankton began to rise out of their watery chambers and magnetize to the *Ourna*'s wooden sides. Soon, the entire hull's surface of the massive ship was covered in a bright neon blue blanket.

Suddenly, the sounds of creaking wood began to break into the choir of koi fish, and the ship's body began to moan and shrink.

The once vastly-sized *Ourna* had now been slowly reduced with dimensions that only held about a quarter of the entire crew.

"Well this is definitely now just a boat," Chase said jokingly while still in shock.

Julissa, Rio, and a small handful of the crew, jumped back onto the main deck in their human forms dripping wet with sea water.

Julissa wrung out her long pony tail and swished it back and forth before saying, "Well? Whaddya think? I was right, eh Chase?"

"Yeah…" Chase stammered. "That was pretty incredible, but why did you shrink the ship?"

Rio wiped away a small piece of seaweed that clung to his face and said, "The river that we will be taking is much too narrow for *Ourna* in her original size, like most rivers on the main lands. We have to do this in order to keep the ship safe from the openness of the sea when we have to restock our supplies."

"But, what about the rest of the crew?" Sam asked worriedly.

"Don't worry 'bout 'em," Julissa replied. "The lot of 'em love to get their fins wet after a long sailin', but they'll be put to work as soon as we get *Ourna* harbored in the river and out scavenging the land for food and reserves or tending to any ailments of the ship."

"The phytoplankton also provide an
invisible shield around the ship," Rio chimed
in. "Only those who sing the gentle spell-song
or who are aboard the ship during the ritual
are allowed to see her. It keeps any unwanted
evils from discovering her. Once we harbor in
and get settled, Julissa and I will introduce
you to your guides."

It took about a two hours for the *Ourna*
and her crew to anchor in the river and set up
camp for the night. Another feast was being
delivered to each crewmate as Julissa and Rio
escorted Sam, Chase, Eton, and their horses
away from the glowing campfires to the border
of the open grassland.

Sam, Chase, and Eton pulled at their
reins to halt their eager horses. The eerie
ambiance of the Great Crossings was making
them edgy.

Julissa stepped forward and called out
into the woods, "I see the Light, and the
Light shall see me!"

Soon after Julissa's words fleeted into
the trees, a loud rustling sounded from the
forest line.

Five white muscular horses and their
riders emerged from the shadows. The hooded
rider in the middle was the first to speak.

"Salutations, Julissa… Rio," a cheerful
female voice greeted. "So, this is the
prophetic child and the Healer's Mastery your
scout told us of?"

"Aye," Julissa replied. "And the third is
their friend, an ex-prisoner of Quar and a
young study of Illusion Magic from when the
Abbey was still ruled by the innocent."

The mysterious rider pulled back her
beige colored hood and revealed a darkly

tanned complexion and a smiling face. A small golden piercing twinkled in her left nostril, and her thick long coffee hued hair lie draped over her shoulder in a loose braid. The deep crème pigment of her cloak swam over the rear of her white steed and was decorated with a maize trim. Earrings of azure beads dangled in the breeze like tiny wind chimes. Across her chest there was a brown leather sash strapped from her right shoulder down to her left hip, and attached to that was a thin crooked wand carved out of an ash tree. It had a fine polished shine to it and lie in waiting for its master to call upon its magical powers.

"Allow me to introduce myself," the enchanting woman announced. "My name is Sabua, the Snake Sorceress, and these are the members of the Light Mafia. To my right is Marthule, the Lion Enforcer."

Marthule was a tall muscular man with medium length light chestnut hair that fell neatly over his ears. The silky smoothness of it glistened in the moonlight just like the gold plated armor that only covered his left shoulder and bicep. It was fashioned with an array of teal stones that also embellished the long handle of a mace that hung from his belt. His deep green eyes were warm and full of fire as they swelled every time the brawny man took a breath. He was not wearing a shirt so his light skinned broad back and defined muscles were quite evident.

Sabua continued, "And next to him is Celtessa, the Peacock Archer."

Celtessa was wearing a hood over part of her face, but it was attached to a brilliant silky white tunic that covered most of her sandy colored pants. A fancy knit pattern of emerald green and silver stitching made a beautiful pattern along the front. She pulled back her hood and exposed her extremely long bronzy brown hair that fell in glorious layers. She sat tall in her saddle with a tan quiver of arrows secured to her back and a matching tan glove on her right hand. Her bow was strapped to the side of her saddle along with a large satchel filled with more arrows. Celtessa bowed her head to acknowledge the individuals before her.

"To my left, we have Christo, the Phoenix Ninja," Sabua proceeded.

Christo's horse neighed and stirred after Sabua introduced its rider. Christo placed a gentle hand on the horse's neck and hushed it until it was calm. Her long thin black hair was pulled up into a high pony tail and was accented with royal purple dangly barrettes that were made out of her own shed feathers. She wore leather gloves that had been cut off at the knuckles to help her control the precision of her deadly metal throwing stars that were safely concealed underneath her black cloak and on the outside of her gray knee-high boots. As the wind blew softly, one could catch a glimpse of her forest green short sleeve shirt and black pants that helped her camouflaged disguise.

"And finally we have Rhodil, the Honey Badger Prowess," Sabua concluded.

The fourth woman of the Light Mafia, Rhodil was slightly shorter than the rest but no less fierce. Her body was covered in a tight leather suit that only showed the flesh of her face, neck and hands. Even then, her left hand wore a deep maroon tinted gauntlet with long metal spikes jutted out from the knuckles. A nicely curled up standard sized bullwhip hung from her right side. The long

leather handle was woven with red threading
and had thin metal filaments protruding from
the lash. Her hair was a rich hazelnut brown
and fell around her like the flowing branches
of a willow tree.

"Four women?" Chase whispered to Sam. "I
can work with that."

Sam elbowed Chase and replied, "It is
lovely to meet all of you. We cannot begin to
tell you how gracious we are for your
assistance."

"The pleasure is entirely ours," Sabua
returned. "If there is a chance to restore the
Light back to Pangea, then we are more than
happy to be of service."

"You will be in good hands," Rio spoke to
Chase as he adjusted a saddle bag on her
horse. "The Light Mafia is the best Alliance
Pangea has. We were lucky that they were so
close to the Great Crossings when we sent our
scout ahead."

"We must leave now while the darkness of
the night still compliments our travel,"
Marthule rushed. "When morning comes, the
trees of these mystical forests awaken and
will prove to be more of a threat than shade."

"It will still take about another two
weeks time to arrive at the Great Abbey,"
Christo sounded. "I hope that allows you
enough time to establish better authority over
your powers, Solaris."

"Um you can call me, Chase," Chase
responded. "But, I hope so, too. Being on a
ship in the middle of water didn't give me
much a chance to practice my control of the
earth elements."

Chase made her hand into a fist, and it
turned to solid earth.

"Fascinating," Celtessa proclaimed.

Eton turned his reins over in his hands and addressed Julissa and Rio, "A thank you to you both, as well. We owe you."

"Ya owe us nothin'," Julissa replied quickly. "Just be safe and get this world back in order, ya hear?"

Sam, Chase, and Eton nodded.

"Time to go," Rhodil piped up.

With that, the Light Mafia turned their horses back to face the Great Crossings' vast forest. Sam, Chase, and Eton kicked their horses to follow and disappeared into the gloomy woodland.

Rio wrapped his arm around Julissa's shoulders and hugged her tight.

"They'll be alright, won't they, Rio?" Julissa pondered out loud.

"They just have to trust what they already know, my darling," Rio replied. "And I am quite certain they will be just fine."

The Darkness Within

"Are you going to tell me why you've brought us here, Quar?" Gelaro asked suspiciously as he descended down the drab hallway to the Great Abbey dungeons behind the deceivingly old Dark Wizard.

"I could not help but overhear that you and your wife are displeased with how the Council is governing the Light Ander situation in the Land of Cassum."

"Don't you mean how they are *not* handling the situation?" Gelaro returned shortly. "Especially those two brothers… I want to wrap my hands around their loud and ill-mannered throats. Even without Neo blood running through my veins, I'm sure I would be able to take them with ease. Let them put their words where their swords are… Then we will see who is more superior."

"Your words are noble and fierce. Come now, let me show you the future, and you'll see you won't need to use your sword to silence the ignorant."

Gelaro continued to follow Quar further into the dark, damp hallway where the roaring cries of the Bolics bounced off the cold walls and into the dark duo's ears. Gelaro shuddered at the eerie howls and with a disgusted look, peered into one of the Bolic cells.

The creature inside had been freshly turned into a wolf Bolic. Its bright yellow eyes flamed in the moonlight sneaking in through the barred window and thick patches of gray fur were scattered over its naked back.

"These are the nasty beasts you've been telling me about?" Gelaro asked. "They look absolutely intolerable."

"That's the idea," Quar replied coolly.

"And Ceros thinks he's the only one that knows about the Fusioning?"

"Yes. As far as the good king knows, he will be the first to gain the pure power of the process."

"But, I thought you said that the process has not yet succeeded on a Neo?

Quar and Gelaro reached the end of the hallway and stood at a thick wooden door, covered in red painted symbols. They were Quar's enchantments, used to keep the prisoner from using any magical powers.

"That is true, and although the Ander subjects are far from sane after the Fusioning, at least they survive. In all my attempts to Fuse Ander blood to a Neo, they die within hours of my spell."

"And you're sure that you can cure the disease of the Fusing Incantation?"

"I *know* I can. I've do-" Quar stopped briefly before continuing on a different track. "As long as you keep providing me with enough sample Anders to work with, I'm certain I can solve the issue."

"That's good to hear, Quar, because I don't want anything bad to happen to me when I undergo the Fusioning. Even in my Bolic crazed state, trust that I will keep it in my mind to kill you if things go wrong."

"I would not question your authority," Quar said smoothly as he bowed his head.

"But, you do not hesitate to rebel and work in secret under Ceros' rule. He is the king and raging with the *Prima Umbros* that you, yourself, endowed him with. Why am I to think you would not betray me as well?"

Quar rested his crinkled hand on the thick prison door and breathed heavily.

"I have my reasons as to why Ceros deserves this. They do not concern you."

"Oh but they do," Gelaro stated crudely. "How am I to trust your actions if I do not know your intentions? How do I know you won't turn around and stab *me* in the back?"

Quar's wicked manner returned as he retorted, "If I wanted you dead, I would have done so already, Gelaro. You're a powerful Ander, why Ceros sought you out twenty years ago, but I doubt you'd last a second in my ill-fated wrath. Besides, the same could be asked of you. Why betray your good king after he raised you from your low stance on this earth?"

"I'm tired of his trivial tasks. I earned my place at the Council table just like everyone else. I am owed equal respect."

"And that, you shall receive once your trust is placed in me, Gelaro. So, before I open this door, shall I trust that both our backs are safe?"

Gelaro stayed silent and nodded.

"Good," Quar continued. "Let's see what we have in store for you…"

Quar cackled and withdrew his hand from the door.

Chanting, Quar closed his eyes and said, "*Aperiro Ostu.*"

As the last word fell from Quar's tongue, the old rusted locks released, and the hinges squealed as the door slowly opened.

Quar turned to Gelaro and stated calmly, "This one may be old, but rest assured, he has much more magical strength than the Magi Order. Once I have perfected the Fusioning ritual, he will be a grand candidate for your blood."

As Quar stepped aside, Gelaro entered the damp cell and stared down upon Friar Sulny who was chained to the wall.

"The infamous Great Abbey friar?" Gelaro said shocked but pleased. "Quar, you've outdone yourself."

Gelaro crouched down, grabbed Friar Sulny by his tattered shirt, and lifted the friar's weak body off the ground. Friar Sulny kept quiet and stared into Gelaro's eyes remaining unmoved and unshaken by the dark Ander's attempt at intimidation.

"A proud one, too? He'll fit well into my character," Gelaro chuckled.

Gelaro tossed poor Friar Sulny's body back to the stony ground and turned to Quar who was standing in the doorway.

"The deal is I send you Anders and you will grant me the full Neo-Ander Fusion when it's been fully resolved?"

"Yes," Quar replied.

"I have to discuss this further with Yura. She will want you to have an equally powerful Neo ready for her blood to fuse with, but I'm sure she will not mind the terms under which you have laid out."

"Good, but I would not wait too long to return, Gelaro. I sense that the spectrum of Pangea is about to turn. Your decision now may be the reason why you live tomorrow."

Concerned with the dark wizard's prophetic words, Gealro quickly responded, "I'll be sure to make haste with a confirmed decision. Meanwhile, I suggest you have your men search for a Neo worthy of my wife."

"Oh… I think I have the perfect fit."

"Outstanding."

Gelaro pulled out a vial from under his black robe and cast it to the wall. Instantly, a swirling vortex opened, the result of Strass and Perone's Shadow creation, and Gelaro stepped inside. The vortex immediately closed and the wall returned to its normal state.

Quar removed his stare from the empty wall and moved it to Friar Sulny who was lying on the ground with his eyes closed.

"The damn Ander knocked his own treasure unconscious," Quar murmured to himself as he pulled the heavy cell door shut and recast his spell to keep the friar's magic confined before returning to his chambers upstairs.

But, Friar Sulny was not unconscious. In fact, he was fully aware of his surroundings and had pretended to be knocked out so that he could cast a spell of his own while Quar's magical barrier was down.

Friar Sulny sat up and looked to a tiny cracked hole in the wall and whispered, "Be well my little friend."

On the other side of the cracked hole, a small white mouse climbed its way out of the Great Abbey's dungeon and out onto the open grassy field surrounding the fortress. After blinking its beady red eyes and shaking off the dirt on its furry coat, it darted off toward the far tree lines at the edge of the Great Abbey's perimeter.

Just beyond these trees, Sam, Chase, and Eton, along with the Light Mafia, had just made camp, hidden in the dark forest.

"Dear God, just shoot me now!" Chase wailed in agony.

"Oh be quiet, Chase. It can't hurt that bad," Sam hushed.

Chase was lying face down on the damp grass. Her shirt had been pulled up to her neck to reveal two large bruises covering the upper part of her back. Sam was sitting next to her trying to heal her, resting her warm hands on Chase's back. The shimmering blue light glistened in the darkness.

"I don't understand. When and how did you even get these bruises? I didn't think that Marthule and Christo were beating you up that badly in training," Sam said concerned.

"They weren't," Chase replied. "Honestly, I have no idea how this happened. I just woke up a couple days ago, and there they were. It feels like there are extra bones in there or something. They keep cracking."

"I wonder why my Healing powers aren't working," Sam said frustrated as she returned her hands to her side allowing Chase to pull down her shirt and sit up as well.

"Hey, don't take it too hard, Sam," Chase consoled. "Remember, these powers are still new to both me *and* you. It might take some time for us to really get a hang of 'em. Besides, the bruises don't hurt that much anyway."

Chase stretched out her arms and wiggled her back.

"See? I'm okay."

Sam was not convinced. Seeing this, Chase scooted over and put her arm around Sam's shoulders.

"Don't worry, Sam. I wouldn't lie to you if I wasn't alright. They'll go away."

Sam sighed and leaning over, resting her head on Chase's shoulder. She could feel Chase's embrace around her. Something about it had changed.

When Chase had hugged Sam, before they arrived at Pangea, Sam could feel love and compassion, but there was an uncertainty about it. Perhaps it was because Chase's emotions were up and down with Cia and the changing current of their chaotic circus lives. Sam was not sure, but now, as Chase caressed Sam's arm in the night's chilly air, there was a sense of maturity and clarity that Sam had never observed of her friend. Whatever it was though, it felt nice, and Sam snuggled in.

As Sam and Chase took in the atmosphere, silence filled the night sky. The stars above sparkled like tiny diamonds in a sea of darkness. The small group below related well to the scene.

As minutes progressed, the Great Crossings got cooler and cooler. Sam could hear the subtle crackling of a fire behind her. It was an incredibly calming moment, which Sam was thankful for considering the past few weeks.

Suddenly, Chase yelled, "Get down!"

Startled, Sam ducked as Chase shoved Sam's body to the ground, and a sharp arrow whizzed by them.

"What the hell?" Chase asked as she lifted herself off the ground.

"That's the ticket!" a shout from the darkness called out.

Sam and Chase squinted their eyes as they tried to make out the mysterious voice's body, but to their surprise, *two* bodies emerged from the shadows. It was Eton and Celtessa.

"Are you crazy?" Chase yelled. "Are you trying to kill us?"

Celtessa laughed.

"Goodness no!" she exclaimed as she drew nearer. "I was helping Eton master his archer skills when we saw you two. Eton figured it might be a good time to test *your* abilities, too."

"Did it ever occur to you what might happen if I *didn't* hear that arrow coming?" Chase inquired.

"Hmm… come to think of it, no. I just hoped for the best that you would. Lucky for us, you did!"

Chase slapped her forehead.

"Oo! It looks like Sabua and Rhodil have started a fire," Celtessa sidetracked. "Perhaps dinner is coming, as well. Come on, Chase. You should be helping them. I loved the grilled bird you made for us two nights ago."

Celtessa grabbed Chase by the arm and started pulling her toward the other members of the Light Mafia.

"Why don't I just teach you how to grill so next time, *you* can do it?" Chase asserted as she rolled her eyes.

"Don't be silly! Then I'd be depriving you of the joy you get when you grill. Beside, it takes too much work, and I like the way you do it better."

Chase groaned as her and Celtessa walked toward the fire. Sam was still sitting on the ground in shock.

"I'm so sorry, Sam," Eton apologized. "I swear it wasn't my idea."

Eton reached out a hand and helped Sam stand to her feet. Sam brushed off her shirt and tossed her hair.

"You have a leaf stuck in your hair," Eton informed playfully.

Sam blushed and shook her hair again to try and set the stubborn leaf free.

"Better?" she asked.

"Nope. Still there. Here, let me get it."

Eton stepped in closer and gently pulled the leaf out of Sam's hair. He held in front of her face and twirled the stem in his fingers.

"This reminds me of that night… Shall we make a wish?" Eton asked wearing a large smile.

"Does that work?"

"Not sure. We might as well give it a go. Just close your eyes and wish."

Sam took a deep breath in and shut her eyes. She could feel Eton bring the leaf closer to her lips.

"Now, blow," Eton whispered.

Keeping her eyes closed, Sam let out all the air in her lungs and blew the feathered leaf into the wind.

"Did you wish for anything, Eton?" Sam finally spoke after opening her eyes.

"Yes. This," Eton grinned as he stepped in and pulled Sam's body into his.

Sam could feel Eton's pulse quickening and racing through his defined muscles. His body was flexed but not tense. Eton rested one hand under her chin and tilted Sam's mouth up to his. Then, he leaned in and kissed her.

Eton's deep breathing beat Sam's upper lip as his hand moved graciously behind her neck. His lips were rough but gentle as they pressed deeper into hers.

A rush of sensation rushed through Sam's body as she wrapped her arms around his strong neck and elegantly kissed him back. Though this was only Sam's second kiss -minus the impulsive kiss to Chase- she knew that this kiss felt better and more fitting than her kiss with Conner.

After the kiss subsided, and Eton pulled away from her, Sam cleared her throat and said, "That was a very nice wish."

"I was hoping you'd say that," Eton replied cheerfully. "To be honest, I've been craving that since I saw you in Chase's world. You looked so beautiful, just as I remembered."

Sam blushed.

"Thank you, Eton. You always have such nice things to say to me."

"Sam?"

"Yes?"

"Do you remember back in the cave, after we had escaped from the Sector… I told you something. Do you remember that?"

Sam politely pulled herself out of Eton's hold.

"Yes," she replied softly.

"Those feelings have not changed. In fact, they've grown quite a bit more since then. They've grown so much more that I feel confident in telling you that I love you. I love you very much. I had doubts, but they have been stilled now by our kiss. Am I right to say that you love me, too?"

"Eton… I do love you, and yes, the kiss was very sweet, but..."

Sam began to fiddle with the moon charm dangling from her neck.

"But, what?" Eton asked eagerly.

"But, with everything that has been going on and everything that is going to happen, I cannot pursue a relationship like this."

"You can't pursue love? That's outrageous," Eton protested.

The flesh wound on his left pectoral began to swell in a subtle glow, growing brighter by the second under Eton's brown shirt. Noticing this, Eton placed his right hand over it and just stared at Sam, waiting for an explanation.

"No, it's not," Sam progressed. "Tomorrow we are going to infiltrate the Great Abbey and save Friar Sulny with only eight Neos, one of which hasn't even fully come into her powers yet. We don't know what kind of evil lies in wait for us or how bad it will be. The last thing I need is to be worrying about losing you in more ways than a friend. It's just not the right time."

"It's not about the right time," Eton continued. "It's about *making* it the time to love. You of all people should know that, or is it that your heart has already been captured by someone else?"

"What are you talking about?" Sam declared though she knew where the conversation was heading.

"I'm talking about Chase," Eton retorted.

"What about Chase? You know it's been my responsibility to keep her safe. It was in the Telling!"

"But, was it in the Telling to fall in love with her? Sure, keep her safe and protect her. *That* was your destiny, not to hold her in your selfish hands and risk what may be the only chance we have at restoring peace on Pangea. I've seen how she loves and who she loves. If you tamper with those emotions who knows what will happen? She's already unstable in her powers, and like you said, she hasn't even fully developed as a Neo. Her heart is the key to her strength. If you damage or meddle with it, we could lose everything."

Sam blinked back a tear.

"Is that what you want?" Eton asked as he stepped forward and tried to put a caring hand on Sam's arm, but Sam stepped back.

"No. That's not what I want," Sam whispered softly as she felt a heavy force weigh down on her heart.

"Well, if you do not choose to share your

affections with me, then at least be aware of your choice of sharing them with Chase. She just realized her love for Cia, and that seems to be helping her powers grow. We need her to focus. We have a very important task to complete tomorrow."

Sam nodded silently, turned, and walked toward the others. Eton sighed with sorrow at the sight of his beloved and followed quietly behind her. He peered down to his flesh wound, and its glow subsided, as always.

"Forgive me," Eton whispered to himself before following Sam.

When they arrived at the camp, Chase and the Light Mafia had already started eating.

"Ah! Sam and Eton, how nice of you to join us," Sabua declared joyfully. "Come, and sit down by the fire before this night air freezes your toes. I think at the rate everyone is eating, there might not be enough food for you to take delight on."

Sam and Eton sat down on a nearby log. Christo walked up to them and handed each of them a plate with a salad and pieces of grilled fish.

"Enjoy," Christo said cheerfully. "I even managed to find some nice tomatoes to put in the salad. I've always liked a splash of color on my dinner plate."

"Thank you, Christo," Sam replied. "It looks delicious."

Christo returned to the opposite side of the fire and sat back down next to Rhodil who was busily filling her hungry mouth with seconds.

"Slow down, Rhodil," Christo laughed. "You'll get a stomach ache."

"I have an iron stomach, Christo," Rhodil assured between chews. "No need to worry."

Sabua finished the last piece of fish on her plate, set it down on the ground then stood up.

"Now that everyone is here, we need to go over our plan of attack for tomorrow evening," Sabua announced.

She withdrew her wand and held it delicately in her left hand.

Pointing and waving it at the fire, Sabua chanted, "*Exor a incenda*!"

With the quick flick of her wrist the flames before the group swirled in enchantment as the bright orange inferno spiraled into a model of the Great Abbey.

"Now *that* is cool," Chase said stunned as she popped a cherry tomato into her mouth.

Marthule patted her on the back and chimed in, "You must wait until you see her arouse the lightning. It's her specialty especially when it rains. Now *that*, as you say, is cool."

Chase playfully elbowed Marthule's mighty body in the side and laughed. Then, she turned to Sam and smiled.

Sam forced a smile back and returned her stare back to the fire as Sabua began explaining their strategy.

"First, we will need to split up into two teams," Sabua began. "There will be one team on each side of the Great Abbey."

As Sabua spoke, the flames played out her every word. Small fire-made images of the group appeared in the flames, one on each side of the Abbey.

"Chase, Sam, Marthule, and Christo will be on the east side and Rhodil, Celtessa, Eton, and myself will be on the west. At midnight, Celtessa and Eton will launch an arrow attack over the western wall because just beyond it, Eton remembers that the stables are located there. As unfortunate as the Devolut horse casualties may be, this will not only bring the guards' attention to the fire but also slow their scout forces from investigating the outside grounds, allowing both teams to close in without being caught."

The fire dolls ran toward the walls mimicking their commanders script.

"Then, Christo will fly up the eastern wall and lay fire to their armory stalls as Marthule, Chase, and Sam charge through the main gates. As the main flow of remaining guards are drawn to them, my team will make our way up the wall and down to the inside grounds. Then, we will search for Friar Sulny as the eastern side distracts the guards.."

When Sabua concluded, the fire settled and returned to normal.

"Wait. I need to be there when you find Friar Sulny," Sam opposed. "We don't now what kind of condition he will be in. I can heal him. I'm going with you."

"No," Sabua instructed. "You will be in the main heat of battle, so you must remain with your group so that if they require healing, you can be there. We can manage to carry the friar out of harm's way."

"She's right," Marthule interjected. "Our best chances lie with their covertness in minimal numbers."

"Once we have the Friar," Sabua continued. "We will start a fire on one of the corner towers. At that point, everyone will split into pairs and disperse into the multiple directions in the woods. By the second morning, everyone will reconvene at the Waterfall Hole north of here. Sam, Eton, do you remember how to get there?"

Sam and Eton nodded their heads.

"Good. Rhodil and Marthule will take the first shift of watching guard tonight. Then it will be-"

Before Sabua could finish, Marthule sprung up and landed hard on the ground, his hands cupped over something.

"What in stars are you doing?" Celtessa asked bewildered.

Marthule smiled.

"I just caught my dessert."

With that, Marthule stood up and was holding a small white mouse by its tail.

"Eew," Christo exclaimed. "Marthule, you can't be so hungry that you'd revert to eating a rodent."

"I have to say, that *is* pretty disgusting," Rhodil chimed in. "And that says quite a bit considering I eat anything."

"Hey!" Marthule defended. "We need all the energy we can get for tomorrow. I'm merely doing that."

Not used to the sight of watching anyone eat a mouse, Chase closed her eyes before Marthule would become the first, but just as Marthule was about to drop the tiny rodent down his throat, the mouse shook fervently and from its body a beaming array of sparkling lights shimmered around it.

Marthule dropped the mouse on the ground.

"What the hell is that?" Marthule exclaimed.

Chase opened her eyes at Marthule's shouting. As the light disappeared, an old man dressed in a white cloak was standing before them.

"Friar Sulny!" Sam cried out.

Indeed, the mouse had transformed into an image of the good friar and was standing in ghostlike form.

"No, my dear Sam'ona," the apparition spoke solemnly. "What you see before you is merely an image of me cast upon this mannerly Devolut. I sensed you were near and was able to send this message to you. The fates were kind to us tonight as they allowed our timings to fall in line."

"Are you alright, Friar Sulny?" Sam asked worriedly.

"Yes, my child. Quar has taken many attempts at stealing my mind, but rest assured my faith in your return has kept me strong."

Sam smiled.

"And I see you have brought Eton back," the white figure noted. "It is good to see that you are well."

"Thank you, Friar Sulny," Eton replied.

Then, Friar Sulny's image turned to face Chase.

"Solaris," he whispered. "You have grown into a marvelous young woman. I see Sam'ona has done a remarkable job at taking care of you."

"She has," Chase said proudly. "It's nice to finally, uh… meet you… sorta."

Friar Sulny chuckled.

"We have met before, dear Solaris, though that was a very long time ago."

"Yeah, I don't remember much from those days," Chase replied sarcastically. "By the way, you can call me Chase. It's what I've grown up with."

"Then it is nice to meet again, Chase," the snowy specter answered. "I sent this Devolut out to lead you directly to me. Quar has many guards and has doubled the amount of Bolics he has here. You will need all the help you can receive."

Christo turned to Marthule and said, "I suppose you won't be having dessert after all."

Marthule folded his arms in jest and returned, "I guess it's alright seeing how the friar has made our job a lot easier for tomorrow. Won't need that extra strength anyway."

"Keep the mouse safe," Friar Sulny progressed. "When you breach the Great Abbey Walls, set it free, and it will lead you to me. Quar has been keeping me in my cell rather than in his quarters, but I never know what trick he prepares to unleash."

"Thank you, Friar Sulny," Sabua spoke up. "We are most thankful for your assistance."

The apparition bowed its head and transformed back into its rodent form. Marthule picked it up and held it in his sturdy hands.

"I'll keep an eye on the thing. I feel bad 'cause I was the one going to eat it."

"Alright everyone," Sabua announced. "It's time to call it a night. We're going to need plenty of rest before tomorrow. We still have to make final preparations before we strike."

Sabua waved her wand for the final time that evening, and the fire was instantly put out.

Marthule and Rhodil remained sitting to start the first round of the night watch as the others prepared their spots on the soft grass to sleep.

Chase walked up to Sam and handed her a blanket.

"You'll probably need this more than I will," Chase started. "You know me, my body's always ten degrees hotter than normal."

Sam took the blanket and smiled.

"Thank you."

"And besides, if I do get cold, I can always come share with you."

Chase chuckled, but Sam did not as she looked down at the wooly covering in her arms.

"Actually, you can keep it," Sam replied anxiously as she returned the blanket back to Chase. "I think Celtessa said she had an extra one packed. I won't bother you with yours."

Startled by Sam's response, Chase stuttered, "Okay, Sam. If you say so."

Chase took the blanket back, and Sam quickly rushed off to Celtessa's side.

"Um… goodnight?" Chase stammered to herself.

Shaking off the awkward moment with Sam, Chase settled down and lied down on her back, staring up at the stars.

"Big day tomorrow. Man, I wish I had a wand like Sabua's so I could control lightning like Marthule said," she whispered to herself. "All I've got is the ability is to control rocks."

Chase turned her face to look at the extinguished fire. She pointed her fore and middle finger together.

"Boom," she whispered again and mockingly flicked her wrist, using her hand as if it was a wand

As she did, Chase felt a swell of air launch itself from her fingertips.

The burst of air shot forward and plowed through the fire pit logs, rolling them about a foot or so from their original spot.

Chase sat up in shock and looked around to see if anyone noticed, but they were fast asleep, and Marthule and Rhodil had walked off to scout the perimeters so Chase lied back down.

Chase put her hand in front of her face.
"All the elements, huh? I wonder what's
next?"

The First of Many

Nysam opened his eyes slowly. His vision remained blurry as he gazed around Quar's chambers. The room was dimly lit by the crackling fireplace and an assortment of candles. Nysam coughed at the rancid smell that stabbed his nostrils.

"Good to see you're awake, Priest," Quar said coldly.

He was leaning his elderly body against the table in front of the fireplace holding a long knife and a bronze goblet.

"How long was I out this time?" Nysam inquired softly.

"Almost a day. Nighttime has fallen over the skies once more," Quar replied.

Nysam let out an agonizing groan. His muscles felt like they had been stretched beyond their limits, and his air felt colder than the Great Crossings' winter winds.

"What have you been doing to me?" Nysam demanded.

"I've been trying to adhere Ander blood to your body. You see, the Fusioning works fine if I inject Neo blood to an Ander specimen, but if I reverse the process, the Neo can only sustain the transformation a couple hours. But, you… You have lasted far longer than any Neo I've worked with."

"You fused my blood with an Ander?"

"Yes, but I have been doing so over the course of a few days, only adding a few more drops into your veins at a time. You haven't died yet, so that means either the more magic a Neo has, the stronger he or she is to withstand the Fusioning changes, or it really will take an elongated time to successfully Fuse the bloods this way."

"You will *not* get away with this," Nysam barked back.

"Oh, but I already have. Take a look at yourself."

Still chained to the wall, Nysam stood up slowly and stared into a dusty mirror that stood erected in the corner. He gasped at the sight of his reflection.

His once brilliant shiny blonde hair had been reduced to a skull covered in his koi fish scales. Nysam ran his hand over his bald head and felt the smooth sliminess that he was used to only underwater in his Neo form. Two large boney spikes also protruded from the tops of both his naked shoulders. Nysam carefully grabbed hold of one and angrily pulled at it. To his surprise, the spike was instantly freed of his body, and Nysam held before him a small jagged dagger.

"I wouldn't touch that if I were you," Quar warned. "They're poisonous."

Nysam dropped the result of his mutation on the ground and fell to his knees in disbelief.

"You're a monster…" Nysam whispered.

"No," Quar started as he walked up to Nysam's shocked and tired body. "From the looks of things, you are."

With that, Quar slashed open a large cut on Nysam's chest. Nysam shouted in pain, which Quar ignored but splashed Nysam with the contents of the bronze goblet.

Nysam's skin sizzled on contact.

Quar continued, "As much as I'd love to continue this experiment with you, Nysam, time is of the essence, and I need you to be the full beast that you can be regardless of your eminent death."

Nysam's eyes widened as he struggled to free himself from his shackles, but it was to no avail. Quar walked back to the table and retrieved his crooked cane, raising high into the air.

"*Inclinio ferra tu nox et silentu luxcio*!" Quar repeated the Fusioning spell.

Nysam howled in excruciating pain as Quar's dark magic wrapped its claws around and sank its fangs into the Water Priest's fragile body. Nysam's transformation finished as he stood back up. His previous Bolic features had remained, but now, he also bore finned hands and feet and a more muscular build. Nysam breathed heavily and stared at Quar, his new master.

Just then, Quar's door slammed open. One of Quar's guards was panting.

"Quar! The stables! They're on fire!" the guard shouted in urgency.

"So, tend to it," Quar said bitterly, frustrated at his servant's ignorance.

"We are, but I think we are under attack!"

Quar smiled slyly and turned to Nysam.

"See? I told you that I would need you."

Nysam roared and broke free of his chains. Then, he took a step forward and waited for his command.

Quar walked confidently up to his new Bolic creation and whispered into his ear, "Kill her."

Nysam let out a howling roar once more before storming out of Quar's room.

The Light Mafia's attack had worked.

Although it was raining, many of the guards had rushed to the stables to try to put out the brilliant flames that Celtessa and Eton's arrows had set.

As the guards raced to the burning stables, Christo, in her grand velvety-purple phoenix form, flew over the Great Abbey walls and unlocked the main gates, granting Chase, Sam, and Marthule their entrance.

"It's working," Christo relayed as she met her comrades at the main gates, back in her human form. "All of the guards went to the other side of the Abbey."

"Good, now it's time to start the second wave of flames," Marthule commanded.

The small group ran over to the armory housing. Chase tried to open the doors but they did not budge.

"It's locked."

"No worries about that," Marthule replied. "There's a reason why I'm called the Enforcer. Step aside."

Sam, Chase, and Christo obeyed Marthule's order as he sprinted back several yards.

In the blink of eye, Marthule had changed into a majestic lion. He tossed his golden mane back and forth then let out a roar before charging forward at the locked doors. Marthule's giant paws beat heavily on the cold ground as he crashed clear through.

Christo turned to Sam and Chase and said, while chuckling, "He loves to show off."

The three scurried to meet Marthule inside. He had changed back to his human form and was strapping on one of the Shadow Force shields to his left arm.

"Sam, Chase… Come and strap on some extra equipment. The Shadow Force troops may be evil, but they do have high quality armor and weapons."

Sam and Chase followed Marthule's orders

as Christo kept watch on the door.

"Hurry. We must not waste any time," Christo urged quietly.

Once Sam and Chase had finished putting on armor and picking up a stronger sword, they rushed back outside. Marthule walked up and stood by Christo's side, just at the entrance of the armor holding.

"Okay, Christo. Let's show these Shadow Force scum what Light really looks like."

Marthule patted his good friend on the back and joined Sam and Chase outside. Christo turned around and stared at the wooden walls that the Shadow Force weapons and shields called their home. She smiled and instantly turned back into a phoenix, flapping her wings so she looked down over the armory.

Closing her eyes, she took a deep breath in, and without hesitation, she opened her mouth and a brilliant gust of flames shot out. The bright swirling reds and oranges flew at the armory as if they had sprouted wings of their own and soared over the fragile wooden surface, instantly setting it ablaze.

Outside, Chase and Sam stood in awe at the sight. They could both see Christo inside, with her incredible wingspan spread open, and her chest swelling with the roaring embers she gave birth to.

Only a few seconds after the house went up in flames, Christo emerged with her human body clean as a whistle, untouched by her fire-driven attack.

Before Chase and Sam could fully comprehend the glory of Christo's powers, a loud stir from behind them distracted their attention.

"It's about time," Marthule said laughing.

Sam and Chase turned around and saw a rush of Quar's guards heading their direction.

"Okay, you two, stick close to either Christo or myself," Marthule continued as he drew his mace from his belt and held it firmly in his hand. "Do not hesitate to call upon us if you need help. We will be right here. Are you ready?"

Sam looked over to Chase for her friend's response. Chase had already unsheathed her sword and was propping her shield up in front of her.

"Ready as I'll ever be," Chase replied as she stared at the charging guards.

Chase turned to face Sam and smiled.

There it was again, that familiar feeling Sam felt in Chase's embrace the night before. Confidence. Certainty.

Passion.

Something in her best friend had changed. If only Sam could feel the same sense of sureness…

Sam smiled back but only slightly.

"Don't worry, Sam," Chase replied to Sam's hesitant look. "You've taken care of me for so long. This time… It's my turn."

A surprising wave of relief swept over Sam's body. She readied her own sword and stared out at the guards that were approaching closer by the second.

Marthule took a practice swing with his mace and reminded the group, "We just have to keep them off long enough for Sabua and the others to locate the friar and get him out. Pay attention to the towers for our exit signal."

The group nodded in return.

"Let the Light be on our side tonight as we make ripples in history," Christo chanted beautifully as she revealed six throwing stars from under her cloak and let the first offensive ammunition of the battle fly into the air directed at the enemy.

With great precision, all of Christo's stars landed at an enemy's throat or head. They fell instantly at the fatal blow, but the remaining charge of guards still progressed. There were about three dozen or so; only a handful of guards had stayed behind to finish tending to the burning stable and horses.

Marthule looked at his fellow comrades and let out a raging battle cry before charging forward. When his body met the oncoming Shadow Force, the striking of his mace to shields, breaking swords, and unexpecting bodies sung in the night air.

Chase gulped and followed in Marthule's lead.

The first attacker she encountered was a brown colored Neo wolf with matted fur and sharp fangs that were dripping with mad saliva. The wolf leaped high into the air, preparing to sink its teeth into Chase's bare neck, but Chase thrust her sword upward directly into the wolf's chest. The wolf let out a whimper as it fell to the ground limp.

Breathing heavily, Chase turned around and looked at Sam who was busy dueling a large burly guard, easily four times bigger than her.

The husky guard slammed his jagged sword down on Sam's shield as she lifted it up to block her thin frame from the attack, but the force of the blow was so great, it brought Sam down to her knees.

Seeing this, Chase dropped her sword and slammed her right fist into the ground. Just like before in the Sector, an earthy vine rose

from the ground and wrapped around the guard's
ankle. After Chase saw that she had a firm
grip on the guard's ankle, she stood back up
and jerked the vine hard. The guard screamed
as he fell on his back, bringing his sword
down with him.

Sam immediately leapt up and cast her
blade into the guard's stomach. The guard
wailed in pain as his vision left him with his
life soon following.

Sam stood over the dead body, shaken up.
Chase rushed to her side and put her hands on
Sam's shoulders.

"Sam? Are you okay?"

"I… I think so," Sam stuttered. "It's
just that… I was raised to be a Healer, to
restore life… not rob one of it."

"I know, Sam," Chase consoled. "This is
still unreal to me, too. A month ago, my
biggest problem was figuring out how to fix
the coffee machine at work, but we're here
now. This is what we're here to do. You taught
me how to be strong and decisive, so I know
you are, too.

I wouldn't be who I am without you. I
wouldn't have gotten my powers without you.
Don't you see? You're my strength, and I need
you, but most importantly, I need you to know
that I'm yours, too. We can do this together.
Do you trust me?"

Filled with Chase's inspiring words, Sam
firmly nodded her head, and using her shield,
she swiftly blocked an arrow that was aimed
toward Chase's neck.

"I trust you," Sam replied.

Chase smiled and ran back to fetch her
sword.

Marthule and Christo were easily holding
their own as more guards charged the

experienced Neos.

Marthule was still pummeling away at the guards as if they were flies, bringing them down one by one with his fierce mace. Many did not stand back up.

Christo's throwing stars whizzed around the battlefield before their opponents could even lay an eye on them. The tiny metal stars were much too fast to be stopped. Screams of pain shot up in the night as the fighting continued.

On the other side of the Great Abbey, Sabua and her group could hear the clatters and cries of the intense battle as they waited patiently in the shadows of the western wall.

"That's our queue," Sabua commanded Eton, Rhodil, and Celtessa. "Here's a great Manipulation Spell for you, Eton. Stand back."

Eton took a step back as Sabua withdrew her wand and held its tip to the smooth stone surface of the Great Abbey.

She closed her eyes and chanted, "*Scala muneo…*"

Then, Sabua opened her eyes and took a few steps back herself. The group stared at the wall as some of the stones within the wall began to shake.

Within seconds, the quivering stones had shifted out of their fixed place in the wall and had emerged just enough to create a makeshift staircase up the entire looming wall while maintaining support to the infamous structure.

"Incredible…" Eton whispered to himself.

Celtessa took the first step.

"C'mon, we don't have much time," she rushed.

The group of four quickly made their way up Sabua's magical stairs. When they

approached the top, Celtessa peeked her head
slowly above the wall-top then suddenly ducked
back down.

"There are four guards still walking the
upper perimeter, and there's about a six
guards below extinguishing the fire at the
stables."

"I think we know what to do here," Rhodil
said directly behind her.

"Right," Celtessa agreed as she pulled
out an arrow from her quiver and set it in
place in her bow. "On my mark."

With that, Celtessa leaped over the wall
and landed gracefully on the curtain wall of
the Great Abbey while launching an arrow at
the guard standing yards in front of her.

The arrow nailed the guard neatly between
his armor plates, and in pain, he stumbled and
fell down to the bailey below.

The other three guards on the roof
screamed for backup as they drew their own
bows out and aimed their weapons at Celtessa,
but as the arrows sailed toward her, Celtessa
keenly ducked and jumped out of each arrow's
attack. With brilliant agility and her long
bronze hair flowing behind her, Celtessa
sprinted along the wall until there was a
brief pause in the flow of shafts raining down
on her. At the slight break, Celtessa quickly
reset her bow and pinned each guard with her
sharp skills and matching arrows. Like the
first guard, the remaining three fell to their
doom as their armor plates were no match for
the power behind Celtessa's zooming arrows.

Meanwhile, Rhodil had also sprung over
the curtain wall. She unhooked her bullwhip
from her belt and jumped down to the bailey
grounds below landing directly on one of
Quar's men. His body breaking her plunge,

Rhodil quickly recovered from her drop and lashed out her whip at the oncoming defense. A guard yelped as the tiny metal shavings at the end of her whip cut deep into his skin. The whip recoiled back, and Rhodil let the whip fly again. This time, the end of the scourge wrapped around the assailant's torso. Rhodil yanked the whip hard to her, and the guard's body shot forward.

Using her free hand, which was shielded by the crimson spiked gauntlet, she swung her mighty fist across his face. He screamed in agony as the metal spikes cut deep into his cheeks. He fell to his knees right before Rhodil delivered one final blow to his chest.

At that point, Sabua and Eton had made their way over the wall. Eton stared below.

"Shouldn't we help her?" he asked nervously as he watched Rhodil battle the Shadow Force guards.

"She will be fine," Sabua assured. "Celtessa will be down to aide her, as well. *We* have more pressing matters to attend to. Follow me."

Sabua ran to the northwest tower door, wand at the ready for any attacker that might be waiting behind it. Eton followed close behind with his sword drawn.

Luckily, when Sabua opened the door, there was no opposition to stand in their way, so the pair made their way down the winding stairs to the ground floor. When they arrived, Sabua pulled out Friar Sulny's mouse from her flowing beige cloak and set it lightly upon the ground.

"Take us to Friar Sulny," she whispered.

The little white mouse shook its head and twitched its whiskers before scampering down the dark hallway. Sabua and Eton ran after it as the commotion outside continued. They could hear more and more guards run out to the battlegrounds to face the Light Mafia under the moonlight and accumulating clouds.

Sabua and Eton darted down another hallway, staying right on the mouse's tail as it guided them through the long corridors. Sabua was just about to turn a corner when she noticed torchlight bouncing off the perpendicular wall. She immediately halted and signaled to Eton to be ready to fight as the voices of two guards grew louder and louder.

But, just as the guards were about to face Sabua and Eton, they screamed in torment. The sound of a whizzing arrow and a flagellating lash echoed in the wide passageway, soon followed by the crashing of metal to the stony floor.

Sabua slowly inched around the corner, wand still poised in her left hand, but let out a sigh of relief as Celtessa and Rhodil stood before her.

"A pleasant sight to see you here," Sabua complimented. "Done with the battle above already?"

"The Shadow Force may give them power, but brains it does not," Rhodil said cheerfully. "They went down before they could blink. They're so lucky they can blink fast."

"The mouse! Where did it go?" Eton exclaimed.

"Down there!" Sabua pointed as the white ball of fur skirted around another corner.

The group ran after it and came to another fork in the hallway. The mouse veered to the right.

"How big is this place?" Celtessa wondered aloud. "It did not seem this big from the outside."

"The Great Abbey is magically enhanced to house more space inside than the actual physicality of it," Eton explained.

Just as Eton was about to describe the enchantments of the Great Abbey further, he noticed a faint shadowy figure float across the far entrance of the left hallway.

"Quar…" Eton muttered to himself, and before Sabua or the others could stop him, he darted down the left corridor instead of the right.

"Eton! Where the hell are you going?" Rhodil shouted after him. "The mouse is leading us this way!"

"I think he saw Quar," Sabua soothed Rhodil's agitation.

"Shouldn't we go after him then?" Celtessa asked.

"I will. You and Rhodil should continue following the mouse to Friar Sulny. Once you get him, head back to the wall from where we came, and get out. Remember to set a fire to the tower to warn the others that they need to leave. We will meet you at the Waterfall Hole when we can."

"You're sure you'll be alright?" Rhodil asked displeased with her friend's response. "I don't think we should split up again."

"If Eton indeed saw Quar, then you might have better success at freeing Friar Sulny while Eton and I keep Quar distracted. Best of luck, friends."

Celtessa gave Sabua a large hug and raced off down the right hallway with Rhodil to find Friar Sulny while Sabua chased after Eton.

As the furtive ensemble separated, the group upstairs banded closer together with the increased flow of Shadow Force guards streaming out into the open courtyard.

Christo had run out of throwing stars and resorted to utilizing a sword and axe to thwart off her aggressors. Even though these were not the tools of her trade, Christo still wielded them as if they were mere extensions of her arms. Her long black pony tail swished back and forth as she swung her left arm down, bringing the sharp axe upon a guard's shield while instantaneously thrusting the blade of her sword backward into the cavity of another who attempted to strike her from behind. After making the stab, she swirled around, grabbed the handle of her sword and kicked the guard straight in the chest, with her black leather boots, freeing her weapon from his ribs.

Just to the right of her, Marthule was clubbing down his attackers with smooth expertise and defined talent for such a crude weapon. His mace beat and shattered each bit of flesh and bone it came into contact with like it was a weak twig. Groups of three or more tried to take on the raged enforcer at the same time, but Marthule's strength was irrefutable. He slammed the guards' bodies down to the ground as if he were gravity himself. It seemed like no one could touch him until a guard standing a few feet away landed an arrow in Marthule's bicep.

Marthule roared at the piercing pain but did not let that stop him. He aimed his mace and hurled the weapon at the archer. The mace struck the guard right on his kneecap, breaking it instantly. Marthule threw back his head and roared as he charged forward toward the archer, back in his Neo Lion form, casting guards' bodies left and right. His golden mane shimmered in the dim moonlight as he stood above the Shadow Force archer and roared one more time before he standing on his hind legs and delivering the final blow.

Just behind Marthule and Christo, Sam and Chase were fighting back to back.

Sam's swordsmanship was surprisingly impeccable. She neatly jabbed and blocked each rivaling blow while staying light on her feet. Though she was still resilient to killing anyone, she succeeded at administering blows to the head or incisions cut just deep enough to render the opposing force unconscious from shock or blood loss. With Chase at her side, the pair were holding out their own for not having as much fighting experience as the Light Mafia members.

By this time, Chase had abandoned her sword and shield and employed her elemental control over the earth. Keeping her fists held tight, she threw knockout punches and blocked threatening blades from cutting her skin with her stony arms.

The battle seemed to be going well and in the small group's favor. The Shadow Force numbers were slowly decreasing, and Sam and Chase were getting much more efficient as a fighting duo while Marthule and Christo persisted in slaying their opponents individually.

The heavy clouds in the sky got darker and larger as the fighting progressed, and rain soon started to fall to the battlefield.

"You see?" Marthule screamed over the clattering and banging of weapons. "Pangea, herself, weeps over how pathetic these demons are fighting."

Marthule cackled as he picked up a charging Shadow Force fox with his bare hands and cast him aside like a rag doll.

Chase turned to Sam and smiled. Despite the circumstances, Chase was feeling great.

The surge of her powers coursed through her veins like a new form of life she had never experienced, even when she was fighting at the Sector.

Finally, she felt free.

The first booming sound of thunder rang in the sky, and Chase turned her attention to the gray billows that blanketed over the tiny sparkled stars. Though the rain was falling harder, making it more difficult to see, Chase noticed a figure standing on top of the northeast tower.

Was it Sabua? Had they already freed Friar Sulny?

She squinted and blinked her eyes rapidly to clear her vision in hopes to make out who the figure was, but she it was to no avail. The figure had disappeared.

"Looking for me?" a strange dark voice from behind her sounded.

Chase quickly turned around to face the stranger.

It was not Sabua who had spoken; instead, Nysam, in his Bolic form, was standing before her.

"Who are you? Chase inquired.

"My name is Nysam, the Water Priest," Nysam breathed heavily.

"Water Priest? Wait! You're part of the Magi Order, right? How did you escape?"

Nysam cracked his neck and withdrew one of his poisonous spikes from his shoulder. Another one grew back immediately in its place.

"I didn't," Nysam responded coldly.

With that, Nysam whipped the body-made thorn at Chase. She ducked just in time as Nysam's spike whizzed right over her head.

"What the hell?" Chase muttered as she

stood back up. "You're supposed to be on *our* side!"

"He has been possessed!" Christo shouted from the sidelines as she and Marthule came rushing toward her. "By the Shadow Force!"

Now ready to defend herself, Chase flexed her muscles and clenched her fists tight as the earth element surged down her arms turning them into stone again.

"I've been watching you from above," the possessed Nysam continued. "I'm impressed with how quickly you've taken to your powers. I take it that you've discovered your heart?"

"Something like that," Chase said sternly.

Nysam laughed, the Shadow Force engrained in his voice.

"I also see that the Healer's Mastery has made it here as well."

Nysam reached out his arm and opened his webbed hand towards Sam. Her entire body was immediately wrapped with a blanket of water composed of the falling rain.

"Sam!" Chase yelled as she made an attempt to run toward Sam.

"I wouldn't do that," Nysam warned. "By my command, I can squeeze her body until it snaps. Lucky me, eh? That it would be raining on our first encounter."

Nysam laughed once more as Marthule and Christo joined Chase with their weapons ready, fallen guards behind them like mere props to a stage.

"Now, that's not fair," Nysam pleaded. "Three against one?"

Evening out his odds, Nysam opened his webbed hands again and pointed them at Marthule and Christo. Just like Sam, their bodies were entirely covered in a swirl of rainwater, controlled by Nysam's magic.

"What do you want?!?" Chase screamed, eager to save her friends before they drowned.

"To kill you, of course," Nysam replied.

The remaining few Shadow Force guards circled around them ready to charge another attack. Nysam held up his hand to stop them.

"No! The rest of you go back into the Abbey and search every hallway. I have a feeling they brought friends."

The guards did not hesitate to follow Nysam's orders and ran immediately inside.

Chase dug her feet into the ground, preparing herself for Nysam's attack.

Nysam chuckled and withdrew two spikes from his shoulder. Again, they quickly regenerated from his shoulders, ready to be used.

Nysam twirled his poisonous spikes in his fingers teasing the nervous Chase. Chase kept her eyes on Sam who was miraculously still kicking and screaming inside Nysam's trap, but for how long?

"I don't have all night!" Chase yelled out, hoping to urge Nysam to make a move so that she could try to save Sam.

"You're right. You don't," Sam remarked snidely.

In a blink of an eye, Nysam launched both of his tiny bone spears at Chase. She knocked the first spike down to the ground with her rocky fist, but the other managed to sneak past Chase's defense and nicked her neck.

Chase immediately grabbed hold of the cut. There was an incredible burning sensation at her skin as it slowly started to flood her bloodstream. The poison quickly took effect, but Chase's stance did not falter. Keeping her right hand over her wound, her left arm dangled at her side, left fist clenched even tighter.

Sam's eyes were slowly closing, as well as Marthule's and Christo's. A charging spark ignited in Chase's chest and spirit.

I have to get them out.

Keeping her hand closed tight, Chase pulled her arm upward, bringing a column of hard soil up from the ground, the resurrected earth latching onto Chase's arm like a simple extension. She wound her arm back and flung it forward, releasing the earthy javelin straight at Nysam with surprising agility.

Nysam quickly reacted and waved his webbed hands in front him, bringing about the drops of rain before him. They collected into the shape of a thick wall composed of water. The viscosity and currents of Nysam's magically endowed fluid slowed Chase's earthy attack before it could strike him. Nysam laughed at the poor attempt.

"Is that all you have for me, Solaris?" Nysam yelled out insulted.

But, Chase was no longer paying attention to him. She had ran to Sam's side and was pulling Sam out of Nysam's watery tornado.

Seeing this, Nysam cast down the rocky spear and reached up into the sky with his hand as he walked towards Chase and Sam.

Though difficult, Chase had successfully pulled Sam out of the water trap by this point who lied on the ground unconscious. Nysam brought his hand back down to his side redirecting a heavy downpour of gathered rain onto Chase. The weight felt like a waterfall and brought Chase down to the ground instantly.

With Chase snared in his watery domain, Nysam picked Sam's limp body up in his arms and traveled up to the top of the northeast tower where he first made his entrance, using the rain to teleport him there.

When Nysam reached the top of the tower, the two fluid snares that held Marthule and Christo in place disintegrated. Both warriors dropped to their knees coughing.

"Chase!" Marthule screamed as he wiped the water from his eyes.

Marthule and Christo rushed to Chase's side to help her out, but the waterfall was much stronger than the one that held them captive. The thick rushing current around Chase's body swirled and twisted in every direction. Each time Marthule and Christo tried to put out a helping hand, the force of the current whisked it out.

From the outside, the water looked to be raging with insanity, but inside, the water was shockingly calm. Chase floated up from the ground and bobbed up and down within the eye of Nysam's hurricane.

Chase could feel the life slowly leaving her as she thought to herself, *I've failed. I've failed them all.*

But, just before the last bit of oxygen fled her lungs and the remaining bit of poison cascaded through her veins, a smooth fin brushed against her face.

Reluctant to open her eyes, but having curiosity motivate her actions, Chase slowly opened her eyes to see what had touched her cheek.

A bright orange koi fish swam before her. Finally, the Tracker fish that Nysam had sent, prior to his ghastly Fusioning, had reached Chase's presence.

Chase's mind was nodding in and out as the brilliant fish floated around.

What is this? *A trick of some kind*?

Before Chase could completely comprehend her own fleeting thoughts, the koi fish spoke to her in a ghostly voice.

"Invincibility it not measured by immortality. It is measured by fearlessness. Set your mind free, and your body will follow."

As the final words were hushed by rushing waters, Chase closed her eyes and filled her head with empowering thoughts.

She pictured Tai sacrificing his life at the hands of Boull. She thought of Julissa, Rio, and their crew working together to brave against the Brevi Ocean's furious storms. She thought of the members of the Light Mafia and all the risks they were taking in tonight's plans. Then, came the thought of all she left behind: Cia, Simon, Leo, the twins, her world…

Chase's heart was immediately filled with the same surge of confidence she had felt when she was fighting Quar's guards only moments ago. She opened her mouth and screamed into the water.

With her muffled scream, she forced her body to combat Nysam's toxins as she compelled her legs down into the current so that could stand on her own two feet again.

After much struggling, she succeeded and proceeded to try out her latest developed power, secretly discovered the night before.

Chase pointed each fore and middle finger together on her hands and crossed her arms over her chest. As the water began to fill her nostrils and drip down her throat, she slowly began to uncross her arms creating two surges of wind from her fingertips that fought against the turbulent waves of Nysam's currents. Her arms shook with fury and resistance.

Slowly but surely, the heavy water screen parted as Chase opened her eyes and saw Marthule and Christo standing before her in shock.

Recovering quickly from the miraculous sight, Marthule and Christo lunged forward and grabbed Chase's arms and pulled her out of the mystical waterfall before it came crashing down again. With Chase free, the torturous water trap dissolved into the ground.

"Are you alright?" Christo asked the coughing Chase.

"Yeah, I'm okay," Chase replied warily. "Where's Sam?"

"Nysam took her up to the tower," Marthule responded. "Don't worry, Chase. We'll get her back. C'mon, Christo."

Chase stopped Marthule and Christo from moving.

"No," she stated. "This is my fight. I told Sam that I would protect her. *I* have to do this."

Using Marthule and Christo as support, Chase stood up.

"But, the poison…" Christo started.

"It doesn't matter right now. All that matters is that we get Sam back," Chase said sternly.

Just as Chase was about to make her way toward the tower stairs, she felt a sharp pain in her back where the unhealed bruises were and was increasingly larger than the subtle stinging of Nysam's poison.

"What's the matter?" Christo continued to ask. "Is it the poison?"

Not wanting to further alarm Christo, Chase lied, "Must be, but I'll be fine. You should go into the Abbey and see if you can help the others locate Friar Sulny."

"We cannot-" Christo began to protest, but Marthule rested a hand on her back before she could proceed.

"Be safe, Chase. We believe in you," Marthule calmly finished.

With that, Marthule and the reluctant Christo headed to the main building of the Great Abbey. Chase cracked her back and used what little strength she had left to race up the tower stairs to the patiently waiting Nysam.

Celtessa and Rhodil were having positive results. Friar Sulny's mouse had led them directly to him in the basement dungeons. They had just finished fighting off the guards and the released Bolics and were attempting to open the cursed door that Quar had secured.

"Luckily, these dungeon corridors were narrow so we only had to fight a few Bolics at once," Rhodil iterated as she smashed her fisted gauntlet into the door, trying to break through.

"Do you really think that this is going to work?" Celtessa inquired. "You've been banging at this thing for five minutes now."

"Do you have any better suggestions?" Rhodil asked as she rubbed her tired hand. "Friar Sulny?"

Friar Sulny walked up to the door from the inside and spoke, "I do. Celtessa, you said that you are an archer correct?"

"Yes, sir," Celtessa replied proudly. "The best in the land. My arrows sail faster than wind itself."

"That's good. Here's what we need to do. Rhodil, tie the end of your whip to one of Celtessa's arrows. Celtessa, I'll need you to get on the ground and fire your arrow underneath the crack of the door. It will have to be with great strength and speed in order to pass through the magical barrier Quar has placed. I'm hoping the magic in your shaft will be able to withstand the curse as it passes under, but if what you say about the agility of your arrows' flight is true, then it should not be a problem."

"Right. Nothing to worry about," Celtessa replied as Rhodil tied the end of her bullwhip to the tail of Celtessa's arrow.

"Rhodil, you'll have to make sure to hold onto the end of your whip very tightly," Friar Sulny continued to instruct. "The curse of the door will either try to pull the whip entirely in or shoot it back out. Once I see the arrow, I will do my best to grab it. At that point, Rhodil, you must be standing directly in front of the door with your hand upon it. I will use your whip to transfer my magic powers to your body as I chant the spell because the curse can only be lifted from the outside. We must act quickly for it to work."

"Understood," Celtessa and Rhodil replied in unison.

Rhodil wrapped both hands tightly around the handle of her whip while Celtessa lied down on the floor preparing to launch her arrow.

"Are you ready, Friar Sulny?" Celtessa asked.

"Yes," Friar Sulny responded confidently.

"Okay. Here it comes!"

Celtessa pulled back the arrow in her bow and let the arrow fly under the open space between the door and the floor. It flew through with exact precision, and just as Friar Sulny had warned, the door tried to spit the arrow back out, sensing the magical ties adhered to it.

Friar Sulny, though old in age, rapidly pounced on Celtessa's arrow and picked up the end of the whip.

"Now!" he shouted.

Rhodil threw her body towards the door and placed her hand upon it, just like Friar

Sulny had directed.

Friar Sulny closed his eyes and repeated the chant that he had heard Quar use the night before when Gelaro visited his cell.

"*Aperiro Ostu.*"

The old heavy door creaked and squealed as the rusty hinges opened slowly.

"It worked!" Celtessa exclaimed as she stood back up.

Friar Sulny hobbled out.

"Friar Sulny, it is a pleasure," Rhodil commented as she bowed.

"The honor, my friends, is all mine," Friar Sulny replied. "I owe you a great deal for saving me."

"Well, we can worry about that later," Celtessa cut in as she brushed off her white tunic. "Let's go find Quar and Eton and get out of here before Quar calls in supporting troops. We'll be lucky if Marthule and the others were able to successfully hold off the outside forces for as long as it's been."

Friar Sulny nodded and followed in between Celtessa and Rhodil as the three went off to the Great Abbey's main floor in search of their comrades.

Sabua had not caught up to Eton yet, as he ran down the final hallway before reaching Quar's chambers. When Eton arrived at Quar's room, the door was shut. He took a deep breath in and tightened his grasp around his sword.

After taking one more huge inhalation, Eton quickly burst through the door.

"Quar?!?" he demanded.

"I can't say I'm surprised to see you here," a dark voice sounded from the shadows.

The fireplace was lowly lit as the last bits of logs were burned, and a swarming shadow, that seemed to have a life of its own, dominated the room.

"Show yourself," Eton commanded.

Quar emerged in front of Eton from behind the shadows of an old bookcase. He hobbled with the use of his crooked cane and stood in what little light the room had.

"But, I have to say," Quar continued coldly. "I didn't expect you to be so enraged when you returned. I would think you'd be a little more grateful considering what I gave you."

"You didn't give me anything!" Eton shouted as he took an eager step forward, yielding his sword in front of him.

"I didn't?" Quar answered, acting insulted. "Sending you to the love of your life, to an entirely different dimension, classifies as nothing after you practically begged me? I'm hurt."

Eton growled at Quar's sarcasm.

Quar proceeded smoothly, "We had a deal, Eton. I wouldn't kill you, or your beloved, if you did your job. I asked for blood, and you bring back an Ander *with* Neo powers! Was the Healer's Mastery too much of a distraction to you that you could not complete a simple task?"

"I know what I had promised," Eton argued. "But, the deal is off. I'm not your slave anymore. Besides, I don't even know who-"

"Silence! Let me remind you what it feels like when you betray me, or have you forgotten? You shouldn't have. After all, it's caught you in your words many times before now."

Quar raised his cane up and pointed it at Eton.

"*Laido exuro*!"

Eton dropped his sword, and it clattered on the ground. He grabbed his chest where Quar's unhealed wound rested and screamed in pain. The residual glow blazed as it did many times before but much brighter than ever.

"Burns doesn't it?" Quar asked mockingly. "'Tis a burden of love, as well, or hadn't you noticed? When jealousy stirs within you, so do the embers in my curse."

Eton grit his teeth in attempt to bear the pain while still maintaining to stand, but Quar walked up to him and jabbed the butt of his cane into Eton's burning ailment. Instantly, Eton collapsed to the ground.

Quar pushed his cane deeper and deeper into Eton's left shoulder and continued, "You should know better not to mess with me, boy. Now that you've broken your promise to me, I'm going to break my promise to you. Rest assured, your girlfriend will die even if not by my hands. I'll see to it."

Quar paused and turned his ear to the window leading to the outside of the Abbey. He grinned as he sensed the aura of Nysam's presence and actions.

"In fact, I do believe it's being taken care of as we speak."

Suddenly, a flash of light blinded Quar's eyes as an overwhelming invisible force threw Quar off of Eton.

When the brightness cleared, Eton squinted at the doorway and saw Sabua standing with her left hand stretched out, wand in hand.

"Are you alright?" Sabua asked worriedly as she rushed to help Eton off the ground.

"I think so," Eton managed to whisper as he wrapped his arm around Sabua's shoulder.

"Hurry," Sabua urged. "Quar will escape

that ball of light in less than a minute. We must reconvene with the others and leave here."

Sabua guided Eton out of Quar's room and down the hallway. When they turned the corner, the pair ran into Marthule and Christo.

"Sabua! Eton!" Christo exclaimed. "What happened?"

"We will have time to explain later," Sabua rushed.

Marthule relieved Sabua of Eton's weight and assisted Eton quickly down the hall with Sabua and Christo close behind.

"Where are Chase and Sam?" Sabua questioned.

"We ran into a situation...," Marthule started.

"What?" Sabua asked.

"Nysam," Christo answered. "Quar possessed the priest's body with the Shadow Force, and something else... He looked different. It was almost as if he was mutated."

"We'll have to ask the friar about that. I pray that Celtessa and Rhodil managed to find him."

Just as the words escaped Sabua's lips, the missing comrades appeared further down the hallway.

"There they are!" Christo announced elated.

Celtessa turned around at Christo's shout and waved. The two groups hurried to each other.

"Good to see you're alright, Friar Sulny," Eton said warily as he leaned on Marthule's strong shoulder.

"The same to you, my child," Friar Sulny responded. "Where is Sam'ona?"

"Sam'ona!" Eton yelled as he remembered what Quar had said. "Quar's going to kill her!"

"Nysam took her," Marthule stated. "Chase wanted to fight him alone. That's why we came down here to find everyone else. We wanted to help but-"

"We must go help Chase," Friar Sulny said sternly. "Although I admire her bravery, she has not honed her powers completely. Nysam has undergone a Fusioning process and although, not have much time to live, he will have an exuberant amount of strength with the Shadow Force behind him. Plus, his level of magic as a member of the Magi Order will only increase that quantity of power."

"I knew we shouldn't have left her!" Christo blamed herself out loud.

"It will be fine, Christo," Sabua consoled. "We will get there in time. Let's hurry."

But, things were not fine on the surface.

Chase had successfully made it to the top of the tower despite her weakened state, but the poison and the ache in her back were taking a toll on her.

Nysam took advantage of it, hit after hit, while Sam lied on the roof of the tower, unawake by the unfair battle between Light and Shadow.

Nysam quickly threw another swift punch across Chase's face. She staggered back, surprisingly able to keep standing. She wiped the blood from her lip and clenched her fists.

Chase's arms did not form into rock as quickly as before. The poison in her body was deterring her focus and disengaging her elemental power.

Nysam laughed, "This is the mighty

prophet we foresaw?"

He walked up to Chase and launched another jab into her ribs. Chase immediately doubled over hacking. Nysam ignored this and wrapped his hand around her throat, lifting Chase into the air.

"To think that we had such faith in you," he continued.

Tired and beaten, Chase managed to spout back, "And to think *I* had such faith in you."

Nysam said nothing.

Chase continued, "A month ago, I was a normal kid, in a normal world, so of course I was scared when I came here, but you know what? I met all these great people that helped me out, stayed by my side, showed me strength, showed me love and faith. It's what brought me here, but that faith didn't just come from the people I met. It came from the stories I heard about even greater people, people like you. You're supposed to be the Light, and look at you. How disappointing."

Chase's harsh words stung Nysam's ears. His breathing softened as he lowered Chase back to the ground and let go of her throat.

A voice from behind Nysam spoke up to follow Chase's speech and said, "She's right."

Nysam turned around and found himself staring at Sam who had woken up from her drowning slumber.

She continued slowly through her regaining awakeness, "Nysam, I know you can find the Light again if you just look to your heart. Remember all the great things you fought for, the wonderful things you taught, and the blessed things that you can still bring. Just fight it. Fight the darkness."

Sam inched closer to Nysam who was now holding his hands over his ears to silence both Sam's and Chase's rebellious words.

"No…" Nysam muttered. "The Shadow… The power… I don't want to…"

Nysam dropped to his knees, and his body started changing.

The scales that coated his bald head slowly began to shed around him as tiny patches of blonde hair grew back in their place. Even one of the spikes, pointing out of his shoulder, began to retract into his skeleton.

Sam cautiously progressed forward to the suffering Nysam. Chase just stood and watched.

"Nysam… you'll be alright," Sam encouraged as she reached out a soothing hand, placing it on Nysam's back.

A small flicker of Sam's blue light palpitated Nysam's pulsing veins.

"No!" Nysam screamed as he grabbed Sam's hand. "Don't!"

Nysam's back arched unrealistically backwards as his body twisted and contorted like a rope.

"Sam, get back!" Chase yelled out as she ran to Sam's side despite the agony she was in.

Sam took back her hand and held it close to her chest.

After heaving and spitting up blood, Nysam warily stood back up with his hand clutched to his side. The air about him seemed different.

"Sam'ona, the Healer's Mastery," he whispered. "It's lovely to meet you."

He smiled.

Then, Nysam's head twitched as the Shadow Force tried to fight its way back to Nysam's spirit, but the Water Priest's returned innocence hushed its dark possessor.

"You'll need to heal Solaris' wounds as soon as you can. My poison will surely kill her if you don't. I'm shocked that she has been able to stay coherent this long."

"I can heal you too," Sam suggested.

"No, you can't," he replied. "My wounds are far too deep for you to heal, for they are not a result of evil, they *are* evil."

"We can save you," Sam protested.

"I'm afraid that is no longer an option," Nysam argued back. "But, allow me to save you instead. There is a collision of Light and Shadow deep within my viscera. Such tension will surely lead to an immaculate release, as conflict usually does. I can take out much of the Great Abbey this way and hopefully Quar's madness."

Nysam gritted his teeth as he fought back the Shadow's tempting urge to travel to his conscience.

"You must leave now," Nysam ordered.

"We won't leave you!" Sam exclaimed sternly.

"Sam…" Chase whispered as she laid a comforting hand on Sam's back.

Sam started to cry.

"What's the point of these stupid Healer's Mastery powers if I can't even use them? Chase, I can't cure your back, I couldn't heal Eton's stab wound, and now, you're telling me I can't help Nysam?" she shouted. "Why was I even given these powers then?"

"There is a purpose to your strength," Nysam consoled. "It will come in time, but this is not it. Go."

Suddenly, Nysam screamed up to the night sky as the rain fell heavily upon his pale skin. He stretched out his arms, and a swirling white and black light collided and circled his body.

"Aaaand there's our sign to leave," Chase voiced as pulled Sam away from Nysam.

Sam was still reluctant as Chase grabbed her hand and guided Sam to the stairs leading down to the main floor, but the chaotic billows expanded outward from Nysam's body, destroying the stony tower roof. The exit crumbled before them like dry leaves.

"Great…" Chase muttered to herself as she looked desperately around the tower surface for another escape route.

Chase felt another twinge of pain from the unexplained bruises on her back. As a result, she hunched over in discomfort. It felt as if something inside her was bursting to escape.

"What's wrong?" Sam asked concerned.

"My back…" Chase replied warily.

Behind them, Nysam's clouds of clashing white and black were getting bigger and bigger.

In the middle of the illuminating tornado, Nysam was still standing, but his arms were no longer stretched out, nor was he screaming. Instead, Nysam stood silently with his arms at his side, tears rolling down his cheeks. He looked over to Chase and Sam and smiled.

"Forgive me," Nysam mouthed as the walls of the black and white swirls enclosed around him.

The tower-roof shook, and the crenulations began to disintegrate.

"What do we do?" Sam asked Chase.

"I have an idea," Chase said unsurely. "Sam, do you still trust me?"

Sam nodded.

for her pupils had been replaced by a ghostly whiteness.

Sam curiously placed a hand on Chase's warm cheek. The Healer's Mastery light shimmered luminously in the microscopic gap between the friends' epidermises.

Leaning in, Sam looked deep into Chase's blank eyes. With the subtle glow emitting from her hand, all Sam could see, was her own reflection. Instantly, a wave of awareness and understanding consumed Sam's spirit like a predator's feeble prey, but instead of panic, Sam felt completely serene.

"Chase?" Sam whispered.

Chase simply smiled and secured her arm elegantly around Sam's waist like a belt. With an enormous flutter, Chase launched the two bodies up into the air.

Following the rhythm, Chase continued to flap and the pair was flying back up to the sky, soaring and leaving a magnificent precipitation of shed feathers over the bloody battlefield.

On the ground, the Light Mafia, Eton, and Friar Sulny were shocked at the sight above them in the sky.

"She can fly, too?" Rhodil asked flabbergasted. "How is that possible? She's still in her human form."

"When the mind caves under the weight of the heart, will one experience the miracle of a prism, and a power will rise upon this naked truth, bringing forth a light of altruism," Friar Sulny replied happily as he watched Chase and Sam soar over the Great Abbey walls to the outside boundaries.

"What?" Rhodil returned.

"I hate to burst everyone's amazement here," Marthule interjected. "But, something up there is going to explode."

The group turned their gaze up to the northeast tower where Nysam was no longer visible. All one could see were the accumulating streaks of eddying lights merging together as the rain above gravitated to the central point of the mystical storm. It was if Nysam's cyclone had mated with nature's tempest, a glorious bomb waiting to erupt.

"Let's go," Sabua rushed as more parts of the Great Abbey shambled to the ground.

The group hustled to the main gates and escaped outside the walls where they met up with Sam and Chase.

Chase had used what remained of her energy to fly off the crumbling tower and passed out in Sam's arms upon their landing. Her wings were gone, retracted into her back, and the bruises had vanished. Sam had already begun the healing process as the brilliant blue light surged out of her hands.

"Please wake up," Sam begged as she held Chase's hand in her own while cradling Chase's limp neck with the other.

The Light Mafia and Eton surrounded the pair as Sam began to weep at the thought of losing Chase. The silent company bowed their heads in honor of the valiant courage Chase had shown despite her severe lack of training against an incredible foe.

Friar Sulny stood beside Sam and rested a caring hand upon her back.

"Why won't my powers work?" Sam wondered aloud. "Friar Sulny, you said that the Healer's Mastery would keep her safe. You said that I would keep her safe…"

"My dear, Sam'ona," he began. "Do you know how Chase was able to fly tonight?"

Sam shook her head.

"She was able to fly because of you. You set her free, Sam'ona."

"No. It was destiny," Sam whispered softly. "The prophecy…"

"A prophecy is a mere prediction, my dear, but we can never be fully certain about what lies ahead," Friar Sulny continued. "We are but guided in life. Destiny… Fate… It seems silly that we would have little control over our destination, does it not?"

Sam shifted her look from Friar Sulny down to Chase. Chase's breathing was getting thinner and less noticeable. Sam closed her eyes and leaned down to Chase's ear.

Though weak, Sam could feel the familiar warmth of Chase's touch. Sam's pulse began to slow to a steady beating inside her chest. She blocked out all noise and bodies around her as Sam focused on herself.

Then, Sam whispered something into Chase's ear. The curious crowd watched in anxiety as Sam gently kissed Chase's forehead and sat back up straight.

At first, it seemed like nothing changed, but suddenly, color returned to Chase's cheeks, and she stirred slightly in Sam's lap.

Chase blinked open her eyes like a newborn child and looked up at the staring faces above her.

"What happened?" Chase questioned. "My head feels like crap."

"That's an odd way of describing it," Celtessa announced. "But, I like it!"

Chase chuckled slightly as she gradually started to sit up.

"I keep forgetting… We're from two totally different worlds," Chase reminded herself.

Before Chase could fully erect her body,

Sam threw her arms around Chase's neck, knocking Chase back to the ground with a thump.

"What the-?" Chase exclaimed, startled.

"I'm so glad you're okay. I thought-" Sam started then realized that there was an audience surrounding the scene. "I mean… we thought that we had lost you."

"Good to know you care," Chase joked playfully. "I'm a little fuzzy on what happened though. Someone needs to fill me in."

A booming clash of thunder responded behind them. The group turned around and saw the Great Abbey walls collapse to the ground in an enormous cloud of black dust.

The majestic structure had perished with the last hidden ounce of Nysam's life.

When the last standing tower plummeted into the ground, the storm finally gave way and the hint of starlight once again peeked its shy eyes into the night's darkness. The tiny Light Alliance band smiled as the enchanting normality of the Great Crossings' atmosphere resumed.

"Did we win? Is Quar dead?" Chase asked.

"I doubt it," Sabua replied. "Quar is a highly skilled wizard. I'm sure he had fled the Great Abbey long before Nysam's insanity broke."

"Still, that doesn't mean we should sit around and wait to see," Rhodil piped up. "Let's get the horses and get out of here."

"We aren't splitting up?" Sam inquired.

"No," Sabua responded as she helped Sam and Chase back up to their feet. "Although Quar got away, we still leave tonight with a much greater success than we had originally planned. I doubt there are survivors, so we will head north to the Waterfall Hole, together. It should take about two days time."

"Ah… Going home," Marthule sighed.

"We can reconfigure our plans there. We have much to arrange and prepare before our next move."

"What would that be?" Chase posed hesitantly.

Friar Sulny interjected, "We must go to the Great Hall in the northern Savannahs to eliminate Ceros and his Shadow Force rule. Heaven hope that the rest of the Order and the Head Nobles are still alive so that when this war is over, we can go back to restoring peace. With the unexpected alliance between all good Neos and Anders, I have faith that our future looks brighter than it's ever been before."

"I could not have said it any better, Friar Sulny," Sabua agreed. "It will be safer for us to travel by night and sleep by day. We will have to worry less about adversary attacks in daylight. Marthule, take Rhodil and Christo with you to fetch the horses from both the western and eastern line of trees. We will wait here for you as Sam heals Eton and Friar Sulny. As soon as you return, we will take our departure."

The three Light Mafia members nodded and ran out into the Great Crossings' forests where they had stashed their horses, safely tucked away from the heat of the battle.

Sam walked up to Friar Sulny to begin the Healing process. She took both his hands in hers and smiled.

"Thank you," Sam whispered softly so that this time, only the good friar could hear.

Friar Sulny grinned as the blue light began to warm his palms and said, "The thanks is not mine to take, but it *is* that of your heart to remember."

Sam turned around to see if the others were paying any attention to them, but Chase was too busy hugging Sabua, Celtessa, and even Eton.

Sam giggled as she watched Chase crouch down to the ground then jump up in the air trying to sprout her wings again and fly.

"She is an audacious character," Friar Sulny interrupted Sam's thoughts. "You did well, Sam'ona."

Sam smiled.

The Healing process was over, and Friar Sulny stretched out his body, reaching high up to the stars.

After he had expanded the length of his body, Friar Sulny rejoined hands with Sam and said, "Just trust, Sam'ona. You will be fine."

Sam let out a forgoing sigh as Friar Sulny whisked around with his new energy and walked up to Chase who was still hopelessly trying to grow her set of wings.

"I can control the earth and now the wind, but I can't control two extra appendages from my back? What gives?" Chase uttered annoyed.

Friar Sulny chuckled.

"Need not worry, Chase, I will help train you so that you may be fully ready for your next battle."

"Stellar," Chase replied.

Just then, Marthule, Rhodil, and Christo returned with all eight horses.

"Two people will have to share," Rhodil stated. "So, get comfy."

Eton limped over to Sam.

"Sam, you can ride with me so that Friar Sulny may take his own horse."

Sam smiled at Eton's offer but first

looked over to Chase to see what her reaction would be.

Chase stared back at Sam, but did not say a word. All she did was smirk. It was the smirk that hung underneath Chase's sanguine eyes, piercing through Sam's soul and assuring her that whatever Sam did, Chase would support her. It was also the same casual smirk Sam recognized whenever Chase knew more than what she was letting on.

Unable and not wanting to unveil Chase's secrets in front of the others, Sam took Eton's hand. He was already sitting firmly in his saddle and had lent out a helping hand to pull Sam up on his steed.

"You can heal me as we ride, Sam," Eton said smoothly as he readied the reigns in his hands.

Sam nodded and wrapped her arms around Eton's muscular body. His injured but warm torso felt nice against Sam's skin. Embracing Eton, she sighed and let any lingering, confusing thoughts out of her mind.

After the entire crew had saddled up, they kicked their horses' sides and made their way north to the Waterfall Hole. The last traces of darkness faded behind them as the sun soon began to peep out above the forested horizon with the brightening promise that they had victoriously bred for themselves.

The Breaking of a New Day

By next full morning, Sam, Chase, Eton,
the Light Mafia and Friar Sulny had
successfully traveled north without any
confrontation. Finding a small pond surrounded
by a collection of hovering trees, the group
decided to stop and make camp.

"What a beautiful place to stop!" Christo
exclaimed as she dismounted her satin white
horse.

Like all other nature born and bred in
the magical Great Crossings, it really was an
amazing sight, especially with Quar's presence
gone.

The water of the pond was crystal clear
so one could see the many small fish that swam
chaotically about as well as the long flowing
water grass fixed to the sandy bottom.

The turf around the reservoir was just as
breathtaking. The swaying blades of grass
shifted back and forth to the wind's noiseless
song and danced under the sun's beaming shine,
and a rainbow of flowers adorned the grassy
plains' edge.

The remaining members of the group
unhorsed as well and started unpacking their
items for the encampment.

"I know exactly what I'm going to do
first," Chase said excitedly as she pulled off
her boots and socks.

Chase walked over to the edge of the
gorgeous pond, sat down on the thick grass,
and gently dipped her feet in the cool water.

She sighed.

"Ah! Exactly what I needed. Sam! Come on

in! The water's fine!"

As Chase laughed, Sam smiled, pulled off her own boots, and joined Chase at the pond's refreshing waters.

"This is nice," Sam agreed as she submerged her bare feet into the pond.

"You know what, Sam?" Chase piped up.

"What?"

"My mind is still reeling over what happened last night. I mean… I know it's been a crazy ride since we got to Pangea, but last night I think was the climax."

"You seemed to have adjusted well," Sam replied.

"Maybe. I get into this motion of what goes on around me, like during the fights at the Sector, but after it's all over, it's like I wake up from a dream and find myself walking around in this world that is still so unreal to me. The only thing that reminds me that this is really happening is you."

Chase let out a sigh and stared into her reflection. She noticed a small figure move under her floating feet. Chase squinted harder and saw, what she thought to be, the same koi fish that had brushed past her face in Nysam's swirling waters at the Great Abbey. The fish quickly scurried back into the pond's reeds before Chase could point it out.

"Chase?" Sam inquired curiously.

Thinking she must have hallucinated the sight, Chase shook her head and continued, "I just don't want to forget where I came from, what I know. Simon, the twins, Leo, the circus, Cia… I know I've got a responsibility to Pangea, but don't I still have a responsibility to our life back home? I mean… that world is where I've built *my* home."

Sam stayed quiet for a moment as she

turned Chase's concerns over in her head. Sam had not even thought about what would happen in the event that they defeat Ceros, returning Pangea to its peaceful state.

Would they stay in Pangea? Would they return back to the circus house in Chicago? Would Sam and Chase even choose the same destination?

Finally, Sam spoke up and said, "After this war is over, Chase, you're allowed to do whatever your heart desires and go wherever your heart leads you."

Chase kicked her feet around in the still waters, making ripples in the calmness.

"Are you going to stay in Pangea, Sam?" Chase asked softly.

"I'm not sure," Sam replied hesitantly. "I suppose I will have to wait and see where my own heart will guide me."

Silently, Sam wished in her own heart that-

Suddenly, one of the horses stood fearfully on its hind legs, neighing loudly. Then, the disturbed white steed galloped off into the brush of the trees.

"I'll get it!" Eton assured to everyone as he took off in the same direction.

Eton darted into the thick canopy of trees and had only ran for about ten minutes until he came across the spooked horse eating an apple from the hand of a black cloaked stranger in a small clearing.

"I thought this might be the only way to get you away," the stranger announced as Eton approached.

The mysterious figure turned around and was revealed to be the crooked senior Quar. His black teeth were in the form of a grin as the white horse continued to be occupied by its tasty treat.

"Sabua was right," Eton stated blatantly.
"You did survive."

"Well, Sabua is a smart wizard," Quar
returned. "But, my concern is more focused on
you, Eton. How are you?"

"You need to leave me alone," Eton shot
back quickly.

"But, I can't. That mark on your chest is
proof. I'm with you no matter what you do or
where you go."

"I told you before that the deal is off,
especially now that Chase has obtained her
powers. I can't kill her."

"Oh, you're quite right. You can't," Qaur
replied coolly. "But, I don't want you to kill
her."

"You don't?" Eton inquired astonished by
Quar's lacking thirst for death.

"Let me show you something, Eton," Quar
responded as he stepped forward, laid one hand
on the horse, and extended the other out for
Eton to take.

Hesitantly, Eton took Quar's hand and
instantly, they were transported to the forest
edge, right where the horse escaped in the
first place.

"What are we doing here?" Eton asked
begrudgingly.

"Look at your comrades, and tell me what
you see," Quar sneered.

Eton obeyed and stared out at the pond's
inhabitants.

Sabua, Marthule, and Rhodil were busy
setting out blankets and gathering small
sticks to feed the fire that Christo and
Celtessa were cooking breakfast over. Chase
and Sam were still at the pond with their feet
submerged into the water. Except now, Sam had

her arm around Chase's shoulders, holding Chase close.

Eton's curious stare morphed into jealousy, and the burning impacted his laceration just as Quar had stated at Eton's first confrontation.

Seeing Eton's reaction, Quar piped up, "They look comfortable. It looks as if they did not even know you were missing. *She* doesn't even look like she cares that you've left. For all she knows, you could have been taken hostage or attacked, but she looks like none of that concerns her."

Eton did not reply so Quar continued.

"Don't you see? As long as Chase is in the picture, I don't think the precious *Sam'ona* will be paying you much attention. What do you think, Eton?"

Again, Eton did not respond. All he could do was stare at the pond with the possible truth of Quar's words echoing in his ears.

"I know what it's like to lose someone you feel so much for. The unfairness of it all is unbearable. Eton, don't lose her. Don't lose her to the only one that stands in your way."

Eton's silence remained, but his breathing intensified.

"Well, if I can't kill her, what do you want me to do?" Eton asked coldly.

"Keep her busy. More importantly, keep Ceros busy with her. I've ignited the fire for you. The good king and the Council have their sights set on her, your beloved, too, but I can grant her safety as promised. You must do as I ask though."

Quar patted Eton on the back and placed the horse's reigns into Eton's hand.

"I will be back, Eton. I trust that

you'll make the right decision. You're not doing this for me. You're doing this for her, and remember, that nasty mark on your chest won't disappear until you fulfill your end of the deal."

"And the blood?"

"Let me worry about that, now," Quar assured. "Things do change, after all."

With that, Quar vanished into the trees' shadows, and Eton was left alone. He steadied his rage, regained his composure, and walked back out into the pond's clearing.

"Thank goodness you found her!" Marthule shouted as Eton retied the horse to the branch that secured all the other steeds to.

"She wasn't too far off. I think it was just a squirrel or something that scared her," Eton replied, returned to his charming demeanor.

"Well, now that you're back, you can help me move those logs over there to the fire pit so we can eat. We may not have a table and chairs, but at least we won't have to eat while sitting on the ground," Marthule joked.

Eton nodded, but before he assisted Marthule, he turned around and returned his eyes back to where Sam and Chase sat.

Sam had playfully splashed Chase with water, so Chase had jumped in the shallow pool to seek her kidlike revenge. They both laughed and smiled under the brilliant sunlight as Chase pulled Sam in.

"You coming?" Marthule shouted.

Eton nodded one more time and followed Marthule to a pile of large logs.

Meanwhile, Quar still lingered in the protection of the forest, but he was not alone.

"Are you sure the boy will follow your

orders?" Gelaro spoke softly.

"He has no choice but to," Quar replied. "The curse I cast on him allows me to know more than what he sees with his eyes. I know every intention that slumbers in his chest. He wants to be with that the girl more than anything else, and he will do anything to make it so."

"A lot depends does on the boy, Quar," Gelaro pointed out.

"You know, Gelaro, Eton's previous failure has shed some benefit on our situation."

"How so?"

"Their next plan is to travel to the Great Hall and take out Ceros. If the child's powers continue to grow as they have, then *she* will be able to kill Ceros. That saves us a lot of work. While he busies himself with that task, you and I can go about our business. We still have an agreement, yes?"

"Yes, as long as I can have someone of the friar's equal value now that he's free. We're risking quite a bit for you, Quar, and our positions in the Council are shaky as it stands."

"Your wife in agreement then?"

"She is."

"That's good. Don't worry. I have the perfect specimen for the two of you."

Gelaro looked pleased the dark wizard's response.

"What should we do in the meantime?"

"In the meantime… we wait," Quar voiced darkly. "Darkness *will* prevail.

As Quar spoke his final words, he pulled one of Chase's small white, golden-tipped feathers from his musty black cloak.

At first, the tiny quill shimmered

delicately in the light, spinning in his
fingertips, but Quar's devilish grin soon
swamped the feather's luster with his
deceitful stare, and it turned into a charcoal
gray.

　　Satisfied with the mutation, Quar blew
the drained feather into the wind. It
combusted instantaneously as Quar and Gelaro
slowly disappeared into the shadows, specters
of the dark, leaving no trace behind.

to be continued...

Want more Solaris?
Visit www.solaristheriseandfall.com

www.ingramcontent.com/pod-product-compliance
Lightning Source LLC
Chambersburg PA
CBHW021425240626
47153CB00001B/33